CARGO TO SAIGON

When tough Dutchman Dirk van Groten offered Rick Mc'Adden the chance to get back on to the bridge of a ship, he could not afford to turn it down. Van Groten hopes to refloat the Greek freighter — wrecked by a typhoon off the Philippines — for its salvage value, plus cargo. But there are complications. The ship finally sails for Saigon, a badly leaking hulk filled with tension and violence. For nothing is as it seems, either with the ship or its cargo.

CHARLES LEADER

CARGO TO SAIGON

Complete and Unabridged

LINFORD
Leicester

First published in Great Britain

First Linford Edition
published 1998

British Library CIP Data

Leader, Charles, *1938 –*
  Cargo to Saigon.—Large print ed.—
Linford mystery library
  1. Detective and mystery stories
  2. Large type books
  I. Title
  823.9'14 [F]

  ISBN 0–7089–5213–5

Published by
F. A. Thorpe (Publishing) Ltd.
Anstey, Leicestershire
Set by Words & Graphics Ltd.
Anstey, Leicestershire
Printed and bound in Great Britain by
T. J. International Ltd., Padstow, Cornwall

This book is printed on acid-free paper

1

The Pussycat Bar

FOR me, trouble usually came in one of three grades; blonde, brunette or redhead. So, when the lush honey with the long black hair slid her dream-like bottom on to the seat opposite it wasn't too difficult even for me to figure out that I was due for trouble. The grey sludge that I like to call a brain began to make definite warning noises. I looked up from my beer, studied her for a moment, and then said bluntly:

"Sorry, lovely, but you're out of luck. I'm a sixth-day abstainer. And for your information that's something like a seventh-day adventist, but different. It means that I don't play with naughty girls on Saturdays. I won't even buy them one little drink."

She smiled sweetly. "But today isn't Saturday."

"And I have no money," I said agreeably. "That makes me religious on Wednesday too. No money — you savvy? No dollars."

The smile didn't fade and neither did she go away. She wasn't even annoyed, just amused. She said calmly:

"You're off course, sailor — way off course. I wouldn't even dream of offending your religion, either on a Saturday or a Wednesday." She turned her head as she spoke and shared some of her smile with a waiter who had appeared to hover behind her with a tall glass on a tray, and added casually, "I've already bought my own drink."

I watched dubiously as the waiter set the glass down in front of her, and the alarm bells jangled even more insistently inside my skull. All women were trouble, and I had a nasty feeling that a woman who bought her own drinks could be deadly. My gaze followed the waiter as he moved off and intercepted a daggered look from one of the regular bar girls who plagued the Pussycat, which meant that the honey sharing my table wasn't another regular. Working girls were naturally jealous of an interloper stealing their pitch, which meant that at any moment there would be a union meeting, followed by a cat-fight with me caught up in the middle. The sensible thing was to get out.

I looked at the girl again. She definitely wasn't a regular. Her smile was too confident, and her English was perfect. Her shape was delicious, but she wasn't showing off any free samples. She wore a dark skirt, and a blue and white patterned blouse that had a small rounded collar and long cuffs, only the sleeves were transparent. Her eyes were black, almond shaped, and the sleek black hair made a striking contrast to the pure white smile. She was taller than the Malaysian girls glaring at her back, and did not have their fragile appearance. Her skin was more fair and I guessed mixed blood. A very beautiful mixture of blood.

She seemed to enjoy my appraisal, and when I failed to comment she gave me a little more time as she tasted her drink. The crest on the glass advertised Tiger beer, so at least she had no fancy tastes. The union meeting had started in the corner, but I didn't leave. I had more curiosity than sense. She knew it and smiled again. Then she put the glass to one side and looked directly into my eyes, and said frankly:

"I think we should be introduced. My name is Louella."

She left it hanging there, so I said cautiously:

"Hello, Louella." And after a moment, "My name is Rick."

She smiled more wisely. "Rick, this is how you say Richard — your full name is Richard Mc'Adden."

It wasn't a question, she was merely revealing an item of pre-knowledge. The warning bells were now quiet in my brain, for they had served their purpose. I watched her carefully, but her smile told me nothing. The smile was a mask, warm and comforting, but as yet still a mask. I said slowly:

"What do you want?"

There was a cat-like streak somewhere in her make-up, playful rather than cruel, but she had to tease. She paused to sip delicately at her ice-cold beer, and then just as delicately moved her tongue to remove the faint traces of foam from her upper lip. Somehow the gesture, the tiny pink tongue snaking along the glistening red lip, carried more sexual challenge than all the blatant glimpses of breast and thigh revealed by the muttering whores' union behind her. And she knew that too.

"I want to help you." The answer came after she had lowered her glass. "I want to offer you a job."

I figured that there was still time to get out; still time to stand up, say that I was not interested, and walk away. But if I did that then she would have to leave the Pussycat alone, and then the working girls would follow and claw her eyes out for trying to poach on their territory. They wouldn't touch her in the bar because that would displease the management, and they wouldn't follow if she left with me, but they would if she had to leave alone. I pretended that I was thinking like a gentleman and stayed.

5

"What sort of a job?"

She smiled blandly. "There is a ship that needs a crew."

"And when did the shipping companies start sending women round the girlie bars to recruit seamen?"

"They don't. But I am not employed by a shipping company. And I am not offering you the job of a seaman." She held back and toyed with her glass, playing cat and mouse again. Then she said quietly, "This ship needs a First Officer."

I stared at her, and little snakes of warning slithered into my stomach. I had been right in anticipating trouble. Before I could only smell it, but now I could feel it. The preliminary fencing was over, and Louella's face was calm and waiting. I tried to keep my own expression blank.

"Then you've come to the wrong man." It didn't sound as casual as I intended. "I'm only a deckhand."

She smiled again, but this time it was a gentle smile.

"We know that you arrived in Singapore as a deckhand, but you have sailed as a

6

ship's First Officer. You were the First Officer aboard a ship called the *Pirahne* which sank another ship in the Gulf of Panama. It was because of that that your papers were taken away."

So my past history had come with me, following me from one side of the world to the other. The official court of enquiry had damned me as being solely responsible for that collision, and had laid the blame for the lost *Conchita* and the thirty-seven drowned members of her crew squarely on my shoulders. After that I had been on the beach, drifting around the ports of Central America, hunting for a job and a ship, any job and any ship. I had got myself mixed up in a crazy treasure hunt in Venezuela,[1] which had at least kept me busy until the collision story had faded into the past. Then I had shipped out of Maracaibo, signing on as a deckhand on the only one-way passage

---

[1] *The Golden Lure*

I could get. It had brought me here, to Singapore.

Now I wanted to curse, but my jaws were clamped tight. The snakes in my belly were shivering, but my face felt as pliable as frozen granite. It had all been for nothing and I hadn't escaped my past. It had all come with me. There had been vague plans for a fresh start under another name, but now they were gone. I stared into Louella's lovely face and hated her.

She was puzzled.

"Why do you look so angry? We know all about you — and we are still willing to offer you the position of First Officer. Surely that is what you want? You should be pleased. To us it is not important that you were the First Officer aboard the *Pirahne*."

My face didn't relax, because the muscles were beyond my control. I was still staring at her, still hating her, but now I was looking right through her. It was a long time since I had stood on the bridge of the *Pirahne* even in my mind, but I was there now. I could still smell and taste the thick night fog that had swamped the ship like an evil shroud. I could still feel the distant pulsing of the ship's engines far below, driving blindly forward at full speed. The helmsman stood like a graven image at the wheel, and the extra lookouts I had posted in the bows and on the wings of the bridge were unseen in the darkness. In hushed silence that might have clothed a graveyard we strained eyes and ears into the night, searching for the first sign that might indicate another vessel in the fog. Normally I would have reduced engines to slow, that was the safe procedure, but I had a dying man aboard and no doctor. The ship's captain lay in his bunk with a broken back and a whole mess of vaguely realized internal injuries received in a bad fall into an empty hold. If he was to live, then I had to reach Balboa at the Pacific mouth of the Panama Canal in the shortest possible time.

I sounded the foghorn at regular intervals, but fog has a muffling effect and those aboard the *Conchita* failed to hear it. Neither did we hear theirs until the last hideous moment when it was all too late. She was an old Panamanian freighter looming like some rusty monster surging out of the sea before our bows. She was coming fast, much too fast, and the impact came before I could even cry a warning. The *Pirahne*'s bows struck the Panamanian just abaft the bridge and smashed her open like a heavy axe blade chopping through an old cocoa tin. I was hurled with the helmsman to the floor, the lookout on the port wing of the bridge was thrown clean into the sea, and the lookout in the bows screamed like a banshee as he was crushed in the tearing steel plates that buckled all around him.

There was more screaming after that, more confusion and cursing. The *Pirahne* heeled over and the two vessels came apart. The *Pirahne* survived to limp into Balboa, where she was later scrapped, but the *Conchita* sank rapidly. I did what was possible in the heavy seas and filthy fog, lowering lifeboats and picking up as many of the Panamanian crew as could be found. Even so, the toll was thirty-seven lost, plus my own two lookouts, and Captain Hugh Frazer of the *Pirahne* who died while I was manoeuvring in the search for survivors.

Hugh Frazer had been more than a skipper; he had been a good friend for many years.

The court of enquiry had later decided that in the circumstances I should have reduced speed to approach the busy mouth of the Canal. And they were right; the captain should have taken second place to the ship.

There was just one point that I wanted to make, and that was that I hadn't expected to meet another ship maintaining the same speed through the total fog. And that was my biggest mistake. The *Conchita* had been going full ahead when she rammed across my bows, and my guess was that she had a tight schedule to keep. But I couldn't prove it, and the Panamanian captain was smart enough to deny it. The court of enquiry believed him, and I took full responsibility. They took away my master's ticket and kicked me ashore.

Gradually the fog cleared, and the black seas swirled away. The screams and curses of drowning men faded into the blurred babble of brash voices and noisy laughter. I had to remind myself that I was still sitting in the Pussycat Bar on the opposite side of the world to the Gulf of Panama; sitting with my body stone-rigid, my jaws still locked together, and staring into the girl's face across the table.

She had said *we* for the second time, but obviously she would not be approaching me on her own behalf. I tried to relax, and to forget that to *them* the *Conchita* and the *Pirahne* were not important. It wasn't easy, but I moved my cramped jaws and said at last:

"I no longer have my papers, you already know that. I can't legally sign ship's articles as First Officer."

She nodded and smiled. "This is not important."

"Then it has to be illegal."

I watched her, but her smile didn't change, and I wondered why I had to be so inane as to quote the obvious. Nobody offered clean work to a man with my record. That explained the whole dubious approach. The job had to be crooked and dirty, something that only a man on the beach with thirty-seven deaths on his conscience would touch. My first instinct had been right and I should have got up and walked away. Now it was too late. I had to know more, even if I didn't take the job. I said coldly, "What's the name of the ship? And why come to me?"

"Then you are interested in the job?"

"Maybe. At the moment I'm just asking questions."

She smiled, and then looked away from the table, behind me. I turned my head and saw a man sitting alone at another small table in the far corner. He was heavy without being fat, with a wave of thick iron-grey hair and a face that had been lined and leathered by sea winds. Louella's glance had been a signal, and as I watched he rose from his table, casually smacked the pert bottom of one of the bar girls who strayed across his path, and then came over to join us.

2

The Skipper of the Zandvoort

DIRK VAN GROTEN was the captain of the *Zandvoort*. Louella made the introductions and I made a wary reply as I watched him pull up a chair and sit down. The *Zandvoort* rang a faint bell and I knew that she was one of the score of small cargo freighters lying in the inner roads outside the harbour. I remembered her from a distance as a pile of scrap and rust somehow holding together in the shape of a ship.

Her skipper was more impressive. He matched me for height, which was about six foot, and the extra weight he carried was mostly across the barrel chest and broad shoulders. I figured he'd been around about ten years longer than I had, and that made him about forty-five. He moved easy, relaxed, but that was because those extra years at sea had made him hard as teak, and he knew that he could prove it any time that it really mattered. His eyes were sharp blue with sailor's wrinkles at the corners. His crisp white shirt was open at the bronzed neck and showed tufts of grey hair climbing up from his chest. His hands were confident with more stiff grey hairs marching down the wrists to the big knuckles, and I noted the fact that those hands could make lethal fists. The completed survey spelled out a very tough and very capable man.

Louella said calmly:

"Dirk, Mister Mc'Adden is interested in the job."

Van Groten matched her smile, and his teeth were in pretty good shape too. Everybody seemed to be in a smiling mood except me.

"I thought that you would be." His tone was matter-of-fact, and the Dutch accent only just showed through. "The sea is like a woman, hey? You can love her. You can hate her. But in the finish you have to go back to her. In your

15

position, I too would be damned glad to get back on to the bridge of a ship."

"And in your position, I wouldn't offer a place on my bridge to a man in my position." I had to say that carefully in case I got it mixed up, and then went back to my bad habit of stating the obvious again. "You must need a First Officer for the *Zandvoort* pretty badly."

"But, Rick, I didn't exactly say that the job was on the *Zandvoort*."

The black almond eyes were shining at me, and Louella's smile was chiding. I felt edgy and began to wish that one of them would scowl, just to give me a break. I didn't like this feeling that everything was so comfortably under their control.

Van Groten was shaking his head.

"You are jumping to the wrong conclusion, hey? My ship already has a full crew. I have a damned good First Officer." He looked to Louella and she nodded her head. A wave of smooth black hair fell across her cheek and they exchanged some more smiles. Van Groten's hand dwarfed and covered her slender white fingers for a moment, and then he remembered me again. He looked around the bar and then back at my face.

"This is not a good place to talk business. My ship will be a better place."

"And if I don't want the job?"

He shrugged. "I will put you ashore again. But after we have talked, I think you will want the job."

I hesitated, but I knew I was just saving a little face. Now that my past had caught up with me the doors would start slamming in my face again. No one else would ever offer me a ship, which meant that I had nothing to lose and everything to gain. The job had to be crooked, but maybe it wasn't too crooked. Smuggling would be okay, as long as it wasn't drugs or human cargoes. Piracy was questionable, depending upon who or what I might have to pirate. Maybe I could do a deal with my conscience. Anyway, I could listen to what the man had to offer, that would cost me nothing. I pretended that I still had reservations and that I wasn't yet

17

for sale to the highest bidder, and said casually:

"All right, let's go."

Van Groten nodded; he had expected nothing less. We stood up and he held back Louella's chair and allowed her to precede us to the door. The regular bar girls watched her with jealous eyes, and I decided that I must have been drunk or dumb to have mistaken her for one of them. She was like a thoroughbred compared to a pack of wild and shaggy mares. She walked disdainfully because she knew it, and suddenly I was jealous of the big Dutchman grinning beside me.

We left the Pussycat and walked out into the street, turning towards the river where it leaked out into the harbour. Singapore was an island city, and the largest port in Asia. A bizarre mixture of modern buildings, neon bars, and hanging shop signs in Chinese characters. It was noisy, brash, and multi-racial, and reeked with the smells of Chinese and Indian cooking from the cheap eating places along Albert Street and around the docks. It had a cathedral, a Sikh temple,

18

a Buddhist temple and a Muslim mosque, and all the vices that a sailor could ask if he knew where to look. Across the river the City Hall was majestically floodlit with a rosy red glow, but the river itself was a stink. Thick with oil and filth and packed tight with sampans and barges, it looked like instant typhoid for anyone unlucky enough to fall in and take a mouthful. Even at night the air was hot and humid.

A trishaw swerved towards us, but van Groten waved it away. He preferred to walk. The Indian riding the trishaw looked at Louella and saw that he could offer us nothing more desirable, and mournfully trod on his pedals to take his creaking conveyance off into the night. The smell of the river became stronger as we crossed Collyer Quay and went down to the water's edge.

Out to sea the massed yellow lights of the idle ships formed a continuous line along the dark horizon, as though there might have been another town out there on some unseen strip of land across the intervening water. Van Groten called to

19

the nearest sampan that sculled quickly towards us.

There was just room for the three of us to get aboard. The sampan rocked beneath our weight, but the little Chinese woman holding it steady just grinned and showed big, uneven teeth. She had a baby tied on to her back and another squatting on the deck of the sampan. She was captain and crew and worked cheerfully at the big oar that reached above her head.

We sat on the single wide seat in the back of the sampan with Louella in the middle, and I could feel the curve of her hip pressed tightly against my own. She kept her knees demurely together, but I ached for her. I hadn't realized that I needed a woman so badly. I wondered if that was the real reason that I had come along, and knew that if it was then I was mad. Van Groten would kill me for it.

I tried to forget that she was beside me and watched the bobbing lights all around. I could smell the salt and feel the wind. The smell was cleaner now that we were away from the mouth of the river.

Louella moved, leaning forward to play with the Chinese baby that had been regarding her from the deck of the sampan with curious eyes. The mother smiled but maintained her slow movements with the oar. The baby gurgled and laughed at Louella's tickling finger. Her thigh was warm against my own, and I had to hold back my hand from stroking down the long, arched curve of her spine. Van Groten was silent, watching the baby, and then he rested one hand on the back of Louella's neck. The fingers caressed her for a moment, absent-mindedly, and then he did what I had wanted to do and stroked down the length of her back. Louella straightened up and smiled at him. The baby looked disappointed, and I was glad when the squat hulk of the *Zandvoort* loomed up before us.

She was about eight thousand tons, her black hull streaked with brown rust. Her single funnel was a dirty yellow with a green band, and apart from the green and yellow pennant at her masthead she sailed under the Dutch flag. The sampan

21

manoeuvred to the foot of the gangway that ran up the freighter's side, and the Chinese woman let go of her oar with one hand and grabbed at the rail. Van Groten helped her steady the sampan while Louella climbed out. Then he paid the woman and told her she could go. I said bluntly:

"Tell her to wait. I might want to go back with her."

He gave me a curious look, then shrugged.

"Okay, I tell her to wait. But I don't think you will want to go back."

He changed the orders and we left the sampan woman tying her craft to the foot of the gangway as we followed Louella aboard. She waited for us on the deck above and looked past me, an enquiring glance at van Groten coming up behind. I didn't see his answering expression because a man moved silently out of the gloom to bar our way. He was short and squat, but there was a hint of threatening purpose in the way he came towards us. He was Chinese, his face cold and yellow in the unflattering electric light that was fixed above the gangway. He wore a soiled vest and trousers and there was a large knife sheathed at his hip. In his right hand was a heavy marlinespike.

One bright slit eye stared into my face, and then he turned his head slightly to catch the light and I saw that his other eye was an empty red socket. The one eye was unblinking, but then van Groten came into view and the man relaxed. The Dutchman must have made some silent signal, for the Chinese moved slowly aside, and then turned and went back into the gloom.

"That was Foong." Van Groten was beside me, unconcerned. "He looks a nasty customer, hey? But he is a damned good seaman. He keeps my crew in good order. Best Bo'sun I ever had on the *Zandvoort*. I think that empty eye frightens the crew, that's why he don't wear no black patch."

"What happened to the eye?"

"A fight, so he tell me. Some bar in Penang. Somebody get his fingers into the socket and tear the eyeball out. Over some woman I think."

Van Groten shrugged as though it wasn't really important, and then led the way forward. Louella followed like a faithful puppy and I brought up the rear. If I reached out my two hands I could neatly enclose the tight, gently bobbing seat of her black skirt, but I had to put that kind of idea out of my mind. When we went up the companionways towards the bridge I had to hang back a pace, and I wondered what the hell was happening to me. It was like I had never been close to a real bedworthy woman before. I thought back to Annette and Venezuela, and realized that that was over six months ago. I felt like I had been starved for six years.

We went into the Captain's cabin. The day-room was big and comfortable, and so far the cleanest part of the ship. The panelling was dark oak, the chairs were red leather, and a framed parchment map of the East Indies covered part of the bulkhead. There was a vase of flowers on the desk-table that confirmed what I had already guessed, that Louella shared the Captain's quarters.

A Chinese steward appeared, but was waved away, curtly. We sat down and Louella fixed the drinks. Then she went into the bedroom and closed the door behind her.

Van Groten raised a whisky-filled glass and said:

"Here's to our partnership, hey?"

I dragged my eyes away from the bedroom door and looked at him.

"We're not partners yet."

"Not yet." He grinned and drank. Then leaned forward, relaxed. "I heard about you, Mc'Adden. Your story was in all the papers, even on this side of the Pacific. I think maybe you had a raw deal — if the *Conchita* was going full ahead like you said."

I didn't answer. I knew it didn't matter whether I had had a raw deal or not. Van Groten wasn't Santa Claus and he still wouldn't be offering me a job that wasn't going to enlarge the stain on my character. He was just being polite.

He waited, but when he saw that I wasn't going to take him up on the subject, he repeated:

25

"Like I say, maybe you had a raw deal. I don't know. But I can still give you a job. Not a regular job, I can't do that. The *Zandvoort* is part mine, I am part owner, but the other half of the ship belongs to the Holland East Indies Steamship Company. They fix my cargoes, so I do what they tell me."

I had placed the yellow and green flag a little before he had spelled it out for me. The Holland East Indies ran half a dozen small tramps plying between the South China and Java seas. But I wasn't interested in what he couldn't do for me. I said bluntly:

"What kind of a job are you offering?"

Van Groten smiled. "First Mate, but not on the *Zandvoort*." He drained the whisky and then got down to facts.

"I am hiring a salvage crew to bring in another ship that has gone aground. She's a Greek boat named the *Kerkyra*. She had a piece of double bad luck. She got caught in a typhoon that ran her on to the rocks. Typhoons are bad out here, worse than a Caribbean hurricane. Most of the crew got ashore, but the Captain stayed aboard with a few of his officers. Then they had the second piece of bad luck. The shipping company in Athens which owned the *Kerkyra* went bankrupt."

He got up, poured himself another whisky and looked at my glass. It was untouched. He shrugged and sat down again, continuing:

"It was the loss of the *Kerkyra* that broke the company. They already had many debts. There was no money to pay wages, no money to buy stores, and no money to salvage the *Kerkyra* from the rocks. What was left of the crew deserted. The Captain stayed because he still hoped to save the scrap value of his ship and his cargo. He was there three months, and then he did a deal with me. He was a sick man and I took him off in the *Zandvoort*. At the same time I left behind my own First Mate with some of my crew and fresh stores. They will stake my claim to salvage the ship until I get back. With the *Zandvoort* I think that I can pull the *Kerkyra* off the rocks. Then I shall sail her to Saigon. That was her original destination. I shall sell the cargo, and get the salvage value of the *Kerkyra*."

"And the Greek Captain?"

"He gets a share." Van Groten paused, and then decided against adding that that wasn't my business. He went on:

"So I need a new crew for the *Kerkyra*. Seamen I can easily hire, but not officers. The *Kerkyra* makes one last voyage and then she is scrapped. A First Mate doesn't look for a six-day berth. That's why I'm offering you the job. I give you normal rates of pay plus a bonus. For you it's worth while, hey?"

I wasn't sure.

"What's the cargo?"

"Fertilizer." Van Groten watched me carefully. "Maybe that don't sound very glamorous, but there's eight thousand, five hundred tons of the damned stuff aboard the *Kerkyra*, and it's worth half a million sterling pounds."

That made me blink. I remembered the glass of whisky in my hand and drank half of it. Then I thought of another question.

"Where is the ship?"

Van Groten seemed to hesitate on that one, then answered:

"She's off the Philippines. A small island off Mindoro. When we get there my First Mate will come back aboard the *Zandvoort*. I'll go aboard the *Kerkyra* and you'll come with me as First Mate on the Greek ship. I'll take my First Engineer as well, the Second can take over the engine-room in the *Zandvoort*. I'll take one of my radio officers too, and Foong. The rest of the salvage crew I'll recruit tomorrow."

I thought about it while he waited, and I had the feeling that it was all a lot less legal than he made it sound. There was something wrong about a half-million-pound cargo left sitting around on the rocks for anyone to come along and help himself, and van Groten was in far too much of a hurry to grab a crew together and get after it.

And then there was Louella. I knew that if I stayed around that woman, then I was going to make a try for her. Already she had got under my skin. I guess you could call it lust at first sight.

I thought about it hard, but again there was no decision to make. Ashore I was an outcast with no future. Here I could have a ship's bridge under my feet, even though it was only for a six-day trip. Here I could taste the sea again, and wear gold braid on my shoulders. Here I could be close to Louella.

The last could prove the most dangerous part of the voyage.

I said calmly:

"All right, you can send someone to tell that sampan woman not to wait. I'm staying."

Van Groten grinned.

"Didn't I tell you, hey? We'll drink to it, Mister Mate."

He stuck out his hand.

I took it.

Then he got up to refill the glasses and bellowed for the Chinese steward.

3

The Devil's Spawn

I SLEPT badly that night, occupying the Chief Officer's cabin, and the bunk of a man now stranded on a holed Greek tramp ship perched on a pile of rocks somewhere off the Philippines. But I didn't sleep badly because I was wondering about the *Kerkyra*, and all the little doubts that should have been flitting through my mind. Instead I lay awake because I was thinking about Louella. I was lying naked because of the heat, for even with the port-holes fully opened the air was still stifling hot. And I wondered if she slept naked too. I wondered if she was lying naked beside van Groten, and wondered whether his hand might be resting casually on the ivory whiteness of her breast or thigh. I was wishing that she was lying naked here beside me.

I wondered what nationality her father

31

might have been. The Malay blood would have come from her mother, but her father must have been English, French or Dutch. Mixed marriages were usually that way around. I wondered how much she meant to van Groten. There had been no ring on her finger, which meant that she was his mistress. But a man could love a mistress as much or more than a wife, and the Dutchman was obviously fond of her. He might kill me for what I was thinking now. I would if she were mine.

I turned beneath the thin sheet, squeezed my eyes shut and tried to sleep. After five minutes I was still awake. I tried thinking of Annette, but Annette was definite past while Louella was possible future. And I still couldn't sleep.

★ ★ ★

The next morning I went ashore to fetch my gear. There wasn't much of it, just a few clothes, shaving gear and a couple of books. It all went into one suitcase and there was no trouble in closing the lid. I

32

checked out of the seaman's hostel where I had stayed and got a sampan to take me back to the *Zandvoort*. It was the same little Chinese woman with the two babies pulling at the oar. I tickled the biggest baby's tummy because he liked it, and gave the mother an extra Malay dollar for a tip. It was Mc'Adden's last grand gesture, because it was also Mc'Adden's last hard-earned dollar.

That was another reason why I had taken van Groten's offer of a job.

I was an early riser, so I was still in time for breakfast, but the officers' saloon was empty. I ate alone, and then went to prowl around the ship. A ship reflects its master and I needed to know a lot more about Dirk van Groten.

The *Zandvoort* was an old tub, worn and tired, the decks hadn't seen a holystone in a long while and she badly needed a fresh coat of paint. On the credit side, the galley was clean, almost spotless, and the lifeboat davits and the winch machinery were well oiled and efficient. She was no floating gin palace, but nothing important had been allowed to rust. There was not much that could be done with an old tramp except look after her vitals and let the exterior suffer, and the *Zandvoort* was as good as any ship that had seen the same number of years at sea.

I looked into the engine-room, but I didn't set a foot inside. Everything appeared to be running smoothly and to pry without concrete cause could make a mortal enemy out of any Chief Engineer. I went up to the foredeck and watched some of the crew jabbering noisily around an open cargo hatch. They were Malays, Chinese and Lascars, not my favourite people, but they worked well. I stood there for some moments, and then I realized that someone was watching me.

I turned and looked into the one cold eye of Foong, the Bo'sun. It was unblinking as before, like the eye of a dead fish, and the empty socket where the other eye had been looked even more repulsive in daylight, just a raw, red slit. He knew all about me and why I was aboard because he didn't ask questions, but the one eye told me that he didn't approve of my snooping around. His Chinese face was like gnarled, impassive wax, but there was feeling in the eye. It was hostile, and I knew that Foong and I would never be friends.

I nodded casually as though I was too dumb to read anything from his stare, and then turned and walked away. I had seen all that I wanted to see. I climbed back up the companionway towards the bridge and I could feel that fish eye watching me all the way.

All that morning van Groten was ashore. He came back about noon, and an hour later a steady stream of sampans began plying between the *Zandvoort* and the quayside. Small groups of men with the unmistakable stamp of seamen scrambled up the gangway where Foong directed them into the saloon. I realized that this must be the salvage crew that van Groten had rounded up for the *Kerkyra* and went to watch the proceedings.

In the saloon van Groten sat behind the big dining table. He was in uniform now and under the golden-braided cap his blue eyes were frosty. He wasn't wasting any smiles with the riff-raff now lining up to sign ship's articles. The rest of the chairs had been cleared back to give plenty of room, but even so the saloon was crowded. The *Zandvoort*'s Second Officer, a tall, sallow man named Schiller, stood by van Groten's shoulder to increase the impression of authority, and a couple of Chinese stewards hovered in attendance.

A Malay was sucking his lower lip and concentrating hard as he made his mark in the big ledger that van Groten had pushed across the table towards him. The Malay had cheap rings in the pierced lobes of his ears and the sickly smile of a queer. The gaunt Lascar behind him was barefoot and his clothes were grimy rags, and his face must have been ugly even before the knife scar had been carved across his twisted cheek. I looked along the line and they were all as bad, or worse, a collection of vice-ridden gutter rats who wouldn't be allowed near a decent ship. Van Groten must have scoured the darkest back alleys of Singapore, and then dredged around in the drains to find this little lot. They smelled of dirt and drink and sweat, and I could understand why van Groten had picked the widest table in the ship to keep them at a distance. What I couldn't understand was why he had gone out of his way to pick out only the dregs. They were all devil's spawn, and there wasn't a man among them I would trust behind my back.

I could see that Schiller shared my opinion, it was there in his withering eyes and the slight crinkling of his nose, but van Groten signed on each man as he stepped up to the table. He asked practically no questions and was in a hurry to get the business done. He scribbled names and they made their marks. None of them could write.

I didn't interfere, but if it hadn't been too late I think I would have walked off the ship. I wanted nothing to do with this crew, but I had signed my own name to sail aboard the *Kerkyra* last night, and I couldn't break the contract.

I watched until the last man had made his mark and left, and nothing but the smell of them was left behind. Van Groten closed his ledger with a bang, pushed back his chair and thankfully stood.

"Thank God that's over, hey? I'm glad they only be aboard my ship a few days before we transfer them to the *Kerkyra*."

He spoke to Schiller, but then looked at me.

"A rough lot, Mister Mc'Adden, but they were the best I could find at short notice. We have to take whatever is available."

"Why?" I asked slowly. "What's the big hurry?"

The blue eyes were frosty for me too. Van Groten had no smiles today. I didn't back down and so he gave me an answer.

"There is hurry because another typhoon could blow the *Kerkyra* off the rocks. That way all is lost, including the men I leave behind. And there is hurry because the *Zandvoort* has regular cargo schedules to keep. I cannot afford to waste too much of my time on the *Kerkyra*."

He didn't invite any more questions,

but shouted for the Chinese steward. The man came running and van Groten waved a massive arm around the cabin.

"You get this place cleaned up, hey? Scrub, scrub, everywhere, you savvy? Get all this damned stink out."

He nodded to Schiller to take care of the ledger and papers that still lay on the saloon table and then went out.

★ ★ ★

I spent the afternoon lying on my bunk, naked again in the sweaty heat, thinking. I had nothing else to do. This time I didn't think about Louella. I thought about what van Groten had said. The *Kerkyra* had been sitting off the Philippines for the past three months, so there was no reason to suppose that she might suddenly get off the rocks and sink. This wasn't the typhoon season. That meant that one of van Groten's reasons for making a fast return wasn't quite valid. The other I wasn't sure about. It was a fair bet that the Holland East Indies Steamship Company knew nothing about the salvage job. Van Groten was going after the Greek ship on his own account and he wouldn't be sharing the profits. So there he did have a valid reason for keeping up the *Zandvoort*'s regular cargo schedules, and keeping her part owners unsuspecting and happy. However, that part didn't worry me, I wasn't concerned over a bunch of company directors who might or might not get cheated some eight thousand miles away in Rotterdam. What worried me was that crew. The crew I would have to handle.

Even taking into account the fact that they had been hastily raked together, they were still a dubious collection. If van Groten had grabbed a score of men at random he should have had a sprinkling of good hands caught up with the rabble, but he hadn't. The crew that had just been signed on looked as though they had all been hand-picked, and all for the wrong reasons. I conceded that the *Kerkyra* would be making only one short trip, but why should van Groten deliberately fill her with scum and villains? It was out of character,

40

because my morning tour had made it obvious that not one of the hands signed on today would have ever been given a berth on the *Zandvoort*.

My thinking got me to the usual place. Nowhere. Finally I gave it up and went to stand under the cold shower. I got dressed and then went up on deck. The ship was still, lulled by the heat, and the other ships lying in the inner and outer roads looked just as lifeless. City noises came from the shore. Singapore was a rat race like any other city. I leaned on the rail, watching, and feeling sorry for the poor slobs who spent their lives running round in the same endless circles in their concrete cages. Then van Groten appeared above me and called me up to his cabin.

I went, hoping for a glimpse of Louella who had stayed out of sight all day. I was disappointed, for the only other occupant of the cabin was a big, fleshy man who sat in the chair I had occupied last night. Van Groten was the friendly host again. He clapped me on the shoulder as I ducked through the door.

"Mister Mc'Adden, I want you to meet Mister Bennet. Mister Bennet has just signed on to act as Second Mate on the *Kerkyra*. We'll need a third deck officer and I can't afford to take one away from the *Zandvoort*."

Bennet stood up and looked at me. His eyes were bloodshot and there was a shimmer of sweat on his face and glistening on the rolls of fat around his neck. He was over-weight and doomed to suffer wherever there was heat. He was American, but I doubt that his countrymen were proud of him. I had never met him, but I knew about him. He had been washed-up in Singapore even longer than I had. I checked to be sure that he was the same man.

"Larry Bennet?"

Bennet nodded slowly, and I knew that this was another man who was never going to be my friend. If I knew his name, then it followed that I knew his story. He was a lush who had been kicked off his last ship for being drunk on watch. And judging by those eyes, he had stayed drunk most of the time since. His mouth made a tight scowl.

I offered him my hand, just to be polite.

He took it for a moment, just to be polite.

I thought what the hell. I didn't need friends anyway. The sudden shock of finding that somebody loved me would probably be more than I could take. It would do awful things to my state of mind.

Van Groten said cheerfully:

"You two better get to know each other, hey? The *Zandvoort* don't have any spare cabins, so you have to share the First Mate's cabin until we get out to the *Kerkyra*. That's the biggest cabin after mine. Okay?"

It wasn't okay, but there wasn't a lot that I could do about it. I just nodded. Bennet looked as though he liked the idea about as much as I did, but he didn't argue either. Van Groten yelled for his steward and told the man to make up an extra bunk in the Chief Officer's cabin.

I showed Bennet the way, but he wasn't very talkative. Once he screwed up his eyes like a man with a bursting head, which he probably was. I had first claim on the cabin and it was obvious that the only place to rig up a spare bunk was on the deck, but he didn't make any comment. My gear was still in my suitcase, because the wardrobe and drawers were still full of stuff left behind by the *Zandvoort*'s First Officer, the man stuck out on the *Kerkyra*. Bennet looked around, but for some reason he was only curious about me. He said suddenly:

"The Captain told me that he only signed you on yesterday. What was your last ship?"

"The *Yankee Trader*," I said casually. I didn't tell him that I had come over as a deckhand. I wasn't going to tell him any more than I had do.

Bennet nodded slowly, and rubbed a finger round the inside of his collar. The sweat was making his neck itch. He changed the subject.

"I've got some gear ashore. I'll go and fetch it. Give the Chink time to make up that extra bunk."

I nodded, just to be polite, and then

he nodded for the same reason and went out. I watched him and wondered how long we could go on being polite.

The Chinese steward came in and I left him to get on with his job. I went back to the rail and watched the sampan that was taking Bennet ashore. To the west the sky and the sea were melting into different shades of yellow, a trick of the sunset. Singapore was already shrouded in dusk, the bright lights flickering to seduce unwary sailors. They snared the wary ones too.

I gave the Chinese half an hour and then went back to the cabin. He had fixed up a bed on the floor, and there was a full bottle of Scotch whisky and two glasses standing prominently on the table. I didn't know whether the bottle was for Bennet or for me. Maybe it was meant to keep both of us happy. I poured myself one drink and then hid the bottle out of sight.

An hour later I had dinner in the saloon. It was a chance to have a good look at the regular officers of the *Zandvoort*, and to let them have a good look at me. Van Groten reeled off the names, but there were only two in which I had any real interest. The Chief Engineer was a bluff, amiable-looking man named van Lynden. The Second Radio Officer was a handsome young lad in his twenties named Hollert. These were the two who would be transferred to the *Kerkyra*. They were all courteous, but I wasn't exactly received with open arms. They were all sailors, and I was a man who had drowned thirty-seven sailors. Nobody wanted me for his bosom pal. The meal was just bearable because Bennet wasn't there, and because Louella was sitting on van Groten's right side. She gave me a smile.

★ ★ ★

Bennet failed to return until midnight. I was a busy man, devoting my time between lying in the cabin and leaning over the ship's rail, and I happened to be on deck when the sampan brought him back. I watched it scull over to the foot of the gangway and then lost

46

interest. A big Chinese junk was nosing in towards the mouth of the Singapore river. I had counted scores of sampans, but this was my first junk. I watched as the big, squared sail was silently lowered, and then heard the commotion coming from the gangway. Bennet's voice was slurred and arrogant, the American twang coming over clearly. There were giggling noises too, and the overall impression of an argument.

I figured that the best thing to do was to keep out of the way. But one of my faults is that I figure out the right thing and then do the opposite. I went to see what was happening.

Bennet was drunk. He stood at the top of the gangway and he had a woman with him, a Chinese slut who might have been pretty once but had been used too often. His arm was around her and he was hugging her close; she was like a flimsy prop holding him up. Facing them was Foong. The Bo'sun was like a watchdog, he was everywhere. Now he was planted in Bennet's path, and the marlinespike was dangling in his hand again. His

47

objection was in three words:

"No womans aboard."

"Go to hell — get out of my way!"

Foong didn't budge.

"No womans aboard."

"Now you just shift your ass. I don't take no orders from any sonofabitch Chink. Move it!"

Bennet wasn't scared by that empty eye socket. He came forward. Foong backed just enough so that he had room to swing the marlinespike and lifted it sharply. Bennet stopped and then pushed the woman away. She looked scared and huddled down in a crouch.

Foong said it a third time.

"No womans aboard. Captain say."

Bennet was too drunk to be scared. Besides, he was American and white, Foong was Chinese, and that was no better than being black. I could read the way Bennet was thinking. And I knew that at any minute that marlinespike would crack open his head. He spat on his hands and steadied his fat bulk.

"Now I'm gonna tell you just one more time. Just shift your ass."

48

I stepped forward, dumb Mc'Adden, sticking my neck out. I said sharply:

"Mister Bennet, sober up! You're supposed to be an officer. You should know better than trying to bring a woman aboard. The ship's Bo'sun has every right to stop you."

They both turned. Bennet was bleary-eyed, even more bloodshot than before. Foong's one eye was cold, as always, wary. Bennet's face twisted into a scowl.

"You're giving orders early, *Mister* Mc'Adden." He put a sneer into the last two words. "I'm not under your command until we transfer to the *Kerkyra*. You got no authority aboard this ship."

He paused, and then gave it to me.

"I found out some facts about you, *Mister* Mc'Adden. Facts that van Groten probably doesn't know yet. When I tell him, I reckon maybe I'll be First Mate aboard the *Kerkyra*, and you'll be Second, if he keeps you aboard at all. So don't bother coming the old bullshit with me."

I was tempted to borrow Foong's

49

marlinespike, but didn't. Instead I soft-pedalled back. I said bluntly:

"Stow it. Get rid of the woman and you can talk tomorrow."

Bennet came towards me, still squared up for a fight.

"How many was it, Mc'Adden? Two ships and how many men?"

I would have thrown him down the gangway, and to hell with everything, but I didn't have to. Van Groten had appeared behind him and Foong stepped smartly back out of the way. Van Groten asked no questions, and offered no warning. He simply lifted one massive balled fist and clubbed Bennet square and solid in the back of the neck. Bennet broke at the knees and I had to skip to one side as he blundered over on to his face. He sprawled on the deck, out cold.

I looked at Van Groten who was rubbing his fist. His face was wooden, but then he showed a bleak smile.

"You don't let him worry you, hey? I take no notice of anything he tell me. You get rid of that whore and Foong and I will put him to bed. He sleep it off."

I looked down at Bennet, smelling the reek of whisky.

"Are you sure you know what you're doing? If it was my ship I'd chuck him back in that sampan and let him rot."

Van Groten shrugged. "He will be okay when he is sober. And I make sure that there is no whisky when we go aboard the *Kerkyra*. I knew he would be drunk tonight. This was just a goodbye session. In port it is no matter. I must have another mate for the *Kerkyra*, and she is only making the one trip."

He nodded to Foong and together they lifted Bennet up. The subject was closed and they carried him away. I watched sourly and then turned to the woman he had brought aboard.

She was rough, but I suppose she wasn't so bad if your sight was blurred. She wore a tight *cheong sen* that was slit almost up to her hip, and she turned to show me her thigh. She wasn't sure what was happening, but she was an optimist.

"You want?"

I shook my head. There was only one woman I wanted.

She smiled hopefully.

"Not want? Why not want?"

I said definitely:

"*Not want*. Not tonight, Josephine. You go back to sampan, savvy?"

She pouted, and it didn't improve her looks any. Then she squared her shoulders and held out her hand.

"Give money. Twenty Malay dollar. Other man no pay. You give twenty dollar."

That was a joke. She might as well have asked for twenty thousand, or twenty cents. I didn't have either. I just pointed down the gangway to the sampan.

She stood her ground and kept her hand out.

"Twenty dollar. Not come here no pay. You pay."

I was tired, fed-up with the whole business, and I wasn't in the mood to stand and argue all night with Bennet's whore. I picked her up bodily and she screamed, but I dropped her over the side before she could claw her nails at my face. She hit the water and came up sobbing and cursing, and I left the waiting sampan to scull round and fish her out.

Somehow it helped my feelings.

4

The Kerkyra

THE *Zandvoort* sailed the next morning. I had no duties until we reached the Philippines, and so I just stayed out of the way. I stood at my usual place by the well deck rail and listened to van Groten giving orders on the bridge, and Foong yelling in Chinese at the seamen in the bows. The windlass whined and the anchor chain rattled aboard, the screw churned and the ship began to move sluggishly. We cleared the Singapore roads and then headed out into the South China Sea. There wasn't a breath of wind and the sun was a white glare that sucked the sweat out of me.

Bennet was still snoring in the cabin, sailing without his gear and making the whole place reek of alcohol and more sweat. I didn't fancy his company and so I climbed up on to the boat deck. I had the deck to myself, so I stripped off my shirt, rolled it into a pillow and began working on my sun tan. I was going to be a passenger for the next few days, so I figured I might as well act like one. Later on I might even offer Bennet a game of deck tennis.

I lay on my back thinking great philosophical thoughts, most of which had been thought before. It was a pity that Plato and Aristotle knew how to write. If they'd kept their thoughts to themselves I could have written a great new book. I might even be famous. I drowsed for an hour and then opened my eyes and found Louella looking down at me. She favoured me with a smile. She knew damned well that smile had me hooked.

"Rick, I envy you. I wish that I could take off some of my clothes and sunbathe."

I said sociably, "It's a free deck."

She accepted the invitation halfway and sat down beside me, wrapping her arms around her knees like a contented

55

schoolgirl. She wore a dark skirt and another high-collared blouse, scarlet this time with pink see-through sleeves. She said sadly:

"Not for me. Dirk says that I must not sunbathe, because it would make the crew restless. There is nowhere that I could be wholly private."

I decided Dirk was right. I was supposed to be civilized, but she was making me restless already. Lay her out on the deck in a bikini and the crew would take some holding back, especially the new crew that had just been signed.

I said, "I agree with Dirk."

She looked at me and laughed, and then asked:

"Is it true that you threw Bennet's woman over the side last night. I heard all the noise, but Dirk made me stay in the cabin out of the way."

I performed the difficult task of nodding my head while lying on my back.

"It's true. Bennet forgot to pay her. I couldn't get rid of her anyhow else."

"I would like to have seen that."
The thought pleased her. "I could have
translated all the filthy names she must
have called you. It would have improved
your education."

I grinned at that, but let it go. She was
silent, looking up at the sky, so after a
minute I said:

"Tell me about Dirk?"

She turned her head, curiously. Her
eyes were like black liquid almonds gazing
steadily into mine.

"Why?"

"Because I'm working for him, and it's
helpful to know something about the kind
of man you're working for."

She thought slowly, then said:

"Dirk is a very good man. One day I
think he will marry me."

I said nothing to that. She was already
his mistress, so van Groten had no real
cause to marry a half-Malay wife.

She gave me that direct look again
and said:

"What you are really asking is about
Dirk and me. How we met?"

I wasn't, but I wasn't going to turn

57

down any information. I stayed non-committal and let her carry on.

"It was five years ago." She was talking almost to herself. "My father was a Frenchman whom I never knew. My mother was a Malay. She married another Malay. He was my real father. A father is the man who takes care of you, and gives you a home. Not the man who puts the seed into your mother. My Malay father sent me to school. I learned English there. Then I got a job in a big store in Singapore. It was a good job, but when my Malay father died there was not enough money to keep a whole family. I had to have a better job, so I went to one of the bath and massage houses."

She paused but I said nothing. She was remembering out loud and I just happened to be there. I wasn't going to break the spell. She smiled faintly and continued:

"You know the places, perhaps you have been a customer there? You pay for a hot bath and then a massage. The girls who give the massage they wear pants and bra. If you like to pay a little more they take off the top half, pay a little more and they will take off the bottom half. If the girl likes you and you can pay, you can get special services. But it is not a whorehouse. If the girl doesn't like you then you only get the hot bath and massage. A girl can make good money there, and you don't have to do anything you don't want to.

"When Dirk came to the bath house I liked him. For the other customers I only took off my top half, for him it was everything. I wasn't a virgin, but he knew that I was new to the bath house. He fell in love with me and took me away. Now I am respectable and he sends money to my family. This was all five years ago."

She finished where she had started and gave me a frank smile. The smile proved that she hadn't forgotten that I was there, and I wondered what she was really trying to say. Was she telling me that she owed a big debt to van Groten, and that I was wasting my time if I tried to change her mind? Or was she titillating little secrets into my ear just to keep my blood burning up. That half-Malay face could be as inscrutable as a Chinese, and I wasn't sure whether she was warning me off or luring me on. She stayed for another five minutes and then made an excuse to leave. I watched her walk away and I still wasn't sure what her motives were.

After she had gone I went below. The sun had started to burn my chest and I knew that I had already exceeded my quota for the day. I found that Bennet was awake, but looking pale and groggy. His red eyes blinked at me.

"What happened last night? Somebody hit me."

I said flatly, "Nobody hit you. You were drunk. You passed out."

He rubbed at the back of his neck, eyeing me dangerously.

"Somebody hit me. They didn't leave a mark, but I can sure as hell feel it." He remembered suddenly and swore. "It was that goddamned Chink. He was behind me with a marlinespike. Damn it, I'll break his stinking neck."

"Somehow I don't think that would be a good idea." I paused and then told him. "It was van Groten who hit you. And he didn't need a marlinespike. He clubbed you with his fist."

Bennet stared at me, and then realized something else.

"Hey, the goddamned ship is moving!"

I nodded. "We left Singapore this morning."

"But my gear is still ashore; I haven't even got a razor."

I shrugged. "You'll have to take it up with van Groten. He's the skipper."

I left him and went out, wondering where I could find some peace and quiet. Behind me Bennet called someone or something a *sonofabitch*.

* * *

It was a four-day voyage and the weather stayed murderously hot. The *Zandvoort* ploughed on a steady course due northeast, and the black filth from her funnel made just about the only cloud in the sky. With two crews aboard, the ship was overcrowded and tempers frayed in the heat. There were fights and arguments among the new hands, and

61

I noticed that Foong never moved a step without his precious marlinespike. It hung permanently from his belt, just behind the big knife on his hip. I don't know exactly how many fights he broke up, but he was a damned good Bo'sun. Van Groten had been right about that. Foong would never win a beauty contest, but he knew how to handle a crew.

Bennet stayed sober but sullen. I knew from experience that coming out of a long, extended drunk wasn't easy, so I stayed clear of him as much as possible. After a couple of days he got rid of the shakes and his eyes began to look almost human. He didn't get any friendlier, and I knew that he had tackled van Groten with the opinion that he should be made First Officer on the *Kerkyra*. I knew too that the Dutchman had brusquely crushed those ambitions down. Bennet nursed his grudge and became more sullen. We stayed out of each other's way and van Groten pretended that he hadn't noticed the enmity between us.

Meals in the officers' saloon were strained. It was as though two hyenas had crept in to eat with the lions. Bennet usually left as soon as it was decently possible, but I made a point of dawdling over the coffee. The Chief Engineer was the most sociable of the officers, he was older, relaxed, and didn't condemn too quickly. I knew that he had loaned Bennet some spare shirts and a reserve shaving kit. He wouldn't be an easy man to draw out, but if any man would talk to me it would be van Lynden. I wasn't looking for a friend, but when we transferred to the *Kerkyra* it would be nice to know that someone aboard wasn't a definite enemy.

On the third night out we finished up with the saloon to ourselves. The Chinese steward had cleared away everything but my coffee cup, and van Lynden was calmly measuring out tobacco and filling his pipe. He was the kind of man who would have been out of character if he didn't smoke a pipe.

I said conversationally:

"How long have you sailed with the *Zandvoort*?"

He looked at me shrewdly. I knew he

would reply, but he wouldn't hurry. He lit the pipe and then said calmly:

"For eight years now. Before that I was Second Engineer with another ship of the Holland East Indies Line. I have been at sea most of my life. Once I got married, but it wasn't any good for a woman who was left behind in Rotterdam while her husband was out on the China seas. I think she would have divorced me if she could have named a ship's engine-room as the corespondent in a lawsuit." He smiled easily at his own joke. "Instead she went to live with another man. She is happy now, I think. And I am happy also — or so I think."

He stopped and drew on his pipe, still watching me, and then he asked:

"Is that what you wanted to know?"

I admitted that it wasn't, and with van Lynden I sensed that only straight questions would get straight answers.

I said, "I was going to ask you about van Groten."

"The Captain, hey?" He nodded gently. "I thought as much. Well, I have known the Captain for eight years also. Dirk van Groten was First Mate when I came aboard the *Zandvoort*. The old Captain retired two years later, and Dirk was given command of the ship. He has sailed these seas all his life, he's a good Captain and a good friend. And for her age the *Zandvoort* is a good ship."

He waited for the next question and I asked:

"And what's your opinion of this new crew he's hired for the *Kerkyra*?"

"They are scum, and I am a little puzzled that Dirk did not wait a little longer to get a better crew. But — " He shrugged. "The *Kerkyra* makes only one last trip, and to waste time is to waste money. I think they will serve their purpose."

I wondered if he considered me as part of the scum, but I didn't ask. He probably had an open mind. Neither did I ask if he considered that van Groten was honest, or if he considered that this present trip was wholly legal. That would have been a mistake, because van Lynden would have answered yes, and it was never wise to anger a placid man.

Later, I tried to sound out Hollert. The Radio Officer spoke only a little English and I was totally ignorant of Dutch, so it didn't get me very far. There was just the general impression that Hollert was a cheerful lad who fully trusted his skipper. He didn't seem to have any worries or doubts. On a passenger ship his good looks would have charmed the ladies too. I really envied him.

★ ★ ★

On the fifth morning we sighted the Philippines. Mindoro was one of the largest of the central islands in the group, and the *Kerkyra* was stuck fast on a rocky islet about three miles off shore. The coastline beyond was white beach with dense green jungle further back, deserted except for the birds in the palm fronds. The sea and the sky were calm and blue, and all of it reflecting the heat and glare of the sun.

Van Groten took the *Zandvoort* close in to the stranded ship, and then stopped engines. The ship slowly became still, and then the anchor chain rumbled out of its hidden locker and sank down into the sea. I stood by the rail and looked out to the *Kerkyra*.

The Greek ship was smaller than the *Zandvoort*, and although her hull had once been painted grey it was now almost pure rust. She had been beached for three months, but from the look of her she might have been there for thirty years. I had considered the *Zandvoort* a tub, but the *Kerkyra* made the Dutch boat look like a queen. My heart sank as I stared at her, and then van Groten was shouting down from the *Zandvoort*'s bridge.

I could take a boat across and start acting like a First Mate again.

It was all a sick joke.

5

Death in the Hold

I WENT back into the cabin and put on a clean white shirt with the three gold bars of a Chief Officer on each shoulder. Those epaulettes had been hidden for a long time at the bottom of my gear, and I still didn't know why I hadn't thrown them away. I hadn't worn them since the night that I brought the crippled *Pirahne* and the pathetic huddle of survivors from the *Conchita* into Panama.

I looked at myself in the mirror and saw that my face had got a lot older and a good deal harder since then. I had never been a particularly handsome brute, but now there was a bleak cynicism in the face that stared back at me. It was a face that had gone sour. I hadn't had the nightmares for a long time, but they had left a definite mark. It hadn't been easy to forget that night in the fog, and if I listened hard enough even now I could hear the screams and curses from men dying behind the curtain of darkness.

Now I had authority again, and responsibility for more lives aboard another ship.

I heard a footstep through the open door behind me, and then there was another face in the mirror. Bennet was there and he made a sneering smile. He knew what I was thinking and he wasn't going to make it any easier. He said shrewdly:

"The boat's lowered and waiting, *Mister Mate*."

I wondered how he had heard about the collision, but that was a question that I hadn't even asked van Groten, and I certainly wasn't going to open the subject with Larry Bennet. The whole story had been written up big by the press, and most of the papers had splashed my picture on their front pages. I just had to accept that although the rest of the world might have forgotten, seamen had longer memories. I turned and said coldly:

"Thank you, Mister Bennet. I'm ready."

I jammed my cap on my head and followed him back on deck. He was wearing one of van Lynden's shirts, and a spare set of epaulettes with the two gold bars of a Second Officer that belonged to Schiller. He hadn't touched a drink since Singapore, which might have been because I had thrown the bottle that had been left in our cabin overboard, and now he wore his borrowed clothes more easily than my own fitted me.

The starboard lifeboat was already resting in the water, with Foong standing in command and a dozen of the new crew sitting at the oars. Van Groten was waiting on the deck, and when we appeared he preceded us down the rope ladder that led down the ship's side into the boat.

Foong cast off and we pulled away from the *Zandvoort*'s hull. I watched the seamen at the oars, mentally noting the ones that looked useful and the ones that weren't. The Lascar with the scarred face was pulling on the port side, and I knew

70

already that he was trouble. Foong had backed him down, but he would still be the one to watch.

We came alongside the *Kerkyra* and Foong grabbed hold of the rope ladder that dangled down her rusty flank. At close quarters she looked like a rotting hulk that was thankful to have found a quiet graveyard. I doubted if she would ever come off the rocks without falling to pieces, and if she did she would probably sink like a sieve. Even Bennet looked as though he was having second thoughts, but van Groten didn't share our opinion. He had a satisfied grin on his face and he was the first man aboard.

I went up the rope ladder more slowly. On the deck above, van Groten was already shaking hands briskly with another big Dutchman who wore twin three-barred epaulettes to my own. It looked like a happy reunion, but the greetings were all in Dutch. I reached the deck and then Bennet came up behind me. Van Groten turned and said cheerfully:

"Mister Pohlmann, Mister Mc'Adden

and Mister Bennet. They are helping me take the *Kerkyra* to Saigon."

Pohlmann was another solid, amiable type. He shook hands in a friendly fashion and welcomed us aboard. I felt that we could be friends, but then I had to remind myself that he didn't know yet that I was the Mc'Adden from the *Pirahne*.

We crossed to the starboard and landward side to see the *Kerkyra*'s position more clearly for ourselves. The deck slanted upwards, which meant that at least she was tilting back in the right direction towards deeper water, but she was still stuck hard and fast. The islet that had stopped her was just a jumble of off-shore rocks, about fifty yards across and covered by a green tangle of fern and creeper. The ship had struck the northern end where the rocks continued underwater, and had been slammed sideways on to those submerged fangs so that she was held amidships, just forward of the engine-room. The typhoon had given her a hammering and parts of her deck railing and one of her lifeboats were missing, but she was stuck so squarely that I guessed it must have been the tail end of the typhoon that had run her aground. In that position she couldn't have taken much of a pounding without breaking her back, and so the storm must have thrown her up and passed on almost immediately. I began to concede that maybe van Groten did have a good case for getting back to her quickly.

Pohlmann saw my expression and said:

"Now it is low tide. At high tide I think it will be possible for the *Zandvoort* to pull her off."

For once, Bennet was on my side. He said doubtfully:

"Yeh, but will she float?"

Van Groten grinned, and I wondered what made him so confident. He said:

"We have a damned good try, hey? Come, let us have a look at the damage below."

Pohlmann nodded and led us towards the forward hatch. The covers were off and in fact there was no sign of them; it looked as though they too had been swept away. We climbed down into the hold and immediately smelled the stink of sulphates. Bennet began to cough.

The floor of the hold was knee-deep in water, although the pumps were going in an effort to keep it down. A network of cables and powerful arc lamps had been rigged up to give light, and it was obvious that Pohlmann and the skeleton crew who had stayed aboard with him had been pretty busy during the *Zandvoort*'s absence. They had patched up the weak places inside the ruptured hull with mattresses held by tarpaulins and braced by a heavy framework of timbers, and they had made a good job of it. Van Groten showed approval, but to me it looked as though a hell of a lot of patching had been necessary, and I wouldn't bet money that it could take any real strain.

Pohlmann said calmly:

"The biggest job was to get rid of the cargo that was in this hold. It was ruined by sea-water anyway, so we dumped most of it over the side. The forward winches were rusted, but we got them going again to lift it out. It was hard, stinking work shovelling that mess into the winch bucket, but we managed. After that the job was easier."

He stepped down into the water and waded over to the bulkhead. The rest of us followed and he picked up a hand light to show us what he had accomplished so far.

"Here there is a big rent in the hull. Underneath the tarpaulin it takes three of the mattresses to cover it, and there is another mattress jammed horizontally into the rent itself. I had the straw taken out and refilled all the mattresses with sawdust. That way they swell when the water soaks into them, and then they wedge even tighter into place."

He shifted the light to the left and added:

"There too the plates are buckled. I patched them up as well as I can and I think that they will hold. The big rent is the main danger; at the best, the ship will keep taking in water and you will need the pumps all the way to Saigon."

Van Groten grinned and said:

"You done a good job here. I got some

timbers aboard the *Zandvoort* that help to strengthen these places. And I think that we will have some time to spare while van Lynden gets the engine-room into shape."

He slapped his Chief Officer on the shoulder and repeated, "A good job, Mister Pohlmann. Now you take command of the *Zandvoort*. Take your own men back with you, they earned a rest. I'll take over here with the new crew I hired in Singapore; let them start losing a little sweat. That will be a nice change for them." He grinned at me. "Hey, Mister Mc'Adden?"

I nodded, and let it pass. Bennet didn't seem to hear and was staring dubiously at the patched bulkhead. He was the last to turn away as we all sloshed back to the foot of the ladder and climbed up and out of the hold. It was good to get out of the acid stench left by the sulphates, and although the glare blinded me for a minute, the sun didn't seem so hostile any more.

We spent the rest of the day transferring men, stores and timbers from the

Zandvoort. The lifeboat made repeated trips back and forth with Foong at the tiller, while Bennet organized a bunch of hands around the forward winch and brought the stores aboard. The sweat dripped from his face and his voice was quickly hoarse, but although he made a lot of noise about it, he knew his job.

Pohlmann had gone back to the *Zandvoort*, and van Lynden came over with the boat's return trip. The Chief's only concern was the engine-room and I knew just how he felt when he made his inspection. He felt the way I had felt when I had first sighted the *Kerkyra* as a whole. He spread his hands helplessly, said that the engine-room was a mess, that it had been shamefully neglected, and that the crankshafts were seized solid and would never turn again. Then he sent for his complete engine crew from the *Zandvoort* and set out to prove himself wrong.

I made a tour of the whole ship with van Groten. We checked the wheelhouse, the charts and the navigation equipment, and then went aft to check the steerage gear. Everything seemed to be intact and workable, despite the outer coating of rust that blanketed the whole ship. We came up on deck again and I asked:

"What about the screw?"

Van Groten nodded and grinned. "A good question."

We threw a rope over the stern and I took off my shirt and cap. When I took off my shoes and socks the deck was hot to my feet, so I didn't hesitate to lower myself over the side. I picked the shady side, otherwise the steel hull might have been hot enough to blister my soles as I walked down. Van Groten leaned over the side and watched.

The screw looked to be in good shape; it hadn't buckled at all and there was no sign that it had struck the rocks. It was an ideal day for a swim, so I dived underneath to make sure. The *Kerkyra*'s hull had a nasty crust of barnacles which I gave a wide berth as I didn't fancy shredding my own flesh, but the screw and the propeller shaft were clear. At least there would be no trouble there. I came up again and van Groten helped to haul me aboard. My report put him in a good humour for the rest of the day.

That night we ate aboard the *Kerkyra*, and it proved a reasonably cheerful meal. Bennet and I now had separate cabins, and also we had plenty of hard work to keep us busy, which helped to ease the strain between us. I knew that another enforced day of the American's company could have led to murder on one side or the other, but now the tension had dropped. Louella had now come aboard to join us and van Groten's good humour persisted. Van Lynden again wore a look of anguish when he was asked about the engines, but he did admit to a thousand-to-one chance that they might be revived again for the one last haul to Saigon. To me it sounded a gloomy forecast, but van Groten knew his Chief Engineer better than I did and accepted it as a vote of confidence. He had no more worries about the engines.

★ ★ ★

For the next two days we worked hard getting the *Kerkyra* ready for sea. Bennet and I worked in shifts, supervising the work in the hold, with the crew divided into the port and starboard watch. With the new timbers brought across from the *Zandvoort* we reinforced the repairs that Pohlmann had already made, bracing the timbers back to the next bulkhead. The pumps never stopped and we got the water level down another six inches. The stink in the hold remained overpowering and we had to limit the time that each watch remained below.

Hollert came aboard the second day and I loaned him a couple of the most intelligent hands to help replace the radio aerials that had been ripped away by the typhoon. Afterwards he fussed around the wireless set, twiddling knobs and replacing valves until he could receive a stream of dance music from Radio Hong Kong. Then he was happy.

All in all, the scratch crew of the *Kerkyra* were knitting together well. Now that they were no longer overcrowded and had work to do, they were shaping up better than I expected. There hadn't been a single fight that I knew about since we had transferred from the *Zandvoort*, and I began to think that maybe we could make the short voyage to Saigon without any further trouble. I should have known better than to start thinking like that, because trouble came as soon as I began to relax.

I was standing on deck, hoping for a glimpse of Louella, who occasionally came to see how the job was going on. I had handed over the work in the hold to Bennet's watch only half an hour before and had only just got cleaned up and washed away the stink and sweat. Then one of the Malay seamen came climbing fast out of the hatchway and ran like a rabbit for the bridge. I knew that van Groten wasn't there and called out sharply as the Malay reached the first companionway.

"You there! Where are you going?"

The man stopped and turned. He was the one with the ear-rings and the sickly smile that I suspected was queer, but he wasn't smiling now. He was breathing hard and he looked shaken. I went towards him and he babbled jerkily:

"Man dead. Mate send, find Captain. Man dead in hold."

I stared at him and he looked more frightened than ever, but I knew it was true. I cursed savagely and then swung down into the hatchway, down into the hold.

When I reached the bottom there was an ominous silence that wasn't affected by the steady chugging of the pumps. The hands stood back with tense, drawn faces and all work had stopped. Bennet and Foong were kneeling over a huddled body that lay half submerged on the floor of the hold and they looked up as I splashed over to join them. Bennet was holding a hand light and Foong was supporting the head and shoulders of the dead man against one knee. I noted that some of the braced timbers had been smashed down, and one lay directly beneath the dead man. It looked as though he had fallen and broken his neck and his back. I said harshly:

"What happened?"

"He fell." Bennet's face was white and glistening in the glare of a light. "The stupid sonofabitch fell."

I looked up. "What the hell was he doing up there?"

"I sent him up," Bennet said flatly. "The bulb failed in one of the arc lights. I sent him up with another bulb."

I could see now that one of the arc lights had gone out. It was high up in the hold and the man must have lost his footing while edging out from the ladder to reach it.

Bennet said, "It was an accident."

I looked at him and nodded, and then looked at the dead man and changed my mind. He was one of the Chinese seamen, a wrinkled old man who should have been pensioned off into the galley. The dead wax face was like a wizened mask, frozen into place. Foong's one eye was passionless as he turned the face to the light so that I could see. I swung back to Bennet.

"He's an old man! Why the hell was an old man sent up aloft? There are younger men here. Men who wouldn't have slipped."

Bennet's face became mottled. He said angrily:

"Goddammit, he's supposed to be a sailor doing a sailor's job. I just picked on the nearest man and sent him up. I didn't stop to ask whether he was young or old. If he wasn't capable, then van Groten shouldn't have signed him on."

"And you shouldn't have sent an old man aloft."

"I told you, I didn't think." Bennet's eyes blazed from his sweating face. "I was busy, I didn't have the time to think."

"Mister Bennet, you're paid to think. Officers who don't think cost men their lives."

I knew immediately that was the wrong thing to say, but it was too late. Bennet stared at me and then he laughed into my face. His mouth twisted viciously.

"That's good, *Mister Mc'Adden*. Coming from you that sounds mighty good. How good was your thinking that night off Panama — the night you sank two ships and thirty-seven men? Go ahead and tell

84

me, *Mister Mc'Adden*, how smart was your thinking then?"

I said nothing. My jaws were paralysed, locked together by the sudden rush of tension that was knotting up all my muscles. Bennet relaxed, no longer bothered by his own conscience, and the sneer stayed on his face.

"I'll tell you something, *Mister Mc'Adden*. I may have been kicked off my last ship for hitting the goddamned bottle. But I never sank any ships and I never drowned any sailors. This guy was an accident and he don't mean a goddamned thing. An accident can happen to any guy. But I never sank any ships. Just you remember that, *Mister Mc'Adden*."

In another minute the old Chinese would not have been the only one floating around the floor of the hold with a broken neck. I balled a fist and was within an inch of smashing the knuckles into Bennet's grinning mouth. Then a new voice bellowed.

"Mister Bennet, you stow that talk, hey? I want no trouble between you two."

85

I recognized van Groten, but I didn't look towards him as he came down the last rungs of the ladder. He splashed across the hold towards us and reluctantly I held my punch. Bennet stared at me for a moment, and then stood up to face the Dutchman.

Van Groten looked down at the dead man.

"What happen here?"

Bennet told him.

I stood up and now I could move my jaws again. I let Bennet finish and then said grimly:

"You'll have to make out a report for when we return to Singapore, and I'll want to make some comments of my own."

Van Groten turned slowly to look at me, and the tension came back into the hold. The weathered face had gone hard and the blue eyes had a shrivelling stare. He said curtly:

"There will be no report for Singapore. The man is dead, and that is the finish. Foong can sew him in a sack and when we get under way we put him over the side. That is best."

There was no query at the end, and that made it an order. I didn't like it, and I said so.

"You can't dismiss a dead man just like that. You'll need to hold a full enquiry and make out a report for the authorities in Singapore."

Van Groten didn't like to be crossed. He shifted that teak-hard body squarely in front of me and planted the big-knuckled hands firmly on his hips. The gold-braided peak of his cap almost cut me between the eyes as he butted his head forward and he said bluntly:

"Mister Mate, this is my ship. I am Captain and I give the orders. And making reports is my business. You just make sure you mind your own damned business and that's all. You understand, hey?"

I understood, and I had more sense than to ball a fist against van Groten. I said harshly:

"Aye, aye, *sir*!"

I pushed Foong out of the way and walked off across the hold. There had been no respect in the way I said *sir*, but van Groten didn't stop me. I climbed back towards the deck and met the Malay seaman coming down. He took one look at my face and shot up again fast to give me right of way. If he hadn't, I would have thrown him off the ladder.

6

A Private Quarrel

I STORMED back into my cabin and was thankful again that I had it to myself. The heat was oppressive as always at this hour of the day, but the sun wasn't the only thing that was blazing. My blood was rushing around at about two hundred and twelve degrees Fahrenheit, or one hundred Centigrade. Whichever way you looked at it, that was boiling point. I hurled my cap in the corner and then stripped off my shirt and flung it down on the same spot. For all those gold bars on the shoulders were worth I might as well be back on the beach.

I stretched out on my bunk and stared up at the deckhead. And then slowly, very slowly, I began to relax. I had to cool down and think. It was a mistake to get riled because van Groten had backed

Bennet in an argument. The death of the old Chinese had been an accident, although Bennet had been careless in letting him work high in the hold. That in itself wasn't important. What made me ponder was why van Groten had been willing to dismiss the whole business so brusquely. The crew were certain to talk about the dead man when they got back to Singapore, and that would mean trouble for van Groten if a full report had not already been made in the right quarters. I felt sure that on the *Zandvoort* he would have stuck strictly to the rules and regulations, but it seemed that the *Kerkyra* was outside the law.

My doubts came crawling back. I had checked the log of the *Kerkyra* at the first opportunity and the entries bore out van Groten's account of the ship's last voyage. The Greek shipping company that owned her had gone bust after she had been wrecked by the typhoon, and her Captain had been forced to abandon her because of illness after being stranded for over three months. And by leaving his own First Officer aboard van Groten had reserved the legal right to salvage. I suspected that the log had deliberately been left so that I could find it and satisfy myself that the whole business was clean and legal, and I was fairly sure that the entries had not been forged. For some reason known only to himself, the Greek Captain had kept his records in English, but his hand-writing was poor and some of the letters strayed into the Greek alphabetical form. It had been difficult to read and would be impossible to imitate. Even so, I could sense that somehow, somewhere, there was something wrong.

It was all food for thought, and so I lay there and let it all revolve around in the grey sludge. Nothing useful emerged, but at least I wasn't concentrating on my wounded ego, which began to simmer down. Half an hour passed, and then I heard a light tap on the door.

I didn't want company, but I was curious. Both Bennet and van Groten would have bashed noisily and made themselves known, and there were few people on the *Kerkyra* who would tap politely and wait in silence for an answer.

I shifted on to one elbow and told whoever it was to come in.

It was Louella. She came through the door and closed it behind her. She wore the blue and white patterned blouse, and a pair of milk-white stretch slacks that hugged her hips so close that for a split second I thought she had nothing on at all. To complete the picture she wore her best smile. She put her finger to her lips, tip-toed over to the bunk and sat down beside me. She said softly:

"Rick, what happened in the hold? I heard Dirk arguing with Bennet, and something about a man being killed."

I wondered why she didn't ask Dirk, but I told her what had happened in the hold. She listened, wide-eyed and nodding seriously. Then she said:

"And you were angry with Bennet?"

"That's right."

"But if it was an accident?"

She was very solemn now, and very close. I had wanted her this close, but suddenly it was too close for comfort. I got up and walked to the porthole, staring out at the *Zandvoort* lying off

92

our port bow. Then I turned back and tried to explain.

"Even an accident should be noted in the log, especially when it results in death. And a report should be made out for the authorities in Singapore. I don't understand why Dirk is disregarding the law."

She smiled, and made a little shrugging movement of her shoulders.

"But, Rick. The *Kerkyra* is finished. We only tow her into Saigon for scrap. There is no need to keep logs and things now. It is not important."

She was telling me in her own bland way that I was making a fuss about nothing, and her smile made it easy listening. I wondered then if that was why she was here, just to smooth down my ruffled feelings. Van Groten had had time for reflection, and perhaps she was here under his orders to calm me down. I decided to find out. I went back to the bunk and said:

"Maybe you're right. Maybe it isn't important."

She smiled more warmly and stood up,

and again she was very close. She said cheerfully:

"Of course I am right. It is all best forgotten. When the officers forget, the crew forget. There is no need for reports and enquiry."

I nodded, as though I was beginning to agree with her, and then asked:

"Tell me something, Louella. Why did you come here?"

She looked up and her eyes were innocent. But her tongue appeared briefly, to leave a glisten of moisture along her upper lip and she knew the effect that could have. She said quietly:

"I think because I like you, Rick. I don't like to see you have trouble with Dirk. That way perhaps you both get hurt."

"And what about Dirk?"

She knew what I meant and said simply:

"I am in love with Dirk. He is my man."

"But you still like me?"

She nodded, and then her right forefinger was idly curling the dark hairs on my bare chest. She looked up again and smiled.

"I love Dirk, but you I like. In some ways you are very much like the man I love."

I didn't try to fathom that. Instead I put my hands on her shoulders. She came closer, touching me, and then she touched her lips to my chest. We stopped fencing then and her face lifted and I kissed her hard. Her mouth was softly alive and she showed every sign of enjoying it. I pulled her close, feeling the whole length of her body burning against my own. I smoothed my hand down her back and across the hard round seat of those milk-white slacks and she didn't mind.

The bunk was just beside us and I wondered how long it would take to get her out of those slacks. For more reasons than one I wanted to find out just how far she was willing to go. I moved away from the bunk for a moment to lock the cabin door, taking Louella with me, but this time Cupid wasn't on my side. There was a sharp knock on the door, and then Bennet came in.

I stopped kissing Louella and she pulled away. She was suddenly frightened and I was just as suddenly mad. Bennet appeared with a set face, looked startled for a second and then recovered his balance.

"Well I'll be goddamned. I'll say one thing for you, Mister Mc'Adden, you sure don't waste a lot of time. You showed a heck of a lot of concern for that dead Chink in the hold, but you sure didn't let it worry you for long."

I tried hard to keep my temper, but my voice came out in a steely rasp.

"And just what the hell do you want in my cabin, Mister Bennet?"

"I came to see you." He ignored Louella and glared straight into my face. "I came to tell you that what happened in the hold was an accident, and I got no objections to a full enquiry and a full report. In fact, I'm gonna make that report myself when I get back to Singapore. I told van Groten the same after you had left the hold."

96

I knew that he meant it, and that he was telling me that I didn't have to go out of my way to make any reports of my own. I nodded and said harshly:

"All right, you've said your piece. Now get to hell out of my cabin."

Bennet grinned. "Okay, I'm leaving. I don't have to be any goddamned genius to figure out why the two of you need to be alone. And don't sweat any that I'll let on to van Groten that you're giving him the doublecross with his woman. Because there'll be other times and I can fancy a piece of that tail for myself. It takes more than one guy to feed a hot woman in the tropics."

I saw red, and I hit him before even I knew what was happening. Louella screamed and jumped back out of the way, and Bennet spun round and slammed up against the door frame. My knuckles hurt and the skin was grazed and broken across Bennet's right cheekbone. He blinked and shook his head groggily. His hand came up as though to feel the spot where the blow had landed, and then abruptly he exploded towards me.

He was fat and he was heavy, but he was a whole lot faster than I had expected. He slammed me just under the belt and the air whooshed out of me as I went backwards and fell sprawling on my bunk. He came at me in another rush and I kicked him square in the chest and sent him reeling off. He cursed and crashed across the cabin, and then I pushed myself up and followed him. I hit him twice, across the mouth and in the middle, and then he flung a flat-edged back-hander that cut me across the side of the throat and left me gagging. Behind me, Louella was still shrieking her head off, and then she got through the door and ran.

Bennet and I backed off, both of us sucking in breath but neither of us prepared to call it finished. We were both glad that it had come at last. His face was dripping and there was the stink of sweat about him, but I didn't let that fool me any. Bennet sweated naturally and it didn't mean that he was puffed out or afraid. He smiled and spat at me through gasps for air.

"You *sonofabitch*."

Then he rushed me again. I hit him in the belly and stopped a clout that almost took my right ear from the side of my head. We both got hurt and we both got mad. There wasn't room for any fancy footwork and we both gave way to a stupid slugging match. When it ended we were both in a bloody mess and the cabin was in a shambles, but it wasn't a decisive finish. Louella had screamed for van Groten and he kicked through the cabin door and barged between us. Bennet fell back panting against one bulkhead and I needed the support of another.

The Dutchman was furious and his own hands were balled into massive fists. He stepped back so that he could face both of us and roared like an irate bull.

"That's enough, hey? If you want to fight, then I fight the damned two of you. Any fighting on my ship and I damned well settle it."

I was mad enough to take him up on that. I pushed away from the bulkhead and he turned towards me. I hesitated and then Foong appeared in the cabin doorway behind him. The Bo'sun held a marlinespike. I looked from the Dutchman to the Chinese, and then did myself a favour and backed off.

Van Groten glanced round. Maybe he didn't need Foong, but he didn't send him away either. Louella returned nervously to the doorway, and now the place was too crowded for anyone to fight. Van Groten gave her a hard look, and then he looked from Bennet to me.

"All right, maybe you better tell me what this was all about?"

I didn't say anything. I hadn't got the breath. Bennet looked worse than I was, but he licked a trickle of sweat and blood from the corner of his mouth and said hoarsely:

"It was private, Captain. Just a private bust-up between the Mate and me. I guess we both lost our tempers."

Van Groten glared at him, then swung back to me again. I had no choice but to back Bennet, and said slowly:

"That's right, just a private quarrel. We've worked it out. I don't think it will happen again."

"It damned well better not."

He relaxed his fists, and then turned sharply on Louella.

"How much you know about this, hey?"

Louella looked startled, then looked at me. Then she shook her head vigorously. She didn't convince van Groten, but he didn't push it. I felt sure then that he knew she had been in the cabin, and that meant that it was he who had sent her. He made a jerking motion with his thumb that needed no interpretation and she hurriedly slipped away. I watched and wondered just how much she would tell him when they were alone in the Captain's quarters.

Foong received another sign to dismiss and quietly retreated, still maintaining his national reputation for an impassive face. When the Bo'sun had gone, van Groten looked slowly around the wrecked cabin, and decided that maybe we had worked out all the bad blood that had been brewing between Bennet and myself. He looked up, pushed back his gold-braided cap and said blunty:

"This is another matter that should go down in the log, hey? But the *Kerkyra* is finished when we reach Saigon. That's why I don't trouble to keep any log. Not for this, not for the seaman in the hold." He paused to let that sink in, and then added a warning. "But there'll be no more fighting, you understand? Any more private quarrels you bring to me. I settle them. Otherwise you keep them until you get ashore. That is understood, hey?"

He shot a look at me.

"Mister Mc'Adden?"

I nodded slowly.

"Mister Bennet?"

Bennet hesitated, then he nodded too.

"That's good." Van Groten relaxed a little more. Then he looked to Bennet again. "You better get below, Mister Bennet. Those timbers have to be replaced in the hold. And see that Foong takes care of the dead man."

Bennet nodded and then moved forward to pick up his borrowed cap that had been trampled on the deck. Schiller wasn't going to be pleased about that. Bennet pulled it into shape again and then fitted it on to his head. Then, without another glance at me, he went out.

Van Groten gave him time to get clear, and then he allowed his weathered face to flicker into a brief, passing smile.

"You go easy on Bennet, Rick. Don't let him wear you down. It's hard for a man coming off the booze. It makes him edgy. You remember that, hey?"

He was being friendly again, and I guess he knew that he couldn't sail the *Kerkyra* unless he healed the peace between himself and his officers. I let it pass with just a brief nod, and van Groten stared at me for a moment and then went out.

I went over to the wash-basin in the corner of the cabin and rinsed the blood off my face and knuckles.

★ ★ ★

That evening I stood on the boat deck, watching the sunset do beautiful things to the sky and the sea. I wasn't a romantic or a nature lover, but sunsets had a soothing effect that helped me to forget a whole lot of other things, and this one might have been laid on specially to take the sting out of my wounded pride. It was all gold, and bronze and red, as though the edge of the world was melting. I watched until the show was over, and then I sensed that someone else was watching me.

There was no one in sight except a seaman standing on the aft deck below. He was leaning on the rail and facing west, but I had the feeling that he wasn't there just to admire the sunset. At first it was just a feeling, but I stayed where I was and eventually I was sure that his eyes had shifted towards me a couple of times.

He wasn't from my watch, which meant that he had to be one of Bennet's. He was another Malay, wearing a dirt-grey vest and shorts, and a scrap of greasy rag knotted around his neck. There was nothing to distinguish him from the other Malay seamen aboard, but then I noticed that there was a tattoo on his arm. It looked like a snake twined around a naked woman, and that rang a bell. He had been one of the men working in the hold when I had gone down to find Bennet and Foong crouching over the dead Chinese. I thought back, and remembered that he had given me a peculiar glance even then.

He had an interest in me, and I wondered what it was. Perhaps he wanted to tell me something. I was tempted to go down and find out instead of waiting for him to pluck up enough courage to approach me. Then Foong appeared on the aft deck. The Malay turned, saw the one-eyed Bo'sun, and hurriedly took himself off.

Foong walked over to the rail, spat over the side, and then disappeared beneath me. He didn't seem to be aware that he had put the Malay to flight, and I stayed on the boat deck wondering.

Finally, I went down to the saloon for dinner. Bennet was already there and I had the satisfaction of seeing that his bruises were even more noticeable than mine. However, van Groten had an announcement to make that was calculated to make us forget our differences of opinion, and one that made me forget the shifty antics of the Malay seaman at the same time; it was simply that on the morning tide we would be making our first attempt to pull the *Kerkyra* off the rocks.

7

West by South

HIGH tide was at eleven a.m., which gave us the full morning to prepare. We didn't want the *Kerkyra* swivelling and grinding herself on the rocks, but with only the *Zandvoort* to pull her off it was impossible to get a simultaneous pull on both the stern and the bows. Van Groten's solution was to take out the *Kerkyra*'s anchor to the full extent of the chain, drop it down, and then winch it back across the seabed until it dragged and took a bite. Then, with the bows held, we could fix the towing cables from the *Zandvoort* to the *Kerkyra*'s stern and try to pull her clear. The main pull at the stern also eliminated the risk of the stern swinging inward and damaging the screw on the rocks.

We lowered the Greek ship's lifeboat,

107

and I went aboard with Foong and my own starboard watch. The *Zandvoort* was standing close by with Pohlmann commanding the bridge, and van Lynden back in charge of his own engines for the tricky manoeuvring that would be needed. The Dutch boat had edged in as close as possible and now it was only a short pull across the intervening water. I took aboard one of the forward winch cables with its heavy steel hook, and with the winch paying out behind ordered the hands to row back to the *Kerkyra*. Bennet was on the Greek ship's bows with a gang of men round the anchor winch. He dropped the rusted, stockless anchor down to sea level and with Foong's help I clipped the *Zandvoort*'s cable hook on to the first link of the chain. Then I backed the lifeboat off and my crew took a rest.

We watched while the anchor was winched across to the *Zandvoort*. Once it was aboard, the Dutch boat reversed engines and began to back out to sea. Pohlmann handled her well, for it wasn't easy to ride an eight-thousand-ton cargo freighter like a harbour tug-boat. Once the chain started paying out the heavy anchor would have probably sunk my small lifeboat, but the weight was nothing to the *Zandvoort*. Pohlmann eased back until Bennet raised both arms sharply to tell him that he had drawn out the full length of the chain. The *Zandvoort* stopped dead, and then a gang of her seamen tipped the anchor over the side with a mighty splash.

The anchor sank from sight into the blue-green depths, and in the *Kerkyra*'s bows Bennet reversed the winch machinery and ordered a slow rewind. The chain rattled in, growing taut and dripping as it emerged from the sea. The anchor was dragging, and I cursed, because if she dragged all the way then the whole sweating process had to be gone through again. Then the anchor took a hard bite, the heavy steel prongs digging deep into the seabed. Bennet snapped an order and the winch stopped, and I wiped the sweat out of my eyes and grinned. The bows were now held fast, and if the anchor should slip free there was still plenty of room for it to drag and bite again. On the *Kerkyra*'s bridge van Groten had watched the overall operation and now he too was grinning his satisfaction.

My crew still had to sit back from their oars and wait, but with the sun blazing down and no shade they were not exactly enjoying it. We watched as Pohlmann did some more fancy juggling with the *Zandvoort*, backing her out to sea and then round in a wide circle to bring her in stern first towards the stern of the *Kerkyra*. They made me think of two slightly devilish old ladies manoeuvring their rumps to play boomps-a-daisy at a polite party. Finally the *Zandvoort* stopped engines again, only thirty yards away, and it was my turn to go into action.

We pulled over to the Dutch ship and took aboard the first of the heavy towing cables that van Groten had brought from Singapore, and then lost some more sweat in pulling back to the *Kerkyra*. Bennet had brought his team aft to receive the cable and make it fast, and with a whole lot of cursing the job was done. The men

110

were wearing heavy gloves, but the gloves were mostly in tatters and the men were not used to this kind of rough work. I noticed that several of them had bleeding hands. One yelping Lascar managed to get his finger nipped between the cable and the fastening bollard, but Bennet was short on sympathy. I wasn't in charge of the deck, so I didn't interfere. The man with the crushed finger went off to find the steward and the first-aid box, while I took my boat back to the *Zandvoort* to fetch a second cable. When that was made fast van Groten came along and declared that we had done enough. It was a fair morning's work and there was still an hour before the tide.

The lifeboat was hoisted back into place on the *Kerkyra*'s deck, and I went thankfully to my cabin to get washed and cleaned up. I was hungry too, but it had been a long morning and van Groten had ordered a second breakfast for both officers and crew. At least he didn't expect hard work on an empty stomach. I went down to the saloon, and now there were only five of us; Bennet, van Groten, Hollert, Louella and myself. It was the most cheerful meal yet, and Louella still felt free to smile at me, which meant that there had been no repercussions yesterday between her and van Groten. I was glad about that.

After the meal we took up our positions again. Bennet and his men in the bows, myself at the stern, and van Groten in overall command on the bridge. The Dutchman had a megaphone in his hand and Hollert standing by to act as a messenger if he felt one was needed. Louella watched from the boat deck, curious to watch the events, but wise enough to stay out of everybody's way, including the Captain.

The tide was as high as it would ever be, and van Groten bawled across the sea for Pohlmann to gently take up the strain. The *Zandvoort*'s screw began to churn slowly, and the two slack cables emerged from the sea. I motioned Foong and the rest of the hands to stay clear, and that was one order they did obey right smartly. They knew as well as I did what would happen if one of those cables snapped.

The ends would fly back like a cross between a dying snake and a flailing buzz saw, and decapitate anyone fool enough to have his head in the way.

The cables became taut, stretched between the two ships like double tight-ropes. All we needed now was a sexy blonde in sequined tights, or a circus clown on a bike, but I couldn't afford to think about jokes. I watched the foam boiling more violently at the *Zandvoort*'s stern, and my whole body was tense, ready to duck.

The *Zandvoort* began to move, easing gently forward. The towing cables stretched, black and glistening with oil and seawater and dripping along their whole tortured length, as though some kind of blood was being wrung out of them. The *Kerkyra* stayed solid, and I knew the cables would have to snap. I was sure of it. I could feel it. And then, when the cables should have blown apart, the *Kerkyra* shifted. The deck shuddered, and then tilted another fraction of a degree. There was a harsh creaking and grinding sound, and I had a horrible picture of what might be happening down in the ruptured hold. The cables stayed intact and the whole stern moved over by several feet, sliding into deeper water. I held my breath, Foong actually began to grin, and then that awful grinding noise began again. I heard Bennet bellow out in the bows, and then van Groten was roaring through the megaphone and telling Pohlmann to slacken off. The Zandvoort stopped. The foam died in her wake, and then threshed again as the screw reversed its thrust. The cables went limp and the crew looked disappointed. I started to breathe again.

I didn't have to go forward to know what had happened. I could hear from the shouted conversation between van Groten and Bennet that the anchor had slipped. As the stern pulled out so the bows had started to move in on to the rocks, starting that merciless swivelling movement that we didn't want. Too much of that and the rocks would bore right through amidships and the ship would never float.

The anchor winch started up on the foredeck and I leaned over the rail to get a glimpse of the chain reeling aboard. Foong and the other seamen lined the rail beside me and we all knew that if the anchor didn't bite then we were finished till the next tide. Link after link crawled up from the sea, and then the chain locked tight again as the double prongs of the anchor found another grip. The winch stopped, and one of the hands dared a ragged cheer.

I could see that Pohlmann had come out on to the wing of the *Zandvoort*'s bridge to watch. Van Groten shouted through the megaphone for another try, and Pohlmann raised his hand and went back into the wheel-house. Schiller was my opposite number in the *Zandvoort*'s stern, and he gave me a similar wave of acknowledgement before backing off out of sight. He knew all about snapping cables too.

The screw stirred up more foam at the *Zandvoort*'s stern, like a witch's cauldron. Again our giant tug began to inch forward and the slack cables tightened. Pohlmann had a master's touch, and I could visualize van Lynden hovering like a confident mother hen with one cool eye on the engine-room telegraph and the other on his monstrous, clanking chick. The pull began and the *Kerkyra* gave an agonizing groan and seemed to shiver from stem to stern. She jerked and slipped another foot and again I could hear her buckled plates grinding on the rocks. She shifted another few inches, her rump sliding into deeper water, and the bows were holding fast.

"She's coming, by God she's coming."

Van Groten roared delightedly from the bridge, the megaphone throwing his voice for all to hear. For a moment I believed him, and then I heard Bennet bawl almost as loudly.

The anchor was a '*sonofabitch*', and it was dragging loose again. The ship was turning her bows, but she was coming free. Van Groten yelled at Pohlmann to keep going, and then the first of the cables snapped.

I didn't need to shout a warning. The cable parted with an explosive bang that sounded as though someone had opened up from the shoreline with a piece of twenty-five-pounder field artillery. The broken end hurled backward like a slashing steel whip, more deadly than a whole barrage of gunfire, but my crew had already hit the deck. In that they were only following the example of their officer, for I dived flat and did my best to bury myself under the hot boards. The jagged end of the cable flailed over our heads, slapped down and spurred a howl of terror from one of the seamen as it gouged a shower of splinters close beside him. For another moment it writhed and thrashed in a frenzy and then it became still. I got up slowly and was relieved to find that nobody had been transformed into a bloody mess. We had all been standing well back, but the cable had snapped in the middle to make a long-reaching whip. We were lucky that it hadn't found a victim.

Pohlmann must have had sixth sense. He had stopped the *Zandvoort* immediately and slackened off to save the second cable which was still holding. There was a moment of sick silence, and then van

Groten was shouting frantically from the bridge.

"Mister Mc'Adden, is anyone hurt down there?"

I checked them again and shouted back the negative.

Van Groten swung the megaphone again to face the *Zandvoort*, and his voice was still tense.

"Mister Schiller, any damage on your side?"

I had forgotten that the other end of the cable must have sprung back on to stern of the *Zandvoort* but after a moment Schiller appeared at the rail. He looked shaken, but was able to shout back that no one had been killed.

Both ships were able to relax for we knew that we had to suspend salvage operations for the rest of the day. I told Foong that the men could take a break and then hurried forward. Van Groten and Bennet both had the same worry and they were ahead of me when I reached the forward cargo hatch. I followed them down into the hold and found that the water in the bottom was knee-deep again

118

and rising fast. The patched hull was leaking badly, with water spurting in from a dozen places. The shaking and grinding that the ship had endured had brought down several of the timbers we had braced between the bulkheads, and the whole patchwork of repairs had come loose.

Bennet had already found a hand light and was picking out the weak place, while van Groten crouched beside him, nodding thoughtfully but making no comment. The splash and trickle of the incoming water had an ugly sound and the hold was like a dank, waterlogged tomb. I waded over to join them and van Groten looked back. He said calmly:

"She twisted too much when the anchor dragged, but we can brace these fallen timbers and patch her up again. There is no more real damage than before. The pumps will get the water level down again. Then tomorrow we pull her off, hey?"

He straightened his back and gave us both an amiable slap on the shoulder. He let his hands rest there, almost holding us down, and despite the stinking black water lapping around us he was supremely confident.

"Mister Bennet, you start work down here right away. Mister Mc'Adden will relieve you in two hours." He grinned again. "A damn pity that rope break, hey? One more pull would be finish. That's all she need. Just one more pull."

I nodded, for to a certain extent I agreed with him. I just wasn't sure whether the *Kerkya* would float, or whether she would slide straight to the bottom. However, I didn't like to be another Cassandra and so I kept quiet.

★ ★ ★

When the two hours were up I took over from Bennet in the hold, and for once he was glad to see me. The pumps were going, but so far they were only keeping pace and the water was still slopping around just above our knees. Bennet showed me what he had managed to do so far, and then he left me to it and led his men up into the sunlight. I watched them

120

go, and there was something familiar about one of the Malay seamen ascending the ladder. Then I saw the snake and naked female tattoo on his forearm and I remembered. Again I had caught him looking uncertainly in my direction, but Foong was behind him, the last man on the ladder, and he scuttled quickly aloft.

I spent another minute wondering, but the sea was still spurting in places through the ruptured plates of the hull, and there was a lot of work to be done. The men were workshy unless I rode them hard and put my own back into it, and so I got busy.

* * *

The next morning van Groten made a careful inspection and decided that the *Kerkyra* was in fit enough shape to try again. The lifeboat was lowered and I took my crew aboard and went through a repeat performance of the sweating and cursing that was needed to get the anchor towed out and dropped at its full length, and again we made the lines fast between the two ships. There was a spare cable to replace the one that had snapped, and by high tide we were ready to make our second attempt at wresting the Greek ship free of the rocks.

I cleared my crew completely off the deck, and made sure that I stayed well back. I didn't fancy a repetition of yesterday and I was bearing in mind that one of those cables had already been subjected to strain. Pohlmann showed the same sure skill in commanding the *Zandvoort* as before, and the Dutch ship manoeuvred so precisely that I felt he must have had some kind of telepathic communication with van Lynden in the engine-room. It was as though the Chief Engineer could sense what was wanted even before the signal could be rung down the telegraph.

The *Zandvoort*'s screw churned, the cables tightened and again the *Kerkyra* shuddered as the struggle began. She creaked painfully in every rivet, and then gave a groaning lurch that tipped her a little deeper into the sea. Pohlmann was wary of snapping more cables and eased back. The *Kerkyra* became still, her deck now at a sharp angle, and I wiped the sweat out of my eyes. I noticed that Foong had come on deck to watch, but I didn't send him back. He was more nimble than I was and I knew that if anything went wrong then he would be the last to get hurt. On the bridge van Groten was shouting through his megaphone.

"She nearly come that time. Mister Bennet, next time try and start the anchor winch. Then we get a pull both ends, hey?"

"Aye, aye, sir!"

I heard Bennet's yell, and then van Groten again:

"Mister Pohlmann, give her one more try."

Again the *Zandvoort* edged away, stretching the cables taut until the deck beneath my feet began to quiver. Faintly I heard Bennet shouting in the *Kerkyra*'s bows, and then the slow clatter of the anchor windlass. The stranded ship seemed to groan and writhe, like a great, rusted grey whale in a spasm of labour, and I moved quickly to the rail. The anchor was dragging and the chain was coming out of the sea, then it held again and the bows were swaying out as Bennet kept the chain drawing in. The *Kerkyra* heaved with more herculean birth pangs, and I was sure that she must break up. Those savaged plates were getting more punishment than they could take. The anchor slipped again and the bows swung in, the stern shifted farther out, and then like a drunken old maid rolling over in bed the ship lifted and slithered off the rocks into clear water.

For a moment it seemed as though she was turning turtle, but then she swayed upright again, wallowed, and then settled with a sigh. Bennet shut off the anchor windlass, and Pohlmann rang down stop engines and came out grinning on to the wing of the *Zandvoort*'s bridge. On our own bridge it sounded as though van Groten had given way to an impromptu victory dance. He was whooping through the megaphone, but he had temporarily forgotten his English, and the result was what might have been a long string of 'Hellelujahs' in roaring Dutch.

★ ★ ★

The *Zandvoort* pulled us well clear of the rocks, and then again it was all hands below to assess the damage. The sea was cascading in again and the hold was thigh deep, and there was no time to waste in reinforcing the weakened repairs. We worked desperately all through the afternoon, but by the time we had stopped the fresh wave of leaks and braced all the timbers back into position we were toiling in water that swirled around our waists. There wasn't a man amongst us who wasn't soaking wet from head to toe, but again the battle was won. The pumps were in control and gradually bringing the water level down.

Van Groten wisely decided to waste no time, for if the *Kerkyra* was to reach Saigon then the only course was to get under way and pray for calm weather. In a storm the ship would sink, but if the seas stayed kind she just might be able to struggle into port.

I went over the side to check that the screw had not been damaged during the salvage operations, and was relieved to find that it was still the right shape. When I got back van Lynden had come aboard, and he had brought just one of his engineers, a fair-haired junior named Drekker. He reckoned that the two of them, with the help of the new engine-room hands signed on in Singapore, should be able to nurse the *Kerkyra*'s engines into Saigon. Van Groten didn't doubt him, and neither did I.

It was dusk when the old Greek tramp trembled into life for the first time in four months. She was battered and rusted, little more than a spent hulk, but van Lynden had breathed some soul into the great pistons of her heart. The screw turned and she shook her old bones to prepare for her last journey. I shared the bridge with van Groten, and on the foredeck below us Bennet ordered the anchor hoisted aboard. Van Groten took the wheel himself and ordered slow ahead. I rang the signal down and the *Kerkyra* moved uncertainly forward. She was low in the water, sluggish and reluctant, but at least she moved. Van Groten brought her around gently, turning her back on the rock pile that had claimed her for so long, and then took her out to sea. The *Zandvoort* stood by to accompany us, like a priest attending the last rites. Van Groten ordered half engines, and then boldly:

"Full ahead."

Clumsily the *Kerkyra* obeyed his command. Louella had ventured up on to the bridge and favoured us both with a huge smile. Behind us a white wake stretched back over the dark sea to Mindoro, a black silhouette coastline of jungle and fading palms. Ahead, the South China Seas lay open to Saigon. Van Groten relinquished the wheel to the helmsman and ordered the course.

"West by south. Keep her steady."

He turned to Louella, laughed suddenly and kissed her. It wasn't a polite kiss, and I was jealous.

8

Man Overboard

VAN GROTEN took the first watch, and I relieved him for the middle watch between midnight and four a.m. It was an uneventful four hours. The *Kerkyra* was old and weary, with no enthusiasm for the job, but she managed a limping ten knots. The stars were brilliant in the dark heavens and the seas were calm. This was the dead watch, silent and lonely and unloved by sailors, and it was reassuring to have the twinkling lights and the faint blurred silhouette of the *Zandvoort* keeping a friendly vigil off our port bow. Bennet appeared to take over the morning watch at eight bells and I went below.

The last two days had been pretty strenuous and just lately I wasn't accustomed to hard work. I turned in and slept the full eight hours until I was due to take command of the bridge once more, and returned on deck just before noon. The sun was blistering everything within reach and made me blink as I looked out on to the port bow. That was when I received a shock. The seas were empty and there was not even a puff of smoke to stain the horizon.

The *Kerkyra* was alone.

I stared all around and then made my way fast to the bridge. The helmsman glanced round from the wheel, looked me up and down, and then turned his attention back to his job. It was the scar-faced Lascar and he didn't look particularly happy. Van Groten was out on the wing of the bridge, squinting through the sextant to take the noon sighting of the sun. His actions were ordered and precise and he didn't seem concerned.

I let him finish and waited for him to come back into the wheelhouse. He knew what was on my mind, but gave me a curt good morning and turned his back as he leaned over the chart table to work out the ship's position with a slide rule and pencil. I let him finish that too, and then he turned to face me. His blue eyes were frosty and I knew that he was prepared to act the iron-fisted Captain again. I kept my face expressionless and asked grimly:

"What happened to the *Zandvoort*?"

"She is returning to Singapore." He was watching me carefully. "I radioed the order to Pohlmann four hours ago. Nothing to worry about, hey?"

Four hours; that meant that he had sent the signal to Pohlmann immediately after he had taken over the forenoon watch. Bennet would have gone straight to his bunk and most probably he hadn't known what was happening either. The crew wouldn't have asked questions, and neither would Hollert, the radio officer. Hollert had too much faith in his skipper. Van Groten had chosen his time well, and now the *Zandvoort* was four hours away. I said harshly:

"The *Kerkyra* isn't seaworthy, you know that! If the weather cuts up rough she'll never reach Saigon. We might need the *Zandvoort* standing by to take off the crew. You must be mad to send Pohlmann away."

"Mister Mc'Adden, I am not mad." His jaw jutted angrily and for the second time he tried to shrivel me with that blue glare. "The pumps are coping well down in the hold, and the weather reports are good for the next three days. There is no reason why the *Kerkyra* should not reach Saigon, and I cannot afford to keep the *Zandvoort* playing nursemaid. There is a cargo waiting in Singapore, and I still have a duty to the Holland East Indies Shipping Company."

I didn't shrivel. I said flatly. "You know as well as I do that weather reports aren't accurate over a matter of days. At the best, they're only guesswork. Another typhoon could whip up at any time."

"This isn't typhoon season."

"Typhoons don't always confine themselves to their seasons."

"Mister Mc'Adden, the *Zandvoort* is returned to Singapore and that is the finish. I can't afford to lose the cargo that waits for her. I don't think there is any danger, but if there is then the

Kerkyra must take her chances like any other ship, and so must you. If you are afraid of the sea, then you should not have signed ship's articles."

He stopped and began to simmer down, knowing that the argument was getting out of hand. I held back because I knew that nothing I could say would make any difference. The *Zandvoort* had gone and he wasn't going to radio for her to come back. We matched hostile eyes for a moment and then he said:

"Take over the watch, Mister Mc'Adden. The course is still west by south."

I nodded slowly, and then he turned and walked off the bridge.

After that it was a quiet watch. I walked over to the helmsman to check the compass reading on the binnacle in front of him, and he had the sense to pretend that he was made of stone. He hadn't seen anything and hadn't heard anything, and he didn't breath a word. I knew he would stay that way until he got back to the crew's mess-room, and I was peeved to find that the compass read exactly west by south. It wasn't the flicker

132

of a needle out and I couldn't even vent my temper on him.

Out of habit I checked the position on the chart. The *Kerkyra* had covered one hundred and sixty-two miles in just over fourteen hours, which meant that she had kept very close to her average of ten knots. Not bad for an old lady with a big hole in her side. I just hoped that hole wasn't taking in too much of the South China Sea.

* * *

The weather stayed calm and sweltering throughout the day, and the *Kerkyra* steamed slowly towards the always empty and ever receding horizon. When my spell on watch was over I went below to check the hold. The water in the bottom was thigh-deep, but the patchwork of repairs was holding firm and the pumps were keeping control. The throbbing of the engines was very close and the vibration was spreading evil ripples across the black surface of the water. I watched for a moment and I wasn't wholly reassured when I came back on deck.

Van Groten stayed in his cabin most of the afternoon, and I knew he had had a repeat performance of our argument with Bennet. The American hadn't liked the idea of sailing without escort any more than I did, but, like me, he had failed to get any change out of the Captain.

I stood my watch on the bridge again at midnight. Van Groten gave me a brief nod of acknowledgement as he handed over command, but he didn't linger to indulge in any conversation. I checked the course, but the helmsman was on the ball. There wasn't much else to do but count the stars and think. So far I hadn't tried to plot my own future beyond Saigon and the end of the voyage, and from here it still looked bleak. Now that my past record was once more tied around my neck, there wasn't much point in going back to Singapore with van Groten and the rest of the crew. There was one hell of a messy war rolling up and down the length of Vietnam, and Saigon wasn't the healthiest port in the world, but maybe it was the best place for me.

The Viet Cong had taken offence at good old Uncle Sam trying to run their country with the aid of napalm and an almighty armada of fighter-bombers, and so the little fellers had formed the nasty habit of slipping high explosive mines into the Saigon River as part of the fight back. That endangered navigation somewhat, and on some ships regularly calling at Saigon crews were scarce. On ammunition ships especially the owners had to pay high danger money, and they might not be too fussy about the men they took aboard. I tried to cast my thoughts a little wider, but in four hours of quiet thinking I didn't turn up any other possibilities.

Eight bells sounded, and Bennet climbed up on to the bridge to stand the morning watch. We greeted each other cautiously and politely. We were on formal terms now, and staying out of each other's way as much as possible. The hatchet was buried on van Groten's orders, but only just under the surface. I handed over the watch and left.

I didn't go direct to my bunk. I was

still pondering on my chances of getting another ship in Saigon, and so I took a slow walk around the boatdeck. It was still dark, with no sign yet that dawn was only an hour away. I stood for a moment by the lifeboat, watching the aft mast rolling gently against the pattern of the stars. And then abruptly I heard the sound of a movement somewhere below, and what could have been the sound of a human cry choked off by an alert hand.

I stood tense, and Saigon was forgotten. Softly I moved aft and looked down on the main deck below. There was nothing to be seen, the decks were deserted in the starlight. I stood listening and watching, and I could detect nothing, but I was certain that I hadn't imagined that faint scuffle and the attempted cry. I wasn't the imagining type.

I was tempted to arm myself with the hand axe that formed part of the lifeboat's standard equipment, but I wasn't sure that I could climb in and out of the boat without making a noise, and I might be too late to learn anything if I wasted time. Then I told myself that I didn't need a weapon; I was supposed to be First Mate of this leaking tub and the gold bars on my shoulders should guarantee some element of control. I moved silently down the first companionway and hesitated again on the next deck.

There was still nothing, and I wasn't sure whether that mere suggestion of a scuffle had come from this deck or the main deck that was still below. I listened and tried to see into the maze of darkness and shadows. There were so many places where a man could hide. The sound wasn't repeated, but I could feel my heart knocking inside my chest. The ship was too quiet, as though someone somewhere was trying hard *not* to make a sound. I was a practical man who didn't believe in sixth sense, and yet I could feel it.

I leaned over the rail of the next companionway, making sure that no one lay in wait in the black shadow immediately underneath, and then I eased down on to the deck below. In front of me lay the aft cargo hatch, then the mast and winches, and finally the poop that housed quarters for some of the crew.

It was all silent and still. There was only the faint pulsing of the engines deep below decks. I moved across the ship to look along the enclosed alleyway running forward along the port side, and then all the stars in the sky dived down from behind and exploded in my brain.

★ ★ ★

I opened my eyes a long time afterwards and recorded the fact that my face was pressed down in the scuppers. That wasn't dignified, so I moved it and promptly recorded another fact; there was a splitting ache at the base of my skull. I pushed myself up on to my feet and leaned against the rail for support, and having a super I.Q. of about fifty-five I eventually managed to work it out that it wasn't the stars that had fallen in on me. Some joker had merely clobbered me hard from behind.

I was still on the aft deck, which meant that they hadn't even bothered to move me. I had been left where I had fallen. The stars were gone and the sky was now grey with dawn, which told me that I had been decorating the scuppers for at least an hour. Whatever it was that I had interrupted, it was long completed by now, and whoever was responsible was tucked up comfortably in his bunk.

I put my fingers to my scalp and it felt as though an extra large cuckoo had laid a hard round egg just under the skin. It hurt to touch, but at least the skin wasn't broken. I had a tough nut, but I wasn't going to be able to comb my hair properly for a week. I found my cap and put it on very gently, and then I looked sourly at those gold bars on my shoulders. I was beginning to realize more than ever that they didn't mean very much to anybody.

I went back to my cabin to feel sorry for myself with the help of a towel soaked in cold water, and at the same time I wondered who had hit me. I started to reason that even this crew of gutter-rats would think twice before knocking down the First Mate, and so I concentrated first on the officers. I felt that I could safely rule out van Lynden, Drekker and Hollert, for those three skulduggery seemed out of character. That narrowed the field quite considerably. Louella I could also cross out, for there had been more than a woman's strength behind the blow that had toppled me into the scuppers, and only three names remained: Bennet, van Groten himself, or Foong. Which one, and why? Bennet had been, or should have been, on the bridge, but I wasn't sure about Bennet. What it boiled down to was that I wasn't really sure of anything. I only knew that whoever he was, he was damned fast. I had been fully alert, but I hadn't seen or heard a damned thing as he came up behind me. Foong would be fast and he carried a marlinespike, but was that too obvious? It could be a mistake not to look beyond the obvious.

I put the main question aside and asked myself another one: was I going to report the attack or not? That was easier, and I decided no. Even if van Groten questioned every man on board, nobody would know anything, especially if it was van Groten who had clobbered me. The better alternative was to keep quiet and let somebody wonder why. That way somebody might betray himself. That was Mc'Adden the psychologist thinking. I hoped he was a damned sight smarter than Mc'Adden the private investigator. My head hurt like hell and I gave it all up and went to bed.

* * *

I survived to do my turn on the bridge at noon, and van Groten was again squinting through the sextant to shoot the sun. There was only the one sextant aboard, so I couldn't double-check, and he didn't ask me to verify his figures. I still had a headache and at the time it didn't seem important. He wrote down that the *Kerkyra* had covered another two hundred and fifty-three miles during the past twenty-four hours, and the line he drew across the chart was continuing direct from the Philippines to Saigon.

I lasted out my four hours and then handed over to Bennet who had the two dog watches. He didn't give me any strange glances, and neither had van Groten, which meant that Mc'Adden the psychologist was faring as might have been expected.

I was still puzzled about last night, mainly because that lump on my skull wouldn't let me forget, and so I made a casual tour of the ship. I tried to look as though I wasn't looking for anything in particular, which was easy because I didn't know what I was looking for. I only knew that the answer wasn't in my cabin, and therefore I had to look somewhere else. I wandered idly up and down the length of the decks, especially where the crew were working, but no one seemed unduly worried by my presence. I saw Foong on the foredeck and called him over. I made my voice sharp and threatening, and deliberately kept him waiting a minute while I stared into that one eye. He wasn't nervous either, and I finally ordered him to come with me and check the hold.

When we came up again my legs were soaking wet and I was still no further forward. Foong went back to his job and I stood steaming in the sun and tried to think. Everything was in order, but I sensed that something was wrong. It was as definite as the feeling that I had had last night. I looked slowly around the ragged villains of the crew who were either working or relaxing on deck, and my glance finished on the pansy Malay with the cheap ear-rings. Something clicked in my brain and I remembered the other Malay, the one with the tattooed forearm who had tried twice to attract my attention. It was so obvious now that I wondered if my brains really had been shifted out of joint, or at least into a slower gear.

I made another tour, and this time I knew what I was looking for, and I didn't expect to find him. I checked the crew's quarters and found the cabin that the Malay shared with three other seamen. There was nothing there but a stink, but I tracked one of his cabin-mates down on to the foredeck. He

143

didn't want to talk, but he knew he wouldn't get away with any lies either. He admitted reluctantly that the Malay was missing.

I went up to the Captain's cabin and reported to van Groten. Louella was there and they both stared as though the news came as a shock. Then van Groten said slowly:

"Mister Mc'Adden, are you sure about this?"

"I'm sure." I said it flatly. "I've checked the ship. It's one of the Malays from Bennet's watch. The man with the snake and the nude woman tattooed on his arm. He isn't aboard."

Van Groten knew I wouldn't joke. He stood up and pulled his peaked cap on to his iron-grey hair. Then he went to the door and hollered for a steward to bring Foong at the double. Then he turned back to me.

"I get to the bottom of this, hey? I have the Bo'sun search the whole damned ship. Everywhere!"

I nodded slowly, but I knew he wouldn't find the Malay. In fact I could have drawn a pretty accurate sketch of how and when the Malay had gone overboard. I watched, and wondered whether van Groten could do it just as well.

9

North-West by North

THE *Kerkyra* was searched from bows to stern and van Groten was not pleased with the result. When Foong finally brought his report the Dutchman's leathery face might have been chipped out of granite, and he stared deep into the Bo'sun's one eye. Foong didn't flinch, the fish eye revealed about as much as the red socket that was its partner. Van Groten told him to go.

We had waited silently in his cabin and he turned to face me. He said slowly:

"You heard. The Malay seaman is not on board. Foong says that he was an alcoholic, always drunk. Last night he found a bottle somewhere. There are four men who will testify that he was drinking heavily when he was last seen. Foong thinks that he must have drunk too much and fallen over the side."

I didn't believe that, and I wasn't sure whether van Groten did. I said bluntly:

"Where would he get the liquor?"

"Perhaps he bring it aboard from Singapore. Sometimes they save a bottle for some festival or celebration, and sometimes they drink it too soon. How do I know, hey?"

He was staring at me strangely. I hadn't yet told him that somebody had knocked me cold last night, and he could sense that I was keeping something back. There was suspicion in his mind and he hit me with a sudden question.

"The Malay was in the port watch. That's Bennet's crew. How is it that you report him missing, and not Bennet?"

That had me rattled for a minute. Louella was watching closely and there was a strange look in her eyes too. She was again wearing those milk-white stretch slacks that made me feel hot and uncomfortable, and I shifted so that my back was partly towards her. Then I told van Groten half of the truth.

"The Malay had a distinctive tattoo, that made him pretty noticeable. And he

147

had an interest in me. Several times I've had the feeling that he was waiting for a chance to talk to me. That's why it registered when he was missing."

"Why should he want to talk to you? He was on Bennet's watch. Why not talk to Bennet? Or me? Why you?"

I said flatly: "I don't know — and now it's too late to find out."

Van Groten thought for a moment, and then looked up.

"Okay, let's go see Mister Bennet."

Louella stayed in the cabin while we made our trip to the bridge. Bennet hadn't failed to witness the buzz of activity as Foong and the hands had scoured the ship, and he turned round to watch van Groten and I as we came up the companionway. His face looked puzzled and I knew he was going to ask what the heck was going on. He came to meet us, opened his mouth, and the words came out.

"Say, what the heck's going on?"

Van Groten told him. Bennet still looked mystified and rubbed slowly at his jaw.

"The Malay guy with the tattoo. Sure, I know him. He's no loss, but I didn't figure he'd be dumb enough to fall overboard. That boy was pretty smart on his feet. He didn't like work, but he knew how to step out of trouble."

Van Groten said quietly, "Mister Mc'Adden isn't sure that the Malay did fall overboard."

Bennet shrugged. "Mister Mc'Adden could be right. With this pack of bilge-rats anything's possible." He stopped and suddenly sensed the implied insinuation. Then he looked at me. "What's on your mind?"

"Just a feeling. The man was waiting for a chance to tell me something, but he didn't get it."

"Tell you what?"

"I don't know."

Bennet was getting hostile again. He said curtly:

"Then neither do I."

We all looked at each other for a moment and I wondered who was fooling who. Or was anybody fooling anybody? Then van Groten decided that it was time to play the peacemaker.

"Mister Mc'Adden, I don't think it matters what the Malay wanted to tell you. He got drunk and four men saw him. He must have been stupid enough to fall over the side. Perhaps he was sick or something. He lean over to spew and lose his balance. It can happen that way. We leave it at that, hey?"

He clapped me on the shoulder to show that there was no ill feeling for having wasted his time, and then looked to his Second Officer.

"Thank you, Mister Bennet. We leave you to finish your watch."

Bennet nodded doubtfully, but made no further comment. Van Groten turned and left, and there wasn't much that I could do except follow him down from the bridge.

★ ★ ★

At midnight I took over the watch again. During the afternoon I had tried to think, but the heat and my headache had made that impossible and finally I had taken

150

some aspirin and slept instead. Now, after a cold shower, the cool of the night gave me some relief and I made another try. All my previous thinking had led to nowhere, but I had to keep at it. If I kept up the pressure even my puny mind had to make a breakthrough sometime.

I was sure by now that there was something wrong about this whole voyage, and after checking that the helmsman was keeping a steady course I went out on to the wing of the bridge where there was a shred of breeze and tried to figure out what it could be. Alone with the stars it might be easier to think.

I started by counting up all the little causes for suspicion. First the missing Malay seaman, and the crack that I had received on the back of the head. Then the dismissal of the *Zandvoort*, and the unnecessary risk of letting the badly-holed *Kerkyra* proceed alone. Add to that the careless attitude of van Groten towards the old Chinese who had died in the hold, and a crew of handpicked ruffians who would have disgraced a sewer. It all spelled up to something illegal.

And yet so far there was nothing illegal. I had checked the cargo and I had checked the log, and it was all in order. The cargo was destined for Saigon, there was a waiting market, and van Groten was entitled to the salvage value of the abandoned ship. It was like one of those crazy Chinese three-ring puzzles where the pieces would fit neatly together or slide neatly apart, if only you knew how. So far, there was something obvious that I hadn't seen.

Two bells rang, an hour had passed, and I moved into the wheelhouse to check the course. The sea was calm, almost benevolent, and the helmsman was having a dull time. I went out into the open again and resumed thinking.

I had to try another tack. Why had the tattooed Malay tried to catch my attention? Why couldn't he have taken his problem, whatever it was, to Bennet? Answer: he was afraid of Bennet. Or was he afraid of Foong? The Bo'sun usually worked with Bennet's watch. He had to be afraid, or distrustful, of one of the two men in charge of his own working party.

152

But which one? And why? And why did he think that I might have been the safer man to approach than van Groten?

I tacked on to another course. The Malay must have been down in the hold when the old Chinese had fallen to his death. Could that have been the problem on his mind? It seemed possible, and yet I didn't think so. Bennet had been careless, but it was unlikely that the fall had been anything other than an accident. The smell there was in van Groten's off-hand dismissal of the whole affair. You couldn't arrange a deliberate accident in front of a hold full of the man's mates, or could you? I told myself that there was no reason, but that failed to hold water. So far there was no concrete reason behind the disappearance of the Malay, but I was one hundred per cent certain that he had been thrown overboard.

Four bells rang. It was two a.m. From habit I checked the course once more and then returned to my thinking position. The helmsman was the scar-faced Lascar. He gave me a puzzled glance, but decided to mind his own business. It was nothing to do with him if I wanted to brood.

I gazed up at the stars, and wondered if I had been right in keeping quiet about that crack on the head. If I had given van Groten the full facts, then he might have been able to hammer the truth out of one of those seamen who had testified that the Malay was drunk. But that was only possible if van Groten wasn't involved. I thought about that drink story and wondered who would have the influence to plant that with the crew. The answer came to van Groten or Foong, and seemed to let Bennet off the hook, but still I wasn't sure.

I toyed again with the idea of taking van Groten into my confidence about that attack, but I could see no advantage. Keeping the fact to myself was the only card I had up my sleeve, and although it was a poor one I couldn't afford to throw it away. I had to watch and wait for someone to make a slip and reveal that he knew about that lump on my skull. Then I might start getting somewhere.

All the thinking was making me dizzy, and I stopped for a bit and watched the stars. The night sky was the only consolation for this dead watch, and they made a glorious sight. There was no cloud and it seemed as though I might be able to reach out and touch the Milky Way. That reminded me of milk-white slacks and Louella, and the questions came creeping back. I had forgotten Louella, and perhaps she could provide some of the answers. She was van Groten's mistress and perhaps his Achilles heel. Perhaps I could trick her into revealing the hidden secret of the *Kerkyra*.

I continued to gaze up at the stars, and vaguely the feeling returned that there was something obvious that I had missed. The questions came back in a revolving whirl, but suddenly the answers seemed very close. The stars blurred before my eyes and my head throbbed, and yet I was on the brink of that promised breakthrough. I tried to concentrate, concentrate hard. I closed my eyes and forced all the known factors through my mind. The answer wasn't there and yet it was still close. I could feel it forming in the back of my brain. It was within reach. It was staring me in the face. That something obvious was about to give agonizing birth, but then the strain was too much and it was fading away. I had to relax, and open my eyes and look at the stars. My mind went mercifully blank, and then suddenly it seemed that my own voice was thundering in my brain.

Look at the stars, you bloody fool. LOOK AT THE STARS!

I looked, and there it was, the obvious, smacking me right between the eyes. I was supposed to be a sailor with at least a rudimentary knowledge of navigation, and yet I had missed it. I must have been blind as well as dumb. Our supposed course was west by south and the north star should have been on our starboard side. But the north star wasn't; it was riding high in the heavens almost directly ahead, just a fraction to starboard of the *Kerkyra*'s bows.

For a moment I stared, and then more obvious facts tumbled into place. Van Groten had the forenoon watch, and he alone had handled the sextant to shoot our noon position by the sun. He was the skipper and no one had been invited to check his readings. He alone had plotted our course, and no one had checked his figures. I had only van Groten's word that we were on course for Saigon. Then I remembered the compass in the binnacle.

I went back into the wheelhouse and looked over the helmsman's shoulder. The binnacle light was clear, a small, circular pool of illumination that showed that the ship was holding steadily on her theoretical course of south by west. The Lascar shifted to one side and looked at me with no expression on his scarred face. I nodded, also without expression, and then stepped back to let him resume his place. Ahead, the north star was still hanging high over our bows, which meant that either the compass or the stars were playing tricks. And somehow I didn't think that van Groten could have tampered with the north star.

I contemplated for a minute, and then told the Lascar to go below to the galley and bring up some coffee. He looked at me stupidly, not sure that he had heard right, and I repeated sharply:

"Coffee, understand? I'll take care of the wheel while you bring me some coffee. And bring some aspirin; I've got a headache."

The last was true, and it was also an explanation for unconventional behaviour. The Lascar moved away from the wheel doubtfully and I took over. Then reluctantly he went below.

When he had gone I let go of the wheel. The sea was calm and the wheel stayed steady. I moved round it to the binnacle, pulled a small clasp knife out of my pocket and went to work quickly. Once I had to reach back to correct the wheel, but the *Kerkyra* was too sluggish to stray far from her set course. The screws holding the glass window of the binnacle yielded easily. Only one was rusted enough to make me swear under my breath as the tip of my knife blade skidded a nasty scratch mark across the glass. Finally I lifted the glass out and felt inside. Immediately I located the small piece of iron wedged under the rim to throw the delicate magnets out of true. The compass card did a frantic job and then settled to give a new reading.

The *Kerkyra* was steaming north-west by north.

I couldn't guarantee too much time before the Lascar helmsman came back, so I replaced everything as I had found it. Then I shoved my knife back into my pocket and steadied the wheel once more. I was thoughtful as I waited for the Lascar to return, but he was longer than I expected. The ship showed no desire to wander, so I left her unattended for another moment and went over to the chart table.

There was no way of knowing how many hours the *Kerkyra* had been ploughing on her new course, but the compass could only have been fixed while van Groten was taking the first watch during the four hours leading up to midnight, either tonight or last night, or even the first night out from the Philippines. I considered for a bit and decided that I could rule out the first night. Then he had been accompanied by the *Zandvoort* and he wouldn't have been able to fix her compass as well. That explained why Pohlmann had been ordered to take the *Zandvoort* back to Singapore. The most likely probability was that the course had been changed a few degrees to the north last night, and then even further tonight, thus bringing the ship round gradually.

I stared down at the chart and ignored the lines that van Groten had pencilled across, for it was obvious now that we were not headed for Saigon. It was impossible to position where we were, but we were most certainly sailing north. That meant only two possibilities: China or North Vietnam.

I asked myself what interest the Communist world could possibly have in a mass of floating scrap metal and a cargo of fertilizers, and then I heard a soft footstep directly behind me.

10

Embargo

I WAS jumpy. I had already collected one nasty crack across the back of the head and I didn't want another. Somebody on this ship moved too fast and hit too hard, and it was a mistake to keep your back turned for too long. The warning was very faint, but it was all that was needed to make me come spinning round like a scalded cat.

Van Groten was behind me.

He smiled bleakly, glanced down at the chart, and then said:

"You get careless, Mister Mc'Adden. The wheel should never be left unattended, not even in a calm sea."

He turned away from me and rested his own hands upon the motionless wheel. He stood there with his back towards me, his feet apart, solid and unconcerned. He looked up at the north star and then

161

down at the binnacle in front of him, and I remembered that my knife blade had scratched the glass. The wheelhouse was very still and silent, and then footsteps sounded on the companionway and the Lascar returned with my coffee. Van Groten turned as the man appeared. He said curtly:

"You, take over the wheel."

The Lascar hesitated, then set the coffee cup down on the chart table and went back to his post as van Groten stepped out of the way. His brown hands gripped tightly to the spokes of the wheel and he kept his scarred face staring straight ahead. He had not looked at me once, not even for support in deserting the bridge on my orders, and I knew that it was he who had fetched van Groten. He had obviously been told in advance to inform the Captain if I found any pretext to send him down from the bridge, and Bennet's helmsman had probably received the same instructions. Van Groten knew that one of us would eventually tumble to what was happening.

The big Dutchman looked at me, and

162

then jerked his head and walked out on to the wing of the bridge. I held back a second, and then obeyed the silent signal and followed. When we were out of the Lascar's hearing he leaned his back against the rail and faced me. His eyes were shadowed by the gold-braided peak of his cap, but his mouth was again shaped into that bleak smile. He said calmly:

"Congratulations, Rick. I was right in making you First Mate above Bennet, hey? You are much smarter than he is. Bennet still hasn't realized that I have changed the course." He looked up at the heavens and now I could see that the smile was also in his eyes as he added, "Perhaps I should not have given you the first watch. The stars are too damned clear, hey?"

I said slowly, "That's right, and now we both know that our destination isn't Saigon. So where are we going?"

He looked at me more shrewdly. The smile and the first-name familiarity wasn't making me any easier to deal with and so he dropped it. His face became harder as he said:

"We are going north. We are taking the *Kerkyra* to Haiphong."

"Why?" I still didn't understand. "You have a legal market for the cargo waiting in South Vietanm. Why should a cargo of fertilizer be of more value to the north?"

Van Groten found another smile for my ignorance.

"Think, Rick, think. The *Kerkyra*'s cargo is eight thousand, five hundred tons of sulphates."

I thought. I was a sailor and I knew a whole lot about ships and the sea. I knew ocean geography and weather signs, how to navigate and a little about astrology, but chemistry had never been one of my serious studies. My knowledge of chemistry was worse than basic, but something did begin to emerge. Sulphates was a fairly general term that could cover various acid salts with a variety of uses. I asked:

"What's the exact nature of the cargo?"

Van Groten said calmly, "Calcium ammonium nitrate." And then he watched for my reaction.

164

The word nitrate was an obvious clue. I stared and said harshly:

"Explosives?"

Van Groten chuckled. "Possibly. The cargo is intended for use as fertilizer, but I believe that it can also be used for the manufacture of ammunions. Perhaps that is why the North Vietnamese have offered me a better price to take the *Kerkyra* to Haiphong. But that is not really our business, hey? We just sail the ship."

I said flatly, "There's a United States embargo on the sale of all military materials to Red China, and I reckon that includes North Vietnam. You're breaking the embargo."

Van Groten shrugged. "Politics are not my concern."

He was still watching me carefully, waiting for me to make a definite stand, either with him or against him, but I stayed neutral and asked:

"Who else knows that we are no longer headed for Saigon ?"

"There is myself, Foong the Bo'sun, and Louella. I have no secrets from Louella. And now, of course, you. There is no one else. Bennet must eventually realize the truth, like you he will notice the stars, but I think that I can handle Bennet. He is just a loud-mouthed drunk. He will argue, but when I offer him a share in the profits then he will see sense. You are also a sensible man, Rick. I am offering you a full ten per cent of the profits if you will continue to work with me. The rest of the crew will not know what is happening until we are entering Haiphong, and then it will be too late."

"And what happens then?"

"It is all arranged. The Vietnamese will take over the ship, and I and all my officers will be given safe conduct to leave the country through Laos. We will all be very well paid. Unfortunately we cannot trust the crew to keep silent if they should be released, and so for our own safety they will be interned in North Vietnam. That is why I did Singapore a favour and cleaned out the gutterrats who will not be missed."

He paused and smiled briefly. "There is no need to worry, Rick. Perhaps I should have told you sooner, hey?

You don't like to be fooled. But this way is best. I don't tell anyone until it is necessary. That makes for less trouble, hey?"

I could understand that perfectly well. His only hope of getting away with it was to keep everybody on board in complete ignorance for as long as possible, or at least until we were so far north that it would be no less dangerous to continue than to return. Foong was already in his confidence, and Bennet and I were the only other dangers. We were the deck officers and the only two who would be likely to read the stars. Bennet he had already dismissed as a loudmouth who could be bought when the time came, and he obviously didn't think any more highly of me. I was a sea-going leper who for all practical purposes had already sunk two ships in the Gulf of Panama, and I wasn't expected to have any morals. It was a familiar pattern, but I began to get mad. I asked bluntly:

"What happens if I decide that I don't want to play along? I might have a conscience."

"That would be stupid, Rick. What could you do, hey? If you try to take over the ship no one would follow you. My Dutch officers have all been with me for many years aboard the *Zandvoort*. They will stay loyal. Foong has control over the crew. Bennet will stand where the money pays best."

He pushed both hands into his jacket pockets, still leaning very calmly against the rail, and finished:

"Ten per cent of half a million pounds should cure your conscience, Rick. And there is also ten per cent of the scrap value of the *Kerkyra*. The North Vietnamese have agreed to buy the ship as well as the cargo. It is a lot of money, hey?"

I said coldly, "I still have a conscience."

"Then you suffer with it. There is nothing you can do."

"Don't be so sure. I wouldn't bet on Foong being able to control the crew when they find out that they're going to be interned in North Vietnam. And I wouldn't bet on your Dutch officers either. I get the impression that van Lynden is an honest man, and as yet he doesn't know anything about this. When he finds out, he might go against you, and I think Drekker will back his Chief. Hollert is doubtful, and Bennet you're welcome to anyway. When the facts get known, I reckon that I can at least split this ship right down the middle."

Van Groten was still watching me; his last smile had long since vanished and his eyes were staring out from under the peak of his cap. He didn't bother to straighten up or shift his weight from the rail, but he brought his right hand out of the pocket of his jacket. He said grimly:

"Perhaps I was wrong about you, hey? Perhaps I make a mistake when I give you those three gold bars. But mistakes can be put right, hey? Perhaps I don't need you any more?"

I looked down at his hand. I didn't know much about guns and pistols, but the ugly black barrel pointing straight at my belly looked like the business end of a German Luger, or rather like my preconceived picture of what a German Luger might look like. Van Groten corrected my thought.

"It's a Japanese make, but it's a good gun, an eight-millimetre Nambu Type Fourteen. I did some resistance fighting in Sumatra during the war. I got the gun then, and I keep her as a souvenir. Now the eight-millimetre cartridges are hard to get, but a few I keep for emergencies. I think this is an emergency, hey?" His eyes were glinting into mine and his tone was guttural and harsh. "I am Captain on this ship. She sails to Haiphong and that is finish. There is nothing that you can do about it."

"And if I try, I get shot, is that it? Or are you just going to club me over the head and dump me over the side — the way you got rid of the Malay? How did he find out that the ship was going north?"

For a moment van Groten looked uncertain, and the wrinkles that led back from his eyes creased into a frown. He repeated slowly:

"The Malay? What about the Malay?"

He wasn't that clever an actor, and at this stage there was no need for him to lie. I stared into his face and realized that there was still at least one unsolved mystery aboard the *Kerkyra*, for van Groten obviously didn't know anything about the disappearance of the Malay seaman. That worried him, for he didn't like the sudden feeling that the whole ship might not be completely sewn-up under his control. I hadn't answered him, and he repeated more sharply:

"What about the Malay? Foong says he fell overboard. He was drunk. If you know anything different, you better tell me."

I still refrained from an answer, and then there was an interruption from the wheelhouse. Neither of us had heard Louella approach, and she had failed to notice the gun held low in van Groten's hand. From behind us her voice said sleepily:

"Dirk, what is happening? I woke up and found that you were not there. Is anything — "

Van Groten's eyes flicked towards her and I took the only chance I was likely to get. I wasn't sure whether he was bluffing or not, but I was nervous with that Japanese war souvenir pointing straight at my middle. As his attention shifted, I chopped down hard with my left hand and knocked the gun spinning across the bridge. Van Groten cursed, but he had been too casual and his own left hand was still trapped in his jacket pocket. I didn't give him a chance, but hit him twice, driving my fists into his middle to double him up. Then I hooked him with a right that slammed his head back and sent his Captain's cap sailing out from the bridge and down on to the foredeck. Van Groten rolled away and I made a dive for the fallen gun.

I reached it and straightened up, but before I could wrap my index finger round the trigger Louella was upon me like a raging tigress. She had been drowsy when she came on to the bridge, but that girl came awake fast. Felling Dirk van Groten was like shoving a red hot needle into her bottom. She was wearing one of the Captain's jackets like a short coat over her pyjamas, but it didn't cramp her style any. She flew across the bridge and knocked me flying, and then she was all kicking feet and clawing nails.

172

She was loveliness turned abruptly into a spitting volcano, and the gun went clattering across the deck again as I tried to protect my eyes. It was impossible to come to grips with that hot, fiery body wriggling furiously above me, and when I did succeed in throwing her off van Groten had recovered and was waiting for me.

I got up just in time to receive a massive fist square between the eyes. A whole mess of stars turned blazing cartwheels inside my head and I went staggering back. Louella yelled as I trampled over one of her bare ankles lying in the way, and then my back hit against the bridge rail. I couldn't see a thing, but instinct told me that van Groten was following up for the grand slam that would knock me clean over the rail, and I dropped into a crouch. I butted my head forward and hit the Dutchman in the middle as he launched a killer punch at the spot where my jaw had been, and as he gasped and sagged back I threw in another low punch with my right.

I barely knew what I was doing, but

173

I knew that attack was the best form of defence. I followed him up with a rush and then it wasn't only my head that was spinning. My shoulder felt as though it had broken under the impact of van Groten's knuckles and the rest of me was whirling like a top. I ended up by crashing backwards into the wheelhouse and dimly saw the Dutchman charging me again. I rolled to dodge the kick that he swung at my head, and then grabbed at his arm to haul myself up. We blundered over to crash against the chart table and I hooked a close jab to his jaw. That rattled him and again I got my fist to his belly. I was seeing stars, but he was badly winded. I hit him low again, and we broke apart. I stepped back and then something hard jabbed painfully into the small of my back.

Louella said shrilly:

"Be still, or I will shoot you."

I became still. I didn't need two guesses to know exactly what was pressing up against my backbone, and the sweat that had oozed out of me during the fight began to freeze all over. I remembered her fury when she had thrown herself into the fray, and I couldn't think of anything that could possibly be more dangerous than an hysterical woman with a gun. To show good faith, I even lifted my hands in the air, but I did it very gingerly indeed.

Van Groten straightened up slowly and wiped a thin red smear from the corner of his mouth. He was breathing heavily and his eyes were savage, and for a moment I thought he was going to take advantage of my raised hands to smash one of those huge fists into my face. Then he relaxed and smiled briefly at Louella. He was still too breathless to speak, but made a warning gesture with his hand to wave her away. He must have thought that she was safer if she was not too close, which meant that at least I didn't look as scared as I felt.

Behind him, the Lascar helmsman had left his post and backed up against the far side of the wheelhouse, where he was staring nervously and doing his best to look invisible. Then there was another footstep on the companionway and I felt a moment of hope. Foong appeared and the hope died. Van Groten turned and was reassured to see that it was only the Bo'sun. There was a marlinespike in Foong's right hand and his one eye gazed curiously from van Groten to me. He said nothing, but waited patiently behind his Captain. Louella had moved round to my right and now I could see the Japanese Nambu held steadily in her pale white hand.

With the three of them lined against me, my one-man rebellion was over.

11

When You Can't Fight Them . . .

LOUELLA was dishevelled, with her sleek black hair falling wildly over her face, and underneath the big navy-blue jacket her pyjama top had burst open to such an extent that even in my uncomfortable position I could still feel hot and bothered. As she moved round to face me I saw that she was limping badly where I had inadvertently trampled some of the skin away from her slim ankle, but mercifully that tiger-cat temper was under control. The hand that held the gun was dwarfed by the overhanging jacket sleeve with the four golden rings, but at least it was steady and she didn't shoot me. Foong was impassive, just a silent threat in the background of the wheelhouse, and van Groten and I were both short of breath. Louella pushed the dark hair out of her

177

eyes with her left hand, and it was she who spoke first.

"Dirk, what is all this fighting about?"

I answered for him.

"Can't you guess, Louella? I've just found out that he's been fooling around with the compass. I know that the *Kerkyra* isn't going to Saigon."

Van Groten touched the side of his mouth again and nodded.

"Mister Mc'Adden isn't as sensible as we thought he would be. He get crazy ideas about taking over my ship and turning back."

I noted that it was Mister Mc'Adden again, and not Rick any more. The honeymoon had been short, and now we weren't even friends. Then Louella was looking at me with those liquid black eyes and her face was mystified.

"But why? There is much more money in taking the *Kerkyra* to Haiphong. Surely it is worth the extra risks?"

"Maybe." I looked at her squarely and wished that she would cover up that distracting glimpse of her smooth breast. It wasn't helping me to concentrate, but I tried. "If this was some ordinary smuggling trip I'd go along, but you're really sticking your necks out by breaking the U.S. embargo. That doesn't worry me so much, but for all practical purposes you're running an ammunition ship to the North Vietnamese. Now I may not know much about politics, and I wouldn't try to argue the right and wrong of it, but I do know that already there's more than enough guns and explosives playing hell in Vietnam. It all makes bloodshed, and like every other war it's the poor bastards in the middle who shed the most blood. And I don't want any part in adding to the mess."

Louella still looked puzzled.

"But, Rick, what we are doing is no more immoral than thousands of other people do every day of the week. Arms are big business. There are millions of people all over the world engaged in the manufacture and sale of arms and ammunition. When you consider the huge amount of guns and bombs that pour out of the factories in Russia and the West, then the cargo of the

Kerkyra becomes just a drop in the ocean. Everyone else is making big money, so why should we not make a little big money as well?"

I said coldly. "Most dealers are choosey about their customers."

Louella laughed as though I was the funniest person on earth.

"Rick, your morals are foolish. What does it matter how you pick your customers when there is always somebody to sell to the other side? If the West sells arms to one country, then Russia will sell arms to its neighbour. And if Russia had sold arms to the first country, then the West would have sold arms to the second. Morals like that make you a hypocrite."

There was something unanswerable in her simple logic. If you dealt in arms at all, then there was no honest way to justify one sale and not another. To try was mere self-delusion. That left me trying to find my own principles again, but after a moment I knew what they were. I didn't want anything to do with running arms and ammunition anywhere or to anybody, period. However, Louella was still talking.

"Wars will always happen, Rick. As long as the world has politicians and priests it will have wars. And when there are wars some people are lucky and make money, and some are unlucky and get killed. We are just trying to be lucky, that is all." She paused, and then thought of something else. "This cargo will not even make any difference to the outcome of the war. If it fails to get through, then it merely means that one more shipment of sulphates will be sent down from Russia or Red China. The only difference is in who makes the money."

She was doing well, but van Groten decided that it was time he began to support her. He said bluntly:

"That is true. It is cheaper for the North Vietnamese to buy this cargo, but if they do not get it they can still buy the raw materials their factories need from the North."

I glared at him and said:

"Sulphates equals explosives. Explosives equals guns and bombs. Guns and bombs equal blood and death. Whichever way you look at it, you can't get away from that basic algebra."

Van Groten glared back at me and then moved round to take the Japanese Nambu from Louella's hand. I might have tried to jump him again, but Foong read my mind and shifted closer with the marlinespike gripped loosely in his hand. Van Groten pointed the gun at my nose and I was so well covered that I felt I could safely lower my arms. They were beginning to ache and I brought them down slowly. Van Groten watched me and then said:

"Mister Mc'Adden, I am tired of this argument. This ship goes to Haiphong. You may not like that, but there is nothing that you can do about it. So now I give you a a choice, hey? You can continue your duties as First Mate, and if you like to protest by refusing your pay at the end of the trip, then that is your business. All I ask is that you keep quiet and do not interfere. The alternative is that I clap you in irons and keep you out of sight where you can talk to no one until the *Kerkyra* reaches port." He put his fingers to the bleeding corner of his mouth once more and finished grimly, "You have started a fight with the ship's Captain, Mister Mc'Adden. That is a criminal act at sea which gives me every right to have you locked up. No one will ask any questions."

His face was uncompromising now, and in the faint light of the wheelhouse it looked like a leather mask framed by the iron-grey hair. I knew that he meant what he said, and that no matter how much I opposed him there was nothing that I could do that would stop him from taking the *Kerkyra* north.

For a moment I thought again of trying to get word to van Lynden and winning the Chief Engineer over to my side, but I knew that it was a flimsy hope. Even if I could split the crew down the middle as I had threatened, it would do no good to start another war aboard the *Kerkyra*. It would be like a chess game, both sides might start evenly matched, but by the time the game was over there would be so many pieces missing from the board that any victory would be hollow. And I couldn't even be sure that the odds would be equal. Van Lynden and the other Dutch officers might be basically honest, but at the best they would have divided loyalties, and my own past record was no recommendation for a take-over bid. On the other hand, I now knew that van Groten was ruthless and that he was determined to go his own way. He had a gun in his hand, and possibly there were more with which he could arm Foong and Bennet if it became necessary. The more I thought about it the more I realized that there just wasn't any sense in starting a massacre.

Louella had watched my face and she knew that I was weakening. She smiled a little sadly and tried to ease the tension with a feminine plea. The fight was forgotten now and her voice was seductive.

"Rick, be sensible. It is foolish to argue, and especially so for you. When I first saw you in the Pussycat Bar you had no job, and no ship, and no money. And that is the way it will be again when this trip is over. This is the last chance you will ever have to wear those gold bars and sail as a First Officer. Remember that they took away your Master's ticket, and that there will be no more ships like the *Kerkyra*. You have no future, Rick. There is nothing waiting for you in Singapore, or anywhere else. But if you work with us you will be well paid when we reach Haiphong. Then perhaps you can buy your future. I don't know, but we are offering you the only chance you will ever have."

It was an argument that I had heard before, in Venezuela, she was right. I was adrift without an anchor, and a man in my position couldn't afford to have high morals and principles. Back on the beach again I would be nothing, but here I was looking a gift horse in the mouth. If I had known the truth in Singapore then I would never have signed ship's articles, but now that I was here and incapable of stopping what was happening then the only sensible thing was to go along. I had no desire to be a martyr, because I knew damn well that although martyrs got their names in history books they rarely changed the course of history. Besides, you needed a death wish to become a martyr, and that I didn't have. It all boiled down to an old philosophy; if you can't beat them you have to join them.

Van Groten had allowed Louella to say her piece, and he had given me time to think. Now he said flatly:

"Well, Mister Mc'Adden, what do you say? Are we enemies, or do we forget our quarrel and carry on? You have to choose."

I swallowed my morals and my principles and slowly nodded my head. Van Groten smiled, but he didn't relax. He hesitated for a moment, and then he shifted his Japanese war souvenir to his left hand and lowered it. His right hand he stuck out in offering.

"We shake on that, hey? And forget all about our fight."

Reluctantly, I took his hand, and then he did relax. Beside him Louella smiled happily. Only Foong failed to show any real joy; he was still watching me doubtfully. Van Groten released my hand and there was an awkward pause. Then abruptly Foong broke his long silence with a sharp exclamation.

"Captain. Helmsman gone!"

We both jerked round. The helmsman had been completely forgotten while we argued and now there was no one at the wheel. The *Kerkyra* was out of control, and while we had talked her bows had wandered slowly away from her set course. The scar-faced Lascar had vanished and there was no way of knowing exactly how much he had heard and understood before slipping silently away from the wheelhouse.

Van Groten swore and grabbed for the wheel. He started to haul the ship back on to her course, and then paused as he realized that that wasn't the first priority. He swung back towards the Bo'sun and his face was savage.

"Where would he go?"

"Maybe tell crew." For the first time that Chinese face was worried and he hefted the marlinespike in his hand. "I go see."

"Wait." Van Groten looked at me. "Take over the wheel, Mister Mc'Adden. You're in command of the bridge."

He stepped back, and after a second I moved into his place. He smiled roughly and then cocked the Japanese Nambu in his hand again. He nodded to Foong and then, with the gun at the ready, he followed the Bo'sun down from the bridge. I watched them go and then turned my attention to the helm. I pulled it hard over to bring the ship back on to her true course, and then watched as the two men came into view again on the foredeck below.

I saw van Groten stop to retrieve his peaked cap, and then they headed into the crew's quarters. Foong led the way, squat and menacing as he hurried purposefully across the deck, and the Dutchman was a massive rearguard behind him.

There was a movement beside me as Louella came close. I looked into her face and she smiled, that calm Oriental smile that seemed to know so much, and then for the first time she pulled the torn top of her pyjamas closer to conceal her breasts. I hesitated for a moment and then stepped back. I said grimly:

"Take over the wheel for me. I'm going after them."

A glint of suspicion marred those lovely eyes.

"Why, Rick?"

"Because I don't change sides every five minutes. Van Groten is outnumbered down there, and some of those gutter-rats that we've got aboard might be drunk enough to jump that gun. I don't want a full-scale mutiny in the crew's mess, especially if I'm still First Mate of this stinking tub."

She believed me. She nodded her head and moved closer to grip the spokes of the wheel.

"I just keep her steady, isn't that right?"

I nodded, and then left her to captain the bridge while I chased after van Groten and Foong.

12

A Small Mutiny

I WASN'T being exactly honest with Louella when I left her at the wheel, for my mind was still shifting from one tack to another without finding any definite course. My truce with van Groten had been made at the point of a gun and so I didn't feel wholly bound by the mere fact that we had shaken hands. My principles didn't extend to purely gentlemanly things like that. I didn't have any honour any more. I was just occasionally troubled by my conscience. I came down from the bridge with an open mind and the only important thing then was to get down fast and find out what was happening in the crew's mess. If things got tough, then maybe I'd side with van Groten and maybe I wouldn't. I'd voted against becoming a martyr, but that didn't mean that I'd sold my soul to the devil. I just wanted to be on hand when the action started, and from there I'd play it by ear.

I didn't look back as I hurried across the deck, even though I knew that Louella would be staring down to watch me. I stepped into the narrow alleyway that led into the forepeak and then I slowed up. There was a jabber of noisy voices ahead, and a curious sickly smell that made me stop and breathe the air. I had been in the East long enough to recognize that odour and I went forward more cautiously.

The opium smell got stronger and it was mixed with the smell of sweat and dirt, and cheap scent. The bulb was missing from the socket of the alleyway light above the entrance to the messroom, and so I held back for a moment in the gloom. Van Groten and Foong both had their backs to me and their voices were raised in angry conflict with a dozen or more of the devil's spawn that passed for our crew. They were all standing up, away from the bare tables and benches where they normally gossiped and ate their meals, and their faces were ugly

191

and hostile. The scar-faced Lascar who had deserted the bridge was their main spokesman, and he was arguing hotly with Foong. I wasn't sure what language they were using, it could have been Hindu, Malay or Chinese, but it sure was one big hell-rattler of an argument.

The stench and the smoke made me want to cough, but with an effort I kept my lungs under control and stayed silent. There was incense burning somewhere in the messroom, and together with the smell of opium and the acrid fog of cigarettes the atmosphere was vile. In a corner one of the Chinese stokers lay on his back on the hard deck with his head propped on a straw bolster. His pipe lay on his chest where it had slipped from his lips, and his face was a blissful smile. He was away on the happy poppy, but he was the only one who had reached dreamland. The others were wide awake and whipped up into a wild frenzy, and the room was filled with shouting faces and brandished fists.

I could feel butterflies in hob-nailed boots kicking around in my stomach, and

I began to wish that I had stayed up on the bridge where it was nice and safe. The situation here was far from healthy. I don't know what they had to celebrate, but it was obvious that these boys had been interrupted in the middle of what would have been an all-night party. There was the taste of cheap alcohol underlying the thicker smells, and those that were not half-drugged were half-drunk. To make matters worse, the Lascar had had plenty of time to tell his story, and with their support he had worked himself up into a defiant rage. If Foong had gone in alone to try and regain control they would have torn him to pieces, and it was only the solid presence of van Groten that held them back. Those who were too drugged or drunk to respect the authority of the gold rings on the Dutchman's sleeves could at least recognize the levelled gun in his hand.

I knew that Foong had had trouble before with the Lascar, but this time the scar-faced man was holding his ground. The Bo'sun was practically screaming with fury, but the Lascar was giving as good as he received and his shipmates were hurling in a continuous jabber of threats and abuse. The uproar was deafening and the air was ripening fast for violence. Van Groten had left the initial talking to Foong, but the Chinese was losing the verbal battle and was being shouted down on all sides. The Dutchman had to intervene, and his powerful roar thundered above the gabble.

"Belay there! Stow that gab, all of you! And listen to the Bo'sun!"

For a moment he won a wavering silence, and it was in the balance whether they would accept the supreme command of the ship's Master. They all knew the law of the sea, the Captain was just one step removed from Lord God Almighty, and to defy him laid them open to a charge of mutiny. They faltered, but the Lascar was their leader and he knew that he was already beyond the point of no return. He shook a knotted fist in van Groten's face and shouted back.

"No listen! No listen anybody! Ship must sail Saigon — no sail ship Haiphong!"

There was a roar of approval and the ring of dark, sweating faces grew tighter. There was murder in their angry eyes, and the gold rings and the braided cap meant nothing. The only authority was the gun. Van Groten neither flinched nor moved, but his voice was a savage bark.

"You sail where I damned well tell you to sail."

"No sail Haiphong!"

The Lascar howled his defiance, his scarred face twisted and almost gibbering with rage. There was another chorus of support and the circle edged closer. Van Groten knew they were beyond control and that at any second they would jump him. He snapped harshly:

"Bo'sun — haul out that man!"

Foong made a fast grab and seized the front of the Lascar's shirt. He too knew that the ringleader had to be felled quickly, and the marlinespike in his right hand started on a vicious swing. A Malay seaman threw himself on the Bo'sun's arm and the blow was checked in mid-air, and then Foong was struggling between the two of them.

"Belay that!"

Van Groten's bellow had no effect and he turned swiftly to wade into the fray. There was a dark face at his left elbow and as he made the turn its owner slipped behind him like a wriggling eel and made a grab for his gun arm.

I had no choice. I had followed with an open mind, but even if I tried to side with the mutineers there wasn't a hope in hell that I could assert any control over their next moves. Where van Groten had failed, so would I. The hands were no longer in a talking mood, and if I allowed van Groten and Foong to be swamped, then I would be next in their path. Murder would be done, and with the Captain, Bo'sun and First Officer all dead the mutineers would be committed to an attempt to take over the ship on their own account. The remaining white officers would be killed and there would be mass rape and worse for Louella. There was no future in that, and self-preservation left no course but to throw in my weight behind van Groten. I had to act, and I echoed the Dutchman's last command with a bull-like roar of my own.

"Belay there!"

Until then I had stayed unnoticed in the gloom of the alleyway, and as I pushed into the messroom I had the brief advantage of surprise. In that moment my shout carried more impact than the Captain's, and there was an instant of silence as all eyes shifted to find me. The man who had dodged behind van Groten's back was no less startled, and he sacrificed a vital second as he looked round in alarm. A second was all that I needed, and I caught him by the shoulder and spun him round bodily before his clutching fingers could fasten on van Groten's arm. He was another dark-faced Lascar and his eyes were horrified as I cracked him down with my fist. His nose busted under my knuckles and he squealed like a ringed pig as he fell. The shock lasted another half-second, and then there was a howl of anger from his mess-mates as they recovered and surged forward.

They were too late; van Groten's back

was saved and now he was fully alert to his danger. I kicked over a wooden bench into the path of the rush, and in the same moment van Groten fired a close shot above their heads. The bench felled a Malay and another Lascar as it banged into their shins, and the wicked crack of the Japanese Nambu sent the others tumbling back. Foong still fought his own battle, but he succeeded in throwing off the Malay hampering his arm. Then he made a second lunge with the marlinespike that split open the head of the Lascar with the scarred face, and the pressure was relieved. With their leader down, and faced with a united front of seven gold bars and Foong's single bloodlusting eye the mutiny fizzled slowly out.

The dark mixture of Chinese, Malay and Indian faces were scared now. The hate and defiance had been abruptly drained out of them and their sweat was the sweat of fear. There was a hushed silence broken only by the nervous shifting of feet and the harsh sound of Foong's breathing. Van Groten towered over them like a combination of the unstoppable force and the immovable object, and the gun in his hand did not waver by the fraction of a millimetre. It was a hand that a surgeon might have envied. He knew that he was in command again, and he was in no hurry to speak. Instead he just let them continue sweating. His eyes sought out each cringing face in turn, and one by one they wilted even further away under that shrivelling blue-eyed glare. Finally he was satisfied, lowered the gun carelessly and turned to me.

"Thank you, Mister Mc'Adden. You time your appearances very well, hey?"

His lips cracked into a smile that was just for me, but the rest of his face didn't move and the lips tightened again as he turned back to the crew. He said coldly:

"Bo'sun, you tell these men that the *Kerkyra* is sailing for Haiphong. But that is my business and not theirs. You also tell them that these two men are charged with mutiny and that they will be kept locked up and then thrown into jail when the ship returns to Singapore." As he spoke he stabbed the toe of his shoe contemptuously at the two Lascars sprawled unconscious on the deck, and then for good measure he added, "You better make that three men, Bo'sun. Lock up the man who attack you also."

Foong needed no second invitation. He stepped forward and dragged out the Malay seaman who had attempted to hold back his arm when he had tackled the Lascar. The Malay was subdued now and came with his arms wrapped over his head in anticipation of a blow from that itching marlinespike in the Bo'sun's hand. He dared not meet that one fish eye, and Foong held him easily with one fist.

Van Groten surveyed the rest of the hands and then continued in the same tone.

"You can tell them that there is no danger in Haiphong. The ship will unload her cargo and then we return to Singapore. When we return to Singapore there will be double pay for every man, but if we have any more mutiny there will be cracked heads and jail instead."

Most of them understood, but Foong translated for the benefit of the rest. I watched their faces carefully, but they were all mute and resigned. They didn't know that neither they nor the ship would be returning from Haiphong, which meant that the Lascar helmsman had only heard the last part of the conversation that had followed my fight with van Groten in the wheelhouse. That was fortunate, and van Groten's double bluff of lies and threats met with no resistance. Some of them actually smiled at the juicy carrot of double pay, and I knew that with the ringleaders removed there would be no more trouble. They were duped so easily that I felt sorry for them, but there was nothing that I could do about it. When Foong had finished, van Groten nodded to him to get on with the job, and then calmly turned away and ducked out of the messroom. I hesitated a moment and then followed him.

I caught him up on the open deck where he stopped to breathe deeply and cleanse his lungs. I needed some clean air myself and we stood for a moment in silence. I was doubtful of the wisdom of leaving Foong to lock up the leading mutineers alone, but I knew what van Groten was thinking. He had reasserted his own authority as Captain, and now it was up to Foong to reassert his authority as Bo'sun. The Chinese had to handle them alone, and now while the fight was knocked out of them was the best time for him to start.

We listened to the sound of his voice snapping orders, and there was no sound of dissent. Van Groten finished his breathing exercises, and then there was the clatter of footsteps coming down the companionway from the bridge. We looked up and saw Bennet hurrying towards us, and then went to meet him. He was still in the process of buttoning up his jacket and fired his questions at us as we approached.

"What the hell's going on down here? I thought I heard a shot."

Van Groten smiled and showed him the gun.

"Just a small mutiny, Mister Bennet.

Nothing serious to worry about. The crew were having a party, opium and drink, and they got a little bit out of hand. But it's okay now. Hey, Mister Mc'Adden?" He glanced to me for support. "Just a very small mutiny."

I nodded, and guessed that he would tell Bennet the truth in his own good time. He could do his own explaining and I didn't want any part of it.

Bennet looked dubious, but it was almost eight bells and he was due to take command of the bridge. Van Groten forestalled any further questions and sent him up to relieve Louella.

Later the three of us shared a drink in the Captain's cabin. Louella was happy and smiling, pleased that I had now committed myself to their side, and van Groten had relaxed and was addressing me as Rick again. It was a casual nightcap to celebrate our new partnership, and although I badly needed the drink it tasted sour. I've never known Johnny Walker's red label to grace bad whisky, so the taste must have been in my mouth.

The *Kerkyra* continued north, a restless ship, quiet but simmering under the surface. We were in dangerous waters now, for the U.S. Navy ruled these seas and would not welcome our intrusion. The crew knew it, and although the mutiny had been knocked out of them they were uneasy. Van Groten seemed to have given up sleeping altogether and spent much of his time on the bridge or on deck, outwardly casual, but inwardly alert for the first signs of aircraft overhead, or the ships of the mighty Seventh Fleet steaming over the horizon. I didn't sleep much either, and I knew that I would be glad when the *Kerkyra* finally limped into port. Any port would do; I just wanted the voyage to be over.

There was a brooding atmosphere about the ship, as though unseen vultures were squatting and waiting on the masts. It had spread quickly from the crew and it could not fail to touch the officers who were still in the dark. Bennet passed comment on the changed attitude of the men, but he had accepted van Groten's version of the mutiny, and did not seem to suspect that anything was really amiss. He had stood the morning watch alone with his helmsman, but he hadn't noticed the stars.

We were seated around the saloon table, eating an early lunch, when Bennet made his remark. Van Lynden was there too, and he looked up and nodded slowly.

"I have noticed a change also in my engine-room. The hands keep muttering amongst themselves, and there are strange silences when either Drekker or myself pass too near. When I ask if anything is wrong they become sullen. They shake their heads and move away. I think last night's mutiny has unsettled them."

He glanced at me as he spoke. I was the officer who had helped to quell the mutiny, and I was expected to comment. I nodded to concede his point and said:

"They were in an ugly mood last night. Foong had to split a couple of heads, and three of them are still under lock and key.

205

The others don't approve."

The Chief's grey eyes still watched me, but I didn't want to go any deeper into the subject. I still wasn't sure whether or not I should try to talk to van Lynden, but if I did decide to talk then I would talk to him alone, not while Bennet was listening. The silence dragged for a moment, and then it was Bennet who broke it. He wiped his mouth with a napkin and spoke with his mouth full.

"If they don't approve, then that's tough luck. You gotta crack down on a bunch like this. Give'em an inch and they'll knife you for a dime."

"Perhaps." Van Lynden was cautious. He could sense something and he was still looking at me.

Bennet was confident, and it was almost as though he had put down the mutiny.

"There ain't no perhaps, you gotta keep these boys in line. They're the worst sonsofbitches I ever handled." He dropped his napkin in a crumpled heap and finished: "Thank Christ it's only twenty-four hours to Saigon. I've seen enough of this trip."

Van Lynden smiled and nodded, but I said nothing. The sailing time was approximately right, but I didn't enlighten them with the fact that we would be entering a different port. Soon after that Bennet left to make his daily inspection of the leaking hold. Van Lynden stayed, and began to thumb golden tobacco into the bowl of his pipe, but then Louella appeared, and it was also time for me to relieve van Groten and stand the afternoon watch.

★ ★ ★

It was three hours later when I saw the junks appear on the far horizon.

13

The Doublecross

THERE were two of them, drifting lazily towards us and directly in the *Kerkyra*'s path. At first they were just fly specks, but gradually the cumbersome square sails took form and shape, and then the square bows and high poop of the clumsy hulls. They were large, sea-going fishing junks, and they made no move to get out of our way as the *Kerkyra* pushed sluggishly on her set course. Van Lynden could still coax only a bare ten knots from the complaining engines, but the gap closed soon enough. I trained binoculars on each junk in turn, but there were no signs of activity. On the nearest vessel two men in black clothing squatted on the deck over a pile of fishing nets, working slowly but not looking up, and on the other the decks were empty. They were too quiet and I didn't believe that they hadn't seen us approach. For no other reason there was a faint flutter in my stomach and impulse made me pick up the voice-pipe to van Groten's cabin. I didn't want to make myself foolish by sounding alarmed, but I did want van Groten on deck, and I tried to pitch my voice between the two levels.

Louella answered.

"Hello, Rick. Is it important? Dirk is asleep."

I hesitated, looking back at the two junks, but I didn't have to make a decision. Van Groten must have been catnapping with one ear open, for his voice came a second later. He sounded harsh and tense.

"What is it?"

I told him. "We've got company. Two junks across our bows."

"Junks!" He sounded relieved, as though he had expected a couple of Skyhawk jets buzzing overhead. Then caution took over again and I heard the creak as he swung off his bunk. His voice said briefly, "I'm coming up."

I hung up the voice-pipe and went

back to stand by the helmsman. He was a new man, one of the Malays, and he was looking to me for advice. The junks were immediately ahead and there was still no scurry of activity to indicate that they had any intentions of getting out of our way. I had the choice of changing course, slowing engines, or ramming into them. I hesitated, but there was really no choice, for the vague warning in my belly was outweighed by the old nightmare that flickered into my mind. That night off Panama had cost me my sleep for too many of the long, sweating nights that had followed, and I wasn't risking another collision at any price. If I merely changed course, one of the junks might wake up and move in the same moment, and the *Kerkyra*'s bows could still knife her under. I moved to the engine-room telegraph and rang down slow engines.

I didn't need the binoculars now, for the junks were less than a hundred yards away. Van Lynden had shut down on the steam and the *Kerkyra* was losing way, but the gap was still closing. I said sharply:

210

"Helmsman, hard to starboard!"

The Malay pulled hard at the wheel, but then I stopped him.

"Hold that! Hold your course."

I had seen the sudden movement that had electrified both junks. They had come alive to their danger and had started to veer apart, the big sails swinging out like opening gates to leave a wide lane through the middle. Their engines must have been idling, for they were shifting fast under power. A handful of men appeared on each deck as they cleared away on either side of the *Kerkyra*'s bows; they waved and jabbered cheerfully and our own hands on the foredeck shouted back. I relaxed now that the *Kerkyra* had a clear passage, and then heard van Groten lumber on to the deck behind me.

"What is happening, hey?"

I pointed to the junks drifting past on either side, and then everything seemed to happen at once. The junk on our port bow swung in again, and her deck was suddenly filled with men flooding up from every conceivable hiding place.

211

They were all dressed alike in baggy black pyjamas, and every man-jack of them gripped an automatic rifle or a sub-machine-gun. The *Kerkyra* had slowed almost to a stop, and the unarmed men who had been waving so cheerfully only a second ago were snatching up the grappling hooks that had lain unseen at their feet. The iron hooks were hurled up in a shower of trailing ropes as the junk crashed against the steel plates of the *Kerkyra*, and then the grappling hooks dragged at our rails and the junk was making itself fast alongside. There was an echoing crash a second later, and we wheeled to our right to see another shower of lines heaved aboard as the second junk closed up on our starboard side.

Van Groten swore savagely in his native Dutch and then made a dive for the telegraph. In the same moment I saw a heap of tangled nets hurled aside from the poop of the junk on our port side, and from underneath the double barrels of a mounted machine-gun swinging up to cover the bridge. I dived forward on

212

instinct and brought van Groten down with a low tackle as the gun opened up. A stream of shells raked along the upper front of the wheelhouse and shattered every window in a hideous cascade of glass. The helmsman screamed and reeled away with his face cut open, but it had been a warning burst that was deliberately aimed high. Van Groten stared back at me as we sprawled on the deck, and then he began swearing again.

"Pirates! Goddamned, stinking pirates! But they don't take my ship!"

He kicked clear of my arms which were still entangled round his legs, and ignoring the carpet of broken glass he twisted round to regain the telegraph. He reached up and dragged the handle down to ring full ahead, and then he squatted back on his heels and pulled the Japanese Nambu from his belt. The mounted machine-gun was silent now, although it still threatened the bridge, and the continuing blaze of gunfire came from individual weapons as the pirates covered each other in the act of swarming aboard.

The helmsman was whimpering in the corner, but van Groten ignored him. He backed up to rejoin me and said quickly:

"The chartroom. There are rifles."

I turned and followed him at a run into the chartroom, but then he was cursing again. There was a tall cupboard on the far bulkhead that was always kept locked, and I had suspected before that there were arms inside. Now the lock dropped away the moment that he touched it and when he jerked open the door there were three empty racks where there had once been rifles. His face became thunderous.

"Who the hell — ?"

He left the question in mid-air and rounded on me, his eyes ugly with suspicion. I shook my head curtly, and then the uproar from outside told him that there was no time to hold an enquiry. We ran back on to the bridge again, and saw the last of the pirates tumbling over our rails on to the foredeck below. There looked to be a score from each junk and they were thick as flies and yelling hysterically as they rounded up our crew.

There had been no response to the signal for full engines and the ship was almost at a standstill. The silent muzzles of the mounted machine-gun still threatened the bridge, and behind it I could see two tense Oriental faces staring up and watching us closely. One man's finger would be on the trigger, and with no resistance from the deck below the *Kerkyra* was taken. Van Groten's face was a picture of helpless rage, he had lost his cap and there was a trickle of blood leaking down from his iron-grey hair. The war souvenir in his hand was about as useful as a child's toy pistol against all the fire-power ranged against us, but his fist was showing white around the butt. Then footsteps clattered on the companionway behind us and we both wheeled round.

Foong stepped on to the bridge, and behind him two of our own Chinese seamen. Their arrival cleared up that small mystery of the broken lock, and I had to move fast and knock the gun out of van Groten's hand before he could do anything suicidal. The three missing rifles were pointing straight at us, and I'm a coward against odds of that kind. Foong was grinning broadly and so were his two companions.

The Bo'sun said, "Captain, ring down engine-room. Stop ship!"

"Like hell I will!"

Van Groten was glaring round as though he wasn't sure whether he had a friend left on board, but he was still rebellious. A vicious gleam came into Foong's one eye and he jerked the rifle sharply.

"Stop ship. Now! That is order!"

Van Groten made a spluttering sound and I had to drag him back. He swung round on me, fuming with rage, and I shook my head warningly. He still wasn't sure which side I was on, but he didn't hit me. He was trapped on the receiving end and he knew it. I left him then and crossed to the telegraph to ring down stop engines. The clang of the bell signalled a return of Foong's smile, but the Captain's eyes were icy. I said flatly:

"The ship is stopped anyway. That just tells van Lynden not to do anything stupid. He could get himself killed and it's too late to help us."

Van Groten saw the sense of that and after a moment he nodded slowly. The tight line of his lips was almost invisible and he did not trust himself to speak.

It was all over bar the shouting, and now there was nothing to do but wait. Then more feet clattered up the companionway and Foong moved to intercept. He was careful to lower his rifle as he faced the new arrivals, but his two friends didn't lower theirs. They were a quiet pair who had always obeyed orders smartly and stayed out of the limelight, and they had stayed uninvolved in last night's punitive mutiny. Now they looked cool and efficient and their slit eyes never wavered. I turned to watch Foong as he greeted the pirates, and then about half a dozen of the little brutes were filling up the wheelhouse. They all had grinning yellow faces and black pyjamas, and there were enough gun barrels pointing at van Groten and myself to shred us into scattered mincemeat.

Their leader wasn't much unlike the rest of them, except that he had a fancy leather belt and a pistol holster, and was waving the pistol instead of a combat rifle or a sub-machine-gun. The belt and holster were polished up like a badge of office, and he had a snappy voice and a strutting walk like a fighting bantam cock. He was highly pleased with himself and jabbered cheerfully with Foong. Then he turned to us, the prisoners, and waved the pistol about some more.

"Please to go down on deck. Quick, quick!"

His English was pretty good, but someone had forgotten to tell him that please was supposed to be a polite expression, for there was nothing polite about the way he said it. However, I wasn't sure whether he had the safety back on that pistol and I didn't like the vigorous flourishes he made to illustrate each point and so I went, quick, quick. Behind me, van Groten was slow in moving and I heard the thud as a rifle butt slammed none too gently in the small of his back. He cursed, but followed me down from the bridge.

Our own seamen had been bundled

over into one corner of the foredeck and stood in a huddled bunch, looking terrified. They were held in check by a ring of automatic weapons, and more steel gun barrels lined up swiftly on van Groten and myself as we stepped down on to the deck. The combined crews of the two junks who were not holding guns on us were doing a lot of yelling and running about as they searched the rest of the ship, and by now I had remembered which army favoured black pyjamas as a uniform. These boys were North Vietnamese.

A few more seamen were dragged out of hidden corners and our Malay helmsman was chased down from the bridge. They were shoved against the rail with the rest of our cowering crew, and I noticed that the Malay was the only one bleeding. At least there were no bodies littering the deck, and it looked as though all that blazing gunfire had simply been wasted ammunition to terrorize the men into instant submission.

A savage hiss of fury from van Groten made me forget about the crew and look up again. Louella was being forced down the companionway to join us and she was half-carrying Hollert who had to lean heavily against her. Louella's face was white, but Hollert was even worse. There was a savage bruise across the boy's right temple and blood was dripping down the side of his face. The muzzle of a rifle jabbed me in the stomach and another held van Groten in the same way, but Louella was allowed to come to us. She said wretchedly:

"Dirk, help me. Hollert tried to use the radio, but they broke in and knocked him down. They smashed the radio with the butts of their guns."

Van Groten looked down at the slit-eyed face behind the rifle that pressed into his middle, and then he pushed the gun aside. I thought he was going to get shot, but there were so many other guns that it wasn't necessary. The Dutchman relieved Louella of Hollert's weight, and the boy stumbled out some apologetic words in their own language. Van Groten's answer was gruff, but not harsh. He badly wanted to blister someone, but the broken face showed that Hollert had done his best.

Foong and his new buddy with the shiny holster came down from the bridge, and then Van Lynden and Drekker were brought up from the engine-room. The two engineers looked dishevelled and Drekker was pale, but van Lynden's bluff features were unflustered despite an unnatural hardness. He said grimly:

"Sorry, Dirk. I couldn't obey that last order. Two of the new hands jumped me when they heard the shooting. They confused things until their friends came down to join them."

It was simply said, but there was a clear oiled imprint made by the head of a large wrench stamped on the shoulder of his stained white overalls. The wrench had missed his head, but it hadn't done a lot of good to the arm that hung limp and numbed by his side. He didn't elaborate and van Groten asked no questions, because there was another disturbing commotion as Bennet was prodded up from the hold.

The round-up was now complete, and the hands who had been helping Bennet with the repair work were sent scuttling to join the rest of the crew. Bennet's fat face was aflame with anger and he clearly didn't care much for being poked up the bottom with a rifle barrel. He was busting to take a swing at somebody, but when he saw the two junks lying alongside and the mass of bandits filling our deck he decided to bottle that urge for the time being. He glared at everybody, and then looked to van Groten for an explanation.

The Dutchman was concentrating on Foong and at last his voice was controlled enough to speak.

"Mister Bo'sun, just what the hell is this all about, hey?"

The words came out with enough menace to curdle the normal human heart into a shivering jelly, but Foong was unaffected. His one eye was as immovable as the red socket beside it and his mouth smiled briefly.

"Very simple, Captain. We now have escort to take us last few miles to Haiphong."

"And why is that necessary?"

Foong smiled again.

"*Kerkyra* is now captured ship. No question of payment for you when we reach Haiphong."

"Why you doublecrossing — "

Van Groten exploded and I had to haul him back. Fortunately he was still hampered by Hollert, and Louella added her own anguished cry. Sanity got through to him again and he stood trembling. The Vietnamese had all tensed, with their fingers curling on a dozen triggers, and I was sweating. Bennet was watching with a baffled expression on his face, and he was the only one who didn't seem to realize that this was a tense moment. He said slowly:

"What is all this about Haiphong?"

Van Groten's fists were still clenched and his mouth was clamped tight, so I gave Bennet his answer.

"We were running the ship to North Vietnam. There's a better market there for the cargo."

He stared at me blankly.

"For fertilizer?"

"For sulphates." I spelled it out for him. "They can be used for making explosives too."

"Explosives — for killing American boys in Vietnam!" It was through to him now, but for a moment he didn't believe it. There was astonishment on his face and then he let out a sudden howl.

"You sonofabitch bastard!"

He came at me so fast that I didn't have a chance to defend myself. His fist took me clean in the mouth and I somersaulted backwards in a flailing crash dive that knocked three of the Vietnamese flying. I hit the deck with my mouth full of blood and spat out one of my own teeth, and then the boys in black got angry and rushed in with their gun butts. Bennet was clubbed down from behind as he tried to follow me up, and went spinning and slithering across the deck. He fared worse than I did, for he was knocked cold.

I pushed myself back on to my feet and stared down at him. The taste of my own blood wasn't pleasant and I was still groggy, but one fact was suddenly and miserably clear in my stupid brain. I had badly misjudged Larry Bennet. He might have been a fat drunken slob, but that didn't necessarily make him into another Judas. I had been influenced by our fight over Louella and my own dislike into believing van Groten's casual estimation that 'Bennet would side where the money was', and it didn't help to know that van Groten had also made a mistake. We had both forgotten that Bennet was American, and it was his countrymen who were fighting in Vietnam. Somewhere underneath all that belligerent fat was a streak of Yank patriotism, and Bennet would have been an ally if I had tried to take over the ship. Now it was too late. What might have been had dissolved into a well-deserved smack in the teeth.

Van Lynden and Drekker were staring hard at me and I wished now that I had let van Groten do his own explaining. He was the Captain and up till now he had shouted the orders. He should have had Bennet's fist and all the accusing eyes. I should have kept my trap shut. Van Lynden started to say something, but the head of the pyjama boys decided that it was time that he made it clear who was boss around here. He said snappily:

"Okay, all is finished. No more trouble."

His flat moon face and the way his pistol jabbed around to point at everybody showed that he meant it. He didn't really mind us slugging each other, but now that he had ordered it stopped it would be a question of his face and his authority. From now on anyone who moved out of step would get blasted. He went on in the same definite tone:

"My name is Phann Ki. I am now Captain of this ship. All men obey." He smiled proudly as he told us his name, but he didn't stay friendly for long. He singled out Drekker and demanded:

"You are engineer, yes?"

Drekker nodded. He was nervous, but that was no disgrace. I was feeling unheroic myself. Phann Ki smiled and showed brown-stained teeth.

"Good. You will go back to engine-room and start engines. Ship must make good speed for Haiphong."

Drekker hesitated and a rifle prodded him impatiently. Van Lynden said quietly:

"Go and do as he says. There is nothing that any of us can do."

Drekker looked to his Chief, and then allowed himself to be herded back towards the engine-room. The rest of us waited, and then Phann Ki said calmly:

"Other men will be locked up. Comrade Foong will sail this ship. Tomorrow we reach Haiphong."

Van Groten fumed, but Foong was grinning broadly.

14

All the Dead Heroes

PHANN KI didn't need anyone else to help him manage his prize, and so the rest of us were marched away to clear the decks. He chose to separate us into two groups; which was a compromise between locking each of us into our own cabins, which would require too many scattered guards, and putting all six of us together in the saloon where we might help each other to evolve troublesome ideas. He had weighed Bennet and van Groten as the two most likely sources of any counterattack and so he took care to keep them apart. He was also aware that Bennet would probably take another dive at me if I was within reach when he awoke, and just to keep a quiet ship I was kept apart from the American. It didn't help my ego any to know that I was rated third after Bennet as a possible source of danger, and I wasn't even sure that I was that high upon Phann Ki's list, but there wasn't much that I could do about it. With *Comrade* Foong leading the way and a host of little black devils shoving with rifles from the rear, I was forced to accompany Louella and van Groten up to the Captain's cabin which was to be our prison. Despite their injuries, Hollert and van Lynden had to struggle with Bennet's unconscious weight and carry him under escort to the Chief Engineer's cabin, while the unneeded members of the crew were herded like sheep into the forepeak, presumably to their own messroom.

Phann Ki was careful to have his men check the cabin for any possible hidden weapons before we were confined inside, and when the searchers retreated the place was a mess and everything pocketable that was of value had disappeared. The strutting little rat-face then informed us that there would be two armed guards outside the door at all times and more within easy call. He saluted and the door was slammed and locked as he withdrew.

Van Groten remained in the centre of the ruined day cabin with his fists balled and his mouth shut tight. He had maintained that exercise in silent self-control ever since I had pulled him away from Foong, but I could recognize a man with pure murder in his heart. I didn't dare speak to him, but moved past into the inner bedroom. That was topsy-turvy too, but I was only interested in the porthole that looked out on to the boatdeck. It was too small for a man, but Louella might have been able to wriggle through. I put my head out to weigh the chances, and the answer was an instant nil. I all but gouged my eye out on the business end of a rifle barrel, and behind it was another wrinkled face with a nasty grin. I smiled back politely and gently eased my head out of the line of fire. I decided then that I was going to be a good prisoner.

Louella came into the bedroom behind me. Her face was still white and there were tiny red specks of Hollert's blood

230

on the breast of her white blouse. She looked at the bedclothes strewn over the deck and there were tears in her lovely black eyes. She stood over the ransacked dressing table, and her fingers were shaking. She said wretchedly:

"They've stolen everything, even my nylons and underthings. Why should they want those?"

"Perhaps they've got sisters or girl friends." I tried to inject a smile. "Or perhaps they fancy them for themselves. They wear black pyjamas, so why not frilly panties?"

Louella didn't laugh; she turned, and the tears were spilling down her cheeks.

"Don't, Rick — please don't. I couldn't bear to think of those horrible little animals wearing my — "

She stopped and then van Groten appeared behind her and put his big hands on her shoulders. He still wasn't smiling or talking, but he turned her slowly to face him and then pulled her face against his chest. She hugged him and I couldn't tell whether she was still sobbing or not. I felt uncomfortable. I was an interloper here, but there was nowhere else that I could go. In that same moment I also knew something else. Mc'Adden had lost out again. No matter how much I wanted Louella, there was only one man that she really wanted for keeps, and that man was Dirk van Groten.

There was an awkward moment, and then from deep below we felt the heave and throb as the engines began to turn once again. That meant that Drekker and his crew were behaving themselves, and I hoped that they would continue to behave. I hadn't got to know Drekker very well, but I had no particular desire to hear that he had been shot full of holes. The throbbing became more definite, causing the decks to vibrate, and then from the bridge we heard the voice of Foong shouting orders. Van Groten looked at me above the top of Louella's head, and his expression had not changed. He said bleakly:

"Listen, Mister Mc'Adden. That's a dead man shouting from my bridge. Dead because I am going to kill him."

I nodded warily, because I had no doubt at all that he meant it. My own position wasn't exactly salubrious, but I was very glad indeed that I wasn't a Chinese Communist named Foong. The *Kerkyra* gave a slow shudder and then began to move, heading north once more for Haiphong.

★ ★ ★

I had plenty of time to think, and privately I thought that there was a grim streak of justice running through the whole affair. Van Groten had tried to fool everybody else and now the Viet Cong had made a neat fool of him. He had lost his ship and there had never been any intention of paying him half a million pounds for her cargo. The fact that I had lost ten per cent of that half-million failed to bother me unduly and was more of a relief than anything else. I didn't want to make money out of a trip like this, but if it had been successfully completed I don't know whether I would have refused my share. The deed would have been done, and to go away broke wouldn't have helped me or anyone else. Now at least my shaky conscience was off the hook.

Louella had made a half-hearted attempt to tidy the bed, and then gave it up and went to sit in the day cabin, saying nothing and staring dully at the deck. Van Groten paced up and down like a penned bull, and I knew what he was thinking. I hadn't thought to warn him and, like me, he had almost got his eye poked out by thrusting his head out of the porthole. Unlike me, the incident hadn't made him acceptable to his fate, and he was still calculating ways and means of getting out. I was letting my brains take a rest, but I didn't give him the benefit of my considered opinion that any escape attempt would be hopeless. Already he wasn't any too pleased with me. I was the dumb goon who had rung down slow engines when the junks appeared, and my only contribution afterwards had been in holding him back. If Foong hadn't shown up as the real traitor in his ranks I might have stayed under suspicion, and at the best I was far from being the Captain's blue-eyed boy any more.

I started thinking about *Comrade* Foong, and a few minor details became a little less vague. I had never asked myself why van Groten should have taken the Bo'sun into his confidence, but now the answer came hand in hand with the question. Foong must have been his initial link with the North Vietnamese, the link through which he had arranged the sale of the ship and her cargo. Probably he had intended to make a legitimate trip to Saigon when he first decided to salvage the *Kerkyra*, but through Foong he had been approached to take the vessel north. Foong had then made sure that a few more Communist agents were included in the new crew; the two Chinese who had helped him capture the bridge, and two more to block van Lynden in the engine-room. It was the kind of doublecross that van Groten should have expected.

The atmosphere was strained and humid in the cabin. I knew that van

Groten was in no mood to answer questions, but the endless pacing and Louella's disconsolate brooding was bothering my nerves. I took a chance on breaking the long black silence, and asked:

"How long had Foong been Bo'sun of the *Zandvoort*?"

Van Groten stopped moving and looked at me. I was sitting on the corner of his desk, and now that he had remembered that I was there he seemed to deliberate on whether he could regain some of his lost authority by bawling me off. Then he decided that maybe he had enough enemies and gave me a sour answer.

"He's been ten years with the *Zandvoort*, four of them as Bo'sun. That's a long time, hey? That's why I thought that I could trust him."

I reflected that Foong had probably been a Communist agent for all those ten years. There were one or two on every ship that carried a Chinese crew in these waters. Normally they just spied on each other or reported on cargo shipments, but this time one of them had been nicely placed to make a real killing. That thought struck another late flash of light up there in the grey sludge between my ears. I was a real clever fellow when it came to seeing the obvious after the event. My voice was as sour as van Groten's when I said:

"It must have been Foong who killed that Malay seaman. He was the joker who slugged me the night the Malay was lost overboard."

"You were attacked?" Van Groten was staring hard. "Why didn't you tell me?"

"Because I thought it might have been you," I said bluntly. "I heard a scuffle that night when I came off watch, so I went to have a look. Somebody knocked me cold."

"Then that seaman was murdered?"

"That's right — and now I can guess why. Somehow he must haved learned that Foong was a Communist agent. Perhaps he overheard Foong talking with the other agents he brought aboard, or perhaps he was one of them who chickened out at the idea of actual piracy.

Either way, he knew, but he didn't know who to approach with his tale. He was in Bennet's watch, but so was Foong, so he fought shy of Bennet. He fought shy of you too, because you were in league with the North Vietnamese. I was the only deck officer left, but before he could get to me Foong fixed him and dumped him over the side."

Van Groten's jaw jutted out. He said angrily:

"You should have told me this before!"

"I couldn't," I reminded him. "I've only just figured it out."

"I mean about the attack, when you were knocked down."

I had to remind him about that too. "Don't forget that you were one of the suspects who might have done the knocking. You, Bennet and Foong were neck and neck at the top of my list. Now I know it had to be Foong. I was wrong about Bennet too."

Van Groten glowered, but at least he had stopped pacing. Louella was watching us anxiously as though she feared that we might start another fight,

238

but finally the Dutchman lowered his hand and let it rest reassuringly on her shoulder. With an effort he dismissed what was past because a heated argument over that was no help to solving our future. He even dropped the Mister Mc'Adden prefix to indicate that we were considered equals again as he said grimly:

"Rick, somehow we have to get out of this."

"We can't," I said bravely. "Foong and Phann Ki have the *Kerkyra* completely under their control."

He said savagely, "These damn vermin have stolen my ship and my cargo. You think I accept that, hey?"

I nodded. "You have to."

"I am damned if I do." His face was thunderous. "Maybe you think I deserve to lose my ship, but there is something else you need remember. Because of this pirate trick these scum are saying that we have no deal. They won't honour the contract they made with me. That means I don't get half a million pounds. Tough luck, you think, Dirk van Groten can go without his blood money. But there was another part to that agreement, and if they doublecross in one way then you can bet they doublecross on the whole deal. That's where you start to share the tough luck. The ship's officers were to have been released, but if we are taken to North Vietnam now, then we will all end up in a stinking prison camp for the rest of our days."

Even my dumb brain had appreciated that, but it didn't change our present situation. I said patiently:

"There's still nothing that we can do. Phann Ki's got the best part of forty men out there patrolling the decks and they're all trigger-happy and armed to the tonsils. There's two of us and we don't have a pea-shooter between us. With those odds any man would stack his hand."

Van Groten said harshly, "There's five of us if we can reach van Lynden's cabin. I know my officers will back me to the limit, and Bennet's got more guts than either of us gave him credit. We take a few guns and — "

I cut him off deliberately. "If you expect Bennet to co-operate with you, then you must be mad. By now he's had time to wake up and refigure things. I got the first smack in the teeth because I was fool enough to do the talking and he doesn't like me anyway. But I'll bet that the man he wants to flatten now is you. The chances are that he's got van Lynden and Hollert thinking the same way." I paused and then finished, "Five against forty isn't my idea of a sporting chance even if we were united; divided we'd get chopped to pieces while we were scrapping with each other."

"But we have to try something!"

"Then count me out. If the going gets rough I might consider suicide in my own good time. But I've no desire to be a dead hero yet."

Van Groten put on his black thunder look again, and then straightened up from Louella and renewed his pacing. He wasn't going to be side-tracked into a quarrel with me and he went back to his thinking. Louella looked helplessly at me and I could only shrug. For the moment I

241

was prepared to take things as they came, and if van Groten wanted to put his brain through a mangle that was his affair. I knew he wouldn't think of any way of escape, because there wasn't one.

★ ★ ★

The *Kerkyra* ploughed on stolidly and the seas were calm. The only hope that I could see now lay in the two things that we had feared most before the pirates had taken over; one was sharp intervention by a flight of screaming U.S. Skyhawks, and the other was a sudden storm that would cave in the leaking side of the ship's hull and sink her to the bottom. There might have been some advantage in a change of disasters, but I wasn't too sure about it and I wasn't wholly disappointed when neither possibility showed any signs of happening. We were sweating in the frying-pan, but fire had a nasty habit of burning.

Throughout the evening we could hear the jabbering of the Vietnamese as they moved about the ship, and at intervals noisy exchanges outside the door when the sentries were relieved. Nobody looked in to see how we were amusing ourselves and nobody thought to bring us any food. We were contemptuously forgotten. The ship quietened down as darkness fell, and we spent a mostly sleepless night. Van Groten took Louella into the bedroom, but I doubt whether he gave her any consolation. He was still racking his brains for an idea that wasn't there. I sat in the armchair in the day cabin and tried not to think about that waiting prison camp. In fact, I tried not to think about anything. Towards dawn I succeeded and dozed.

★ ★ ★

I awoke as though an electric shock had been plugged into my backside and found that I had already jumped high out of my chair. It was still dark but not pitch dark, and outside it sounded as though all hell had been let loose. A sub-machine-gun was hammering out a clatter of bullets somewhere near the back of the boatdeck, and the sound was almost drowned in an uproar of howls and shouts. Somebody gave a death scream that sounded as though his guts had been ripped up with it, and then a dozen of those powerful combat rifles seemed to open fire in the same moment. There were curses, another howl, and the sub-machine-gun that had started the battle was abruptly silenced.

There was a crash behind me as van Groten bulldozed through the door from the bedroom. He stopped short when he saw that I was still there and that we were still locked in. I could see his face dimly in the gloom and his expression was one of helpless frustration and agony. He knew his friends were dying, but he said nothing. There was nothing that either of us could do except stand there like two wax dummies and listen.

The battle outside was fierce and brief, and finished almost as soon as it had started. There was another echoing stream of shots from a combat rifle, or perhaps it was several rifles firing in quick succession, I couldn't really tell; a final death shriek, and then a pregnant silence. The next sound that came was a low moaning from someone who had been hit, and then a growing chorus of excited yelling in shrill, alien voices. Louella came slowly out of the bedroom and her face showed up like a shiny white moon. Van Groten put one arm around her and we waited.

It was only a minute, but it was an hour of sweat. Then there was shouting outside the cabin door. The voices were urgent and full of purpose. The door rattled as it was unlocked, and then it was kicked open. It crashed back wide on its hinges and anyone standing behind it would have had his face mashed flat. The light was switched on and half a dozen angry yellow faces surged in behind a barrier of threatening weapons. They screamed at us like infuriated monkeys and there was only one sensible response. We raised our hands respectfully above our heads and backed up against the bulkhead.

They held us there for another three minutes, and then Foong appeared with Phann Ki. The little rat-face was burning up with anger and it was he who did the talking. He waved his revolver at us and cried hysterically:

"Come! All men come see. If you seek escape I show you price of failure!"

His men cleared a path and we were taken up on deck to view the bodies of Bennet, Hollert and van Lynden, all laid out in a neat and bloody row.

15

Haiphong

I HAD expected nothing less, but it made me want to retch; all three of them had been practically shot to pieces, butchered at close range of high-velocity rifles that could kill at over a mile. Louella gave a shuddering cry and quickly turned her face against van Groten's chest, almost fainting. The Dutchman held her tightly as he stared down at the dead men, and his face was old and hard. It was a grey face, blending with the iron-grey hair and the darker grey of first dawn.

Foong and Phann Ki stood side by side, watching our reaction with malicious eyes, but saying nothing. A tight ring of black-dressed Vietnamese supported them with levelled weapons, but all their faces were blank. I looked around and saw that there was plenty of blood on the deck, long smears of it where the three corpses had been dragged into position, and more smears where other corpses had been dragged away. The killing hadn't been all one-sided, but Phann Ki was too good a psychologist to let us see his own casualties. I wasn't sure that I could control my stomach and looked out to sea. The two junks were still there, running with both sails and engines, and the nearest was close alongside. The mounted machinegun on her poop deck was angled upwards to cover the *Kerkyra*'s bridge once more, and I guessed that she had hurried up in support as soon as the firing had started. There was plenty of time to look around, for we were intended to have a good, long look at our dead friends.

The waiting seemed longer than necessary and the sky grew lighter. Van Groten's face was stone and mine must have been identical, and we both sensed that it was a matter of face not to break the silence. Phann Ki wanted to see us weep, or rage, or threaten, but at least he wouldn't have that satisfaction. There was also another reason for the delay, and the silence was finally disrupted when Drekker was hustled into view from the companionway.

Maybe they fed the workers, for Drekker was very sick. He took one look at van Lynden's bloodied form and his stomach heaved. Phann Ki smiled, but I couldn't blame the boy. I had been very close to it myself, and van Lynden hadn't been my Chief and tutor.

There was another moment while Drekker coughed and recovered, and then Phann Ki decided that it was time to make his speech. He had a full audience now, and he meant to rub in the warning. He stepped forward and yapped:

"All men have good look-see. Make trouble is no good for you. This man — " He indicated Bennet with a casual kick. "This man attack guard and take sub-machine-gun. Other men stupid and follow him. They try to attack bridge, but fail. Now they dead. Any more trouble — same thing happening."

He looked round ominously, but no

one answered. He didn't like that and began to wave his revolver, demanding sharply:

"All men understand, yes?"

Drekker was too ill to talk and van Groten was undergoing another stiff session of rigid self-discipline. Keeping his mouth shut was all part of keeping his feet anchored in the same place. If he relaxed anything he would explode. That only left me to speak up.

"We understand. There'll be no more trouble."

I didn't say it meekly, but I didn't say it boldly either. Phann Ki gave me a dubious look, but then he decided to let it pass. He shouted out a whole string of orders, and the pyjama boys jumped at the double. Drekker was taken back below to carry on working in the engine-room, and the rest of us were bundled back into van Groten's cabin. It wasn't done gently and the door was slammed and locked with unnecessary violence.

When they had gone van Groten said harshly:

"I want to be alone."

He disentangled himself from Louella's arm and without another word went into the bedroom. He shut the connecting door with another vicious crash that almost collapsed the cabin, and even Louella did not dare go in to console him.

* * *

The hours passed and the *Kerkyra* ploughed slowly northward. The sun got up and the cabin got hot and stifling, but I no longer pined for the open decks. There were too many stains on the boards and no amount of scrubbing would ever get them clean and white again. Louella was pale and miserable as she sat in her chair, and for the first time I had no desire for her. Her dejection was complete and there was nothing that I could say. Van Groten stayed behind the closed door in self-imposed isolation, but I knew what he would be thinking. It was starkly clear that escape was suicidal and he could only be blaming himself for the deaths of his Dutch officers. I could mourn

251

for them too, but the man more closely on my mind was Bennet. I had been so catastrophically wrong about Bennet, ruled by my own instant dislike for the man, and now he had died in trying to do what I should have done long before those pirate junks had loomed up over the horizon. Bennet was a dead hero, and I was a live coward. That wasn't easy to live with; it could be as bad as the *Conchita* and the *Pirahne*.

It was noon before the cabin door was unlocked again. One of our own Chinese stewards was shoved inside and the tray of food he was carrying was almost pitched in our faces. He recovered his balance and hastily put the tray on the big desk-table. He didn't say anything, because he was hauled out just as sharply as he had been pushed in. His frightened yellow face was shut from view by the slamming door and as the lock turned we heard him being harried away.

I had been hungry before that scene on the deck this morning and now my appetite was beginning to return, so I took a closer look at the food. There were three plates of a messy stew that the steward would never have dared to serve in the saloon, but with an extra forty mouths to strain the catering I hadn't expected too much. I was surprised that they had remembered to feed us at all.

The noise had disturbed van Groten and he emerged to see what it was all about. His face was bleak and beginning to show grey stubble, and when he saw the food he started to turn away. I said bluntly:

"It may be another twenty-four hours before they feed us again. We're only filthy capitalists, remember. You'd better eat."

He glared at me, but one part of his mind was still cold and logical and he accepted that there was no sense in starving himself into weakness. He came back and picked up his plate and spoon. Phann Ki had probably given orders that we were not to get our hands on anything sharp or pointed, so there were no knives and forks. We both ate, but there was no taste in the food. It was a lousy stew even if you didn't have a constricted gullet.

Louella refused to watch us and her own plate was left untouched.

Ten minutes later the door was banged open again. The steward came in to grab up the tray and practically ran out, but only one of the guards followed him. The others came inside, making hostile signals with their rifles, and we were backed up against the bulkhead. Then Phann Ki strutted in with Foong behind him. The Bo'sun had exchanged his marlinespike now for a nice new combat rifle, but he was still only second-in-command. Phann Ki's rat-face wore an unexpected beam as he said cheerfully:

"All men have eat. Good. We look after prisoners very well. Now one man work."

I might have known there would be a condition, and he was pointing at me. I said warily:

"What kind of work?"

"On bridge. You First Officer. You take over ship."

I wanted a future, so I wasn't going to refuse, but I wasn't going to crawl too quickly either. I looked at our ex-Bo'sun and risked putting a sneer into my voice.

"I thought *Comrade* Foong was sailing the ship."

Foong stayed impassive. His speciality was the stab in the back and he left the talking to Phann Ki. The Vietnamese looked at me a little more coldly and said:

"Ship near Haiphong. It is best if officer take her into port. You will come up to bridge."

I saw the picture now. Foong was confident enough in the open sea where he had plenty of room to make mistakes, but taking the *Kerkyra* into port could prove a little more tricky. There was a lot of sea sloping around inside that leaking hold that was making the ship sluggish and unpredictable. She needed careful handling and that was why they preferred to have either van Groten or myself on deck. Then if anything did get rammed or sunk it would be criminal capitalist sabotage instead of stupid Vietnamese incompetence. I was the fall guy because they knew better than to trust van Groten. They had both figured that to me the

Mc'Adden skin was of first priority, but that was another insult that I had to accept.

Van Groten said nothing as I was hustled out of the cabin. He just stood back with his arm around Louella and watched with bitter eyes. On the way up to the bridge I reflected that there wasn't anything else that he could have done.

There were a couple of pyjama boys with sub-machineguns standing guard in the wheelhouse, and one of Foong's Chinese pals was at the helm. More guards with combat rifles were posted on each wing of the bridge where they could cover the boatdeck behind and the foredeck below, and the whole ship was sewn up pretty neatly. I reckoned that it would take a small army to wrest control from this sharp-eyed lot, so I carried on being a model prisoner. I noticed that the two junks were still patrolling off our bows and that there was land and palm trees both to port and starboard. The *Kerkyra* was already entering the estuary of the Red River and Haiphong was directly ahead. I crossed to the telegraph and rang down half engines.

Drekker was still doing as he was told, for the response was almost immediate. The *Kerkyra* began to lose way and I gave the helmsman an order to bring her bows round to the centre of the channel. Phann Ki came to stand beside me and showed his unlovely brown teeth in a smile of satisfaction. I didn't look round, but I knew Foong was behind me with his rifle casually aimed at my spine. His face was certain to be blank.

Haiphong was an unimpressive port, and I was sure that I wasn't going to enjoy my stay. It was a drab town, factories, warehouses and a cement works, and nothing to indicate any of the shoreside comforts that were a sailor's usual demand. Apart from a few junks and sampans, the only ships in the docks were three small freighters all flying the hammer and sickle. Only the Chinese and the Ivans traded with North Vietnam, and the Chinese didn't have many ships. It was a gloomy prospect.

A motor launch put out from shore to meet us, and on Phann Ki's instructions I stopped the ship while it came alongside. Another boatload of grinning monkeys came aboard, and the wheelhouse was filled up with their crowing, jabbering faces. I guessed that they were government and port authorities, for they wore suits or uniforms instead of pyjamas, and they were all filled with that popinjay pomposity that only worthless bureaucracy can give. The ship was expected and this was the welcoming committee, and Phann Ki was all smiles. Everybody was happy except me, but nobody cared about me.

Phann Ki finally ordered me to get the ship moving again. He jabbed me in the belly with his revolver just to show his friends that a big fellow like me wasn't really so tough. One of them spat on my boot and they all laughed. They were too pleased to get really nasty, but it was all hilariously funny. I tried to ignore them and concentrated on docking the *Kerkyra*.

One little ape with a squint eye was obviously some sort of pilot. He stepped out in front and folded his arms across his chest as though he was the Imperial Emperor of all Indo-China and began barking out directions. Phann Ki entered into the spirit of the game and tried to make the translations sound even more fierce. I gave curt orders to the helmsman and with a whole lot of shouting and cheering taking place we slowly entered harbour.

One of the Russian freighters slid past and her rail was lined with fur-capped Slavonic faces returning the waving and cheering from our decks. They probably didn't know why they were cheering, but they could recognize a celebration when they saw one. I started to get irritated and there was a strong temptation to wipe the smiles from some of those smirking faces. The helmsman was obeying my commands implicity and he obviously didn't understand the pilot's Vietnamese. It would have been easy to slip in a crisp *hard-to-starboard* in the same tone of voice, and the odds were that he would swing the wheel round before he realized that I had spoken out of turn. Then the *Kerkyra*'s bows would mangle a few dents into Ivan's newly-painted hull. The only trouble with that idea was that a certain Richard Mc'Adden would get dented and mangled immediately afterwards, and so I didn't do it. Instead I brought the ship round gently and placed her alongside an empty length of quay, exactly where the pilot-type wanted her to be placed. I rang down stop engines, and then watched as the ship was made fast. Our own deckhands were handling the ropes in the bows and stern and they worked a hell of a lot faster than they had ever done before, but perhaps the guns in their backs had something to do with that.

The ship was motionless, but I hesitated for a moment with my hand on the engine-room telegraph. The voyage was at an end, but it was the *Kerkyra*'s final voyage, and it was hard to ring down finished with engines for the very last time. She was a battered old tramp and no more than a stain on the seas, but she deserved better than this. Then I told myself that sentiment was stupid and not even a luxury, and pulled the handle hard down.

The engines stopped and I was out of a job.

★ ★ ★

I was marched back to the cabin, and after I had been pushed inside van Groten was taken out. The welcoming committee wished to thank him for delivering the ship and her cargo safely to North Vietnam. It was a calculated joke and humiliation, devised by someone with an evil sense of humour, and when he was returned the Dutchman was almost white with suppressed fury. He tripped as he was shoved over the threshold and Louella had to grab nervously at his arm as he swung round to snarl at Phann Ki and the guards. The sound became a hiss as he managed to bite down on his tongue, and then Louella pulled him away. Phann Ki was smiling and I risked a question before he withdrew.

"You've got the ship — now what happens to us?"

He had been saving his best contemptuous

261

shrug especially for this occasion, and said smugly:

"That is not important. It will be decided later. Now I must help Comrade Foong to supervise the unloading of the cargo."

He made a mock bow and then backed out. The door slammed in our faces and once again the key rattled in the lock.

16

Air Attack

THE babel of noise and movement that filled the *Kerkyra* gradually died down and the ship became quiet. The only interruption was when Drekker was thrown inside to join us. They didn't need him in the engine-room now and they didn't see any need to keep him under a separate guard. The fact that the Captain's cabin was getting overcrowded was irrelevant in their eyes. The guards remained outside and although they were more careless than they had been at sea it was too late to try any tricks. They were home and dry and they knew it, and they could afford to relax. Van Groten knew it too, and he had stopped his pacing and thinking. Now he was as gloomy as Louella. Drekker was tired and haggard after being forced to work twenty-four hours non-stop with the engines, so he failed to contribute any joy to the party. On the whole we were a pretty silent and miserable bunch.

We passed another practically sleepless night. Louella and van Groten took the bedroom while Drekker and I lay back in the two armchairs in the day cabin. Exhaustion finally closed the boy's eyes, but it was a long time before I could follow his example. I felt as physically beat as he looked, but my mind wouldn't close up and go blank.

Dawn was a relief that didn't bring any breakfast. We had nothing to do but suffer until mid-morning, and then Phann Ki appeared with his usual six-strong armed bodyguard, and van Groten was taken away. There was no explanation, and although the little Vietnamese was still shrill and strutting, his rat-face didn't wear quite the same Supreme God of Creation look. He made heroic gestures with his revolver, but I guessed that he wasn't the real top dog any more.

Louella was worried and I put a hand on her arm to steady her. We could only watch as van Groten found and put on his cap with the gold-braided peak that had once spelt authority, then he was taken out and the door locked behind him. Beside us Drekker still looked haggard and he hadn't yet got rid of the red rings around his eyes. I kept thinking of him as a boy, but suddenly I realized that he wasn't a boy any more. He could only be twenty or thereabout, but experience aged faster than years.

The waiting lasted thirty minutes. Then we heard the tramp of feet again. The door was unlocked and van Groten was hurled roughly inside. Beyond him I saw Phann Ki standing well back behind his men and there was a cold look of anger on his face. Then the door crashed shut. Van Groten had caught at the table for support, and it was a moment before he could straighten up. He hadn't behaved, for his cap was missing and his face would have made a passable double for a slab of raw meat. There were bruises everywhere and an open cut above the eyebrow that obliged him to blink slowly in order to keep the splashes of blood out of his eye.

Louella gave a muffled scream and ran to him.

I helped him to sit down and gave him time to recover. None of us were going anywhere, so there was no need to rush the questions. Louella found a handkerchief and some Elastoplast and we patched him up as well as we were able. Fortunately the cut wasn't too deep. Then finally he told us what had happened.

"They had a paper for me to sign. It was a very good fairy story; all about how we were taking the *Kerkyra* to Saigon so that the American war criminals could make more bombs to kill innocent Vietnamese. It was the usual confession thing, but it was all so twisted that it wouldn't make sense to anybody. I don't think it would have mattered much if I had put my name on the bottom, but instead I told them to stick it up their — " He remembered Louella and stopped, and then his lips cracked a smile at the memory. "They didn't like that, not one little bit." The smile faded and he added: "Then they got tough."

266

I said grimly, "Perhaps you should have signed. Nobody gets fooled by these screwy confessions."

He scowled and retorted, "Perhaps they fool their own people with them. I don't know. But Dirk van Groten is a clean name, and I don't want any dirt on it." He gave me a frigid look. "Your turn comes next. Then it's up to you, hey? If you want you can write Rick Mc'Adden on their damned paper."

He was right. They didn't come too quickly because they wanted me to hear van Groten's story, and get acquainted with the new shape of the Dutchman's face, but eventually they came. I had had two hours to think it over and I still wasn't sure whether it was worth a beating up for an empty principle. Phann Ki's ugly face suggested that it wasn't, and his black pyjama boys had obviously been warned about not being too gentle as I was marched away.

They took me into the saloon where three fat little Vietnamese officials were seated behind the large dining table. They each wore military uniforms and had a lot of gold stars on their shoulders. They might have been Generals or Brigadiers, but I didn't really know. To me they looked like the three wise monkeys, except that the mottoes would have to be reversed. This trio had seen and heard plenty of evil, and they weren't about to croon sweet nothings at me over the table top. There was a huge flag of North Vietnam hung up behind them and they looked very smug.

I was pushed over to stand in front of the table and then someone rammed a chair hard against the back of my knees. It wasn't a polite way of inviting a man to sit, but it sat me down pretty effectively. A lot of rifles pointed at my back and Phann Ki's revolver wasn't far from my head, so I didn't complain. There was a large blotting pad in front of me, and a long sheet of typewritten paper and a cheap pen.

Hear No Evil, that was the one in the middle, appeared to be the big wheel. He spoke English but didn't clean his teeth, or at least he hadn't done so lately. He said pleasantly:

"You are the ship's First Officer, yes? Your confession has been prepared for you. You will sign it, please."

I hesitated for a minute and then picked up the paper. As van Groten had said, it was so screwy it was a laugh, but these jokers were dead serious. There was a lot of stuff about American atrocities and imperialism, and something called shameful escalationizing, all of it badly phrased and spelled and pretty pathetic even for propaganda. All of this, according to the text, I vigorously condemned, at the same time applauding the heroic efforts of the People's Army of National Liberation of North Vietnam. I also confessed to my own crime of attempting to take a cargo of basic war materials to South Vietnam, and I was now repentant and even pleased that capture of the *Kerkyra* by the noble Viet Cong Lieutenant Phann Ki had diverted this criminal cargo to the North. I had seen the error of my ways and now I begged the forgiveness of all those whom

I had wronged. At the bottom of the page there was a space for my humble signature.

Everybody watched me read it, and the rank and file were all itching to have a go with their boots and rifle butts when the big stupid Englishman refused to sign. I thought about it for a moment, and then picked up the pen and signed on the dotted line.

Phann Ki smiled like a Cheshire monkey, if there is such a thing. Some of his pals looked disappointed, but the three wheels showed no reaction. I turned the paper round and passed it over to them, and then I prayed.

Hear No Evil studied the signature dubiously. Speak No Evil and See No Evil leaned closer on each side and they too studied what I had written. Then the middle one looked up. He said curiously:

"Mister — er — Ullshit?"

I nodded. I hoped that they hadn't taken the trouble to check up on my name, and I hoped they weren't too bright, otherwise I could join van Groten in hiring our faces to a butcher's window. The joke was only funny if they didn't find out too soon. I said politely:

"The B. stands for Brian."

I was sweating, because I prefer my beatings to be postponed into the future, but eventually they appeared to be satisfied. See No Evil made a solemn nodding movement of his head, and Hear No Evil signalled my dismissal with a contemptuous wave of his hand. Somebody yanked my chair away and I almost fell over backwards, and then the rifle muzzles were prodding me out towards the door. They did it viciously and by now I probably had a string vest pattern of circular bruise marks all over by back and ribs, but at least I wasn't getting carved up yet.

I was halfway through the door when the sirens sounded. They howled out like metallic banshees, and my nerves must have been wearing thin because I jumped almost a foot in the air. The noise was appalling, as though Haiphong was full of giant tabby cats that had all had their tails chopped off in the same moment.

Everyone froze and listened, and it was a full minute before the wailing died down. The monkey faces all around me weren't quite so confident any more, and those nearest the door were looking through and up at the skies. They were blue skies, flawless and brilliant, but there was death up there and everyone knew it. The sirens stopped and then we heard a shriek of thunder from overhead. Nothing crossed the patch of blue that was visible through the open door, but the jets were low and very close. They roared in and away and left behind the crash of exploding bombs. The U.S. Air Force was making one of its routine calls over the town.

As the first layer of bombs came down the Vietnamese burst into agitated movement. Half of them hit the deck and the three wise monkeys made an undignified scramble to get under the solid oak table. Phann Ki stayed on his feet and began yelling furiously; he was afraid for himself and mad at his men. Nobody wanted to venture out on to the decks, but two of the braver souls finally did as they were told. I had no choice but to go with them, and this time they were really in a hurry to move me along. Phann Ki led the way, and we scrambled up the companionway to the boatdeck. He wanted me safely locked up in the Captain's cabin again, and for once we had a common interest, but then the U.S. Air Force decided to come back.

They swept in low over the harbour; a flight of six rocket-armed Skyhawks that had almost certainly been catapulted from one of the giant aircraft carriers that were based off the coast. They were ducking in under the anti-aircraft cover that was hurled up all around Haiphong, and it looked as though they intended to clip off the *Kerkyra*'s masthead on their way in. There was a deafening roar as they showed us their bellies and howled overhead, and again everybody hit the deck. That is, everybody except me.

The two pyjama boys had dived head first under the nearest lifeboat, and Phann Ki had dropped down on to one knee. He was cursing and screaming at the Skyhawks and banged away into the air

273

with his revolver. I acted on a sudden impulse and kicked him hard in the back of his head. He spilled over on his face and sprawled across the deck, and then I took to my heels and ran. I dodged around the funnel, but no shots chased after me. I guessed that the two guards had their heads down still, but I wasn't waiting to find out. I shot down the opposite companionway to regain the lower decks like a rabbit bolting for its hole.

I didn't know where I was going, I just knew that I had to keep going. The decks had cleared like magic when the air attack began and there was nobody to stop me as I sprinted forward along the starboard alleyway. The gangway was down and the sentries had vanished just like everybody else, and within a matter of seconds I was down on to the quay. At any moment I expected a shot in the back and I can't think of any better incentive to make a championship runner. I fled like one of those crazy cartoon characters who have their feet spinning in frantic circles, and I didn't stop to snort for breath until I had put a couple of warehouses between myself and the *Kerkyra*.

I stayed there, gasping for breath, and listened to the rockets playing hell on the outskirts of town. The dockside was deserted and I guessed that the natives had had plenty of practice in getting under cover when the sirens shrieked out their brief warning. They would stay in their bolt-holes while the Skyhawks were buzzing around over-head, but the air raid couldn't last for ever and I had until it ended to get clear of the docks. After that Phann Ki would get his boys organized and it wouldn't take him long to hunt me down. I didn't like to think of what he might do when he caught me, and so I got going again, fast.

During the next few minutes I qualified for another couple of Olympic golds in hurdling and running, and my assault course tactics were no dawdle either. I went over a mess of railway tracks, through two lines of parked trucks, and did a final breakneck scramble over a ten-foot-high fence of wooden palings. I dropped down into a street outside the docks, fell on my face, practically somersaulted to my feet again, and kept on running. I would have made a fortune in a circus, except that I would never be able to do the same trick again in a million years.

Another wave of Skyhawks made a diving run from the sea to clobber the outskirts of the town with bombs and rockets, and the streets of Haiphong were as empty of human activity as the docks had been. Theoretically the jets were only aiming for the fuel dumps and the railhead to Hanoi, but everybody knew that mistakes were made, so they played safe. That suited me, and although I was scared stiff by the crash of exploding bombs I kept hoping that this raid was going to be a long one.

I was blowing hard and there was a needle pain under my ribs, but I couldn't stop. I had turned left on leaving the dock area and my only thought was the vague aim of getting clear of the town. My progress was almost blind because of the sweat running into my eyes, and I had only the dimmest recollection of the drab streets through which I ran. The pain was getting sharper in my side, and then I was lucky and found a bicycle. It was a rusty old thing that somebody had hastily dropped in the gutter when the air raid began. Its owner was probably hiding in the cellar of one of the dilapidated houses that lined either side of the road, and that was his tough luck. I added bicycle-stealing to my long list of crimes and mounted up. The bike wobbled, but then I got going and pedalled furiously on my way.

I kept my feet flying round for another ten minutes and I doubt if that old bike had ever moved so fast in all its long and battered life. A dozen times we hit ruts and bumps that should have buckled the bouncing wheels, and the bike was airborne more often than it was on the road. I hunched low, fought to keep the handlebars straight, and suffered agonies from a pointed, iron-hard leather seat that must have been designed either by a masochist or a sadist. The odour of poverty and blocked drains became less noticeable

277

as the unattractive houses thinned out around me, and ahead lay an open road through water-logged ricefields. I wasn't escaping from Haiphong any too soon, because the explosions and the sounds of aircraft had all died away. There was an ominous hush that was worse than the bombing had been, and there were palls of ugly black smoke dirtying the sky to the north.

That pain in my side was a hot dagger stabbing right through me, and although I hadn't been going so very long I had burned up so much energy that I was exhausted. Also the local population had started to emerge, and scattered figures were beginning to rise up from the fields. It was obviously my turn to get out of sight and I looked around desperately for any kind of cover.

The only possibility was a clump of palm trees and jungle that lay about fifty yards from the road, and I didn't have time to be choosey. I abandoned the bike and slung it into a ditch that was knee deep in water, hoping that it would stay unnoticed, and then I was running again, splashing and stumbling through the ricefield. I fell over twice, smothering myself with mud and almost drowning before I could flounder back to my feet, but at last I reached that scruffy clump of greenery. I plunged into the middle and flopped down in the thickest part where I could lay unseen, and for the next ten minutes I was as helpless as a brand-new baby. I was utterly drained and my whole body simply collapsed.

17

Basic Algebra

LUCKILY for me, the patch of jungle that I had chosen was just a little higher than the swamped paddy fields all around, so at least I had my nose out of water as I sprawled on my face. After ten minutes I managed to roll on to my back, but apart from that it was half an hour before I felt fit enough to move any farther. My chest was heaving like the biggest set of bellows ever built and that dagger in my side was on fire. My legs ached and my heart did a crazy imitation of a hopped-up jazz drummer playing *Skin Deep* at double tempo. I was a wreck, and if I had been seen the natives could have dragged me out of my hiding place without any resistance. Mercifully, I had not been seen.

I listened closely, but I could hear no voices or sounds of any kind, and finally I plucked up enough strength and courage to crawl back to the edge of my tiny island. I lay between two bushes and looked out over the flat, shallow lakes with their green rows of young rice shoots. In the distance I could see peasants working, black figures with large straw hats, bent over like crippled hunchbacks as they pushed more young plants into the flooded earth. There was traffic along the road that I had left, a few bicycles, a cart drawn by a slow ambling bullock and a few people walking. It was a changed scene, quiet and peaceful except for the black fog of smoke that overhung Haiphong. Air raids were common and it seemed that they were soon forgotten when the attack was over.

There was nothing I could do except resign myself to a long stay in the bushes. I'm a pretty big, round-eyed, foreign white devil, and if I moved out into the open it would be all too obvious to any Vietnamese who looked up from his planting that I wasn't one of his countrymen taking a casual stroll.

In fact my presence would probably find only one explanation in a Vietnamese mind. There had just been an air raid, and I would be fingered as a ditched pilot who had somehow managed to bale out unseen. Then everybody and his brother would grab up a hoe or a pitchfork and the fun would start. I didn't fancy that at all, so the only sensible thing was to stay put until darkness.

It was going to be a long wait. The sun was almost directly overhead and although the cluster of palms and jungle gave me some shade I was still sweating. The green shimmer of the surrounding water made me realize that my throat was parched and dry, but I knew that it was all undrinkable. Then my belly began to rumble emptily to remind me that it was now twenty-four hours since I had eaten my last meal. I was uncomfortably bedraggled and caked with mud, and now that I had time to think about it my attempt to escape had been a pretty stupid impulse.

My next move was as vague as it could possibly be. I could just remember the shape of Vietnam on the map and it seemed that whichever way I went I would be headed for trouble. East lay the sea and I couldn't quite see myself swimming anywhere, north lay Red China, but it was most unlikely that Chairman Mao would hang out the welcome flags for one Richard Mc'Adden, and to the south all kinds of hell were raging. The only alternative that remained was west toward Laos, and even Laos was partially under Communist control. There was also the small matter of some two hundred miles of jungle between here and the Laotian border, and God alone knew how many more before I found a link with any civilized town. I wasn't even sure that Laos had any civilized towns, and all things considered my position was about as enviable as that of a plump white missionary who strays into a cannibal village at the wrong end of an acute famine.

There was only one consolation, and that was that I soon got rid of the slight guilt complex that came with deserting van Groten and Louella. They were better off than I was, and now that I had had time to reflect I might have given myself up and rejoined them if I had not been dumb enough to kick Phann Ki halfway across the *Kerkyra*'s deck. The Vietnamese would want to see at least a few of my bones broken in return for that, which meant that I would only stay in one piece while I stayed out of his reach.

I decided then that when darkness fell I would attempt to steal some food and then head west. I didn't expect to last for very long, but I would continue moving by night and hiding by day until I was recaptured. I had nothing to lose and at least I could make a run for the border. It was better than admitting defeat.

When my mind was made up I tried to give it a rest and watched the peasants working in the fields. They were moving closer, and by the end of the afternoon there was a group of a dozen women working only fifty yards from the island where I lay in hiding. Several of them had babies tied to their backs and there were five or six children clustered around them. The elder ones worked with their mothers while the younger ones played. I edged a little deeper into the bushes and became very still.

The younger children worried me; they had to amuse themselves, and I hoped that they wouldn't decide to investigate my island. There were two boys and a little girl, noisy, cheeky little devils who chattered shrilly as they scampered up to their knees in water and chased each other in circles. The women worked stoically and paid them no attention, their backs ever bent as they pushed and pulled at the rice. They were thinning out the young shoots, and this was the end of the day when they were too weary to gossip. It was getting dusk and only the children were lively.

Despite the threat that they unconsciously offered, I found myself smiling at their antics. Kids were kids the whole world over, and it's the world's biggest tragedy that they have to grow up and be taught to hate each other. These kids were just as carefree as any English kids playing in a puddle, except that they had a much bigger puddle in which to play. They shrieked and splashed each other like children anywhere. Occasionally one of the women would lift her head and smile, or shout an exasperated demand for good behaviour which she didn't really want. The babies watched from the uncomfortable security of their mothers' backs with the solemn, wide-eyed curiosity that babies always have.

It was almost dark and I was waiting for them to go, and then abruptly the sirens sounded again over Haiphong. The children stopped playing and the women straightened their backs. My own muscles tensed and we all stared in the direction of that hideous caterwauling rising up from the black silhouette of the ugly town. The sirens reached a frantic wail and then died slowly into silence. The peasant women still stood upright, looking all around the darkening skies, and minutes passed before we heard the first howl of a jet engine high overhead.

This time it wasn't the Skyhawks making a return attack. These were heavier jets coming in over land from the west, and I guessed that they were the more powerful Thunderchiefs operating out of the U.S. bases in northern Thailand. The anti-aircraft batteries opened up to spread a murderous curtain of exploding shells across the skies, but still the jets screamed in to unload their bombs. I had a ringside seat to watch the black, red-cored mushrooms that sprouted all around the beleaguered city. The earth shook under that rain of death and the blasts of sound slammed repeatedly at my eardrums.

The children had run close to their mothers and the women were crouching low in the paddy field. They were silent now, huddled and frightened, and they could only wince and watch as great flashes of light lit up the agony of Haiphong. The earth and skies were being torn apart, and it seemed that the centuries of martyrs to the endless wars of past history must have wept in their meaningless graves. The raid lasted for fifteen minutes and the only thing to surpass man's criminal inhumanity to man was his blind, colossal insanity.

287

At last the bombing stopped, the planes began to retreat in a series of fast roaring climbs and headed back for the safety of Thailand. The peasant women straightened up from the mud and I began to relax again. The big guns on the ground were still throwing up a noisy barrage of flak and it was a moment before I realized that there was still at least one jet lagging behind its companions. The pilot was in trouble and he was still circling to dodge the flak. Finally he came down in a dive to get underneath it and levelled out to come low over the ricefields. The jet engine screamed a frenzied warning and then I saw it approaching through the thickening gloom.

It was one of the Thunderchiefs, and his tail was wobbling and leaking a trail of black smoke. He was going to pass directly overhead and in that one sickening, psychic moment of foresight I knew exactly what was going to happen. I knew and I have never felt so absolutely powerless in all my life. I could just distinguish the evil, pointed snouts of the bombs still hanging underneath the Thunderchief's belly, and I knew why that lone sky jockey had come down and turned away from Haiphong. He was hit and he was losing height, and he had failed to unload his bombs on the target. He had to drop that load somewhere and so he was going to ditch them over what he thought were empty ricefields.

Except that they weren't empty ricefields. Those women and kids had ducked down again and they were too scared to scatter and run. The pilot probably didn't know that he was making another of war's unfortunate little mistakes, and even if he did it would probably rate only a couple of lines in the Western press. The bombs fell from its belly like a string of broken beads and then with a deafening howl the Thunderchief soared over my head and began its rapid climb to safety. Behind it the six seven-hundred-and-fifty pound beads crashed down.

I clapped my hands over my ears and buried my face in the dirt, and the earth itself seemed to disintegrate around me. It seemed that my eardrums must have shattered and my island shifted and heaved beneath me. The ricefield erupted into a gigantic cascade of mud and water, and a tidal wave flooded over my covering body in a surging rush. I was sure that I was dead, but then the water drained away and I realized that I was alive. There was a hideous ringing sensation inside my head, but at least I was in one piece. I looked up slowly, but I could see nothing of the peasants at all.

I got to my feet and began to run. The bombs hadn't scored a direct hit, but they had been close enough and most of the women were dead. Some had been blown to pieces and others killed by the blast. A woman with her arm missing was crawling around in the mud with her mouth open in a scream. At least I think she was screaming, because I was deaf except for the ringing inside my own head, and she died before my hearing came back. I could only find one of the children, just one of the little boys. He was about five years old and he sat up to his waist in water. His face was a mask of blood that trickled from his mouth and ears and nostrils, and I crouched beside him, tearing off my shirt and desperately trying to staunch the flow of blood. I think he was whimpering, but I couldn't hear, and I lifted him into my arms and on my knee as I tried to clean his face. The blood was coming much too fast and at last I stopped and realized that I was holding a five-year-old corpse.

I knelt in the mud and I was sick in my heart. A few minutes ago a child had been playing happily in a lovely big puddle, and now there was only a lump of pathetic bloodied flesh in my arms. A doll's leg floated past a few inches away, but it wasn't a doll's leg because that too was leaking a faint smear of red; it was all that was left of one of the babies.

Vietnam was a war of two giant political ideologies that mercilessly crushed all those unfortunate enough to be caught in the middle, and in that moment I hated all power politics. I hated all political creeds and doctrines and spheres of influence, and I hated and loathed all politicians. From where I stood with a dead child bleeding in my arms there wasn't a cent's worth of difference between Ho chi Minh and Lynden B. Johnson. Neither of them would place children before politics.

In that moment I also hated someone else, and he was a cowardly rat by the name of Rick Mc'Adden. I hated myself because I had suddenly remembered what I had told van Groten about basic algebra: sulphated equals explosives; explosives equals guns and bombs; and guns and bombs equals blood and death. The man who started the chain was as guilty as the man who pulled the final trigger, or pressed the final button, and I had helped to start a chain. There was absolutely nothing I could do to stop the bombs that the Americans were dropping on Vietnam, but I knew now that the introduction of any explosives of any kind and to any side in this senseless and hopeless war was morally wrong.

I lowered that poor, bloody little corpse

into the mud and I knew exactly what I had to do, and it wasn't anything crazy like trying to walk to Laos. Instead I was going back into Haiphong to destroy the cargo of the *Kerkyra*.

18

Captain's Duty

IN that particular field there was no one left alive, so there was no one to raise the outcry that might have stopped me. My shirt was a useless, bloodied rag that I threw away, but I picked up a floating straw hat to improve my overall silhouette before I hurried back to the raised road. I fished my bicycle out of the ditch and then mounted up and rode back towards Haiphong. I hunched my body as small as possible and hoped that in the darkness the large conical hat would provide sufficient disguise to get me through. The odds were like playing five high against a hand of known aces, but it was an improvement on walking to Laos.

I took it easy until I started to encounter people, and then I made the old bike shift again. I worked on the

294

principle that if I pedalled fast enough I would flash past so quickly that no one would have time for a close second look, and I made sure that even a bat out of hell would have needed overdrive to stay on my tail. There were a lot of fires burning around the city and the inhabitants were slow in coming out of their burrows, and that was the biggest thing in my favour. Also the streets were badly lit and swirled with smoke, and although I flushed a few startled faces and attracted some angry shouts, nobody seemed to fully realize that the wild man on the bike was an alien. Speed and the poor light were my only allies, but I made every possible use of them.

I couldn't remember exactly which roads I had taken during my flight from the docks, but my sense of direction was good and I trusted more than a little to luck. It almost ran out when I bowled over an old man and knocked him into the gutter as I came round a blind corner, but I grabbed up my hat and my bike and was away again before any of his neighbours could reach the scene.

Hostile yells followed me as I raced on, but even then they failed to mark me as a stranger, and the hue and cry did not carry ahead. My route lay through the most tumbledown back streets where the lighting was almost non-existent, and donning that peasant's hat had been my only stroke of genius.

The old bike was rattling fit to fall apart and my bones were taking just as bad a shaking, but I didn't dare to let up. I knew that once I stopped and one of the local population got a good look at my face then I would be finished. That damned needle came back into my side and the sweat was running into my eyes, and I thought that I was lost. Then I hurtled out into a wider road and running parallel I recognized the high fence that encircled the docks. The road looked empty and I prayed that there was no one watching from an upstairs window as I skidded the bike to a stop. I leaned it against the fence and after a hasty look round I used it as a ladder in order to scramble up and over the top. I dropped down like a sack of bricks and then lay flat and listened.

There was nothing, no challenge from within the dockyard, and no denouncing cries from the buildings on the opposite side of the road I had just left. I managed to crawl into a dark hole between some stacked timber and there I waited for my heart and lungs to get back to normal, and for the pain to ease in my side. I was a long way from my goal, but at least I had reached the docks, and that in itself was a good omen. I had got through simply because nobody had expected to see a big, barechested Englishman riding like a homicidal maniac through the streets of their town, and those who had witnessed my frenzied passage were probably still rubbing their eyes and wondering whether their sight was playing them tricks. Human uncertainty had combined with the smoke and darkness to get me this far, and I could only hope that my luck would continue.

I took my time once I was sure that my arrival had not been seen, for I had the rest of the night to accomplish the task

I had in mind. I rested up until I felt fit for anything, and only then did I begin to move. It was wholly dark and there was enough cloud to blot out the moon and stars, and I felt confident that the conditions were all in my favour. In fact it was almost too dark and I lost my way in a tangle of railway sidings and parked trucks. I tripped over the rails and then had to lay up for another ten minutes while two men worked their way along one of the lines of trucks, tapping away at the wheels with light hammers. They carried a lamp each and I waited until the twin pools of light and the sounds of tapping were well ahead before I wriggled through the trucks behind them.

It was a relief to get out of the railway tracks, for I had already cracked my ankles a couple of times in the dark. The waterfront lay ahead through rows of warehouses and I could hear the clank of chains and winches. Two of the tall dock cranes were working and there were pools of light along the quayside, but when I worked my way in close I saw that the cranes were unloading one of the Russian freighters. The *Kerkyra* was still out of sight farther along the quay.

I edged back into the shadows and then began to circle around the warehouses to my left. I saw no one, but I kept my head down and stayed close against the wall. The docks must have certainly been searched on my behalf during the afternoon, but I wasn't going to assume that because they hadn't found me the searchers had all given up and gone home. The obvious thing was for them to leave a few soldiers to make occasional patrols with dogs, and I was taking no chances.

I soft-footed down another alleyway between two long unloading sheds, still with my back to the wall, and gently eased my eyes round the corner. There she was, the familiar rusted grey hull and the smoke-grimed funnel. The old tramp-ship looked as unattractive as ever before and she was lying low against the quay. Before the night was over I hoped that she would be lying a hell of a lot lower; to be precise, on the bottom, with her cargo ruined and jamming up the harbour.

She was quiet and there was no activity round her. In fact the only bustle of movement was around the Russian ship, and it seemed that there was no night shift to work the rest of the docks. That suited me fine, for to the best of my knowledge the Vietnamese had not yet started to shift any of the *Kerkyra*'s cargo. I didn't know the reason for the delay, perhaps it was simply that ships which had another voyage to make had priority, but I was grateful that all eight thousand tons of sulphates were still buried in her holds.

I stayed back and watched for a moment. There were lights along the quayside and on the ship itself, and there was no easy way of returning aboard. I could see two guards standing at the top of the gangway, wearing the usual black pyjamas and with sub-machine-guns slung across their backs. Another guard stood in the bows and it was impossible to guess how many more had been left aboard. A dozen would probably be a low estimate, plus Phann Ki and Foong if they hadn't gone ashore to receive their medals.

I was wary of that guard in the bows, and so I backed up and again circled to my left. I didn't dawdle because I didn't want to hang around long enough to be seen, but I didn't want to be heard either, and I was careful where I put my feet. I managed to reach the next gap between the unloading sheds without blundering into anything, and cautiously I moved back to the quayside. I looked out level with the *Kerkyra*'s stern and I was relieved to see that there was no sign of a guard on the afterdeck.

I had to take a gamble now and make a dash into the open, and my heart began to quicken its beat. I was getting edgy because I was still worried by the possibility of patrols and dogs, and it seemed that I had been dodging about and pushing my luck for just a little too long. However, this wasn't the time to think about failure, and so I checked that those two guards above the gangway were looking the other way and then I pushed my luck again. I ducked low and ran hard for the edge of the quay.

It was less than twenty yards and I was there in a matter of seconds. I crouched down behind the big iron bollard that anchored one of the stern mooring ropes and tried to shrink and stop my heart kicking a hole through my ribs at the same time. Nobody yelled or got trigger-happy, and with an effort I relaxed. The guards hadn't heard the quick scuffle of my feet, nor seen the fleeting movement of my body. I risked a peep to check that they were still facing forward and then reached my legs over the edge of the quay and rolled on to my face. I let my body slither back and down and then caught a hold and hung at arm's length a few feet above the water.

Another gamble now, a gamble with sound, but I couldn't climb down and so I had to drop. The splash sounded clumsily loud and I hoped that that was only because I was in the middle of it. The water was filthy and I came up spluttering amid an abominable smell of oil and scum, and pieces of floating driftwood and broken packing cases butted me in the shoulders. I took a deep breath and then dived down under it all and swam through the stinking blackness towards the *Kerkyra*'s stern. I came up close to her screw and quickly pulled myself round to the seaward side and waited. No one appeared on the quayside to investigate the splash and now I began to feel that I really had a chance.

The water was cold but I didn't mind that, and after wiping the worst of the oil away from my face I began to swim slowly forward alongside the ship. After twenty yards I found a rope ladder dangling down her rusty flank. I guessed that it had been thrown down for the pilot boat that had come out to meet us when I had brought the *Kerkyra* into harbour, and through carelessness nobody had brought it back inboard. The pyjama boys giving the orders were not seamen, and the crew were no longer troubling themselves about keeping a tidy ship. As First Officer, I would have bawled them out, but in the role of night intruder and saboteur they could not have served me better.

I waited for almost five minutes,

listening very carefully, but there was no sound from above. Then I tested the ladder with a strong pull, listened again, and finally began the climb up. I made no sound but for the water dripping back from my body into the sea, and gingerly lifted my head over the rail. The afterdeck was empty and it took bare seconds to haul myself aboard and dart quickly into the patch of black shadow beneath the nearest companionway.

I stayed there until I had stopped dripping, for I had no desire to trail pools of water all over the deck. If I did that some sharp-eyed guard might find them and start to follow the trail. That gave me a minute to think more clearly about my next move, and for the first time since I had pedalled away from the ricefields I felt a moment of indecision. I knew what I intended to do, but previously I had spared no thought for van Groten and Louella. Now I remembered that they might still be aboard, and Drekker too. Maybe I owed them something, and maybe I owed them nothing, but I couldn't leave them to go down with the ship. I hesitated for a long time, but at last, instead of moving directly forward, I moved upwards towards the boatdeck.

I knew why I was doing this, and it wasn't for Drekker or van Groten; it was for Louella. But I did it anyway. When the ship went down it was possible that Phann Ki would be mad enough to leave them all locked up to drown in the Captain's cabin, and I couldn't risk that. My conscience was suddenly hitting back at me from all angles.

I reached the boatdeck without meeting anybody, and gingerly I moved around the funnel towards the bridge. My heart was getting jittery again, but I kept it under control and moved silently through the shadows. Then I saw that the guard was still there outside the cabin porthole. He had a combat rifle slung over one shoulder and he looked to be dozing as he leaned back against the bulkhead.

He was going to be easy, but I had to remember that he would have at least one buddy guarding the door on the opposite side of the cabin, and there would be more higher up on the bridge. It wasn't enough just to take him; I had to take him in silence.

I hesitated again, wondering whether I was right to jeopardize the main job for a side issue, but then I put all my doubts aside. I wasn't prepared to consider failure of any kind, because it was only complete confidence that would carry me through. I had a lousy hand, but I couldn't throw it in, so now I was pushing all or nothing on my luck.

My shoulder blades rubbed against the blackened steel as I kept my back to the funnel and circled it slowly. I was holding my breath and stepping gently as though my feet were red hot and the deck was fragile ice. I never took my eyes away from the dozing Vietnamese guard, but he stayed motionless until the corner of the cabin hid him from my view. I breathed again and listened, but the only sound that disturbed the night was the distant rattle of a winch and faint, faraway voices from the Russian freighter farther back along the quay. The *Kerkyra* was as still and silent as a grave.

I left the shelter of the funnel and swiftly crossed the few open spaces that brought me up against the rear bulkhead of the Captain's cabin. There I froze again, but nothing happened, and finally I edged right to the corner. I could hear the lazy sigh of the guard's breathing only a yard away, and I knew that he was still relaxed and unsuspecting. There was no sense in any delay at this stage, for that might give him time to detect my breathing in turn, and so I came round the corner fast. I grabbed with my right hand and my fingers closed over his throat, pinning his head back against the bulkhead. His eyes opened and stared at me in horror, and then he was wriggling frantically. I hit him hard in the belly with my left fist and he stopped kicking, and then I caught the combat rifle that had started to slip from his right shoulder. My right hand continued to choke him and he succeeded in making a little gagging sound before he went limp. He was only a little fellow and I felt almost ashamed of myself as I lowered him to the deck.

The rifle was Chinese-made and surprisingly light, and it felt good resting in my hands. I looked warily up to the bridge, but it was reassuringly quiet and dark. Then I stepped over the first guard and carried on with the job. I circled round the cabin as silently as before, and when I stopped at the second corner I could only hear the sound of one man breathing on the far side.

This time I didn't have to do any strangling. I simply stepped round the corner with the rifle levelled and pointed it at the guard's middle. His mouth opened and his eyes boggled, but then he recovered his wits and hurriedly lifted his hands and hugged the top of his head. I didn't have to say or do anything, so I must have looked pretty frightening. He started to quake in his black pyjamas and I felt like the school bully as I made him turn to face the door he was supposed to be guarding and then cracked him across the back of his head with the rifle butt. I caught him with one arm as he sagged to the deck, and disentangled another rifle from his shoulder in case it made a clatter.

I found the key on his belt, tied there by a piece of string, and quickly opened up the door. I went inside and closed it again fast because the light was on and I didn't want too much of it to escape and attract attention.

They were all there. Van Groten and Drekker were seated and their heads jerked round. Drekker almost jumped out of his chair and couldn't stifle a gasp of surprise, but van Groten simply went tense and stared. His face was still too raw to show any definite expression. Louella was standing on the far side of the cabin and she too turned sharply as the door opened and closed. Her lovely eyes went wide and she couldn't stop herself as she cried emotionally:

"Rick, oh, Rick!"

She started towards me and then stopped, and I never knew whether it was because of the rifle that I still held in my hands or because she suddenly realized that her outburst might have been heard. She held back uncertainly, and I tried a smile and lowered the rifle. Van Groten got up slowly and faced me.

"So you come back, hey? Why, Rick? I thought you would be still running."

I killed the smile and said bluntly:

"I have my reasons, but they don't concern you. I've cleared the guards away and I'm giving you a chance to get out. You'd better take it."

Van Groten continued to stare at me. He was puzzled, and it showed.

"I don't understand, Rick. Why did you come back for us, hey? You find you can't make it alone?"

"I didn't come back just to release you. I came to do a job."

His eyes narrowed. "What sort of job?"

I hesitated, but I couldn't afford to stand and chat all night, and answers were the quickest way to dry up questions. I said grimly:

"I came back to make sure that the *Kerkyra*'s cargo doesn't get used for manufacturing explosives. I'm going down into the hold to knock away the timbers wedging up the repairs we made to the ship's hull. Once the sea pours in the ship will sink and the cargo will be ruined. There's deep water here; I noticed that when I docked the ship, it might even cover this cabin, so I'm giving you a chance to get ashore."

"You are telling me that you are going to sink *my* ship?"

There was something in his tone that made me lift the rifle again. I said coldly:

"That's right — and I don't intend to let anyone stop me!"

His eyes showed anger and his body tensed, but he was still as uncertain of me as I was of him.

"You came back just for that? Why?"

It would take too long to tell him about a child playing in a puddle, so I made it brief and simple.

"Because I've found my conscience; because I rated Larry Bennet as a slob and he died a hero; because I should have opposed you and this whole trip right from the start when I found out that you'd fixed the compass. There are a whole lot of reasons."

Van Groten said harshly, "So you found your conscience over Bennet, hey? Well, what about van Lynden and Hollert? They died too. They were my officers, van Lynden was an old friend and Hollert was only a boy. You think that I don't have some kind of a conscience too?"

His big fists were clenched and he glared at me savagely.

"No, Mister Mate, you don't sink my ship. I am still Captain of the *Kerkyra*, and a Captain has a privilege and a duty to be the last man to leave his own vessel. If any man sinks my ship that man is going to be me." He swung away from me and snapped curtly, "Mister Drekker, you will take Louella ashore and take care of her. I make her your responsibility. I am going down into the hold with the Mate."

312

19

Sink or Swim

I HESITATED, but then I believed him and lowered the rifle. His motives and mine were completely different, for I suspected that he wanted vengeance not only for van Lynden and Hollert, but because he had been double-crossed and robbed by the Vietnamese, but as long as our objective was the same then his motives were unimportant. I had intended to do the job alone, but that didn't make me dumb enough to turn down any offer of practical help. With Dirk van Groten on my side, the odds were getting better.

I shifted the spare combat rifle from my shoulder and gave it to the big Dutchman. He weighed it easily in his hands and smiled his first real smile since Phann Ki's pirates had stormed over the ship's rails. Then I said grimly:

313

"Switch out the light, and then we'll drag in those two guards where they won't be so noticeable. We may need a little time and we don't want to be disturbed too quickly."

Van Groten nodded and switched out the light. With Drekker's help it look less than a minute to pull the two unconscious guards inside, and I checked that they were going to be out cold for a long time. Then we locked the cabin and got moving, fast but quietly. I led the way back across the boatdeck with van Groten at my shoulder and Drekker and Louella bringing up the rear.

We hurried down the companionways to the afterdeck, and then paused again in a patch of shadow. I let them close up behind me and then pointed out the rope ladder that I had used to climb aboard to Drekker. I said softly:

"That's your only escape route. There are two guards with sub-machine-guns at the top of the gangway, so you can't go straight down to the quay. You'll have to go over the side and swim back until you can climb up. The water's cold and it's filthy, but you'll have to suffer that."

Drekker nodded, and then van Groten said:

"Find somewhere to hide and then wait for us, but if you run into trouble you give yourselves up. Don't make a fight and get yourself killed for nothing. You understand, hey?"

Drekker nodded again. He was tense and scared, but I felt that he was reliable. He said in a whisper:

"I understand, sir. I'll do my best."

Gestures were more silent than words, and so it was van Groten's turn to nod. He pulled Louella close and kissed her, and then reluctantly pushed her back to join the boy. She said in anguish:

"Dirk. Dirk, please — "

He didn't let her finish. His hand gently covered her mouth and then he kissed her again, very gently on the forehead.

"Go with Drekker," he said. "That is an order."

His iron-grey head jerked in a final nod and Drekker understood. The young engineer pulled at Louella's arm and before she could make any further protest he led her away to the ship's rail. He climbed swiftly over the side and on to the rope ladder, and Louella turned for one last silent glimpse of van Groten and myself before she followed. We waited with the rifles ready in our hands, but no one saw them go and after a minute we turned our attention back to the main job.

We moved forward along the port alleyway, on the seaward side of the ship, and before we came out on to the welldeck below the bridge I warned van Groten about the guard in the bows. We crouched down at the forward end of the alleyway to look and listen, but there was nothing to be seen. The guard that I had spotted earlier was either well forward or he had moved off the foredeck altogether. The ship was cloaked in dark silence and our main worry was the bridge. We had to move out into the open directly below to reach the hatch into the hold, and if there was a keen-eyed guard up there then our fun and games would be over before they started.

We had one advantage and that was that the hatch was already open. I remembered that Bennet had been working down there when the pirates had taken over, and that from that point on the *Kerkyra* had become a sloppy ship. The hatch had been left uncovered for the same reason that the rope ladder had been left trailing over the side; there had been no ship's officers to give the necessary orders to tidy the decks.

After a moment van Groten leaned close and murmured in a low voice:

"You want to make the first run, Rick? If you have to come back I cover you with the rifle."

I inclined my head in assent, and took another long look upwards to the silent bridge. Then I headed fast for that open hatch, still crouching as low as possible. As I reached it I hooked the strap of my rifle over my shoulder and swung inside. It was pitch black, but practice and instinct told me exactly where to find the iron rungs of the descending ladder and I dropped down out of sight. The rifle butt struck against one of the rungs and I became still. My heart was thudding, but by now I had become accustomed to the accelerated beat and I didn't let it worry me. I waited a few seconds and when there was no outcry I carried on descending until I touched the first of the tween-decks. There I waited for van Groten to join me.

I realized then that there was no one to cover his run, because I couldn't do it from inside the hatch without getting in his way. However, it was too late now to change the running order. A minute passed as I stared up at the square patch of stars that was visible through the open hatch, and then a dark figure suddenly vaulted into the opening like a great swooping bat, and the ladder rattled briefly as the Dutchman hurried down beside me. We waited again, listening for any sounds of alarm, but none came and I sensed that van Groten was grinning in the darkness.

I led the way again and we climbed deeper into the hold, descending blindly through the familiar smell of sulphates. I thought I knew exactly where to find the lights when we reached the lower levels, but my memory played me tricks and I had to grope around for several minutes before I could switch them on. The arc lamps were still in position and nothing had changed since my last visit. The bottom of the hold was still a crazy jigsaw of braced timbers holding up the patched hull, and black water still lapped around them in evil ripples. The pumps had been stopped and already a lot of water had seeped in through the weakened repairs. I surveyed the scene and smiled when I saw that Bennet's last working party had been obliged to leave their tools behind. All that we needed in the way of crowbars and sledgehammers were close at hand, laid out upon the higher timbers and practically begging us to go to work.

We scrambled down the last rungs of the ladder and the water washed around our hips before our feet touched the floor of the hold. We used the straps of the two combat rifles to tie them loosely to the ladder rungs above water level, and then we waded over to the downed tools and each selected a fourteen-pound sledgehammer. Now that we were forced to show a light and make a noise there was no time to waste, and without any hesitation whatsoever we smashed into those braced timbers and hammered them down.

It had taken a lot of time and sweat and effort to build up that patchwork of repairs, but a timber that had taken an hour to cut and wedge into exactly the right position took only minutes to knock away. The whole structure had been built to resist pressure from outside the hull, but it was vulnerable to a determined attack from the inside. Van Groten and I were both big, powerful men and we swung all our weight behind the pile-driving blows of those big hammers, and the struts tumbled away like ninepins. Both of us knew exactly which timbers were taking the biggest strain and it was these that we assaulted first. More seawater began spurting in through the ruptured plates as the tarpaulins and sawdust-filled mattresses began to slip, and the black water began to rise quickly up to our waists.

That water was icy cold, but above water the sweat streamed down from my neck and shoulders as I worked in a frenzy of destruction. Van Groten spared himself no less, for we both knew that out time must be limited. I struck at a stubborn timber that refused to budge and my arms ached as I rained down blow after blow. It had been easy to knock the first of the timbers out of the way, but as we progressed we shifted more weight on to those that remained and the job became harder. Van Groten had started out by swinging his fourteen-pounder like a toy drumstick, but soon even he was beginning to pant and blow. We were tiring, but there was no time to rest.

We were making an alarming racket and every single hammer-blow reverberated around the hold as though we were working in a great, water-logged echo chamber. We were deep down in the ship's bowels, but even so the noise had to carry upwards eventually and we continually darted backward glances to the steel rungs of the ladder stretching up into the darkness behind us. The dazzling glare of the arc lamps that were shining down put us at a disadvantage, and we both knew it.

I wiped the sweat out of my eyes and made another furious assault on that stubborn spar. Van Groten joined me and we both smashed down in unison, and the end of the timber gave an agonizing creak as it scraped across the bulkhead. We swung the hammers again in another simultaneous double blow and the timber gave with a shuddering crash. The whole jigsaw started to fall apart, and a great gout of water spurted in above our heads. More jets like giant hosepipes opened up all around the edges of the sagging patch, and in a fit of eager triumph I rushed at the next bracing strut.

Van Groten paused to take another look behind us.

"Rick, look out!"

He bawled a frantic warning and I floundered sideways as a rifle sniped at my back from above. The vicious crack resounded like the clanging of a crazy church bell around the steel walls, and a mess of splinters churned up from the timber nearest my face. I fell backwards, but another timber slammed against my spine to stop me from going under the surface, and for a moment I was helpless.

Time was frozen and I saw the squat, unmistakable figure of Foong crouched on the catwalk high above. The Chinese had descended silently, and now he was close beside the yellow glare of one of the big arc lights. He probably thought that he was behind the dazzle, but instead he was clearly visible. He was very cool and precise as he tucked the rifle against his shoulder and aimed for another shot, and his face was like an ugly mask of hateful wax. He didn't have to squint and I could see that raw, empty socket gazing blankly down the barrel as he looked through the sights with his one good eye. Our own rifles were a dozen yards away and we were up to our waists in water, so he had no cause to hurry. He could see exactly what we were doing and he meant to pick us off like ducks in a shooting gallery.

I thought that we were finished, but

I had forgotten what van Groten had once told me — that Foong was a dead man. The big Dutchman whirled that fourteen-pound hammer around his head and let out a fearsome roar.

"*Mister Bo'sun!*"

Foong looked up, startled by the shout, and then van Groten released the hammer. It soared up into the roof of the hold in a great, flailing arc, and behind it was every last ounce of strength that remained in those massive wrists and arms. It was the promised payment for treachery, and retribution for Hollert, van Lynden and Bennet too. It was hurled with all the pent-up fury and savage anger that came from the indignities and beatings of the past three days, and for Foong it was destiny and the Day of Judgement. The Chinese screamed as the hammerhead smashed into his one remaining eye, and the whole front of his skull was caved in as his body reeled round and he toppled down into the hold. His dead fingers still gripped the rifle and as he hit the water it fired an aimless bullet with another ringing crack.

There were more men behind him; Vietnamese in their black pyjamas who were invisible in the upper darkness, but we could hear them scrambling down the ladder. However, van Groten was already ploughing through the swirling pressure of water to reach the two combat rifles that we had captured from the guards outside his cabin, and he shouted harshly over his shoulder:

"Finish the job, Mister Mate! While you work I cover your back."

I saw him tear down one of the rifles and aim it upwards, and then I took a firmer grip on my own hammer and renewed my frenzied attack on the last of the braced timbers. There was an exchange of shots behind me that was deafening in the close confines of the hold, but I didn't look round. Instead I swung that sledgehammer for all I was worth. It became a toy again as necessity gave me my second wind, and another timber splashed down and floated away. Another, and another, and then the sea was washing around my chest as it cascaded in through the great rent in the ship's side. I was drenched now and my hands were blistered, but even though I was working under a veritable waterfall there was still one strut that refused to let the main structure fall completely away.

More shots crashed behind me and I heard a shrieking death scream followed by another heavy splash as a body pitched into the hold. There was a full-scale battle blasting away behind me, but I didn't dare look to see who was winning. That last timber was my only concern and I had to batter it down before the final bullet smacked home between my shoulder blades.

The water was rising over that one awkward spar and that made the job more difficult. I had to wield the hammer above my head and my arm muscles were screaming out again as I cursed and struck and cursed and struck in gasping desperation. I was almost sobbing with each blow, and then suddenly the timber shifted and moved. I raised the sledgehammer for the last time and brought it down with all my strength, and on the point of impact the timber was gone. There was a bang like thunder as the sea exploded in through the ship's side and I was lifted off my feet and hurled backwards. The huge inrush of water carried me clear across the hold and then I was drowning in the black flood.

During the next few minutes I was bruised and battered and knocked all but unconscious by the tumbling mass of flotsam that my efforts had made. The flood-tide swirled me around, sucked me under, and then spewed me to the surface. I tried to swim, but it was impossible with my arms and legs striking blindly into that mass of heaving timber, and the black waters poured over me again. I choked and swallowed on salt brine and I thought that I was dead, and then I came spluttering to the surface yet again. A jagged spar smashed me in the shoulder and I could hear the hissing roar as the sea continued to surge into the hold. The arc lights were spinning above me in a fierce yellow dazzle, and then the dead body of Foong was carried past with its crushed, nightmare face leaving a trailing red stain. The empty eye socket seemed to be taunting me, as though calling me to the grave. The tumult of the waters tore us apart and then mercifully an iron hand clamped over my wrist and dragged me to a stop.

I had been swept past the ladder and van Groten hauled me up bodily until I was able to take a grip on the lower rungs for myself. He had been fast enough to scramble upwards out of reach when the full force of the sea broke in, and he still had one of the combat rifles slung over his shoulder. I had to spit and retch, and shake my head to get rid of the salt water streaming down past my eyes and ears and nostrils, and slowly I realized that there was no more shooting from above. Van Groten looked down at me anxiously, and when he was sure that I was capable of understanding he had to bellow to make his voice heard above the rush and gurgle of the sea filling the hold.

"The rats have all fled aloft. They ran when they saw the sea break in. I think we better follow them, hey?"

I nodded weakly, because the sea was

already climbing up to my knees once more and it was obvious that we could not stay here. The ship was starting to list and we hurriedly climbed higher. When we reached the catwalk by the arc lights I saw that there was another huddled Vietnamese lying dead. There was a neat hole between his eyebrows and I wondered where van Groten had learned to shoot.

There was no time to ask, for he was already scaling the next flight of the ladder, and I kept close behind him. He paused on the tweendeck immediately below the open hatchway and drew me in beside him. Then he said grimly:

"Perhaps they wait for us on deck, but we cannot stay here, so it is a chance we must take. I will go first."

I was still too puffed to argue and he went ahead of me up the ladder. If the pyjama boys were waiting, they could blast his head off as he emerged, but, like the man said, we couldn't stay here. We could only cross our fingers and hope that the Vietnamese had all kept running to get ashore.

20

A Smile from Lady Luck

VERY slowly and deliberately, van Groten raised his head above the level of the hatch — and nobody shot it off. He jumped out quickly then, and I wasn't slow to follow him. There was no welcoming committee and it looked as though the Vietnamese had temporarily panicked and fled ashore. Phann Ki must have been absent on some other business, and with Foong dead there was no one to control and organize them effectively. That huge gush of water spurting into the hold had been an unnerving sight, and already the *Kerkyra* was keeling over at an awkward angle and settling low at the bows.

We started to run, but we didn't make for the gangway or try and jump down to the quay. That was where the Vietnamese would rally and wait for us, and only an idiot would walk into a crossfire. Instead, we ran back along the port alleyway to the stern of the ship. Half-way along, another thought stabbed at my conscience and I grabbed at van Groten's arm.

"The crew! If they're still in the peak they'll drown!"

He answered briefly:

"They were marched ashore this afternoon. Come on."

I didn't delay any more and we raced out on to the afterdeck. The rope ladder still trailed over the port side and I went over and scrambled down fast into the sea. Van Groten followed me, but he was slower, and I saw that he was still hanging on to that damned rifle with one hand. He entered the water more carefully, and kept the rifle dry above his head. We began to swim as quietly as possible, and van Groten rolled on to his back and swam with one hand while he held his precious rifle out of the water.

If we had been seen from the quayside we would have made good target practice for a lot of angry little men with rifles, but fortunately we were not seen. We swam for over a hundred yards through the stinking, oil-stained waters of the harbour, and then we found the steel rungs of a ladder leading up to the quay. We swam towards it, pushing through scum and floating debris, and van Groten went up first. Again he offered his head in slow sacrifice, and again there was no one there to blast it off.

He climbed on to the quay and crouched down with the rifle held across his knee until I joined him. Away to our left the quayside immediately in front of the slowly sinking *Kerkyra* appeared to be deserted, but we weren't fooled by that. It was a dead certainty that the unloading shed directly opposite was filled with hidden snipers just waiting for us to show our big stupid faces. I hoped that they were all too dedicated to even think of looking away from the ship, because if just one of them happened to look right during the next few seconds then we were going to be in trouble again.

We made our run together, because that halved the number of seconds during which we could be spotted. There was an alleyway between the unloading sheds only a little to the right of our landing place and we dived inside with all haste and no dignity. We froze, and stood there with our chests heaving and our backs against the walls, but there were no shouts or shots cracking after our heels. My heart was still doing nineteen beats to the normal dozen, but I started to relax. Then there was a movement behind us.

Van Groten whirled with the rifle. I was faster by a split second and recognized the two figures who emerged dripping from the gloom. I knocked the rifle down just in time to prevent Drekker from getting shot, and then Louella was running into van Groten's arms.

It was an emotional reunion and Drekker was a little embarrassed. He turned his eyes away from them and concentrated his attention upon me. He said uncertainly:

"I am glad that you succeeded, sir. Miss Louella and I found that same ladder to climb up on to the quay. I guessed that if you had to swim away from the ship then you would climb up in the same place, so we waited here."

I said, "That's fine. You did a good job."

We had to wait until van Groten chose to free his neck from Louella's arms, and then he said:

"Well, Mister Mate, we've fixed the ship. What's your plan now, hey?"

I said bluntly, "There isn't one. I didn't think beyond this stage."

Perhaps I should have told him that before, because the silence that followed was somewhat ominous. Then he shrugged and tightened his arms around Louella. She was staring at me, but he turned her face away and kissed her on the nose. In the circumstances I suppose it was about as useful a move as anything. Then Drekker said nervously:

"Captain — "

We all looked at him, and van Groten nodded.

"Captain, I had time to look around while we were waiting for you. There's a big motor launch moored farther along the quay, and I don't think there's a guard. Perhaps — "

He didn't finish because van Groten was already grinning his approval.

"How about it, Mister Mate? We give it a try, hey? All we need is a little smile from Lady Luck."

I had been prepared to accept my fate, but now I decided that I wasn't in any hurry about it. Lady Luck had been with me all night, and only a fool quits on a winning streak. I nodded and said:

"Another smile might just be possible. Let's go."

Drekker led the way, circling back behind the unloading sheds and putting an even healthier distance between ourselves and the *Kerkyra*. We moved at a run, and it took us only a couple of minutes to reach the promised launch. It looked like the big government boat that had come out to meet the *Kerkyra* when we docked, but I couldn't be sure.

Drekker had been right and there was no guard, and we swiftly climbed aboard. The cabin was locked with a padlock and chain, but van Groten soon wrenched it away with the barrel of his rifle. The big Dutchman stepped back and then stayed in the stern to watch out for any unwanted company as Drekker and I pushed inside the cabin and got busy with the engine. There was no ignition key, but this was Drekker's world and even while fumbling in the dark he very quickly succeeded in joining up the wiring underneath the panel. It was as simple as stealing a car, and the engine started on the first attempt. Once it roared I left Drekker to handle the wheel. Louella was crouching on the open deck and I bundled her hastily into the comparative safety of the cabin behind him, and then scrambled ashore to cast off the moorings.

The sound of the engine stirred up a hornet's nest of activity, and chaos and confusion became the order of the night. I heard frantic shouts and yells and the rush of feet, and looked back towards the *Kerkyra* to see a dozen running figures coming like hungry wolves along the quayside towards me. A stutter of sub-machine-gun fire blazed through the darkness above my head, and then van

Groten made them drop and scatter with a quick burst of shots from the combat rifle. Somebody screamed as he scored a hit and that made the others a little less eager. They were all throwing themselves flat and I didn't give them time to sort themselves out. My fingers scrabbled at the last rope and flung it down into the harbour, and then I jumped back aboard and yelled at Drekker to take her away.

The engine snarled and then we were speeding away from the quayside. The sudden movement and the shock of my own arrival almost tipped van Groten and myself into the sea, but we recovered our balance just in time. Drekker opened the throttles wide and hurled the boat's bows round in a tight circle to line her up on the open mouth of the Red River estuary. Then the Vietnamese were opening fire with everything they had in a last desperate effort to stop our escape. Van Groten added to the general uproar by empting the last burst of shells in the magazine of his own rifle, but I don't think anybody scored a hit. Bullets threw up spurts of water all around us, but the

Vietnamese were poor shots from a prone position, and the launch was bouncing and jumping too erratically to allow van Groten to take any proper aim.

The shooting stopped, and then there was only the roar of the engine as we pulled clear and headed out of the harbour at full speed down the estuary. Van Groten lowered the empty rifle and stepped back beside me, and far behind us we saw our last glimpse of the *Kerkyra*. The old tramp ship was wallowing with her decks awash, still sinking slowly but very surely. She was going down at the bows, but she was rolling, and soon the sea would start pouring into the aft cargo hatches and then she would settle gracefully to the bottom. It was an ungallant and unspectacular end, but it was the end.

★ ★ ★

Night covered the rest of our escape from Haiphong and the mouth of the Red River, and when dawn came we had a fair start on any possible pursuit. We stopped the engine to save a little juice in case of emergencies, and van Groten and I combined our skills to fashion a clumsy sail from a rolled tarpaulin that we found stuffed under a locker. We had to tear up a couple of deckboards to make an improvised mast, but after an hour's work we had rigged our sail and a friendly breeze was nudging the launch slowly but steadily towards the south. That suited us fine, for now that we had cleared the twelve-mile limit that the Vietnamese claimed as their territorial waters our only chance of being picked up was to keep heading south as close into land as possible. When we had brought the *Kerkyra* into the Gulf of Tonkin we had circled wide to avoid attracting any American attention, but now the position was changed and we were ready to stand up and wave at anything that was flying the Stars and Stripes. We knew that the U.S. Navy had ships permanently stationed close off-shore for the sole purpose of fishing out their downed pilots who couldn't make it all the way after their bombing raids over Haiphong and

Hanoi, and if our luck lasted we hoped to be caught in the same net. Anyway, it was better than having no hope at all.

We were adrift for another twelve hours, getting hungry and dehydrated, and endlessly searching the empty sky and the sea. We were well aware that it could quite easily be Communist junks that found us first, so we dared not relax, and our eyes ached and our faces blistered under the burning glare of the sun. Then we received that final smile from Lady Luck and late in the afternoon a flight of Skyhawks hurtled overhead once more to plaster a few more tons of high explosive around Haiphong. We were ready for them when they came back, and we stood up and waved shirts and things like howling maniacs. Someone must have seen us and radioed down to the nearest pilot-retriever, for soon after that a helicopter came whirling up from the south-east to take a closer look.

The chopper had U.S. Navy written all over it, and it made a beautiful picture as it circled around in the deep blue skies. When it was satisfied that there was nothing else in sight and that we weren't some kind of a hostile enemy trap it settled down slowly, directly over our heads. The disturbance thrown down by the spinning rotor blades made the motor launch rock and wobble in a flurry of unnatural waves, and the helicopter crew made another long, dubious examination. We could see curious faces with Martian-type helmets looking down, and then they made up their minds and lowered a wire cable with an empty leather harness on the end. We sent Louella up first, and I guess that she was the best catch they had ever made, because after that they quickly hoisted the rest of us aboard. A colourful character with a Missouri accent and a bright yellow flak jacket held a not-so-friendly gun on us until he was sure that we were not Commies in disguise, and then he began asking questions.

I let van Groten do the answering while the chopper headed for home. The parent ship was a sleek, grey-painted destroyer in charge of search-and-rescue operations that was positioned some twenty miles off the North Vietnamese coast, and by the time we were landing van Groten had made a passable run-through of our story as he meant to tell it. He had changed a few of the earlier facts to make it appear that the *Kerkyra* had been on a genuine and legitimate voyage to Saigon when she had been boarded and turned north by the pirates, and so far he was getting away with it. The helicopter crew thought he was on the level. I hoped he stayed as convincing, because it was my neck too and the interrogations were going to get a lot tougher before the U.S. Navy decided to turn us loose. In the meantime Dirk van Groten was welcome to do all the talking.

I was as rich now as I had been when Louella had picked me up penniless in the Pussycat Bar, but sometimes it's a relief just to be alive. The chopper bumped down on to the destroyer's deck, and this was one of those times.

THE END

A FOOT IN THE GRAVE
Bruce Marshall

About to be imprisoned and tortured in Buenos Aires, John Smith escapes, only to become involved in an aeroplane hijacking.

DEAD TROUBLE
Martin Carroll

Trespassing brought Jennifer Denning more than she bargained for. She was totally unprepared for the violence which was to lie in her path.

HOURS TO KILL
Ursula Curtiss

Margaret went to New Mexico to look after her sick sister's rented house and felt a sharp edge of fear when the absent landlady arrived.

THE DEATH OF ABBE DIDIER
Richard Grayson

Inspector Gautier of the Sûreté investigates three crimes which are strangely connected.

NIGHTMARE TIME
Hugh Pentecost

Have the missing major and his wife met with foul play somewhere in the Beaumont Hotel, or is their disappearance a carefully planned step in an act of treason?

BLOOD WILL OUT
Margaret Carr

Why was the manor house so oddly familiar to Elinor Howard? Who would have guessed that a Sunday School outing could lead to murder?

THE DRACULA MURDERS
Philip Daniels

The Horror Ball was interrupted by a spectral figure who warned the merrymakers they were tampering with the unknown.

THE LADIES
OF LAMBTON GREEN
Liza Shepherd

Why did murdered Robin Colquhoun's picture pose such a threat to the ladies of Lambton Green?

CARNABY
AND THE GAOLBREAKERS
Peter N. Walker

Detective Sergeant James Aloysius Carnaby-King is sent to prison as bait. When he joins in an escape he is thrown headfirst into a vicious murder hunt.

114162701

CU

W

MALICE OF THE SOUL

When elderly Mrs Peters appears to suffer a stroke at her nursing home, only Diana Knightson knows the truth: her colleague, Marguerite, has deliberately terrified the old woman and isn't as she seems. Then when Phil Walsh, Diana's fiancé, is seduced by Marguerite he turns against her and her life is in danger. But Diana gains an ally in Jarvis, Mrs Peters' son. He's determined to avenge his mother's death — and together they fight the forces of evil.

Books by Brian Ball
in the Linford Mystery Library:

DEATH OF A LOW HANDICAP MAN
MONTENEGRIN GOLD
THE VENOMOUS SERPENT

BRIAN BALL

MALICE OF
THE SOUL

Complete and Unabridged

LINFORD
Leicester

First published in Great Britain

First Linford Edition
published 2008

British Library CIP Data

Ball, Brian, *1932 –*
    Malice of the soul.—Large print ed.—
Linford mystery library
    1. Nurses—Fiction 2. Murder—Investigation—
Fiction 3. Suspense fiction 4. Large type books
I. Title
823.9'14 [F]

ISBN 978–1–84782–446–2

Published by
F. A. Thorpe (Publishing)
Anstey, Leicestershire
Set by Words & Graphics Ltd.
Anstey, Leicestershire
Printed and bound in Great Britain by
T. J. International Ltd., Padstow, Cornwall

This book is printed on acid-free paper

1

I couldn't take my eyes off Marguerite Friend when I first saw her. My job brings me into contact with very many girls, so it's not unusual for me to come across a strikingly pretty one occasionally; but real beauty is rare.

Given exquisite features, glossy hair, shining eyes, and a perfect shape, many girls can be attractive and enticing and achieve prettiness, but beauty is something more. It's composed of all of these desirable attributes, the exquisite face and the shapely figure, and something else, which I find difficult to describe. The nearest I can get to it is to say it's found with serenity.

There is a serene assurance in a beautiful girl or woman. It comes, I think, from the possessor's knowledge of, and acceptance of her beauty.

But there's something disturbing about it.

I felt disturbed when I first saw Marguerite Friend. She was truly beautiful. She had poise too, for though she must have been aware of my staring at her, she appeared not to notice it.

She was sitting in the part of the office where we park our clients until their social worker tears himself (or, more usually, herself) from the routine jobs of answering the phone, writing up reports, or simply from finishing the coffee and aspirin that makes the day bearable. She was poised, glamorous, and utterly enviable.

She was wearing a neat two-piece linen outfit in black and white, with a gold chain at her throat and delicate Italian sandals on her slender feet. I wondered briefly why she wasn't in the standard teenagers' gear.

Her powerful personality reached out to me, and I was uneasy. What kind of trouble is she in, I asked myself in an attempt at professional detachment, but I couldn't keep it up. I already knew that she wasn't in the office to ask for the help of the Social Services Department.

I sensed in those first few seconds that

she would bring me great suffering. I was still looking at her exquisite features framed in the thick, dark, glossy hair when Pauline Hart noticed me.

'Di, have you got a minute?'

Pauline has her own office. She's a Group Leader, so she doesn't have to pig it with the rest of us in the main office-cum-reception area. She is a lath-like woman of thirty-two married to a central heating engineer. Her standing joke is that the gasman came to put in the heating and she got turned on herself.

I accepted the cup of coffee she offered me, together with an inviting-looking cream cake.

I promised myself I'd pay the calories back later, and I happily took a big bite. Before taking a second, I realized I was being set up.

'You want something, Pauline.'

'It's nothing much, Di.'

'I'm not taking the Phillips kids to be de-loused again.'

'It's not them.'

I drank some coffee and finished the cake.

'I don't get the soft treatment unless there's some kind of pay-off.'

Pauline smiled a little guiltily. 'Well,' she admitted, 'I do need a favour.'

'That sounds like my Group Leader talking.'

'It's the job scheme, Di. Read this, it'll tell you about the Cadet.'

I gave a grimace. I'd heard about the scheme to introduce Cadets. Now I was to have one.

Her name was Marguerite Friend, according to her application form. I read about her.

She was seventeen, single, with a clutch of creditable exam successes, and she was interested in much the kind of thing that most girls put down on their application forms. She played badminton, read a lot, made most of her own clothes, went fell-walking, and most importantly, since it had got her the job in our Department, she had been a volunteer for the Age Concern people.

'Not a Cadet,' I groaned. 'Do I have to?'

'I can't ask any of the others.' She

4

catalogued their overloaded schedules, and finished off with their home commitments. 'Di, she needs someone not too much older than herself, who's sympathetic. You score every way. You know, she could be useful with your bad girls.'

It was certainly a point. Mostly I have adolescent girls on my caseload. I did get bad girls mostly, as Pauline had pointed out. I shouldn't call them bad, for the poor little bitches are ruthlessly exploited by everyone they come into contact with, and they had only their youth to keep them from despair. Badness existed in their exploiters, though I did have one truly bad girl.

On the other hand, it seemed I had a good girl too.

'How long would it be for, Pauline?'

'Say a couple of days, till I can get something organised for her?'

'Just today,' I bargained.

'Today and tomorrow morning.'

'Okay.' It wasn't too bad. We grinned at one another again.

'How's Phil?' Pauline asked.

'He's got a cold.'

'Give him my love.'

'I'll say you asked about him.'

I was waiting for my divorce to come through, and I didn't feel altogether secure about any woman sending her love to my new man, not even Pauline.

'How about bringing Phil round for a meal soon? Say a fortnight today?'

I looked down at the application form again. What was wrong with the Cadet? A cream cake was one thing, a dinner invitation quite another.

'I'll see what Phil's doing,' I hedged, and looked at the application form again.

'She's an orphan, Di.'

'Yes. Go easy on her.'

I nodded. 'When does she come?'

'She's here now.' Pauline indicated the outer office.

And still I didn't put two and two together. 'I suppose I'll be stuck with the dark femme fatale out there too.'

Pauline laughed. 'That femme *is* the Cadet.'

'Damn,' I breathed quietly. 'Her. A Cadet.'

I should explain about the Cadet

scheme. It's part of the government's Job Creation programme, and we take them on because we're ordered to.

The girls are usually pleasant enough, but they come to us at seventeen and they're quite useless. They're little more than a burden, and they can't be left all day at the office looking like personable dummies; so they're allocated to one of us to take around on our visits to clients.

Pauline interrupted my thoughts. 'Thanks, Di.'

'For what?' I muttered, hackles raised.

Pauline smoothed me down as we went into the main office. We're good at it, and Pauline is one of the best. We're professionals. The calm, non-patronising smile is our trademark.

I wasn't smiling when I was introduced to the Cadet.

'Oh, hello Mrs. Hart,' she said, getting up.

I looked her over and could find no flaw. She was willowy, elegant, but well-rounded. Maybe five-six or a shade taller.

'This is Mrs. Knightson,' Pauline said.

'She's going to look after you for the next day or two, then we'll fix a proper schedule for you.'

'You may not find it very interesting,' I warned.

'But I shall, Mrs. Knightson!' she said. 'I'm sure of it!'

She smiled at me, and I saw the glint in her dark eyes as though it invited one to look into a small secret place and share her thoughts. Her smile was right too, very warm and rather shy, just like any other gauche teenager's smile. Trust me, it asked.

'Then that's settled,' Pauline said brightly. 'I'll leave you to get on with it.'

'Right, Miss Friend,' I said when Pauline had gone. 'We're on our way.'

'Please call me Marguerite, Mrs. Knightson.'

'If you wish, Marguerite. My car's in the parking lot. This way.'

'I know we're going to get on well together, Mrs. Knightson,' she said as we walked along the corridor. There was a certainty about the way she said it that made me pause.

'Really?'

'Oh yes!'

We faced one another. She looked young and eager to please, and I almost softened. But I couldn't. I felt unease in her presence.

'That's interesting, Marguerite,' I said. 'How can you tell?'

I envied her. At twenty-seven I felt dowdy and middle-aged, and I had never felt remotely like that before. I envied her flawless skin, the rose-flush along her cheekbones that emphasised the ivory glow of her face, in fact I was plain old-fashioned envious of everything about her, even her clothes.

'Oh, I *know*, Mrs. Knightson,' she said quietly. 'See.'

She held out something that glittered on the gold chain at her throat. It was solid gold, there could be no mistaking it. A solid gold scorpion.

'I'm a Scorpio too, Mrs. Knightson,' she said, and pointed to the very ordinary brooch in my scarf, a tinny silver-plated scorpion. 'We're thoughtful, passionate, we work hard and we're loyal,' she said,

9

her dark eyes holding me. 'We're good to have as friends. And we have to be careful about our diets.'

For a moment I felt again the sense of looking into a secret place far removed from anything to do with a suburban Social Services department. I remember feeling something of the dizziness I had experienced about the third day of a bad flu attack, when things got slightly disoriented.

'Oh,' I said. 'That's nice.' I couldn't think of anything else to say.

She let the golden symbol drop, and it was only then that I realised she had been holding it out to me for the last couple of minutes. I felt its dull radiance still.

'In fact,' she went on, 'we're going to be good friends. I can feel it. Can't you?'

This was altogether too abrupt for me.

'I can't feel anything but a desire to get on with some work, Marguerite,' I said, and I felt as I got the words out that I sounded forty, frumpish and schoolmistressy.

'I know how you feel,' she said.

I started. Just for a moment I had the

feeling that she was far older than her seventeen years — not just ten or twenty years older, but old with centuries of vast experience and enormous knowledge, and not any of it good. I shook off the feeling.

'You can't know how I feel,' I said sharply. 'Strap yourself in, don't talk whilst I'm driving and remember tomorrow to wear something more workaday. Our clients won't appreciate the outfit, neither will they like to have a teenager around who's got a fortune around her neck.'

'Oh, I've got to wear it,' she said. 'It was a present from my mother.'

I let the clutch out too fast and the car lurched forward.

'Oh, I'm sorry.'

She didn't touch me, but I felt as if she had. 'It doesn't matter, Mrs. Knightson,' she said. 'I've not seen her for many years.'

I could have kicked myself. I'd lost my parents in my teens, and I knew how isolated she must feel. I stopped the car.

I'd been a bitch to this charming girl,

and it was up to me now to put things right.

'Everyone calls me Di,' I told her. 'We use full names in front of our clients though. They expect it.'

Marguerite Friend's great dark eyes regarded me. They were clear and shining, but there was a cloudy and remote place at their centre that confused me most terribly, again just for a moment.

Her zestful gratitude dispelled my confusion.

'Thank you, Di! And I'll wear something more casual tomorrow.'

I didn't think about guile or mockery or my unease, not for some time after that. I restarted the car, and drove better now that my social conscience was clear.

The first call was easy enough.

I had to make sure that one of my erring girls had not picked up what is coyly and erroneously called a social disease during her last series of attachments to various lorry-drivers, commercial salesmen, motor-cycle kids and the rest who'd made use of her.

Marguerite Friend found it fascinating.

'How curious,' she said when I gave her a brief rundown on the girl's recent history. 'But she always comes back. Why?'

I had wondered about the same thing myself. Jennie Webb always came back to our part of Hertfordshire, or rather sent word that she was ready to come back from Glasgow or Southampton or, once, Hamburg, and one of us would have to go and collect her, usually me.

'I think we're as near to a family as she's likely to get,' I told Marguerite, after some reflection. We were waiting for the results of the blood tests. 'Yes, I think that's it.' I felt quite maternal towards my runaway Jennie, and part of the maternal glow extended to the exquisite young woman beside me. 'Jennie wakes up one morning and looks at the man she's with and she starts wondering if she really wants to be there.'

'Your client is clear,' said a nursing sister disapprovingly to me. 'The girl is clean.'

Marguerite giggled at her retreating

back. 'I'm sure she thinks I'm one of your bad girls, Di.'

'You don't look the type,' I said.

Her eyes narrowed oddly. 'I suppose your Jennie's what you might call a liberated spirit.'

'Anything but,' I told her firmly. 'She's in chains. Any man who tells her he cares for her is able to exploit her.'

'It bothers you, doesn't it, Di?'

'I hate the damage this casual sex causes.'

'Maybe that's all they want.'

'You can't believe that, surely!'

'I suppose not.' She smiled at me in contrition. 'But it must be a fascinating way of life.'

'It makes them hate themselves.'

I wondered as I said it about Marguerite Friend's way of life, and I realised that I hadn't yet considered her as a person. So far I had only reacted against her. She was obviously quite well-to-do, and her self-assurance suggested a harmonious background. I thought there might be a slightly older boyfriend, say a student, and a set of well-off grandparents.

I should have taken more interest sooner, I suppose, but we can't know these things.

'Poor Jennie,' said Marguerite.

'At least she won't have to attend the V.D. clinic. Anyway, you'll see something far removed from Jennie and her problems on our next call. A very different kind of thing.'

I was to encounter something very different from anything I had ever known before too. It was to be my first warning, but I didn't recognise it as such.

Nevertheless it was a warning, the first cold intimation of horror.

2

I deal mostly with erring girls, but we're supposed to handle a spread of clients. We use the term 'generic' to describe our caseload.

I had at the time a number of geriatric clients, one of whom was Mrs. Peters. My job was to make sure that she settled into the retirement home called The Meadows, and when I was sure that she was happy and comfortable I would write her off my caseload. I expected it would be soon.

She was an interesting old lady. Her life had been spent for the most part in Brighton. She had married a wine-importer in a small way of business, and, as she had disliked travelling, she had spent much of her time alone with her son when he was young, and quite alone for a good part of the time when he had grown up. Her husband had died at about the time the son took over the business, and she didn't see much of him.

He had written to me to say he appreciated what I was doing for his mother; in reply I'd told him I thought she'd settled well. I didn't mention her insomnia.

It wouldn't have been a problem if her hobby had been something other than playing the piano — she had become an accomplished musician over the years of separation from her husband. After two midnight recitals, the Warden took to locking up the key of the piano.

Her other main occupation had been gardening, and this led to a harmless eccentricity on her part: she now believed that the deaf young men employed as gardeners by a benevolent local authority were in her employ. They smiled cheerfully at her advice, and submitted to her haranguing with perfect unknowing good temper.

We found Mrs. Peters in the rose garden. It was an unlikely setting for the macabre scene that developed.

She was a small, stout woman with red cheeks and an alert expression. Her chin nodded in time with a blackbird's beak as it pecked at a piece of cake.

I held Mrs. Peters' hand and watched with her. I have a compulsion to touch very old people.

'She's eighty-eight years old,' I told Marguerite. 'She's rather deaf. I don't think she needs to be on caseload any longer.'

'She's very old,' said Marguerite.

I looked at the thin, blue-veined hand.

'So old,' I said, and I felt curiously light-headed, what with the scent of roses and the warmth of the sheltered garden.

'Do you think you'll live to that age?'

It was a strange thing for Marguerite to say.

Usually people say something like 'I don't think I'd like to live to that age' when they hear of great age.

'I don't know whether I'd want to,' I said, and I felt cold suddenly. One of my childhood friends had died in childbirth a year ago. I sometimes thought of her lying in the dark and the cold with her child.

I shook myself, not for the first time that day.

'Look at Mrs. Peters,' I said. I tried to explain my compulsion, the contact thing. 'She remembers quite clearly back to her sixth year, and some of the things before that. Eighty-two years ago.'

I held up Mrs. Peters' blue-veined hand.

'Tuck-tuck-tuck!' she went to the blackbird.

It continued to watch us from time to time, but it knew Mrs. Peters was no enemy. She had more cake. She wasn't ready to talk to me yet, but that was her way. The contact with my hand was enough for the time being.

'When I touch her hand,' I said to Marguerite, 'I feel I'm reaching across the centuries, can you understand that?'

I was amazed that I was telling a stranger about it. But I felt I had to tell her.

'Tell me, Di,' she said, interested.

'All right. When I touch Mrs. Peters' hand, I think of her knowing and talking to and touching a man who was in Paris when Napoleon Bonaparte made his return from Elba. It was her great-great-grandfather. He saw Napoleon.' I went on

19

with a rush, 'The family are wine importers. They've been buying wine for centuries from France. They've close connections throughout France, and the wars didn't much affect their business dealings. Mrs. Peters tells me all sorts of stories about the dead and gone Peterses.'

The old woman appeared to be nodding off to sleep, so I went on babbling about her and her family, whilst Marguerite stared down at the greedy blackbird and never said a word.

'She told me once that *his* father had seen them chop the King's head off. And the Queen's too.'

Then Marguerite did look up.

Her strange dark eyes seemed to flare. I couldn't make out their colour. They could be dark grey or dark brown, but momentarily they glowed with a fiery intensity.

'In Paris?' she breathed.

'Oh yes, in Paris.' Then, without thought, I opened the gateways to Hell. 'Old Mr. Peters often went to Paris, didn't he, Mrs. Peters?' I said in a shrill voice that I knew would penetrate her semi-deafness. 'That was where his grandfather saw them chop the heads off Louis and Marie Antoinette, wasn't it?'

I shouldn't have harped on about Paris. But would that have changed anything?

Mrs. Peters cackled and dribbled more cake to the blackbird and said the words that began it all. Maybe it wouldn't have changed anything, but I wish she had left the words unspoken.

'They saw everything!' she laughed. And for a second or two she was lost in past memories of a great-grandfather holding her hand and mumbling and complaining and then dredging up shocking little bits of reminiscence to frighten his six-year-old great-granddaughter with, and all with no regard at all for the effect it might have on her.

'Oh, his daddy saw them chop the King's head off all right, and do you know what his grandfather saw, eh girl?'

She meant me, but I was stunned at the implications. Mrs. Peters was in touch — literally in touch, for she had held the man's hand, sat on his knee, brushed against his thin white beard — of a man

21

who was alive some two centuries ago, and he, in his turn, had known a man who must have been born a century before that.

I found it intensely exciting. Suddenly I could see the pictures forming in my head, sharp and clear, pictures of armed men and a great skeletal framework at the top of which glittered a huge blade; and I could see wolfish eyes and shocked, white faces, and then a blood-blackened basket to catch the heads, and the great blade sighing through the air, and bound hands straining as the blade thudded down.

Marguerite was staring intently at Mrs. Peters too, but she hadn't yet noticed the Cadet's presence. She was in her memories of her great-grandfather and his tales. She was six years old again, and she wanted me to be shocked, just as she had been.

And I was!

I had to answer her.

'Tell me, Mrs. Peters,' I said. And I was afraid, without knowing why I should be afraid.

The blackbird shrieked and flew away.

'Eh?' said Mrs. Peters. Memories are short at her age. Geriatrics can forget the present, so keen is their awareness of the past.

'In Paris,' said Marguerite Friend, very coldly.

The old woman didn't appear to hear her, but she stiffened

'What?' she said to me. 'What, dear?' She didn't want to tell me what she had intended to say. Her hands were shaking, and her face was drained of colour. She didn't look round, but she knew Marguerite Friend was there.

'What happened in Paris?' Marguerite said again, and her voice had a steely inflection that chilled me. 'Tell me!'

'She doesn't want to,' I put in, and I felt weak and helpless and unable to intervene as I should have done. The old woman was clearly terrified, but I tried to rationalise the symptoms of terror: she was shaking, but so one would expect, since she was suffering from Parkinson's disease; she looked old and haggard and grey, but she *was* old, and she needed her morning doze. Why shouldn't she shake and go grey, at her age?

But I knew she was terrified, nevertheless. And I felt a chill of pure horror as I saw the expression on her face. She looked blindly round at the exquisite face of Marguerite Friend and said the words that have echoed round my head ever since:

'His granddaddy saw a witch burn.'

It was a child of six speaking, the voice high and treble and afraid. Her face was suffused, grey and blotched, and awash with terror. Odd bird-like noises came from her throat, and her hand came up shaking with palsy in front of her face.

'Get the Warden!' I shouted.

'Poor Mrs. Peters,' said Marguerite Friend. 'I'll stay with her.'

The old woman tried to scream, and all that would come out was a succession of odd half-sounds. 'She's had a stroke!' I said. 'I'll get the Warden.'

'I think someone's coming,' said Marguerite.

An assistant had noticed that I was on my feet waving my arms and shouting for help. I tried to say something to

Marguerite Friend, but I couldn't find the words. I knew that a corner of Hell had been flicked aside, and that I would suffer greatly, but I didn't want to admit anything of the kind to myself. I wanted to recover my composure: why should I feel that this was anything but the maunderings of a demented old woman, in conjunction with the natural interest of an intelligent and concerned adolescent?

She made the right kind of sympathetic noises until the strong, capable assistant took charge. I explained that the old woman had got over-excited, and when Bill Pedley, the Warden, came along, I sounded rational again.

'I've sent for the doctor,' he said. 'Why don't you get a cup of tea in the kitchen. And you, Miss,' he told Marguerite.

'She's an old dear,' said Marguerite. 'I hope she's going to be all right.

'I'll ring later and see how she is,' I told the Warden, when the tension was gone.

He didn't seem too worried. 'She's had attacks before. She'll get over it.'

But I drove badly when we left The Meadows.

'I shouldn't have let her talk for so long,' I said to Marguerite Friend. 'I feel so ashamed of myself. If I hadn't got her talking about her great-grandfather, none of this would have happened.'

'You shouldn't blame yourself, Di.'

'She was so frightened! I couldn't do anything for her!'

Marguerite didn't answer, not for a while. I felt utterly dejected, and as usual I found that I was to blame for the macabre little scene. Oddly, I began to be reassured by Marguerite's presence. It sounds completely illogical that she should frighten me, that I should have known she had terrorised Mrs. Peters, but that afterwards I felt something like warmth towards her; but I did. I remembered that she had told me we should become friends, and that was how I started to think of her, as a friend.

I felt a remoteness beginning to take shape in my life too. It was like being tranquilised. I felt slightly dizzy and slightly disoriented, and that was to be how I would always feel when I was with Marguerite Friend or even when I thought about her. I pulled up at my next call, a shabby terraced house.

'I'm sorry about that, Marguerite,' I said.

'Don't let it bother you, Di,' she said to me. We were talking about Mrs. Peters, but I was telling Marguerite that I feared her. 'You know, I'm glad Pauline Hart said I could come with you. I know I'm only a beginner, but I can see that I'm going to learn quite a lot from you.'

Why should that sound like a threat?

'I won't be long,' I told Marguerite when I went to see the plain, plump girl of sixteen who couldn't shake the habit of pilfering from Woolworth's, though the store detectives sighed when she walked through the doors and phoned for me.

'More bad girls?' said Marguerite.

'Routine,' I told her.

'It's fascinating,' she told me again.

By four-thirty, I'd had enough. I took Marguerite back to the office and found Phil waiting for me. He had his arm round Maggie Henderson, one of our clerks, but as she was fifty-eight or so and motherly I couldn't object.

'Well, that's all for today,' I told Marguerite.

Phil disentangled himself. Maggie looked her over. So did Phil.

'Hi, Di,' he said, but he was looking at her. I watched him become almost numb with embarrassment. Every man who had seen her had watched till she was out of sight, and I was tired of it, edgy, envious and tired.

'This is Mr. Walsh,' I told her.

'I'm Marguerite,' she said.

'Hello, yes, hello. Oh.'

Phil's an extremely articulate man when he's comfortable with people, but his work in research laboratories hasn't given him much social ease. It's a case of education narrowing the mind with Phil. I wanted to be rid of Marguerite, for I certainly wasn't going to give her time to become acquainted with him.

'Di's been showing me some most interesting people,' she said.

'Marguerite's just going home,' I said. 'We're pretty well finished now. I'll see you in the morning.'

'All right, Di,' she said. 'Thanks for all

28

you've done today. Goodbye,' she told Phil.

He watched her go.

'You look like one of our dossers,' I told him. 'You need a clean shirt.'

'I can't afford clothes and you, woman!'

'I'll take you to the Oxfam shop,' said Maggie.

'Women!' growled Phil, and he did his chauvinist pig bit, one of our games. 'I'll get me a chubby little Indian girl straight off the plane and keep her barefoot in the kitchen.'

'Hungry?' I asked.

'What else?'

I should have said 'And pregnant?' but somehow I couldn't. I was still numbed by the bizarre little scene in the rose garden. I had reached further back in time than I had ever thought possible. I looked down at my right hand and thought of Mrs. Peters holding her great-grandfather's hand as he rummaged amongst his memories, and then how he in turn had held the hand of a man whose father had seen a witch burn. Centuries reeled in my head, all those years and years and years.

I couldn't think of our silly game, not now.

'Wake up,' he ordered. 'We'll eat early.'

Maggie smiled at me. 'He's getting masterful.'

'That's the way I like him,' I said sincerely.

I busied around the office clearing up a few queries and thought about Phil and my impending divorce from that charming whiner Tony Knightson, and the things I had endured from him.

My husband, though not for much longer I hoped, was that worst of all males, a charming whiner. Tony Knightson couldn't make up his mind whether he was a mother's boy or the great lover.

At one time he'd be cutting a sexual swathe through the ranks of the bored housewives on the estate where we lived, and then he'd find one who rejected him and he'd come back to me in tears and want me to be his mother. He was a good-looking, smiling man with curly blond hair and grey eyes and a slim, well-muscled body. He dressed well and could afford to. He looked like an ad for shirts, and he drove fast cars (he got his money from the family estate agency he'd inherited) and altogether he was God's gift to women — and to me too until I got bored.

I looked at the top of his curly head one day as he sobbed out his apologies to me, and I felt like putting his head under the cold water tap. I knew that respect had long since gone, and love with it. How he whined when I left him! He got mean about money and our joint possessions, but I got a good lawyer and eventually got agreement to a fair settlement.

Tony whined about that too, and I was woman enough to enjoy hearing him whine. I'd had enough of good-looking thirty-year-olds who wanted to be mothered.

Phil was altogether different. I met him about a year before my separation from Tony. He was quiet, self-confident, larger than Tony and a few years older than him, and he had long since told his mother that he didn't need her advice any longer. He listened with patience to what I had to say and then generally did what he had decided to do; and it was usually right. By profession, he was a bio-chemist, living on a research grant for work on tropical diseases; I teased him about his appearance, for he was as casual as Tony had been snappy, bearded where Tony was fastidiously clean-shaven, and quite uninterested in his own appearance — though when he did put on a well-cut suit, he looked marvellous.

I was in a bit of a dream as I moved about the office. Maggie joked with Phil, and I said the right things in the gaps in the chat, but I didn't listen to the words. It wasn't until Maggie said, 'I put a bomb in your drawer and it's going to go off in three minutes,' that I realised they both knew how abstracted I was.

'Pardon?' I said, as they laughed.

'You haven't been listening for the past five minutes,' Maggie chided.

'Tired, love?' asked Phil.

'I'm sorry,' I told them. 'I'm a bit abstracted. It's been an unsettling sort of day.' Maggie remembered something. She pointed to my desk.

'Pauline left two referrals in the drawer,' she said.

'Thanks, Maggie.'

It was more work. She smiled and said goodnight.

'Sorry I was such a dream,' I told her as she left.

More work, I thought. Referrals were what we call the blue forms made out when someone is referred to Social Services by a member of the public, or some official person or body, as in need of care. Just when we all had far more work than we could cope with, since two members of our team of eight were away on holiday, and another had been away sick for months, the usual thing, nerves. I looked at the referrals.

'Can't they wait?' said Phil.

'I suppose so.'

'We'll pick up special fried rice from the Chinese and go and watch the Walter Matthau film on telly. Come on, Di.'

I hesitated. I had to look at what Pauline had left for me.

I wish I hadn't. It was another part of the pattern of evil that was to enmesh me. I could have avoided this part of it, I suppose. All I had to do was to tell Pauline to give them to someone else, that I was too busy to cope with more work; but I don't suppose it would have made any difference, not in the end.

Marguerite Friend had already marked me down.

Phil sighed. 'You and your social conscience.'

3

Phil sat down whilst I read through the referrals.

The top one seemed simple. It was a self-neglect case reported by a neighbour. The only thing that puzzled me was the address, The Red House, Old Campsall Lane, out on the London side.

Old Campsall Lane is a pleasant road with large redbrick Victorian semi-detached houses on each side with lots of well-grown trees in the gardens. Many of the houses had been converted into flats; I'd been to one not long since to investigate a case of baby-battering, a sad experience. The baby lived, but the mother killed herself in remorse. She had been living at number eighty-seven.

There were no names along Old Campsall Lane, just numbers. It had never been quite the class of area for names.

'Di?' said Phil. 'Something bad?'

'No, it's nothing. Some old duck reported missing, according to a neighbour, but she's turned up again. A Miss Vardy.'

'How about the other one?'

I skimmed it quickly. It was potentially a nasty one, though there was no urgency about it.

'A fostered teenager's playing up. The foster-parents want him out. They can hang on a few days, though.'

'Let's go for a drink.'

'Isn't it too early?'

'We'll drive out to the Bell slowly,' Phil said.

Phil doesn't run a car, though he claims to be nifty on a bike. I've yet to see him on one. We headed out for our favourite pub in my car.

'You're going a long way round,' he told me, as I turned into Old Campsall Lane.

'I want to look at a house.'

'Getting broody?'

'It isn't for us. It's that referral, the one about the old duck.'

'Can't it wait? Why the interest?'

I was looking along the row of elegant redbrick villas, thinking about when they were built in Victorian times, and how different it all was then. I have this thing about the past, and I was translated back in time as I saw the sun glowing on the red brick and catching purple, green and orange glass in the stained glass of the front-room windows. The roof had steep gables, and every house an oriole window. I began to speculate about a family.

'I'm looking for the old duck's house. It's niggling me, I can't remember seeing a house with a name. It's called The Red House. Can you see it?'

'Stop about halfway down,' he said. 'Then we can see round the bend.'

Old Campsall Lane curved gently to a crossroads, then it became Crow Lane after the junction for London. Crow Lane was the posh end of town.

I stopped about halfway down.

'I can't see anything but semis,' said Phil. 'Ask that old lady.' He pointed to a stooping figure in a nearby garden.

The woman looked to be about eighty,

and she had a pair of secateurs in her hand.

As I approached her garden, I noticed the number thirty-two on the gate. 'Excuse me. Where's The Red House?' I asked, using my shrill voice. 'Do you know, please?'

'I can hear you, I'm not deaf. Down the dirt track.' She pointed towards the junction with the London road. 'On the right!'

We drove on slowly, and it wasn't long before Phil saw it.

'There it is, Di. It looks like someone's drive, but it isn't. Anyway, it's half-hidden by the lilacs.'

It was a cinder-track between two pairs of semi-detached houses, and about fifty yards from the London junction. It hadn't got a nameplate, so it must have been listed as part of Old Campsall Lane for postal purposes. I hesitated.

'Go on,' said Phil. 'Or we'll never get that drink.'

I was reluctant to enter the gloomy lane. I drove up the dirt track, wondering why I didn't want to look at the house. It had a forbidding air, overgrown as it was by a tunnel of trees and shrubs. And yet when we'd gone about a hundred yards, the track opened pleasingly to a small field on the right and the grounds of a distinguished house on the left.

The house was a delight, but it was poorly maintained. It stood back from the track in about a half-acre of gardens. The evening sunlight mellowed the brick and heightened the regal proportions of windows and doors, especially the French windows to the left of the porch; but the woodwork was rotten, and neglect was everywhere. Bright yellow roses trailed from a half-fallen timber arbour; the lawns had not been cut and were feet high in couch grass and thistles; clumps of perennials, lupins, phlox and peonies, reared up from the overgrown flowerbeds, but couch grass had strangled the more delicate flowers.

'Where's the neighbour who made the report?' asked Phil.

'Neighbour?' I said, and then I realised what he was asking about: there weren't any neighbours. The dirt track ended just after the gardens of the house in a fence with straggly hawthorn bushes supporting it. And on the other side of the track was only a field. Beyond the hawthorns was a meadow, with three cows visible, all of them staring at us.

'Snap out of it, Di,' said Phil. 'You're as zestful as a zombie.'

'Don't be peevish. Isn't it a restful house? I thought the whole town was under concrete, and look at this. It must be an old house.'

'Mid-eighteenth century. Look at the windows.'

Georgian, then. I was right. Phil knows about houses. I saw myself in it, and momentarily I had a glimpse of dark oak panelling, brilliant mirrors in gold frames, the dull magnificence of tapestry, and the glitter of gold, blue and gold, and the glinting of lights that swayed oddly; it was only the whisper of a thought, no more, but it was intense. It was like seeing an old photograph for a half-second and retaining a jumble of detail.

'I'll have to bring her here,' I said, and I hated the thought.

'Who? Where?' said Phil.

'The Cadet, Marguerite Friend. Here.'

'That dark young girl? I don't follow, Di.'

'There's something I can't take to in her. Maybe I'm just tired, I don't know, but I don't think she's right for our kind of work.'

'She's only a kid, Di.'

Confusion swept through my mind again. I had this wretched ambivalence about Marguerite. I *knew* that she was alien to me, but I had to tell Phil that I liked her. Even though I didn't like her, even though I thoroughly *dis*liked her.

'Oh, she's fine,' I said. 'We'll get along just fine together.' I looked at the splendid warmth of the solid Georgian house and wondered why my fingers trembled. 'We'd better go now. Waiting around might frighten Miss Vardy, if she's at home. I don't think I'll visit just now.'

'Too right,' Phil said. 'Beer first. I'll take over the car, you've had enough for one day. I don't mind you getting broody, but I don't want you sad. I'll drive.'

As we drove to the pub, I suddenly felt

41

threatened, and spiteful.

'Did you think she was pretty?'

'Who?'

'The new Cadet.'

'Marguerite? So-so.'

'She's beautiful.'

'So what?'

'You were watching her.'

'I'd rather watch you.'

I felt like weeping. 'Would you Phil? Then that's all right.' And I thought it was.

At the pub, though, I had to talk about her again.

'Marguerite doesn't seem real,' I told Phil. 'I mean, how can a bloody orphan afford clothes like that?'

'Like me. She buys at the Oxfam shop.'

'And she's wearing a fortune in gold about her throat . . . I like her, but she worries me.'

Phil put down his pint and smiled at me. 'You don't have to take her around after tomorrow, do you?'

I'd told him about the arrangement with Pauline.

'No. Just tomorrow morning.'

'Then why worry about her? I'll get you another gin.'

Phil went for my drink and when he came back I tried to explain my unease.

'Mrs. Peters. At the Meadows.'

He frowned for a moment, then: 'You mean the woman who bosses the gardeners around? The one who comes from a line of wine-bibbers?'

'Wine importers. I told you about my touch thing with her, and how it all gets creepy when I think how far back this touch-to-touch goes.'

Phil sipped his beer. 'I remember that time we went to Hampton Court. You were hanging onto that staircase as if you were glued there. I've never seen anyone in such a trance, Di.'

I'd felt a tingling sensation as I held onto the curved iron railing, and a dream of glittering pearl-decked dresses swum before me. I could almost see the ghosts crowding around me.

I said defensively, 'Catherine Parr could have put her hand on that rail.'

'Nonsense!' growled Phil. 'The rail wasn't put in till a couple of hundred years later. It wasn't a sensory impression of good old Catherine Parr, you just had a chilblain, Di.'

'I felt something,' I snapped.

'Sorry, love. Well, what about Mrs. Peters?'

'She was scared. Why?'

'You tell me, Di. I wasn't there.'

'Marguerite Friend was. I was telling her about my hand-to-hand transference, you know, the way it reaches back through the generations. I told Marguerite about reaching back to the time when Mrs. Peters' great-grandfather saw Napoleon ride into Paris.'

'It's a disturbing idea,' Phil said sympathetically. 'I can see that.'

'Mrs. Peters went one better. She remembered that he'd said his father had seen the revolutionaries chop Louis' and Marie Antoinette's heads off.'

'That beats Hampton Court.' Phil was looking uncomfortable now.

'And I could see it! I saw the drums,' I said quietly. 'I could see the sticks beating on the pigskin of the drums, and I saw the basket for the heads. The blade was trembling against the sky for a tiny fraction of a time, and it came down so slowly at first.'

My voice had risen now, and people were looking.

Phil looked as if he wanted to leave, but he wasn't sure whether I'd fuss or not.

'I'm all right, Phil. Let me tell you the rest. I won't shout.'

He got himself another beer, and when he returned I was quite composed.

'More memories, more dreams?' he prompted.

'No. Something real. About Mrs. Peters, and the way she reacted to Marguerite Friend.'

'I was forgetting we started with her.'

'She terrified Mrs. Peters. I know it, and I don't know why she affected her in this way, but I'm sure she did. Mrs. Peters didn't know she was there whilst I told her about the touch thing and as far back as the story from her great-grandfather, but the old woman was stone-cold terrorised and terrified after that.'

'She's only a kid! It all sounds a bit far-fetched — '

'But she's normally such a level-headed old duck, Phil! She hates any kind of display of emotion, and when she tells the gardeners off she does it in the most ladylike kind of way. But Marguerite seemed to be able to turn her into an abject idiot — she started speaking like a six-year-old and she came out with some nonsense that took all this historical stuff back another hundred years or more!'

Phil stood up, and he gently got me to my feet. I hadn't any choice.

'It's all been too much, Di, and I know what you need.'

'She said something that could have come from a kids' story book. Something about seeing a witch burn.'

'It probably was from a story book. Look, the answer's simple. Don't take Marguerite Friend there again, Di.'

'I won't.'

'Chinese special fried rice, four cans of lager and the charm of Mr. Matthau. How does that sound?'

'Marvellous.'

I put work out of my mind. I had been overreacting to a straightforward set of events, that was all; tiredness had put things into an absurdly disproportionate light. We ate, went to bed, and I got to sleep eventually, well into the early hours.

By immense self-control I had not told Phil that I had seen the street where the witch burned.

I left him still sleeping at seven-thirty that morning full of envy at his tranquility.

4

It was a mistake to go into the office so early.

'Take ten minutes to get your breath back, then you're off to Birmingham,' said Pauline Hart.

'I've already got more than I can cope with today.'

'Elsie Thacker's absconded again. You'll have to pick her up.'

Marguerite Friend watched me. She smiled and I felt myself responding to her charm. It was so confusing. All I had to do was to look into her strange, secret eyes and I forgot my resentment and suspicions.

'I'll need an escort, Pauline,' I said.

'Charlie Gurr will go with you,' she said. 'His car or yours, it doesn't matter.'

'His.'

'You can stay around the office,' Pauline told Marguerite Friend.

I had half-expected her to offer to come with me.

'All right, Mrs. Hart,' she said. 'Have you time for a coffee if I make one, Di?'

'You nice girl. Make two,' said Pauline.

I needed the coffee. The thought of a confrontation with Elsie Thacker was daunting. She was my worst client. I've seen hardened little bitches by the score, but I've never known one remotely as bad as Elsie. She had the knack of intimidation. I've seen robust approved school matrons flinch when Elsie Thacker was returned to their care. Elsie was as near to being evil as any person, young or old, I've ever known.

Pauline was right. I'd have to go to fetch her. She could see that I was low.

'Elsie's at the New Street police headquarters. They want her out as quick as we can do it.'

I didn't doubt it. 'Where is Charlie?'

'On his way,' said Pauline. 'Make three coffees, Marguerite!'

'Coming, Mrs. Hart.'

'She's a good girl, that one,' said Pauline.

'She is,' I said, and wondered why I sounded so enthusiastic. 'I've got a couple of calls to make, Pauline. Won't be long.'

I rang The Meadows. Mrs. Peters had had a restful night, which meant fairly heavy sedation.

'How is she this morning?' I asked the Warden.

'Tired but not ill.'

I hesitated, unsure how to phrase the next question.

'Here's your coffee, Di,' said Marguerite.

I nodded my thanks. 'She's got over her attack, has she?' I asked. 'I mean, she's not distressed, is she?'

'Now why should she be distressed?'

The Warden didn't like that at all. Old ladies didn't get distressed at The Meadows; it had a reputation as a peaceful and contented institution.

Marguerite was watching and listening.

'Oh, no reason,' I said. Then, hurriedly: 'I'll be in as soon as I can.'

'Don't worry about her, Mrs. Knightson. She'll be fine,' he assured me.

'I couldn't help hearing,' said Marguerite. 'How is the old lady?'

It sounded a perfectly genuine enquiry.

Marguerite's clear eyes expressed only concern, yet I had heard her reduce Mrs. Peters to imbecility. Something clicked in my head and I told Marguerite that Mrs. Peters could expect the occasional odd turn at her age, and Marguerite wasn't to worry too much.

'Oh, but I shall,' she said, and I saw that my hands were trembling, trembling for no apparent reason.

'Have a good trip,' she said.

I thought of something else. 'Pauline, that referral. I went out to the house last night.'

'It didn't sound urgent, Di.'

'It wasn't. I'll call round soon, though.' And I remember with unusual clarity seeing the blue form on my desk. I remember too looking at the name: VARDY, printed, and saying to Pauline. 'It's rather lonely out there. I'll see Miss Vardy soon.'

Pauline didn't look at the referral. I'm sure she didn't. But I remember seeing it, with the name VARDY neatly typed, and a corner turned down, and even a splash of coffee where I'd stood the cup of instant on my desk. I did see it. I wasn't doped, and I had come round after my almost sleepless night.

But I don't remember what Pauline said next. I wish I could, but my regrets couldn't alter the past.

It was another small part of the pattern, only a little thing, but it had its importance in the whole.

Charlie Gurr burst in just then knotting his tie and tripping over his shoelaces.

'My car,' he called. 'I need the mileage money. Di, don't let that nasty little bitch talk during the trip, I'll go out of my mind if she talks about poisoning dogs again.'

That was Elsie Thacker.

At the last children's home she had been placed in, she'd found herself treated firmly and threatened with the loss of privileges such as going out in the evenings and having pocket money if she didn't conform. The Matron was a believer in discipline, a middle-class woman who believed that children weren't bad, only misguided.

Poor Mrs. Gordon had spoken sharply

to Elsie, and once had been enough. Elsie found it easy, for Mrs. Gordon had only two loves in her life, the theatre and a Harlequin Dane called Pobbs.

The gangly creature had taken hours to die, and the vet had looked murderous. It had been fed ground glass. After that, Mrs. Gordon became just another tired, defeated, half-frightened background figure in the Child Care service.

The worst of it was that Elsie left broad hints with the other children, and with the staff, and with me too. I had seen the sudden indrawing of breath and the downturn of her lips, then a feral look come onto her thin, freckled face; and I'd known that she was about to strike with all the malignancy of her intuitive and venomous skill.

'Ready, Di?' said Charlie Gurr. 'Let's go and pick the little charmer up.' He turned to Marguerite. 'Thanks for the coffee.'

She smiled at him as he knotted his tie. He tripped over his shoelaces and looked back to see if she was laughing at him. She wasn't, I was. The things one remembers.

It's odd but I can't recall the dreary journey to Birmingham. What sticks in the memory is the smell of Elsie Thacker as the cross-looking policewoman brought her from a detention room. It's one of the crosses we have to bear, this self-neglect by the young, and their stench.

An Inspector stood by the door watching us warily. The policewoman exchanged glances with him and I knew Elsie had got to them.

'Phew,' said Charlie. 'They might have given her a bath.'

Elsie was a skinny little girl of about ninety pounds, wiry and freckle-faced and pimply. She had whored for money, never for her own delight, and she was a liar, a thief and a sadistic killer of animals. The burly Inspector sensed the evil in her. I tried to keep things calm.

'Time to go back,' I told her. 'Did you eat your breakfast, Elsie?'

'Bleeding sausages. I threw them at her.'

The policewoman's expression didn't change, but I saw her large right hand ball into a fist. The Inspector stared stolidly ahead, not looking at Elsie.

'You're not very good at making friends, are you, Elsie?' I said brightly, and immediately I regretted making such a fatuous remark.

'I don't need friends, do I, Mrs. Knightson. But I've got to like you, haven't I? I mean, you being my social worker. And you've got to like me, haven't you? You've no bleeding choice, have you?'

The Inspector tried to silence her. 'Be a good little girl,' he said patiently and with a heavy ironical tone to his words. 'You've had your bit of fun, and now it's time to go back home. Next time you run away, don't come to Birmingham. We'll soon pick you up.'

Elsie glared at him, and he didn't look at all confident.

'I remember faces,' she said. 'I'll remember you, pig.'

She turned to me. 'You know who had the right idea about kids, Miss?'

I couldn't follow the workings of her devious mind, but I knew that something ghastly was coming.

'I just wanted to tell this fat-faced pig. I expect he's got kids.'

'Come on, Elsie!' Charlie Gurr said, but he didn't get hold of her. She'd have screamed assault. And I had already lost what little control I had over her.

'Myra Hindley, that's who, pig!' snarled this vicious little girl, who wasn't a child any more, and probably never was one.

'Elsie,' I begged. 'No more, Elsie. Please?'

She looked tired. The effort of such vituperative hatred had drained her. The Inspector looked stricken. A tough mature policeman had been reduced to a trembling wreck at the deadliness of her threats.

She didn't give any trouble on the drive back to Hertfordshire, nor at the Remand Home.

Charlie Gurr dropped me at the office at about three-thirty. The first thing I saw was Marguerite Friend reading a file on my desk.

I started to tell her that files were confidential, but she forestalled me.

'Pauline said I should get to know

56

something about procedures and the filing system,' she said. 'How was the trip, Di?'

I felt the beginnings of the odd ambivalence that came to me whenever she was near me or in my thoughts. It was wrong for her to be allowed to breach the confidentiality of our records: she was, after all, only seventeen, and working with us only on a temporary basis. Our strict rules forbid inessential access to the files.

None of this seemed to matter. Marguerite's friendly smile was fixed in place, and her eyes were cloudy and remote. I couldn't seem to make my mind up as to what I should say; then, suddenly, I knew.

'Oh, the trip was fine. Yes, go ahead and look through the files. If you're going to be around, you might as well make yourself useful and you can only do that if you know what's going on. That's right, isn't it, Marguerite?'

I was fascinated by the golden scorpion at her throat. She was wearing a low-cut blouse, and the golden scorpion glowed against her smooth skin.

'That's right, Di,' she smiled.

I felt an urge to tell her with some vehemence that I was proud of her.

'Whose file is it?' I asked.

Marguerite showed me. It was Elsie Thacker's file.

I didn't see much of Marguerite Friend for the next week. I had other worries.

Worries about Phil.

We still had separate dwellings, me a flat and Phil a house left him by his grandparents whilst he was still at Oxford ten years before. It was their town house, apparently, and when the tenants moved out he moved into the rather nice but small stone cottage. We had ideas about selling the two places and buying a house with some space around it, and I thought he was working on it when he didn't pick me up from work one evening — I'd got used to him calling in around five and chatting for a while before we left for his house or my flat, usually my flat.

I told myself he was out looking at houses, or maybe he'd got an important experiment cooking in the lab. And then he didn't turn up on another evening.

Nor did he ring.

We didn't always sleep together, but we saw one another daily. I went round to the laboratory, where a technician told me she didn't know where he was. I went home and tried to ring him at his cottage. There was no reply, not then nor when I rang later.

It wasn't until eleven that he answered.

'Where have you been?' I asked abruptly.

'I had a game of squash and a couple of beers, Di.'

'That's twice this week you haven't picked me up.'

I waited. He didn't answer.

'Well, are you coming over to the flat?' He couldn't refuse. How could he?

'I think I'll leave it tonight, Di. I need some sleep.'

'I can't sleep!'

And still he wouldn't come over.

'See you tomorrow, Di?'

I slammed the phone down and picked it up at once, but I'd broken the connection.

I went to bed and tried to sleep, and

when sleep did come at last it was full of odd memories and sudden glimpses of angry scenes.

In the morning I told myself I was upset because of the impending divorce. Tony was being awkward again, my solicitor told me. He wouldn't sign some papers — all in all, he was making things as difficult as he could for Phil and me. That was why I was tense; so I told myself.

I had enough sense to go to see my doctor, who put me onto a stronger drug. The Multivals slid down, and peace followed. I was having a lousy time, but I managed to conceal it from my colleagues; anyway, the last thing they expected was for me to crack — not Di, they said, so I heard later, surely not Di?

I got into the office late and saw Phil drinking coffee, very much at his ease. He didn't stay long. He offered no apologies or explanations, and I was relieved by this; I was gently hyped up and at the same time slowed down on the new pills. I didn't want any dramatic exchanges, and he judged my mood well. All he said was that we'd eat at his place that night, and I was providing the food.

'And it had better be good!' he growled.

And that was all. It made me want to weep with happiness, quite the wrong kind of response for a liberated woman. The feeling didn't last. I soon learned that happiness was a thing I could forget.

The small things that had begun to frighten me were beginning to add up during that week. The weirdness was noticeable, but I put the first incident down to the new drug.

It was the day that began so well, with me humming around the office and the Multival spinning a gentle web over my thoughts.

I was thinking about going out to see the foster-parents who were anxious to get rid of their surly ward, but thinking more of the meal with Phil.

Then Marguerite came into the office.

I don't know why she was there, nor did I ever find out.

The office was quiet. No one came buzzing in or out. There was myself,

Marguerite, and Charlie Gurr.

He was sitting in a far corner writing up reports, quite oblivious of anything around him. No one but me saw Marguerite walk across to the wide window that overlooked the main street.

And I alone saw what I can only describe as the diabolical expression on her beautiful face.

This is what happened.

She came into the office, looked at a pile of papers on a desk that Pauline Hart uses sometimes, and then she stiffened and whirled to face the window. She didn't see me, not then. I don't think she was aware of anything but what she sensed in the street below. It was like watching a graceful and deadly animal.

She paced across to the window and looked down into the street.

I could see down into the street without changing position. My desk has the best situation in the office, that is, if one likes the passing show. The big stores are there, and there's a pleasant little pub. There's always something to look at.

What was she looking at?

'Marguerite?' I said. Charlie Gurr didn't look up.

I scanned the street full of curiosity at what made the girl's body so tense. Two girls from the local comprehensive school swung past gesticulating and laughing. Were they Marguerite's school friends? A traffic warden was writing out a ticket for a Saab with every appearance of satisfaction. That could hold little interest for her. What then?

I was about to reach out to touch her arm when I found that my arms wouldn't make the movement. There was an aura about her that seemed to repel me with a powerful intensity. I couldn't touch her arm. Then I looked out of the window again and immediately saw what she was staring at. He was in the doorway of the pub, a middle-aged man in a dark suit. I could see that he was looking up at the windows of the office as intently as Marguerite Friend was staring down at him. His hand was raised as if he were warding off a blow.

A bus passed, and momentarily the man was hidden.

I saw Marguerite Friend's face then, in that mask-like hideous expression. A hissing noise came through her lips, and I was frozen into horror as I felt the loathing and venomous hatred which she radiated both in her expression and with the power of her body.

I looked down again and the man had gone.

Eleven o'clock. That was what the jeweller's clock read. A taxi was driving away.

I shivered, and I tried to ask myself why. All that had happened was that Marguerite had raced across the office in a swirl of elegant clothes, and she had looked out of the window; and a solidly-built man had stared up at the office.

They couldn't have seen one another. The windows are tinted to keep out the sun's glare, so there was no way they could have seen one another. So how could they have exchanged such stares of mutual antipathy — because they *had*!

I knew at once that they were aware of one another's presence, and that each feared the other. But I didn't let myself believe it. I blamed the drugs: I told myself firmly that I had seen nothing of significance.

But that could be said about everything to do with my encounters with Marguerite Friend. Each one, by itself, was meaningless. Yet they ran around my head like clockwork rats.

Marguerite watched the taxi drive away, then she walked out of the office without a word. I hadn't the nerve to follow her. I slunk out and put on my brisk, self-assured manner as I sorted out a few social problems, but all the time I felt the tracks of those horrible little clockwork rats.

I could see Mrs. Peters turning rigid with fear, and I heard someone shrieking in the flames; I saw Elsie Thacker's face and Marguerite absorbed in the details of her frightful career; I felt the warmth of the red-brick house down the cindered track and knew that The Red House had its own special significance: and I saw a powerfully-built man stand in a doorway looking upwards in blind torment. I knew that I was under a sinister influence.

Only misery remained, and that would soon come.

I found out soon afterwards that I had lost Phil.

It was a Friday, I could remember that.

5

The office was busy that Friday, but then Friday is always a series of catastrophes in our department. A couple turned up with their eight children demanding shelter, all the family noisy, lousy and abusive. A young layabout came in and ordered us to provide instant psychiatric help or he'd commit various forms of nuisance. I had to spend a few hours in the office to help sort things out, and it was a long, long day. I got the family a temporary home in a caravan, and I persuaded the police to eject the layabout. Those were my successes.

Round about four o'clock I stood back and drew breath. My head was aching badly, for I'd cut down on the Multival and I was experiencing withdrawal symptoms; that was why I'd been so peremptory with the young druggie I had ejected.

Sandra Jackson came over to me

shortly after four o'clock. She was the duty Social Worker, handling all the urgent phone messages. 'I've got to go out,' she said. 'It's an emergency. The Area Director's yelling for me to go to the Arbuckles' — it's all gone up there.'

I knew that the Arbuckles were a tempestuous family who could literally maim one another when the mood took them; and it seemed it had. That left me very much alone in the office. Marguerite Friend came to take over telephone duty.

She shouldn't have had the responsibility for handling duty calls, but by this time she'd so impressed everybody by her competence and her willingness that we'd let the rules slide. I was walking to my desk when I heard her answer the phone. She had her back to me. 'Hello?' she said. 'Sexual Services, what would you like me to do for you?'

I stopped at once. Had I heard right? Our normal reply is 'Social Services, can I help you?' A formula we're trained to use; we should sound calm, kind and dispassionate. I didn't think about it, I just said,

'What did you say, Marguerite?'

She turned, and I saw the mysterious depths of her eyes. Yet she had a smile on her face.

'It's for you, Di.'

'Just a minute. When you answered, what did you say?'

'Why, did I say something wrong?'

I felt a dark confusion in my mind, and tiny fragments of fear drifted around my body. She ignored my questions.

'He's in a hurry, Di.' She was deliberately ignoring my questions.

'But what did you say?'

'Why, did I say something wrong?'

'Yes,' I murmured, without conviction. She handed me the receiver.

'Hello?' I said, trying not to look at her.

'Who's that?' Phil said, rather sharply. I needed a pill, I couldn't cope with this situation. 'Is that you, Di?'

I looked at the phone as if it were a snake.

'Everything all right?' whispered Marguerite.

My senses reeled, and faintly I heard Phil making excuses. He was in a hurry, he was committed to a game of squash in

69

a league, and afterwards he had to go straight back to look after some microbes. The Madagascar strain, I remember that outlandish word. 'Look,' he told me, 'I have to rush.'

I put the receiver on the desk and went away to swallow the drugs. When the Multivals had cast their spell and saved me from hysteria, I could face the fact that Marguerite was my deadly enemy. I knew she had answered the phone to Phil with that titillating parody of our normal reply. 'Sexual Services,' she had said to him. 'What can I do for you' or something of the sort.

I couldn't challenge her, though. I didn't dare. I left the office soon afterwards and waited for Phil to call me. I knew he would. He can't leave ends loose; it's the scientist's training.

At half-past-six he asked if he could put off our dinner.

'Definitely no,' I told him. 'No. No!'

'Di, I've got three lots of cultures going and any one of them might brew up. It's this new strain. I think I'm near the breakthrough.'

It was very important professionally. I wasn't sure about the details, just that it was a hideously poisonous virus, and that if Phil came up with the information he was looking for there'd be promotion, worldwide recognition, and maybe a prize.

'I cancelled the squash,' he said. 'It really is important.'

'No. Come here. I want you here tonight.'

'I can't.' He sounded calm and determined.

'You'd better!' I shouted. He waited for a while, and I felt the distance between us stretching into infinity. Surprisingly he gave in.

'It won't be until about twelve, Di.'

'I'll have a meal ready.'

'I'll look forward to it, love.'

It was too late for the local shops. I needed meat and wine, which meant a late-night supermarket near the town centre. I had plenty of time, so I walked into town.

It was a pleasant evening, with great white clouds and the sunlight quite warm on the hills and the market gardens. In a few minutes a few drops of rain fell very softly and I looked up to feel them on my face. I don't mind wet weather.

I walked past the town library as I got to the dessert stage of my planning. I'd decided on a fresh fruit salad.

By now, the Multivals had done their work and I was in quite a euphoric state of mind. It was going to be such a marvellous meal when Phil came to see me at midnight.

Then I saw her.

She was standing outside the information centre, just around the corner from the town library, with a group of girls about her own age. They all turned my way as my wooden sandals clacked slower and slower along the pavement. There was no way I could avoid them.

Marguerite Friend's face was unsmiling, and she had seen me.

I picked out faces I knew. I was unsurprised when I saw who the girls were. I'd known already that Elsie Thacker figured somewhere in Marguerite's plans, so when I saw her spiteful little face I felt only that things would take their pre-ordained course. Jennie Webb, my runaway, was there too, and another girl I specially disliked but who wasn't one of my clients, Caroline something-or-other, whose mother had given her an elementary training in prostitution and theft.

Caroline Jones, that was it. Another of the girls was heavily pregnant. I couldn't be sure whether I knew her or not, but I fancied I'd come across her when she was much younger. I didn't know any of the three or four others.

'Hello, Di,' said Marguerite. She was dressed in a linen suit the colour of oyster-shells, greys and subtle white shades, and the golden scorpion seemed to coil itself ready to strike. I still tried my best. I saw that Elsie Thacker was in a new outfit.

'You look nice, Elsie. I like the skirt.'

'She nicked it,' said Jennie Webb.

I looked at my watch. It was half-past-seven, and I knew that Elsie Thacker should have been back at the Home by seven even if she had been granted evening leave, which I doubted.

'You late, Mrs. Knightson, are you?' she said.

She stared at my faded jeans and the dowdy blouse. It was an unmistakable challenge to my authority. Marguerite had a small half-interested smile on her face. Her eyes were smoky and remote, and if I hadn't had experience of the hallucinatory power of those eyes I'd have said she was stoned on some mild drug. I shook myself and looked back to Elsie Thacker.

'Have you got permission to be out, Elsie?' I asked.

'Course I have. I gave myself permission, Mrs. Knightson,' she said, then she exploded into laughter and turned to look at Marguerite Friend, and that exquisitely beautiful creature nodded slightly as if granting permission for her to continue in her baiting of me.

I should have felt furious, but I didn't. I could only feel the menace of the little group of teenagers. And still I tried, though my nerves were jangling.

'Go back, Elsie. It's better that way.'

'How would you know?' she said, and

she wasn't giggling now. 'How would you know what way's best? I mean, what way have you been getting it lately?'

Her shining eyes and half-choked breathing made it impossible for me to miss the innuendo.

They watched me carefully, even the dull-witted pregnant girl. Marguerite had a detached air about her; she wanted to know how I would react.

'Getting what?' I asked lamely.

I didn't think even Elsie would be explicit, but she was. 'This,' she said, making an unmistakable gesture. Her face was set in a wild, feral expression, and her eyes glinted like those of a night creature. Her lips were cruel, and they matched exactly the malice on the face of Marguerite Friend.

I turned to her. 'What are you doing with these girls?'

Jennie Webb answered for her. 'Why shouldn't she talk to us? We're not dirt, are we? She's a social worker just like you, and she doesn't say we're rubbish! She talks to us the same as she talks to anyone else.'

Jennie Webb was a heavily-built girl with a plain face, but she had something of vitality and a curious helplessness; I'd always thought of her as honest and open, and I'd been good to her. She knew I valued her, and this attack left me without an answer for her. Instead I asked Marguerite, again, to explain herself.

'What have you done to these girls?' I said.

'What's troubling you, Di?' she half-whispered.

'I've got to talk to you!' I said loudly. 'Not here. Come with me.'

'I know your kind, Miss,' Elsie Thacker said, leering. 'I wouldn't go, Marguerite!'

'Bent,' hissed one of the girls I didn't know.

'She's a dyke,' said another.

They all intended me harm. It was still daylight, we were at a busy intersection in the middle of a pleasant market town; and I was being subjected to a vicious bullying attack. I thought of Mrs. Peters' extremity of terror: it had come from this exquisite and terrible girl. I was suddenly angry.

'You shouldn't be with these girls!' I yelled. 'You're not their social worker — you're just a kid yourself.'

I found myself staring at the evil little head of the golden scorpion, and my vision blurred. I heard Elsie Thacker say something hurtful, and Jennie Webb declare that Marguerite was her best friend, then I could see properly again.

'Aren't you well, Di?' Marguerite said soothingly.

'Too much brainwork and not enough bed,' Elsie Thacker jeered.

'Elsie,' warned Marguerite. 'Di's a bit tired, that's all,' she went on. 'It's the strain of the job.'

The girls came closer to me, and I felt an overpowering sense of menace.

I had just enough strength left for one outburst. 'You knew you were talking to Phil!' I yelled. 'You did say 'Sexual Services' to him, you bitch!'

'Language, Miss,' said Elsie delightedly.

'That your boyfriend?' came from one of the strangers. 'Has he gone off you?'

'You imagined it, Di,' said Marguerite. She turned those hitherto curtained eyes on me. I was allowed to see deep into the dark pits beyond, right through to the core of writhing evil that was Marguerite Friend.

'Imagined it?' I heard myself say.

'She's flipping,' said Elsie Thacker.

Marguerite signed for her to be quiet.

'Diana?' taunted the malevolent girl. 'Thinking, Diana? Thinking of imagining what you never heard?'

'I didn't imagine what you did to Mrs. Peters! I didn't imagine what you said to Phil either,' I said.

'It would be better if you stopped asking questions, Di,' she said imperturbably. 'Really, it would.'

I was bold with terror. 'I'm going to have you thrown out of the office,' I said.

The girls crowded nearer once more. Their eyes gleamed with delighted malice.

She caught my eyes again in the net of her evil. 'Mrs. Peters doesn't need you, Di,' she whispered. 'It would be better if you wrote her off your case-load.'

'You'd better do what Marguerite says,' warned Elsie Thacker.

Marguerite smiled indulgently at the

girl. 'Di knows,' she said. 'Di won't ask any more questions. She won't trouble about things that no longer concern her. Will you, Di?'

I was confused. I wished to fight back, but that too-familiar sensation of bewildered compliance was with me again. Marguerite was just a Cadet whose position was clear: she should not undertake any of our duties or make any decisions about our regular clients. I knew it and Pauline knew it. Yet Pauline, I myself, and even those higher up in the Department had come to regard Marguerite Friend as different from other cadets.

Why? Why was she here now, at the centre of a mocking group of delinquent girls, frightening me?

A little anger remained in me.

'Keep away from Phil!'

'Phil?' she murmured silkily.

'What do you want from him?' I asked, and now I was pleading with her.

'Ask him!' She smiled cruelly. 'If you dare.'

'She daren't,' said Elsie.

Marguerite's eyes spun, and I listened,

all fight drained from me.

'Go and finish your shopping, Di.' I realised that she knew about my dinner with Phil, but that thought was immediately locked away. 'You'll feel differently about things in the morning.

'Start walking, Miss,' said Elsie. 'Better not report me. You hear?'

'Di won't want to cause us any trouble,' Marguerite said. 'Not after tonight. Mother said so.'

'Mother — ' I began.

'*But surely you're an orphan,*' I wanted to say. '*Like me.*'

Marguerite's cold face stopped my question instantly. She nodded slowly at me.

'Yes, Di. Mother wishes to see you. You'll come out to the house soon.'

'But — '

'Go.'

I gave in, and all the despair and confusion was erased from my thoughts. I concentrated on the meal ahead, and the lovemaking afterwards.

But the thought returned. 'After tonight, *what*?'

6

I was bright and cheerful and happy for Phil. The wine and the mutton were both excellent. Phil talked about his work and I nodded and smiled in the right places as the Multivals kept me dreamy and smiling. We'd finished the fruit and I'd just poured the coffee when the drugs began to wear off, and I felt the easy, serene state slipping away.

'Who answered you today?'

He hesitated. 'When, Di?'

'Today.' I knew he was going to lie to me, and I could have screamed in fury, for he was avoiding my eyes.

'Good meal, that, Di. You mean when I rang you at work?'

'This afternoon.'

'I can't remember, love. You all sound alike on the phone. Very brisk, very professional.'

I tried to believe him, God help me. I tried.

But I had heard her! I made an effort to dismiss it.

'I haven't seen you all week, Phil.'

'Things to do, love, microbes to cosset. Bigger and better bugs to look after.'

I couldn't leave it. 'Didn't Marguerite Friend answer the phone?'

'Who?'

He was lying. He should have put his arm round me and asked what I was worrying about, and shown me that I was absurdly jealous. It was the way I'd hoped the scene would go. I'd got the scene wrong.

'Oh, you mean the Cadet,' he said, when he saw the extent of my distress.

I started to weep, then I ran into the kitchen. Phil turned the late night movie on, and I could hear the forties music alternating with gunfire from the lousy old gangster B-movie. I swallowed a couple more pills.

'I'm going to bed,' I told Phil when they'd started to work. My head crashed with violent pains. He didn't look my way, and I didn't give him time to say anything, for I still had a remnant of hope.

I went to bed and floated off into a fog of despair mingled with doubts about my sanity.

I didn't hear Phil come to bed, however I could hear his breathing when I woke up some time later, and I was comforted at once. If he'd been offended, he'd have returned to his cottage, and, I reasoned, if there was anything to my suspicions, surely he wouldn't have come to bed with me?

'Phil?' I said, but he didn't wake. I fell asleep again, and my dreams were shot through with sudden glimpses into nightmare. Then I would find myself awash with terror, for no reason at all. I would wake sweating and instantly fall into that frightful dream world again.

It was still night when I felt the weight pressing on my legs and I thought I was still in a dream-state. 'Go away, Tao,' I ordered, for I had been dreaming that I was a child again, eight years old, and my Siamese cat had sneaked upstairs into my bedroom. I kicked out, and the weight shifted slightly, in fact it crawled along my leg and half-across my left thigh. In the same moment, I heard a wet slithering sound, and I was full awake. I opened my eyes and saw the edge of the window where the curtains didn't quite fit. Moonlight rimmed the edge, but little of the light filtered into the bedroom.

The whole room was a dense and solid mass of blackness, except for the sliver of moonlight at the window. But there was movement in the blackness.

I started to reach out for the bedside light, and then I sensed the movement on my legs, and felt the coldness of the dead weight, a bitter chill that burned my legs numb.

I admitted to myself then that there was a *thing* on the bed. On *me*!

It moved again, and I heard a thin, wicked sound, full of malice, and then waves of a foetid, graveyard stench filled the blackness, and there were sounds of a dank, cold progress as the thing slithered closer.

'No!' I breathed. 'Oh God, no!'

I couldn't stir. I couldn't move even the muscles that controlled my breathing. I could no more scream for help or try to wake Phil, than I could reach down to the ghastly thing slithering along my body.

I was rigid with horror. A frozen wave of air flicked across my cold face.

The thing sighed with delighted malice. Moonlight suddenly broke into the room, and I heard a low weird sound. I couldn't identify its source for a little while, then I knew that I was making the noise. It wasn't through any conscious impulse — I seemed quite separate from the frozen woman on the bed.

And then I looked at the thing, because now I could see something silhouetted against the treacherous moonlight.

It was a bulky mound that slowly raised itself, so that less of the frozen bulk pressed on me. I fancied that I could see huge, pale eyes, but I was sure there was one glimpse only, and, just afterwards, a hint of a blubbery mouth and needle fangs, and then my muscles responded at last to the ultimate horror of the thing, and I could find a voice to express my torment.

I screamed. And the noise blotted out the slithering sounds, and the mocking gulps of evil laughter. I could close my eyes too, and it was a release from the nightmare.

I wound myself around Phil, vaguely conscious that the room was flooded with warm, safe light, but I wouldn't open my eyes and I couldn't stop making terrified, whimpering sounds. Phil shook me.

'Di, stop for a moment! Then you can tell me?'

No, I thought; no, no. I'll keep whimpering for the rest of the night, I'll not allow any questions because I daren't think of answers.

'Let me get you a drink — some tea. Whisky, no, tea.'

But I wouldn't let him leave me. I'm strong enough for that, and though he tried to disentangle me with some firmness I wouldn't allow it.

'All right, Di. I'll stay.'

He sounded weary. And something else. I picked the note up instantly. Maybe a hint of annoyance, but whatever it was his sympathy didn't ring true. I couldn't work out what it was. What I needed was light, warmth, someone to hold me; safety, that's what I needed. I knew, though, that my safe days were over.

I couldn't sleep, and I wouldn't let Phil sleep. He tried once or twice to move into a more relaxed position, but I held on more firmly still. We avoided cramp by moving slightly, but only slightly. The light stayed on, of course. Phil knew better than to turn it off. I stopped whimpering around four in the morning when the moonlight faded. He sensed my tension gradually diminishing.

'What was it, a bad dream?'

A bad dream? Couldn't he see that I was still in a state of shock? Couldn't he feel the chill in the room when the night-thing stirred? I had *seen* it: couldn't he guess just a little of my terror?

I'd seen dead people, some who'd been dead for days. There is a graveyard stench, and it had been in our bedroom, and I could still smell it.

'It wasn't a dream,' I told him.

'Did you take a pill before you went to bed?'

'Two.'

'It couldn't be side-effects?'

'No.' I had to explain, at least try to tell him about the thing.

'Look on the bedcover.'

'Right. What am I looking for?'

'Feel down the middle of the cover. Is it wet?'

I could feel the raw edge to my voice. I waited, holding my breath. He had to have felt something on the bed.

'It's not wet, Di. Spill something?'

'No. Is it very cold — the bed cover?'

He patted the cover again. 'No, it's not. Is this something to do with your nightmare?'

What could I begin to tell him? Especially when my mind refused to accept that I had seen the full ghastliness of it?

I pointed. 'It was on the bed.'

'Tell me about it.'

'I can't!' and I started to scream again when he got out of bed.

'All right, come with me! And don't yell, you'll wake the kids next door.'

We went into the living room, and Phil poured large whiskies with not much water. I knew Phil thought that I had experienced nothing worse than a bad dream; I knew he was bored with me.

'Are you ready to tell me about it now, Di?' he asked.

I couldn't tell him, because I had seen worse than boredom on his face, just for a moment; women have finely-tuned antennae, infinite perceptiveness with the men they love. I wish I hadn't seen that look.

'I'm sorry I woke you,' I told him.

Phil poured another drink. 'Get it down, Di. You know, you had me worried there. You've looked abstracted a lot lately.'

'Have I?'

He wasn't good at scheming and looked nervous.

'Di, I don't mean to sound over-anxious, but don't you think you could do with a rest?'

'I know I could.'

'Just for a few days,' he rushed on. 'You could stay at your aunt's at the coast. She'd be glad to see you.'

'I could get a few days off.' Our administrators realise that when the pressures get to be too much for us we need to have leave of absence, so they keep our leave-schedules flexible.

But Phil was transparent. He hadn't got my interests at heart, and he was playing some devious game of his own.

'That's fine, Di!'

'When do we go then, Phil?'

He looked at me stupidly. 'We? Sorry, but I just couldn't get away, Di! I have to be in the lab night and day for the next few weeks.'

'Couldn't one of your assistants look after the bugs for a few days?'

'There'd be nothing left when I got back, Di!'

'Don't you want to come with me?'

The look of disgust was there again, he couldn't hide it. I began to admit certain things to myself. Phil and I were through. He disliked me, and I knew why. The bitch, I said to myself. *The conniving bitch*.

But I'd stop her. I knew how.

Somehow we got through the weekend with a pretence of mutual affection. We didn't mention Phil's idea of my going to the coast again, though.

7

I found Pauline Hart busy with a couple of detectives in the office.

'I doubt if Jack Gallagher's involved,' she said, 'and anyway would I tell you if he was? I don't really care if he's stolen a bit of chicken wire and a few half-inch nails, not really, not when we're trying to get him to believe he's rather more than the lump of dirt you've told him he is.'

One of them grinned at her, and she relented. 'He's only fourteen. I'll have a word with him.'

When they had gone she told me the lad was building a rabbit hutch.

'I want to talk to you,' I said.

She caught the note of tension. 'In the office then. Coffee?'

'Just a talk. About Marguerite Friend.'

'All right, Di,' Pauline looked business-like.

'She's evil through and through.'

'You serious, Di?' Pauline's expression

didn't alter. 'I mean, it's not that she's annoyed you in some way we can put right?'

'And if she had annoyed me?'

Pauline is very shrewd. 'Don't get defensive, Di. I'm your friend. You and I can talk to one another without evasions. If Marguerite's offended you or one of your clients, I'll have her transferred to another area. Has she?'

It struck me with some forcefulness that I had so little to argue with. For instance, what had she actually *done*? I knew she had terrorised Mrs. Peters; I knew she had seduced Phil, I had been openly threatened by the girls in the middle of town: and all of these things were the manifestation of a vicious spirit. But when I started to tell Pauline about them, my confidence drained away.

'It was when Mrs. Peters started talking about the Emperor. She's the one at The Meadows. A lovely old lady.'

Pauline nodded. 'I know.'

'You know I have this thing about old people — they're our link with those they've known and touched in the past.'

'You've talked about it before, Di. Yes.'

'But it's never been so vivid as this, Pauline. With Mrs. Peters I can reach back hundreds of years! Back and back, until it frightens me. Back in time to before the execution of Louis and Marie Antoinette.'

'Memories,' Pauline prompted. 'Executions. But what happened at the home? From what I gather, Mrs. Peters was very distressed.'

'She wasn't distressed, she was terrified! That hypnotic bitch glared at her with her witches' eyes, and she went out of her mind with terror!'

Pauline waited for a moment or two, then said quietly: 'The doctor reported that she'd had a mild seizure, Di.'

'They should have sent for a priest. He'd have seen that the poor old woman was bewitched.'

'You can't believe that, Di?'

'Oh yes, Pauline. Truly.' And then I started sobbing.

She pushed me back into my chair when I tried to get up.

'Shut up, Di.' Like all really calm

people, she can radiate the area around her with peace. 'Shut up altogether for a minute or two.'

'Yes.' I wept silently. I felt half-dead with fatigue and terror.

'Now Listen. Marguerite Friend came to see me yesterday at home. She said she saw you on Friday night.'

'Did she say who was with her?'

'Some of the Department's clients, all about her own age. She mentioned Jennie Webb and Caroline Jones.'

'Did she say Elsie Thacker was there too?' I said, but I knew that Marguerite Friend would have told her story well. 'Elsie's the one who poisons dogs and admires a child-torturer.'

'She's not all bad, Di.'

'If you believe that, you're a fool, Pauline. Elsie Thacker's all bad — she's evil. And that's why Marguerite Friend has taken up with her.'

'That's not what Marguerite says, Di. She believes she can help some of our disruptive teenage girls. The especially badly-deprived ones. She's talked it over with Ed Callison, and I've been impressed by what they've come up with.'

Ed Callison is the next up in the hierarchy from Pauline, coming between the Area Director and Group Leader levels. He's Group Coordinator, with special responsibility for children. Ed is a naive and rather lazy man of around fifty, easy meat for Marguerite Friend. I could see the way she'd worked it well enough.

'She and Ed came up with the idea that she could do something with the bad girls. Liaison work.'

I was recognised as the teenage girls specialist in our group. I said shortly: 'Why didn't she come to me first?'

'I expect she was rather in awe of you, Di. You can be quite a formidable person, you know.'

'And Ed's easier to handle.'

Pauline smiled. 'Not exactly. But Ed approved her notion of meeting the girls on their own ground. Under supervision, of course. Ed thought he could do that himself.'

'And what do you think, Pauline?'

She was no fool. 'You're the obvious person, naturally, Di, but I feel you've enough to do without supervising untrained staff. And besides, we at our age might be a little out of touch with teenagers, don't you think?'

She'd done it so cleverly. Marguerite Friend had succeeded in manipulating the intelligent and over-kindly woman who was my friend, as well as Ed Callison who would be a pushover for her. I did my best.

'I can't see the Director approving this kind of arrangement, Pauline. The Friend girl shouldn't be with clients out of office hours. In fact, she's no official standing at any time.'

'Oh, I wouldn't call it an official arrangement, Di. No one's suggesting that Marguerite's doing social work.'

'Then what is she doing?' As I said it, I wondered too what Marguerite wanted with the bad girls. I could see what she and Elsie Thacker had in common: they could dominate others easily, one by the use of her hypnotic beauty and the other by hinting at the frightful. But what could Marguerite Friend want with poor, overweight and under-loved Jennie Webb?

And the others, too: what did she want with them?

'I expect she's got the usual adolescent conscience, and this is her way of helping put the world to rights. There's no harm in that, surely, Di?'

'Pauline,' I said calmly enough, though I felt like screaming, 'she threatened me.'

Pauline Hart didn't flinch at that. We're well-trained. 'Go on, Di.'

I felt bitterly cynical, but I told her.

'That bitch scared me. I accused her of interfering in my private life, and that she had no right to take up with clients. I got mad with her and told her I'd have her kicked out of Social Services.'

'How did she take it?'

I hesitated. I needed a Multival. My resolution was ebbing away, and I didn't want to talk any more. I couldn't tell Pauline I was doped up, and my thoughts were full of shadowy doubts and misery.

'Di, what did Marguerite actually *say*?'

'What did she say? She told me that it would be much better if I stopped asking questions.'

Pauline gave me a few moments to

recover, for I was exhausted and she could see it.

'Di,' she said, 'let me tell you what Marguerite said about meeting you on Friday. But first, I want you to know that she admires and likes you. She made a point of saying it, then she told me how sorry she and the other girls were.'

'But they hate me!'

'No, Di. They knew you were a bit distraught. They saw that you'd been crying, so they tried to show that they cared about you by involving you in their conversation. Marguerite says you might have misunderstood what they were trying to do, but they were sincere in trying to help you.'

I found myself in a daze. It all sounded so very reasonable. Was I, after all, just a paranoid woman whose trouble was over-work and a failed marriage? Then a violent reaction made me furious with myself. I couldn't have been mistaken! I could see the enormous hostility in the girls' faces, I could hear Elsie Thacker's mocking tones, and I could feel the surge of power in Marguerite Friend's deep, dark eyes.

'I wasn't mistaken,' I said bitterly. 'She threatened me. Get her out, Pauline.'

'But I can't see any reason to, Di. Everyone speaks highly of her. You did too, for that matter.'

I held back the outburst and the tears. 'Since she came into this office, my life's been hell.'

'Maybe you should have a break, Di. How long is it since you had a holiday a — real holiday, not just a weekend?'

'In March. We went to North Berwick.'

'Scotland. Yes, I remember seeing the photographs. Suppose you take some time now, a week or two?'

'I won't be hounded out of here by that evil bitch.'

Pauline's temper remained cool.

'I'll keep her out of your way when you get back,' she offered.

'I'm not hiding from her, either!'

'Of course not. I didn't mean that, Di.'

'I'm staying. I want to know what she's up to, Pauline — no one else seems to care.'

Pauline thought about it. She tapped on her desk with her long vermillion nails, obviously thinking of some bland subject to introduce. 'By the way, I was thinking about you and Phil. How is he?'

'Phil? What's that hell-bitch been saying about him?'

She was astonished at my anger. But she knew that I was talking about Marguerite Friend nonetheless.

'Di, no one's been talking about Phil. I just asked because it's time we had that meal together.'

'I'd love us to come to dinner, but the fact is, Phil's very busy these days. And these nights. I don't see much of him now.'

Gently, Pauline said, 'Then we'll leave it for a while, Di.'

'I expect we'll leave it for a long time, Pauline.'

'Want to talk?'

'Phil's vulnerable,' I told her. 'He's not known many women, and anyway he's straight. It would be easy for her.'

I left it at that. Pauline didn't reply, and I couldn't tell what she was thinking. That was the last time I attempted to confide in her.

There was a sharp rap at the door, and this broke whatever was left of our rapport.

'Go away!' yelled Pauline, but Ed Callison came in beaming.

'I'm taking a few days off,' he said. 'Wealth at last. My great-uncle finally snuffed it.'

The great-uncle was over ninety, and, according to Ed, he was an insufferable misery. Ed had been living on his expectations for years. The funeral was likely to be memorable.

'We'll cope in your absence, won't we, Di?'

He produced a scrap of paper. 'One of the clerks gave me this.' He handed it to Pauline. 'Wealth,' he said as he left. 'Lovely.'

'Still worried?' asked Pauline when he had gone. We hadn't resolved anything by this long and harrowing session. I still hadn't told her about Marguerite Friend's unambiguous lasciviousness when she answered the phone.

'I'll get over it,' I said.

I looked at a corner of the cheerful

office where the sunlight left a dark area, and the darkness seemed to hold movement. I was shaking again.

'See a doctor, Di.'

'I think I will,' I said, though I had.

'Look, Di, why don't we go for an early lunch?'

'I'm meeting Phil.' It had been arranged, mostly because I'd insisted.

Pauline looked embarrassed. 'He sent a message. It was for you, not me. He just brought it in.'

Phil hadn't troubled to make excuses. He'd written, 'I can't make lunch. Sorry, Phil.'

'Bastard,' I said quietly. Pauline pretended she hadn't heard. 'Ready?' I asked briskly.

I'd have gone out with anyone. After Phil's rejection I was desperate for support. Anyone would have done, man or woman. It happened that Pauline was around,

Lunch was very good.

We're both good conversationalists, and we enjoyed one another's company. The time passed agreeably, and not once did we mention my personal concerns. We ate well, and two salesmen who came in jokingly chatted us up and bought us large glasses of Armagnac. We left the pub in high spirits.

'Look, let's pay a surprise visit,' said Pauline.

We were already in the car. I didn't catch immediately what Pauline had said. She was driving, the radio was blaring pop music, and the Multival was doing strange things with the Armagnac, so I didn't properly realise what we were doing or where we were heading till she turned into The Meadows.

'Oh good,' said Pauline excitedly. 'I was hoping she'd be here.'

The alcohol ran cold, and the Multivals smashed into my brain. She was there, very serene, as beautiful as a cobra, smiling dazzlingly.

'Dear Christ,' I breathed, and it was a plea for help. 'Marguerite.'

8

There were raindrops on her delicate skin, and I marvelled at her beauty as I had marvelled the first time I saw her. Then, though, I had not known the reason for my instinctive fear of her.

She smiled and came up to the car. We got out.

'Di, I'm so glad you came! When I rang Pauline she wasn't sure you could spare the time. I wanted you to see Mrs. Peters — she's been asking for you.'

'Let's get out of the rain,' said Pauline.

She'd set this up, it was all planned to get me to The Meadows. All in my best interests, of course.

'Mrs. Peters has invited us to tea,' said Marguerite. 'Please come, Di. Please?'

I looked fully at her. The dark eyes were smoky, with a dull blaze somewhere deep within the irises, then I felt dizzy as the irises seemed to spin, and I had no will to act. I was guided towards the shelter of the home.

It took me a few minutes to recover, and by this time I was sitting in one of the smaller lounges with Pauline Hart, Marguerite Friend, and two old ladies, Mrs. Peters and her friend Miss Tillot.

It was like some ghastly children's tea party where the children are playing at being polite. Both the old women were deaf to some degree, but both were determined that the occasion should be a success. They had dressed up in starched summer linen, and their smiles were firmly in place, with the dentures too large for their shrunken gums. At any other time I would have been touched by their solicitude for me.

'It's lovely to see you, dear!' said Miss Tillot, a lady I'd met before.

'Shall I pour the tea?' mumbled Mrs. Peters. 'I'll give Mrs. Knightson her tea, shall I?'

'You pour the tea, Ivy!' Miss Tillot called back. 'They must be parched after coming such a long way.'

We didn't offer to help as the old woman clawed at the teapot and swung it dangerously over the cups. Old people resent the aid of the young. I couldn't have done much to help anyway, for I was in a curious mood where I felt heavy and slow.

Then, suddenly, the fog on my mind lifted. I knew why we were at The Meadows.

It was a demonstration of power.

Only I saw it, naturally. Who else would have believed that Mrs. Peters was under the sway of a malignant teenager? I was meant to see it, and to learn from what I saw. And what did I see?

I saw what I was meant to see, the subjection of one will to a stronger one.

Marguerite Friend was tapping the table with one long fingernail, and Mrs. Peters watched her. On the face of the old woman was the anxious, placatory expression I've seen on the faces of beaten children: they are determined that they will not be hurt again if a show of utter subjection can keep away the blows.

The tapping stopped, and Mrs. Peters turned to me. 'I don't know what I'd do without Miss Friend,' she mumbled loudly, as if the words were rehearsed. 'We all love her here. She's made such a difference to our lives. My friend Miss Tillot wouldn't come out of her room except for bingo, but Miss Friend talked to her and now she comes out for all her meals, don't you, dear?'

A sidelong glance implored approval from Marguerite.

'This is what I wanted you to see,' said Pauline to me. 'The warden says he's never seen such a change in a person. Miss Peters is fully socialised where before she was extremely introverted. And then there's Miss Tillot too.'

'Good.'

'Tea, Di?' said Marguerite.

I looked at the mess in the saucer. Mrs. Peters looked at me in a terror of anxiety.

'It's Darjeeling, dear, very nice. Isn't it, Miss Friend?'

She had begun in a chiding voice when talking to me, but her words to Marguerite had an awed tone to them. She smiled ingratiatingly at her and Marguerite nodded approval.

She said earnestly, 'Don't you think,

Di, that working with old people is extra specially rewarding? I mean, they've so much to offer people in my age group. There's so much stored experience they can call on — they've seen so much in their time, and they've been in contact with years and years of living and chains and chains of people going back far beyond their own lifetimes. Isn't it thrilling to think of it, Di?'

'Is it?'

Pauline listened with the half-smile of someone who has achieved a master-stroke of diplomacy and organization, had, so she thought, reconciled the differences between me and Marguerite, and after this touching scene how could I, a mature and caring social worker, maintain a grudge against such a dedicated young person?

'Well, you should know, Di! You told me about it first. You know, how people can be in touch with events hundreds of years back in time.'

'Di's mentioned it to me, too,' said Pauline.

The Multival kept me from raging, and

108

some other force prevented me from actively questioning Marguerite. I was sure I had been brought to The Meadows for a good reason: I waited. I would know soon. It centred on Mrs. Peters.

'So I have, Pauline,' I said. 'Marguerite and I were talking to Mrs. Peters and she told us about her great-grandfather.'

'Oh, it goes much further back than that, Di,' Marguerite said. 'Why, don't you remember, she had a direct contact with someone who had spoken to and touched a man who had been at the court of Louis the Fourteenth. You know, the Sun — '

'I don't remember her saying anything about the court,' I said. My throat had dried, and my hands shook. The strange deep eyes glowed unnaturally.

'Di,' she laughed. 'You know, the really interesting things happened at the court when it was at Versailles.'

Pauline was unaware of anything but an odd conversation, which, I think, slightly bored her.

'We were at Versailles last year,' she said. 'It rained. Just like today. And it was so cold in the galleries.'

Miss Tillot snored gently, though Mrs. Peters followed every word. When Marguerite spoke, she flinched and screwed her eyes up in concentration,

'I've never been to Versailles,' I said listlessly. 'Have you, Marguerite?'

'Of course!' she said. 'But not for years.'

'You're not that old, Marguerite,' said Pauline, plainly bored now.

Marguerite looked at me. 'Things aren't always what they seem. I could be a lot older than you realise.'

Pauline didn't react at all to that, but Mrs. Peters began to whimper. Curiously, Pauline didn't notice that either. She got up and said briskly,

'I think you've developed a very good relationship with these old ladies during your time here, Marguerite. Don't you agree, Di?'

I began to shake my head, when Bill Pedley joined us.

'You can leave Marguerite here as long as you like! She's doing a first-rate job for a youngster. Mrs. Peters here follows her around everywhere.'

'Like a dog?' I said, and the blazing fury in those weird eyes made me flinch, just as Mrs. Peters flinched whenever Marguerite spoke.

The warden looked at me uncertainly.

'I suppose you could say that,' he said, and he looked to Marguerite.

She went over to Mrs. Peters and patted her thin arm. 'I think of Mrs. Peters as I would of my own mother,' she said.

'Oh, but I thought — ' I said, and again I stopped, for the shadowy uncertainty was there again.

'Don't get too involved with old people,' warned Pauline. 'They come to depend on you, Marguerite, and when their time comes you find that their death can hurt most terribly.'

'I expect so,' she said. 'I'll be careful, Mrs. Hart. Oh, by the way, Di,' she said to me as we walked down the path towards the car. 'I'd love you to come out to meet my mother. She's got some interesting contacts too. I think you'll find that you'll be quite stimulated when you see her.'

I looked back, to see Mrs. Peters. She looked like a dead woman. I shuddered at a memory that wouldn't go away, then I lost contact with it, except for the dread that remained.

What was happening to my memory? There were things I should be asking Marguerite Friend. What things, though?

The bad girls? No, not them. Pauline had cleared that up for me — *Mrs. Peters?* Not her, either. She was a contented old woman, so Pauline insisted and that had to be good enough for me. *Phil*.

No, I told myself. Not Phil. I must lock that one away in a cupboard in my head, and throw away the key. Otherwise, there would be more nightmares.

So what was happening to my memory? I knew, of course. At the onset of a nervous breakdown, memory is one of the first things to go faulty, in the way that a car's electrical system is the first to go on the blink when it's getting old. A breakdown is remorseless. You can watch yourself sliding down the ice towards the chasm of desperation, where the darkness waits and there are ice-fangs in the blackness.

'Di?' said Marguerite with a deadly sweetness.

'Yes?' There was a vivid rainbow over the fields. I wondered if it would bring somebody luck.

'You won't forget to come to meet my mother?'

That was what I had forgotten.

'But I thought you were an orphan, Marguerite?'

The treacherous eyes held me, and the irises spun. 'We lost my father quite a while ago,' Marguerite said. 'But mother and I live together still. We don't see many people.'

'You should go,' said Pauline. 'Mrs. Friend can't get about easily. Unfortunately, she suffers from dystrophy.'

What had Marguerite said? *I could be a lot older than you realise.*

Shadows beat with a malignant sound in my head. What was wrong with me?

Time: that was wrong. 'How long ago did your father die?' I asked.

'It seems an eternity.' She was deadly serious.

I thought of eternity, and I saw it in her

eyes. I caught a glimpse of stars wheeling in an ancient blackness, then I had to look away.

I saw the rainbow die away into a blue and white sky.

'Where do you live?' I asked Marguerite.

'Surely you remember, Di?'

'I must be going mad,' I said. Of course I knew where she lived. I'd seen a glimpse of dark panelling, heavy furniture with vividly painted panels, and the glitter of lights that wouldn't hold still and steady. 'I can't seem to remember the simplest things now, Marguerite. Of course I know where you live. I was there the other evening. The house is called — '

' — The Red House. Yes, Di.'

In Old Campsall Lane. I shook my head to clear the muzziness. 'Would this evening be all right?'

'Yes, come this evening, Di. Mother will be so pleased to have company. She's been alone too long.'

'Well, that's fixed,' said Pauline. 'Back to work for all of us now.'

I looked back as Marguerite went into the day-lounge. Mrs. Peters followed her with a blind look on her faded old face. Then Marguerite saw me looking and I knew what I had been shown. It was the power of evil. That was what Marguerite Friend had shown me.

When Pauline and I got back to the office, she said, 'Take those days off we were talking about, Di. If you leave at lunchtime on Friday and don't bother to come in on Monday morning, it'll give you a goodish break. You've done a lot of extra hours lately. Go to the coast.'

With Phil, I thought. But that wouldn't happen.

'She's won, hasn't she?' I said.

'Sorry, Di,' said Pauline. 'I've got work to do.'

I knew Phil wouldn't want to see me that evening, but I rang him out of habit.

'Are you coming round to the flat later?' I said.

'I wasn't expecting to get away, no,' he told me.

'What were you expecting to do? And who with?'

He must have detected the desolation in my heart. I think he still cared for me a little. At least I like to think so. He sounded embarrassed about it, but he said he'd try to call in late. The bugs had to be seen to, he said.

'When you've tucked all the little bugs in,' I said. 'Please, Phil?'

'I have to be careful at this stage,' he said. 'They kill in minutes.'

'Don't bring any home with you.'

There was a longish silence, then: 'I'll see you later.'

'Yes, please.' I despised myself for pleading, then I said I'd work something out. I was, after all, a trained social worker so I should be able to work out my personal relationships. As I made my calls during the later part of the afternoon, I kept visualising little scenes where Phil and I talked things out and restored our trust in one another. He would be calm and reasonable when I told him about my jealousies and fears, and he'd smile at all the absurd things that troubled me: Christ, the way we deceive ourselves! I made up one little play after another, and I took some comfort from them.

It wasn't a bad afternoon, and I'm pleased when I look back at it. It held no major triumphs, but it wasn't an unhappy afternoon. One of my bad girls had found a job and her mother thought she'd hold on to it. I also found a home for the disruptive youth who had been referred to me when the Vardy case came up. I'd remembered an oldish couple who ran a smallholding and who'd asked to be foster-parents. The strong, surly youth would suit them.

So, I'd done my job and I was content. I went home and swallowed a Multival. When I was asked later about my actions on that day, I was able to recall them easily enough up to this point. I went home, drugged myself with one Multival, added a third of a tumbler of whisky, which I filled to the rim with water; and I may have taken another Multival after that, I'm not sure. The total could easily have been three or four, so that when it was suggested to me that such a large intake of powerful drugs could have caused a considerable distortion of reality, I had to agree.

I was bombed out of my mind.

So, I was asked patiently, couldn't it all have been a hallucination?

The answer is no.

What happened that evening wasn't a hallucination. All right, I was distraught, I was drunk, I was hopped up and my hormones were playing up too, but half my female acquaintances are in much the same condition for most of the time. It happened the way I told it later. I did go into the house, and inside it wasn't our place or time, no way. And I did see the woman who called herself Marguerite's mother.

I saw these things. I did.

9

The rain was back as I drove down Old Campsall Lane, and it was dusk. It should have been gloomy, but I couldn't feel depressed. I hummed a tune as I drove, one that Phil liked. I turned into the dirt track and thought of Phil making jokes the last time we'd been along the track.

The cows in the field stared at me. Their flanks glistened with rain. I shivered then.

The house was as I remembered it except, of course, for the rain. Water streaked the brickwork where the gutters leaked, and I noticed that the rain of the past few weeks had put another three or four inches on the couch grass. There weren't many flowers showing out of the grey dankness. And still I couldn't feel gloomy, even though the house was a depressing sight, lonely and neglected-looking in its overgrown gardens. I was almost light-hearted, and the reason was that I was going to meet Marguerite's mother.

There was a curious doorknocker made of a dull-grey metal. I reached for it, then saw two eyes staring from a moulded head on the striker. When I looked closer, I saw that the thing was in a familiar shape, a stylised scorpion, and that it had a curled tail ready to sting. When I touched it I found it to be needle-sharp. I was still staring at the venomous metal beast when the heavy door swung open on oiled hinges.

Marguerite smiled at me. 'How nice to see you, Di! Why, what's the matter?'

'Nothing.' I indicated the scorpion. 'It's sharp.'

There was a similar symbol on the heavy golden chain at her neck, another little beast with its glittering tail curled ready to strike.

'I'll get you a plaster, Di.'

'No.' I sucked the blood. 'It's nothing. 'Am I late?'

I was very anxious not to be late, and I had another cause for anxiety. I should have brought a gift.'

'Come in, Di. No, we weren't expecting you until now.'

'I'm afraid I didn't bring your mother anything. I meant to bring her a present. You know how it is with older people, Marguerite?'

'Don't give it another thought. Do come in, Di,' she said again, for I hesitated, I don't know why. 'How do you like the house?'

I had seen it before. I looked at the dark, panelled walls, and I remembered the grain of the rich, dark wood, and the intricate arrangement of small panels. And there was the wall hung with a glowing tapestry that filled the sombre hall with reds and golds. It showed a hunting scene: a magnificent stag scrambled up a river bank as lean dogs bayed and yelled in frozen excitement, urged on by courtiers who waved their plumed hats and whipped on tired horses, for this was the moment of triumph, the kill. And the tapestry had the unmistakable sheen of new and freshly-worked silks.

'The tapestry is magnificent,' I said. I wanted to add an oblique question about its age, on the lines of I didn't think they made hangings like that any more, but I couldn't. My will had collapsed, and I could not find the resolution to resist Marguerite Friend.

She didn't answer my comment, and I felt the need to placate her.

I complimented her on its richness. 'It must have cost a fortune,' I said.

'It did. But then we could afford it.'

'Could afford it?'

'We could afford anything we wanted.'

I looked past Marguerite and for the first time I noticed that the wide curving stairs were lit by a soft and yellow light that shifted subtly and gave an alien and unreal quality to the scene. There were traces of odours that disturbed me, a hint of henbane, and musky perfumes. The hall and the stairs were too large, and the furniture and hangings would have graced a palace. And the light was candlelight.

I looked up. 'I've never seen a candelabra in use before,' I said. It was gold, with cut-glass pendants that winked and shivered in a million diamond flashes.

Marguerite smiled. 'No, I don't suppose you have.'

Marguerite's eyes held me, the strange irises spinning slowly, so that I felt myself to be unreal too, an intruder in this gorgeous place.

'This should be The Red House,' I heard myself saying. 'It isn't though, is it?'

'We've made some changes, Di. Mother and I, that is.'

'I thought someone else lived here, not your mother.' I could hear myself talking, and I could hear the fear and wonder in my voice, but it seemed that it wasn't me at all. I felt sorry for poor Di Knightson. How had she got herself into this mess?

'It's time to meet my mother, Di,' the exquisite and baleful creature said.

'Who *are* you, Marguerite?' I heard myself say.

Marguerite had her hand on my arm, and suddenly I panicked, for the hand that rested on my sleeve seemed momentarily to become not that of a young girl, but a withered claw-like thing of bare bone and decayed flesh. I gagged, and then the eerie smell of musk and henbane and hellebore choked me and I tried to move away.

'Come this way!' she grated.

'Marguerite, who *are* you!'

I looked at her face and I saw the malice in the creature hidden behind the beautiful mask, and then I had to walk, I had no will of my own; I put my feet out and they led me to a closed door. We walked softly on a silken carpet with a pattern of lotus and acanthus leaves. Marguerite tapped on a lacquered and inlaid panel, but the hand was smooth, and white, and young again.

After a moment, she said, 'It's all right, we can go in.'

She opened the door and I gasped in sheer incredulity at what lay before me.

The room was huge, and it was ablaze with gold.

Mirrors flung back the yellow light of a thousand candles, and all was gold, the mirrors in gold frames, the paintings in heavy, embossed gold frames, and the tiny figures in a stucco frieze were golden. Candles blazed in recesses, and the brackets that held them were caryatids with evil smiles on their gilded faces.

Every piece of furniture was magnificent, all of them designed to match the grandeur of the interior. There were tables, a writing desk: and a sumptuous bed, canopied in blue and gold damask, and none of the furniture was old, or antique, it was shining new.

My mind whirled, for the room was not a collection of museum pieces gathered to recreate a past splendour. Time was different here.

'Mother,' said Marguerite, and I was startled, for I had forgotten her. 'Mother, we have a visitor.'

There was a small movement in one of the chairs.

It was the kind of winged chair that is now called *en confessional*, I don't know why, but it had served to hide the presence of the woman.

'So this is your colleague, Marguerite,' she said.

I moved so that I could see her. She was old and frail and as beautiful as Marguerite, and I saw the serene face looking at me with an expression of infinite kindness. She was beautiful, as I've said, though her skin had the pallor of one who spends most of her time indoors. I looked from one to another, from mother to daughter, and I felt thrilled by their presence.

I was bewitched, I'm sure of it, but their spell was only partially effective. Reality kept breaking through. Though I could see the golden dress, the gold-shot silk of her high-heeled slippers, and the gold-flecked lace cap she wore, and marvel at the magnificence of her appearance, I could see beyond the apparent realities to something below the surface. Just as I had caught a glimpse of a grave-rotted hand on my arm. Outside this golden room, so now I saw a tiny vision of the old woman's face, a frightful and fortunately fleeting instant of time when I saw a skull flecked with shreds of withered flesh: it passed in less than a second, and the woman was transformed into a most beautiful and regal lady, but I had seen that moment of horror, and I was to remember it. Though what, I was to ask myself, was reality?

And just what *had* I seen?

'How sweet of you to come to see an old cripple!' the woman said, in a honeydew voice.

'Not at all,' I found myself saying, 'I so wanted to meet Marguerite's mother. We've become such good friends since she came to work in our team, and she's told me a good deal about you.'

'And I've heard about you, too, my dear.'

What could be pleasanter than this banal little exchange of civilities, I asked myself. Why should I have thought that Mrs. Friend was saying something quite different to the words I heard, and that these words were not in English, but French, and not uttered by a polite middle-class Englishwoman, but by a vicious coarse-featured slut who spoke in an argot that was barely understandable?

I speak French well, but I could only make out a word here and there, and what I seemed to be hearing made little sense. She seemed to be talking to both Marguerite and myself and it was all surface politeness — about the office, about the weather, about clothes — but occasionally I had the distinct impression that I was the subject of the two women's talk, and that there were bitter, mocking, and contemptuous remarks about me.

'I'm sure your friend would like some tea,' the older woman was saying. 'Will you order it, Marguerite?'

That's what I heard, though I could swear that there was something said about poison. *Poison*. And that Marguerite was chided by her mother. One set of words masked another.

'Yes, I'll have tea brought for all of us,' said Marguerite; but '*I'd like to see her biting her guts out*,' was what I also heard her say.

'Thank you, dear.' said Mrs. Friend. but I also heard her hiss a warning in that strangely accented French. Two sets of words were exchanged. I'm sure I heard both.

But how could this possibly be? Who *were* these women?

I examined the older woman more carefully than hitherto, because I was shocked into an unnaturally hypersensitive state where my whole energies were channelled into this question. *Who were they?* Malevolent daughter and evil mother.

She had the same overall physical characteristics as Marguerite. She was about the same height, but rather slighter of build; and she had the uncanny beauty that was Marguerite's including the wide, deep, secret eyes. But the skin of her neck was scarred.

At some time she had been burned. And her hands too. Neck and hands were a mass of scar tissue. She had suffered badly in the flames, and for a moment a vision of fire and acrid smoke filled me, and I could feel only an overwhelming sympathy with the poor victim, so I said,

'I wish I could be of more help, Miss Vardy. I know how you've suffered.'

Behind me, I heard Marguerite's hissing intake of breath. She said something in French, so I turned and said,

'Marguerite, I do wish you'd speak in English. I can't make out half you're saying!'

Amazingly, I didn't feel afraid of

Marguerite; I was so intent on offering help to her mother that I forgot my terror of her.

She reminded me.

'Mrs. Peters would understand,' she said, with a deadly softness that almost sent me reeling. Then the older woman grasped my arm.

'Marguerite!' The older woman's eyes blazed.

'She called you 'Miss Vardy'!' hissed Marguerite.

'Did I?' I said. 'How stupid of me — '

'Leave Mrs. Knightson with me,' interrupted Mrs. Friend. 'Leave us, Marguerite.'

Marguerite looked once more at me, and the hatred was gone from her face.

'Of course, Mother. By the way, her friends call Mrs. Knightson 'Di'.'

'It's for Diana,' I said.

'Then I'll call you Diana.'

Mother and daughter exchanged a look of understanding, then Marguerite left. From that brief glance I knew that I was amongst those who loathed me. The house and everyone in it were inimical to me, and I was in the most deadly danger. I knew it, but I wished the women to be my friends.

Examined in detail, long afterwards, it made a kind of macabre sense, but at the time I could not make any kind of sense of any of it. I knew, in one part of my poor, fragmented brain, that the woman before me should have been a Miss Vardy, and yet it seemed proper that Marguerite's mother should be where she was.

I knew too that both mother and daughter had spoken over me in an odd kind of French, and yet even this seemed to be far from unnatural. All I felt was a sense of melancholy, and a dreary awareness of death all around me. I sighed in misery.

'Be still,' ordered Mrs. Friend. 'Diana, keep quite still.'

I trembled, though I did as she ordered.

She put her thin, almost translucent hands over my eyes. I felt cold at first, and then the hands were pleasantly cool. Things seemed much simpler when she at last removed her hands; for a minute or two I stared into space at the gorgeous blues and golds of the room, and I wasn't Di Knightson at all, but an extension of the old woman's will.

All I knew was that she was my deadly enemy, but I must do what she said without question, without thought, even. I tried one last time, more out of habit than any reasoning ability, for I was, after all, a trained inquisitor.

'Who are you?' I said quietly. 'Please tell me.'

The scarred hands gripped one another convulsively.

'Why, my dear, I am Marguerite's old mother, and soon I shall give you some tea, and do you know what we'll do after that? Why, we'll look at the cards for you, that's what we'll do!'

'I don't think I want my fortune told,' I said.

'Oh, you do, Diana! Every young woman wants to know what will happen to her! You're no different from all the others I've read the cards for. I know about these things.'

Her eyes spun, and I could see a

glimpse of the evil in her.

'I've known about these things for a very long time,' she said softly.

I wanted to ask her how long a very long time was, but I believe now that I already knew. There had been sufficient clues for me. I looked at the burned hands, and then up at her face, and I couldn't ask my question.

'Sit there,' she told me, indicating a chair opposite the winged chair I had first seen her in. Between the two chairs was a small low table with a delicate green and blue marble surface. 'Tea,' she said. 'Diana, we shall have our tea.'

Someone stirred behind me.

'Your tea, Madame,' I heard, and I froze as I recognised the voice. I didn't turn. I couldn't face her.

'Put it on the table,' I heard Mrs. Friend say.

I had to move then, I could not bear the thought of the terrible girl near me. I got up and faced Elsie Thacker.

'Do sit down, Diana,' Mrs. Friend said in an iron voice.

I realised that Elsie Thacker wasn't

looking at me, but at the frail old woman, and the look she regarded her with was one of awe.

'Elsie?' I said. I was afraid of her, almost as much as I feared the women who dominated my soul.

'Hello, Mrs. Knightson,' she said. 'I brought the tea.' There was no hint of mockery, in fact her demeanour suggested an effort to be conciliatory, to make me feel at my ease.

'What are you doing here?' I said. It was the obvious question, and again it was force of habit that prompted it. Elsie looked for guidance to Mrs. Friend.

The old woman smiled at her. 'Tell Mrs. Knightson about your Community Services Project, Elsie,' she said encouragingly. 'I'm sure she's very interested to hear what you're doing.'

I fumbled for my wits. Community Services? Yes, I'd heard of the idea, of course I had. It was one of the current notions, that vandals and the like should make some kind of restitution for the damage they'd caused. But Elsie Thacker doing this kind of thing?

'It's like Mrs. Friend says,' Elsie told me, and it all sounded so bloody reasonable, so public-spirited, all so praiseworthy. 'It was Marguerite's idea. We were talking about it when we saw you the other night in town. Marguerite's got us kids on probation and in care, that kind of thing, to do voluntary work for old people. Mrs. Friend lets us come here, so we do jobs for her.'

'Do pour the tea, Elsie, then you can go,' said Mrs. Friend. 'Milk or lemon?' This was to me.

'Milk, please.'

'Thank you, Elsie,' said the old woman when Elsie had carefully poured out the tea. 'That's all for now.

I looked at the teacups and thought of the last time I had seen Elsie Thacker. The girl had altered. There was a quiet confidence about her that was different from the bitter arrogance she had previously shown; it was as though some great secret had been revealed to her, giving her more power than she had dreamed existed.

'Drink your tea, Diana,' said Mrs. Friend. She laughed coldly. 'It isn't poisoned, you know!'

That frightened me, as it was intended to frighten. Memories surged back, and I was in the blackness of my bedroom again, with the cold weight on my legs, and something silhouetted against the thin, pale moonlight.

'You sent it, didn't you?' I said, my breath coming fast and the words only half-formed. 'You sent it in the night! I know!'

She smiled, and I had another insight into the thing she was, or had been, for I distinctly saw the coarse features again, and the malice in them, all from another time, another age. In almost the same instant, she became a frail and beautiful old lady again though, a sweet old lady who smiled at me and reached to take my hand.

'It won't happen again, Diana,' she whispered.

I clutched at hope, for I knew I should lose my mind if the thing came to me again. I felt myself sliding down a frozen slope, at the bottom of which was only pain and misery and the darkness of the tomb.

'Nothing is going to harm you, Diana,' she said, and her eyes burned red, and I knew she owned me.

'Please don't send it to me. Please?' I whimpered.

I felt the injustice of it, like a child in the playground who stares hopelessly at his tormentors mutely asking for a reason for his misery.

'If you remember that moonlight is dangerous for you, and that questions should not be asked, Diana. If you remember, then you will not be harmed.'

'Thank you, Madame,' I said, choking with gratitude.

'Now you can drink your tea,' she said, and the black mood lifted and I looked round, blinking against the light.

And, after all, it was very good tea.

'Move the tray and bring the cards,' Mrs. Friend ordered briskly. 'I'm going to tell you your fortune, my dear!'

I found the cards where she pointed, on an ebony cabinet inlaid with painted panels. I gave them to her, and her fine, thin hands riffed through them professionally. The cards were much larger than any I had seen before.

'Shall we look into your future, Diana?' she said.

'Yes, please, Madame.' It seemed right to call her that now.

'Now,' she said. 'A guide for you.' Quickly she placed twenty or so cards in a circle, and the rest of the pack she put at its centre.

'Point to a card, Diana. Don't turn it over.'

The silken cards glistened in the candlelight. I hesitated, then I saw the picture on the back of the cards. There were figures in moonlight, indistinct, yet so well portrayed that they seemed to be in motion. Maybe it was the flickering of the candlelight, but I thought I saw figures of men and women half-hidden in a wood. I felt fearful, yet excited too. Mrs. Friend smiled at me when I touched one of the cards; she moved it next to the pack in the centre of the circle.

'There, my dear. You've chosen your guide, but we won't look at it yet; it isn't time.'

'No. Of course not.'

'Now. Let's find your card of Destiny.'
She made a larger circle around the first
one with the rest of the cards. 'Once
again, Diana. Choose a card.'

'This one,' I said.

She caught my hand. 'Blood?'

The little prick hadn't yet stopped
bleeding.

'It was the doorknocker. I'll bind it up.
It's nothing, Madame.'

'So, our little scorpion stung you,
Diana. But you're a Scorpio too, like
Marguerite.'

'Yes, Madame.'

She smiled evilly. 'You must beware of
Scorpios, Diana. Always remember.'

'I shall, Madame.'

'Now turn the card over. That one.'

I did so. Nine red swords blazed on a
white background.

'The Nine of Swords,' she said. 'That's
Death.'

'Death!'

'Death in your power, Diana — the
card gives you power over Destiny. You
can use it, my dear.'

My senses reeled, for there was a hint

of age-old decay and centuries of corruption, and I saw the corpse-face once more. A grating voice was asking me again and again,

'Who is your enemy, Diana? Who stands in your way? Who do you wish dead, my dear?'

I couldn't reply. She wasn't talking about cards and my future, she was talking about death. *Murder.*

I was being offered the opportunity to murder someone. It was grotesque. Diana Knightson, who had devoted her life to one of the caring professions, could kill. I was sure of it. The dreadful creature had that power. And yet, there was a sly thought somewhere in my mind that told me, yes, it would be easier for me if —

'A man!' the woman grated, laughing. 'You needn't be troubled by men. They're weak creatures. They die very easy, my dear! And he will, the one you wish dead.'

'I don't want anyone killed!' I said. 'Please, Madame, no more!'

She couldn't hear me. Her thoughts weren't on me and my pleas. She was in a trance, and I had no part in it.

My hands shook, and I couldn't look away from the bright red of the swords for long moments. I've had my fortune told before, by self-proclaimed experts and by amateurs, and none of them has stirred me into a shred of belief in their powers; this was different I knew if I expressed a murderous intent, then there would be a killing.

She slowly turned to me again, and the blindness went from her eyes.

'Go now,' she said.

'Yes, Madame.'

'And remember.'

She had no need to say more. The yellow light blazed suddenly and the room seemed to spin in a vortex of yellow and gold. Somehow I got to my feet, and keeping her in sight I staggered to the door.

It was open. So was the front door.

No one tried to impede my departure, and I thought for a moment that I should be able to run out into the night air and drive away without having any more to do with the weird creatures. But I had not finished yet.

'Di!' said the low, sweet malicious voice.

I turned.

Marguerite stood at the foot of the stairs, and with her were the same girls I had seen in the town centre. They were grinning at me. Elsie Thacker was no longer under the restraint of the older woman; she made an obscene gesture and bared her teeth. Jennie Webb giggled and thrust her tongue out, but she looked pathetic rather than malignant. The others grinned from hate-filled faces, yet Marguerite's steady gaze was worse than the adolescent anger of the others.

Her antipathy brushed against my soul.

She held me captive with that fearful gaze for a few moments. Then she said gently,

'You will remember what my mother told you?'

'Yes.'

'Worse things can happen, Di. Remember!' She nodded in dismissal.

'I will!' I sobbed, then I found I could run out into the rain towards my car.

The engine fired first time and as I

fumbled with the gears I tried to imagine that everything was back to normal, and that I could resume my busy, useful and satisfactory life, where it had left off before the Friends came into it. I wanted safety.

The rain slashed down, and I nearly spun the car off the dirt track in my hurry to be out into bright light and traffic and, above all, to have people around me.

By this time I was screaming.

I turned into Old Campsall Lane and got myself under control. I couldn't get to the Multivals in my handbag, but I forced myself to stop screaming with the promise of an extra jolt of drugs. I took a wrong turning, then I realised I'd been heading for the house Tony and I used to have.

'Stupid!' I said aloud. 'Phil will be — '

Waiting, I was going to tell myself. Good, safe, reliable Phil would be waiting, but he wouldn't, would he?

'No,' I told myself.

I'd have to settle for being alone.

10

I didn't notice that the lights were on in the flat, I simply headed for the spare bottle of Multivals in the bathroom. The two I had in my handbag weren't going to be enough.

I fumbled the top off and scooped water from the cold tap.

Someone touched my shoulder.

'Hi, Di,' Phil said.

'Don't do that!' I screamed. 'Don't ever creep up on me again!'

'You look like a half-drowned rat. Get that jacket off.'

I stared at him. I was trembling and shaking and couldn't speak yet. Everything was wrong again. Phil was here, Phil with the broad face and the kind eyes: he was here, in the flat.

My senses began to function. I could smell onions and bacon cooking; and cabbage. Phil was cooking. I looked at the pills in my hand and started to say something about them, but he hadn't noticed them.

I still couldn't believe Phil was here, and he was caring for me. And, for a little while longer, I was able to persuade myself that the ghastly incidents of the past weeks hadn't happened. I blinked and put the pills back in the bottle. He didn't seem to notice them.

'I wasn't sure you'd be here tonight,' I said uncertainly.

'But I told you I was coming. I left a message.' He looked puzzled. There was no guile in his clever brown eyes.

'A message?'

'Didn't you look in your message book?'

Unbelievably, I started to hope for belief in him. Women will hope and hope, even against direct and incontrovertible evidence to the contrary, that their lovers will be faithful. I hadn't looked in my message book. At least, I couldn't remember doing so.

'I'm sorry. Phil,' I said. 'I normally check.'

He came towards me and offered to

hold me, but I motioned him away. Unthinkingly I looked down at the pinprick where the scorpion had drawn blood. It hadn't healed, even then.

I busied myself putting a small jet of plastic skin on it. Phil watched without commenting.

'You haven't been here lately,' I said. 'Have you, Phil?' Butterflies raced around my stomach. I dearly wanted Phil to say something to reassure me.

He said the right things. How busy he'd been, how much he thought of me.

'You know I've been busy, Di! I've got to get the results on this strain — it's quite new. I can name it myself when I've finally proved it out as a new species. But it's got to be right, all the tests have to show that there isn't a family resemblance to another species.'

It made only the vaguest kind of sense to me. I was listening instead to the tone, trying to identify the truth behind the words.

'Half-right won't do, Di, not on this one. It's lethal. I've had to be there night and day, to make sure it doesn't change its form without leaving a record of the change. But I'd far rather spend my time checking your form, Di. I've missed your lovely body and as for canteen meals — hey, my cabbage!' He ran into the kitchen.

I began to believe it could be all right. Would he talk like that if he didn't want me? In the mirror I asked my white face if I believed him. I found myself saying no one could find me desirable. I looked closely and discovered wrinkles I hadn't noticed before. My eyes were muddy, and there were hollows on each side of my nose. I looked like a drug addict.

'Get out of those clothes!' Phil shouted from the kitchen.

'Yes, sir,' I called and I smiled at myself. I found hot towels and wrapped myself in them. Phil bounded into the bathroom.

'That's how I like my women. Warm and loosely wrapped.'

'Don't leave me,' I pleaded quietly.

'Got to get back to my cabbage,' he grinned.

I changed into a bathrobe and followed

him into the kitchen.

'We'll eat here,' Phil said. 'How about a lager with the meal?'

'You won't leave me, will you?'

'Not for all the bugs in Madagascar!' It was all right. He loved me. Everything could be explained. I was sure of it.

I popped the rings of two cans of Heineken and handed him one. It felt like a new beginning for the two of us. Phil's face was red from the steam in the kitchen and his laughter as we drank the beer and ate the meal he'd prepared.

'It's delicious, Phil. It really is.'

Phil laughed. 'There are two things I can do well for you, Di Knightson. One is to feed you with my delicious fried cabbage.'

What a fool I had been! I laughed aloud at myself and my imaginings.

'I had the weirdest experience today, Phil. I acted like a complete idiot. I don't know why — everything was perfectly normal, but it seemed to be odd at the time.'

'I expect you've had a hard day, Di. It's not an easy job.'

I had to tell him. It came out with a rush.

'I mean, I thought I was in a room that couldn't exist outside a museum. It was like being at one of the grand houses like Hampton Court Palace, but it was all *new*. It didn't seem old at all. I must have been imagining things.'

Phil got two more lagers. 'Come on, love. Have another. You need one after that cabbage.'

I looked at his face and he looked back at me with his especial considerate smile, a little weary and indulgent, and full of good nature. Or was there a hint of calculation there?

Deliberately, I said, 'It was at the house we went to.'

He couldn't look at me. 'Forget it, Di. You've had a bad day.'

'It was down Old Campsall Lane. The turn-off down the dirt track. You were with me four weeks ago. It was a Tuesday.'

He drank some of his lager.

'I'd picked up a couple of referrals at the office, late. You were there. It was about — '

Who?

'You must have got it mixed up, Di.' But I hadn't. I could remember back to that early evening and see the house again with its mellow red brick and the flowers lost in the long grass.

'I'm sure it was that Tuesday. We had a couple of drinks at the Bell afterwards. You must remember, please, Phil!'

'Di, your memory is like a sieve at times,' he chided. 'I have a regular game of squash on Tuesdays with Charlie Gurr, then a few drinks. It's about the only relaxation I get from the bugs. Surely you know about it, Di?'

More to try to convince myself than him, I said.

'One of the referrals wasn't much, I remember sorting it out quite soon afterwards, but the other puzzled me. It was an old lady who hadn't been seen for a while — '

He was shaking his head.

'It was! Her name was Vardy — Miss Vardy!'

Phil got up and held my arm firmly. 'Let's drop work for tonight, Di. I think

150

you've been under a strain and thinking about it's making you feel worse. Let's go to bed, Di.'

'Don't you remember me saying she was called Vardy?'

'Bed, Di.'

I gave in. 'All right, Phil.' Either he was lying, or I was mad. If he was lying, I had nothing to live for. I was desperately tired, so I preferred to think I was going mad. Or rather that I was about to undergo a nervous breakdown.

'Stop worrying,' Phil said, as we retired.

I wasn't worried, I was scared, and scared to the depths of my soul.

'Don't,' I told Phil when he wanted to make love to me.

He seemed relieved to hear it. He grunted a few times and then turned on his side away from me. I couldn't summon up the illusion of happiness, and I didn't get any comfort from his presence in my bed. At least, though, I didn't stay awake long, and there were no nightmares.

I slept very deeply for a long time. It

was the sound of Phil's voice that drew me from sleep. I told him to shut up, but he didn't so I reached out for him. And, of course, he wasn't there.

I could hear the murmur of his voice, and at first I thought I was still asleep and dreaming. The voice went on with an insistent tone; evidently he hadn't realised how thin the walls of the flat were. Or was he utterly contemptuous of me by now?

The bedroom door was ajar. It was a mistake on Phil's part, for it meant I could see a part of his face by merely moving over to his side of the bed. I knew by his expression that he was talking about me. He looked furtive and spiteful as he spoke into the receiver, and he was talking in a very low voice.

He should have known he would awaken me. He should have known that distraught women are hypersensitive in their vision and hearing.

'Yes. She's asleep,' he said insistently. 'She's snoring like a pig.'

A pig. That was me.

I could supply the questions at the other end of the phone. It was clear enough who he was talking to.

Marguerite.

'She did,' Phil said, after a while. 'Yes. Yes. I kept having to head her off from it, but she wanted to talk about it.'

I'd wanted to talk about the evening's visit. Of course.

'Yes, she'd got the address right. And the name. Vardy.' Phil glanced towards me, but I was in darkness. He looked angry.

He listened again, and his smile was unpleasant.

'Of course she's asleep. The amount of dope in her blood would keep a U.S. Marine down.'

She must have ordered him to make sure, for he suddenly shouted: 'Di! You awake?'

Instead of answering I moaned contentedly. Phil turned away, but he had noticed that the door was open. He told her to wait, then he shut it. His words still came through the flimsy door clearly enough for me to make out what he was saying.

'But darling,' said Phil, as impatient

and as fawning as any love-sick youth, 'can't you make it sooner?'

He didn't like the answer. 'Why not?' he said sharply.

There was a considerable silence, and I could imagine the honey in her voice and the iron too. She knew how to handle Phil.

'Of course!' I heard him say. 'Just as you say, my dear.'

He hadn't once mentioned her name, but that didn't matter. I had identified my enemies, and I knew my aims.

I gloated when I thought of Phil's discomfiture. He wasn't having an easy time of it with Marguerite.

I wanted bad things to happen to him, though, and I revelled in the thought. I didn't swallow any more pills — I had a purpose, and women with a purpose don't willingly slide into the darkness, not voluntarily.

I had hatred to sustain me. Hatred cryatallised my fears. I could look at them and examine them almost with detachment; and to some extent being able to examine them lessened them too.

I knew my enemy, and I knew my aim. She called herself Marguerite Friend, and I would destroy her.

All that was left was to work out my strategy for her destruction.

Or so I told myself.

11

I kept looking at Phil as he was eating breakfast — I'd never noticed before that he didn't so much eat the food as dissect and ingest it.

Occasionally he would reach out and pat my arm or my hand. I had to tolerate his deceitful fondling of me. You see people in a new light when trust goes. His skin was coarse, and his beard had grey patches.

'Don't work too hard,' he told me when I was ready to go. 'I'll leave the flat tidy. 'Bye, Di,' he said, just as if he loved me.

My head crashed as the car door slammed so I kept to aspirin when I reached the office. It kept the pain down, and the muzziness slowly cleared. The long night's sleep had helped — oddly enough, it was the best stretch of sleep I'd had in weeks. It had given me a chance to put things into perspective.

There was no doubt that I had been

through a mystical experience. By some extra-sensory means, I had seen things that could not possibly exist. The furnishings and fittings belonged to a more elegant age; and the dimensions of the room and the hallway did not belong to The Red House. They couldn't have existed as I saw them.

It followed, therefore, that I'd undergone an illusionary experience, and the Friends, mother and daughter, were part of the same experience. So it was likely that the monstrous pair had worked on me to influence my perception of reality.

And it was clear that they would continue to hold me in their spell if they could. As for their reasons for influencing me, this was something that I dared not inquire into yet. It was sufficient that I had an immediate goal. My long-term strategy could wait.

For the moment, I would find what I could of the link between a redbrick house whose owner should have been a Miss Vardy, and the creatures who were known as the Friends. Full of hate — and determination — I entered the office.

But my confidence didn't last.

It wasn't quite half-past-eight, and there were no typists or clerks around yet; this was, of course, why I was in the office so early.

I riffled through the pile of referrals in my tray. To my dismay, I couldn't find what I was looking for. The referral for Miss Vardy, who lived in old Campsall lane.

I looked more carefully. The blue referral form should have been in the tray on my desk. I thought of the cards and the talk of death, and I shivered. Death, the old woman had whispered. Death and power.

I got panicky when the door opened and a couple of young clerks breezed in chatting about the disco and barbecue they were going to.

I decided to look in the files. It's our safeguard against any comeback from officious councillors, relatives, journalists, or liverish administrators, that we photocopy and date stamp the original referral and then keep the photocopy on file.

I looked in the files. The photocopy

wasn't there either.

I asked two of the clerks about it, but they didn't remember a Miss Vardy. I checked with more as they arrived, but again without any result. I insisted that one of them must have taken the call and made out the blue sheet. Vardy was an unusual name.

'Vardy,' I said to Maggie Henderson when she arrived. 'She was called Vardy.'

There was a look of pity in her face when she told me that if her clerks said they hadn't taken the referral, then they hadn't.

Pauline Hart came into the office as I was getting distraught. She listened to the tail-end of our conversation, then said:

'Lost something, Di?'

I laughed unconvincingly. 'Nothing serious. Just the Miss Vardy referral.'

She frowned. 'Vardy? The name doesn't ring any bells.'

'Look, Pauline,' I said, 'I saw the referral. It was there in my drawer. I saw the name and the address. Phil and I went out to see her.'

'And did you see her?'

159

'No. No, we didn't go into the garden.'

'Maybe you're thinking about someone else?' said Pauline. She was talking very quietly so that only myself, Maggie Henderson and Pauline were involved in the discussion.

Maggie waited, but when I didn't reply to Pauline, she said,

'Di, we're good at keeping records here. If there was a Miss Vardy, she'd be down on paper.'

'She's not just a paper person,' I said, shivering again. 'You can't make her a non-person. Can you?'

Pauline took my arm. 'Of course not, Di!'

'And she wasn't Miss Vardy,' I said, picking my way through my anguished doubts. Pauline had enough professional curiosity to want to find out what it was that troubled me.

'Then who was she, Di? I mean, if there wasn't a Miss Vardy, who did you go to see?'

I said the first thing that came into my head. 'Oh, some lost soul or other!'

Pauline looked anxious now. I could

160

tell what she was thinking, that Di Knightson was only hours away from the nice men in white coats and the helpful nurse with the needle. I had to be careful now.

'Pauline, I expect she's one of those poor lost souls like the old-age pensioners who got swallowed up when the computer went wrong last year — don't you remember, the files got wiped out and we lost all our records and had to chase them up again?'

'Oh yes,' she said. 'I'd forgotten.'

'But referrals don't go into the computer, Di,' said Maggie.

'Then I expect there's some other simple explanation,' I said firmly. 'Anyway, I'm going to forget it until I find the original. There's quite enough to keep me busy as it is.'

Maggie went away, but Pauline wasn't convinced.

'Don't get obsessed by this,' she told me. 'It could be just a slip of memory.'

I smelled danger. I didn't want Pauline consulting Marguerite Friend.

'Pauline, I've made a mistake. We all do

it, but that's an end to it. All right?'

She seemed satisfied. I had been a fool, I realised it now. Marguerite had her confidants at all levels in our department; I felt a chill on my neck.

Still Pauline stayed. 'Di, will you do me a favour?' she asked. 'Before you do anything chancey, call me. Will you?'

She was very sensitive to my moods, and she was offering to help me. But what could she do for me? Like the poor delinquent girls, like trembling Mrs. Peters, like everyone else around the hell-bitch, Pauline was bewitched by Marguerite Friend. No matter how much she might think she was helping me, she would deliver me to my enemies if I confided in her. Pauline could not accept that the Friends were involved in some diabolical plot against me, and against the others too. Nor could Pauline truly help me.

Sincere Marguerite Friend could encompass the total destruction of the original owner of The Red House — if she could make Miss Vardy disappear so that no trace of her remained — then what would happen to me if I were seen to be a danger to the Friends? At the very least, there would be a visit from the thing in the night. At worst, what?

No, I couldn't confide in Pauline Hart. I would have to work alone and in secret, and much more circumspectly.

'Now why should you think I'd consider doing anything I shouldn't?' I said, leering at Pauline. 'If I decide to elope with the Area Director, I'll send you a postcard, though, Pauline.'

Pauline nodded. She watched me walk away, smiling tightly to myself.

But mentally, I was squirming. I was thinking of flames, and something was writing in the fire.

12

Over the next few days, I tried to establish a pattern of normality. I saw to the welfare of my clients with exemplary efficiency and compassion, and I arrived at the office looking neat and calm. Fortunately Marguerite Friend didn't cross my path, otherwise I might have cracked.

As it was, I didn't make any attempt to investigate the disappearance of Miss Vardy. I was sure every last trace of the referral would have been removed from the office, and I hadn't yet summoned up the resolve to return to the neighbourhood of The Red House. But a new development strengthened my resolve.

Mrs. Peters died. I learned about it on Thursday afternoon.

All week I had masked my anxieties. Phil rang a couple of times in the evening, but I was sure it was on instructions from the hell-bitches who owned him. He would be making sure that I was at home and reasonably cowed, and unlikely to make indiscreet inquiries. From his tone and the probing questions it was obvious that he was simply checking up on me.

I made the right replies and he seemed satisfied with them. I was quite determined to keep away from Marguerite Friend.

I wanted to be away from her and her terrifying mother for a long period of time — their influence could only be diminished by days or weeks of separation from them. I didn't want their spinning eyes and their subtle, evil smiles on me; they could damage my will to the point where I believed they owned me, and their spell worked on me for days. When they were near, I trembled and obeyed.

So, if it was possible, I would do my work and keep Marguerite at a distance. I would recover my nerve. And, when I was ready, I would revisit The Red House.

The next time I visited The Red House I wanted to be certain as to how much was hallucination, and how much reality.

I couldn't trust memory, not now. I was

too far gone into my impending break-down. I knew the signs too well to place much reliance on recollected events. I delayed. I made excuses to myself.

The days passed, and I said, tomorrow, maybe tomorrow I'll go and buy a camera with the kind of lens that will adapt instantly to changes of light. Tomorrow I'll get a new tape for my little micro-recorder so I can keep a minute-by-minute recording of what I saw and heard. Then, on Thursday, I heard that Mrs. Peters was dead.

There was a message in my message-book: 'Ring The Meadows'.

'Di Knightson,' I said.

'Bill Pedley,' said the Warden. 'I thought I'd better speak to you myself. It's about Mrs. Peters.'

I knew she was dead from his tone. He would be thinking that all the social workers in the district would be putting in a claim for the vacant bed. He sounded rather defensive, and something else too: if anything, there was a hint of puzzle-ment in his voice. *Marguerite Friend*, I thought.

I felt a cold chill like frozen lightning. 'What happened?' I said.

'It was a virus infection. She went last night, I'm afraid.'

'She was very happy with you,' I managed to say. 'I know she could be difficult, but she was a sweet old thing.'

'That music of hers!'

I waited. There was something else he wanted to tell me. About Marguerite Friend?

'The doctor looked, in, so there won't be an inquest.'

It made things less complicated for me. 'Good.'

'Marguerite looked in, just before the old girl died.'

I thought of that exquisite harpie watching Mrs. Peters die and I was full of a violent anger. Rage shook me. No one but I knew it, but murder had been done.

'And did her visit comfort Mrs. Peters?' I said bitterly.

There was a pause. 'I can't say it did. Funny thing that. The old girl got a bit upset.'

I had been too cowardly to act. All

week I had built up my strength for the confrontation, hoarding it, but I had none to spare to save Mrs. Peters. I felt sickeningly ashamed of myself. The gentle old lady with the odd quirks of character had died in fear for her soul.

A gloating thing from nightmare had killed her.

'You still there, Di?' said the Warden of The Meadows.

'Yes. Did the doctor examine her?'

'Of course he did!'

Yes. They were punctilious in such matters. 'I was fond of her,' I said.

I don't think Bill Pedley had cared for her much. But she had been a source of great comfort to me during some of my bad times. In an oblique way she had said things that had made me able to face another day, another client, when I was especially low.

'There'll be a place,' said the Warden. I tried to sound grateful. He was offering me a bed for one of my old ladies.

'I've got just the client for you,' I told him. I had. She was a cheerful old cockney lady of ninety who couldn't quite cope with life alone any more. She'd cheer the place up.

'Oh — nearly forgot. Most important thing of all.' I felt my heart lurch. There was something odd about the death, after all. Marguerite was involved, I was certain of it. I panicked.

'I can't come to the funeral. I mean, she's not on my case-load — oh, Christ, she's dead anyway!'

Bill Pedley waited. 'One of the relatives wants you to get in touch,' he said at length. 'The son.'

So that was why he'd rung me. Normally, I'd not have been involved at all. A notification would have reached me in about a week's time, and that would have been that. But the special circumstance in the case was the son's request. Not Marguerite.

I sighed. 'What does he want?'

'I'm sorry, he didn't say. He left a telephone number and asked you to ring, if you could. He has an answering service, he told me to tell you.'

'He's abroad a lot,' I said, thinking aloud. 'Her son's not here in this country much. Mrs. Peters said so.'

'He called here this morning. I tried your office when he asked for you, but he couldn't wait. He fixed up the funeral.'

'Good.'

Things had to be organised. Bill Pedley would approve of a brisk approach.

'So you're sending me a Cockney, are you?'

'You'll like Mrs. Bartholomew.'

Mrs. Peters' epitaph was brief.

'I hope she doesn't play the piano.'

I wasn't going to ring Mrs. Peters' son. I had important things on my mind, and I sensed, in Bill Pedley's voice, a puzzlement that still had not been resolved by his conversation with me. The Warden of The Meadows was a shrewd and sensitive man, for all his apparent unconcern at Mrs. Peters' death.

He had sensed something puzzling in the son's attitude. I wasn't going to try to enlighten Bill Pedley by questioning the son; nor introducing a further complication into my life by having the son question me.

Like so much during that frightful

time, I was wrong about that too. I hadn't finished with the Peters family.

The next day I went to the office early. I think Pauline must have quietly put the word around that I was having a bad time and some of the other social workers must have passed the word on, for I got no irritating phone calls and the customary bitching and bawling around the office ceased. I heard from Phil in the afternoon. He was fishing again to check on my attitudes.

He suggested he come round, but I put him off and he seemed relieved. I'd told him I was repapering the lounge so we could have a party in the flat soon. I could imagine his guilty laughter as he told Marguerite what a fond idiot I was. It made me shudder when I thought of our intimacy now. I couldn't sleep with him again — there was no sadness any more, just a feeling of helpless detestation of him.

I completed my preparations that afternoon.

I bought a new tape for the office micro-recorder, then I drove out to a nearby town to buy a camera. I explained that I wanted to take pictures in unusual lighting conditions, which didn't suit the professional in the photographer. No, he said, not without flash; but when I said the cost didn't matter too much, he found me a German camera that might be suitable. It seemed easy enough to operate.

Action brought the illusion of progress.

I got back to my flat and ripped off some wallpaper in case Phil called unexpectedly. Then I tried out my new tape and my new camera.

The recorder was fine, but I'd have to get the photographs developed. I made sure, of course, that the new tape was of a different make from the office cassettes — I didn't want our typists accidentally typing up my report on my visit to The Red House.

The weekend passed. No one called in, and I didn't go out further than the corner shop for my Sunday newspaper. I slept a good deal, and I was thoroughly rested by Monday.

Jarvis Peters rang me at the office as

soon as I got in. 'Who?' I asked. Jarvis was an unusual first name.

'Peters,' he said. 'Jarvis Peters, Mrs. Knightson.' His voice was calm and deep.

Mrs. Peters had shown me a photograph of a young man looking athletic in some sort of outdoors clothing — skiing or climbing, something like that. She was very proud of him. I think she told me he had been married but it hadn't worked out.

'I'm sorry about your mother,' I said. 'It was very sudden.'

'Mrs. Knightson, I left a message for you. I asked if you'd call me. It's very important that I see you.'

Why was he worrying me? I wanted to forget about Mrs. Peters and concentrate on what was left. I wanted to wind myself up for my next visit to The Red House, and Jarvis Peters was distracting me.

'I can't really discuss clients, I'm afraid,' I said. 'It isn't Department policy.'

It was untrue. We could make our own rules up as we went along, so long as what we did was in our clients' best interests. And anyway my client was dead.

Pauline Hart naturally chose that moment to look in and chat to one of the assistants. She looked at me inquiringly. I smiled back and gave her a mock grimace.

'Did you hear what I said, Mrs. Knightson?' said the resonant voice, still calm, but with a depth of passion that set up echoes inside me.

'Of course, Mr. Peters.'

'I shall be able to get away from town tomorrow. For the funeral. Afterwards, will you meet me?'

And risk meeting Marguerite, who would surely be there?

'No!' I said firmly. 'I'm afraid I'm too busy at the moment — '

'I know what troubles you,' he said.

Pauline went away. I wanted to put the receiver down but I couldn't. If this man said he knew, then he *knew*.

I hesitated, uncertain. 'I'm afraid I don't understand.'

'My mother sent me a letter. She told me about you and the danger.'

'What danger?' I wasn't acting any more.

'My mother wrote to say she was afraid, and that you too were afraid.'

She had sensed their power, and she knew her own danger.

'Really, Mr. Peters, I don't want to seem impertinent, but — '

'It isn't over.'

Cold fingers traced ice patterns on my neck.

'Keep away from me,' I whispered.

'She said in her letter that the fires of Hell burned, and the fires were near her. And near you, Mrs. Knightson, you too.'

'Oh, Christ.'

'My mother was psychic. She would know her end was near.'

'I'll have to put the phone down.'

'I'm going to the funeral on Tuesday. It's at three in the afternoon. I know you won't be there, but may I call on you in the evening? There are things you should know.'

'No!'

'You having trouble, Di?' said Pauline at my elbow.

I could feel my skin prickling. 'No, no Pauline. Look, I can't possibly help you,

I'm afraid.' I searched desperately for some convincing phrase. 'Why don't you try a priest?'

'I have,' said Jarvis Peters, and I slammed the phone down hard.

'We get some weirdos,' I said.

Pauline made me a coffee. She didn't comment. I sat with my coffee thinking about the phone call. *Danger*, Mrs. Peters' son had said. He knew about the danger, and he knew it wasn't over.

I so much wanted to have someone tell me that I wasn't going mad, and that the things I had seen were real and manifest, and that I was truly the victim of a conspiracy, not a paranoid woman jilted by her man and seeking revenge on the new loved one.

Jarvis Peter's calm had given me a moment to look at myself and feel sorry for what I saw. Poor Diana, I wept silently.

Could I trust him?

No.

Trust happens deeply only once, and that was gone.

I threw myself into my work, and when

I went home I began filling in the minute cracks in the ceiling meticulously. I had chosen a wallpaper that was difficult to match, and I sanded down the painted doors and windows with exemplary patience. I made a dozen meals for the freezer, washed all the curtains, looked out all the junk for a jumble sale, and my time still hung leadenly on me.

I thought a good deal about where I should start in my investigation into the Friends. We've all watched TV movies: the techniques of detection are familiar to us all. I could have checked on things like the Land Registry, the rating office and the public utilities to establish who was the owner of The Red House; I know how to do such things anyway, without any help from TV. It's part of my job to know, those things and much more.

I knew, too, that if I did begin an investigation, I would leave a trail. Direct enquiries were out. I had decided to be a spy, and I revelled in the thought. I wanted to revisit The Red House. I wanted to be involved personally, I actually desired the kind of confrontation that had seemed impossible to be borne a week or so before.

Hate kept me glowing with life.

I easily avoided Jarvis Peters. He rang me at the office on Tuesday, but I shook my head when one of the assistants told me who was calling.

He was politely informed that I wasn't available.

'I'm seeing him soon,' I told the assistant. 'I just can't deal with him now. You know how it is.'

She did, she told me. But she looked puzzled. It must have been my smile, which was pasted on, and which was distorted by an occasional twitching.

I examined myself clinically that evening as Jarvis Peters rang the bell of my flat. I looked at my whey-coloured face and my dowdy hair. The bell rang insistently for five minutes, then a note appeared in the hall. I heard his heavy steps, then I was alone with my reflection.

Tears rolled down my face.

I let the note lie in the hall for a while, then I picked it up. He had written it at the door, so it was short, and scrawled:

'Please let me see you. We need to talk. My mother's letter explained a lot, but not all. I have things to do, but I'll be in touch soon. *Take great care, Mrs. Knightson.*'

The last was heavily underlined.

He signed it 'Jarvis Peters'.

'Good,' I said when I'd read it. I had easily avoided him, and I was glad of it. I don't know what kind of a fool I would have made of myself if someone had said just one or two kind and reassuring words: probably I'd have poured out the whole inconsequential and bizarre story, and convinced him that I was mad.

I was grateful that he had gone away without causing me any more strain.

On Wednesday I picked up the photographs I'd taken. Again I used the nearby market town where I'd bought the camera. The shopkeeper was quite complimentary about my efforts: the pictures I'd taken of the flat weren't at all bad, whilst the studies of night time street scenes were well composed. He recommended a slightly faster film, which I bought.

All I had to do was to return to The Red House. I had to go back. It was the centre of the enigma.

It held the creatures who had somehow supplanted a woman called Miss Vardy; it was the focal point for the strange group collected together by Marguerite Friend — the bad girls who weren't really bad, except for Elsie Thacker. The redbrick house in its overgrown gardens was the only solid fact I could come back to in my fearful imaginings.

All the rest was insubstantial: The Red House was solid and inarguable. I was ready to revisit it, but when?

The problem was solved for me by Pauline Hart's efficiency.

She had ensured that a notice of a meeting of the new Community Services Youth Group was included in our weekly information bulletin. Miss M. Friend was the organiser, so we were informed, and the meeting would be at her home. All those interested were invited to get in touch with her, though the meeting on Saturday, 3rd September, was for members.

This Saturday, I thought.

It was all arranged. I rang the remand home that had consented reluctantly to house Elsie Thacker, and learned that she had permission to stay overnight on Saturday at the home of the leader of a Community Services Youth Group: Marguerite. I didn't give my true name. I pretended to be a policewoman. The Matron sounded relieved to be rid of Elsie for at least one night.

The rest of the week passed in a haze of drugs. Phil rang a couple of times, and I reassured him. Yes, I was working hard on the redecorating. Yes, I was staying home at nights. No, I didn't suspect him of disloyalty: I nearly said, no, I'd rather you slept with the hell-bitch, but I bit the words back. I felt insanely pleased when Saturday dawned overcast, and I smiled when the rain came down.

I wanted a dark, misty night when I returned to see if I had been wrong about the house that contained that palatial other-worldly room of glass and gold.

13

I left my car a good distance away from the house. I didn't try to use the dirt track, in case one or other of the girls came late.

Instead I found a route through a jungle of undergrowth in a field beyond the rear of The Red House, where a lane led to a small development of small, cheap houses. I parked in the lane and negotiated the undergrowth.

I wore training shoes, left over from the days I jogged with Tony, and a dark anorak. I'd wound an old college scarf, guerilla-style, over my face, for I'd read somewhere that it's faces that can be seen in the dark. I felt foolish at my precautions, but I made them carefully nonetheless.

My camera was in a case slung over my back; the micro-recorder fitted into one of the pockets of the anorak. It wasn't full dark yet, that wouldn't come until well after nine o'clock, but the rain and the mist made visibility poor. I wouldn't be seen.

I reached the edge of the field. The traffic noises were muffled, and the street lights only a yellow glow through mist and trees. There were noises in the darkness.

A shrill cry immediately above me had me cringing in terror. It was a bat or a hunting night-bird, but my trembling limbs and shaking hands told me otherwise: I could see a reptilian shape in the darkness and feel the cold of the grave: and I could picture something moving in the weird silken pattern of the Tarot cards on the table in the room of glass and gold. I could hear other noises, too.

Past memories of horrors began to merge with the night-shapes. I held my breath for long moments, too frightened to breathe. My skin crawled.

A heavy black shape came out of the gloom, then it suddenly snorted violently and rushed away with a splash of hooves.

I remembered the cows.

Cows in the darkness, more afraid of me than I of them. Already I was confusing reality with fancy. I took the recorder out of my pocket.

'September 3rd,' I began, habit forcing me to be methodical. 'Nine-twelve p.m. I thought it was earlier, but I've just looked at my watch. I must have been standing here for nearly twenty minutes. I nearly turned back just now because I got jumpy. First it was a bat squeaking, or maybe an owl. I'm still in the field with the cows. One came near me just now. I wish I was back in the flat.'

But what for, I asked myself. The machine whirred on for a second or two until I remembered to switch it off. No, there was no reason to retreat now that I had come so far.

So I went on.

There was a wall between the field and the garden with thick clumps of thistles and nettles on the field side. My training shoes got soaked, so did my cord trousers; I scrambled over and found myself in more thick clumps of nettles. My hands began to sting.

I made my second recording.

'I'm in the kitchen garden at the back of the house. I can't hear anything from the house. There's a wall ahead with only one window. The window's the wrong height for either the first or the second storey. Maybe it's a staircase window.'

Don't speculate, I told myself. You'll need fixed points of reference. For instance, what's the time.

'Nine-twenty-one p.m.,' I said, adjusting my scarf as it began to slip off my head. 'I'm scared. I think they can sense me. No, they can't! I can't possibly be seen if I keep still. There's no light on me, and I'm not outlined against any light source. I can't be heard more than two or three yards away, and I'd know if anyone was near. I'm going to stand still for five minutes. There's bound to be some sign of movement, or some sound from the house.'

I thought: what if I were to be challenged?

Run. I'd simply run. Alone, afoot, and dressed as I was, they would be in no doubt about my reasons for being there.

Something rattled in the dead stalks under the nettles.

The rain came down steadily, sweeping through the thin material of the anorak. I heard a small squeaking noise, and I almost laughed aloud in relief

'I've just heard a hedgehog,' I said into the recorder. 'I've been here for five minutes now, and all I've heard is a hedgehog squeaking. I'm going round the corner of the house furthest away from Old Campsall Lane to see if there's a window I can look through.'

I trod on something soft. The recorder slipped from my pocket as I half-fell into soft, viscous dankness. I could smell rotting vegetation, and then I could distinguish another group of smells too.

I had smelled them before, on my previous visit to the house. I scrabbled around for the little recording machine, my hands shaking. It took me a minute or so to locate it.

When I managed to press the switch, I said,

'It's happening. I think the hell-bitches are getting to me. I can smell the incense.

It's coming from somewhere near. I know what it is, I've smelt it before, but it wasn't so strong then. There's something about it that makes me think of horrible things.'

I made sure the machine was recording and started again.

'I trod in some rotten vegetation just now, and there's no reason why I should be afraid of some rotting undergrowth. But I feel sick to my soul. It's the smell of the incense. It makes me feel putrid in my soul.'

I rewound and listened to the last few seconds of the tape. It sounded shaky and high-pitched.

'I said I felt a rottenness in my soul and I do. I don't know what my soul is except I've been told it's the immortal part of me that goes back to God when my time comes. That's where I feel imperilled, I think. The hell-bitches don't make me just doubt myself, they make me feel I'll go on forever with this knowledge of evil. I think they could kill me and destroy whatever comes after too. I think they can do that.'

My breathing was difficult, and tears joined the rain on my face.

'I'll go on with the recording whilst I can,' I whispered into the machine. 'Whilst I'm still in command of myself. I know I can smell rue and myrtle and henbane and that I can depend on my senses. I am still in possession of myself, though I am sure that they know of my presence. I can feel their influence all around me. They may not know I'm spying on them, but they know something threatens. But I'm going on, to find out what I can.'

I felt better when I'd said that. I moved along the wall with the rain now a steady downpour from the broken guttering.

There were two small windows a little further along the wall, both curtained, both in darkness. I listened at the glass. There was no sound. Far away, I heard the sudden shriek of brakes and then the sound of rubber trying to grip the wet road. There was no hollow bang, so the car must have negotiated the crisis.

Another sound hung in the wet air for a moment, and at first, I thought that this sound too was from the road. But there was a familiar and plaintive quality about it that I recognised as something distinct, but which as yet I couldn't identify.

It was something small, and afraid.

I switched on the recording machine.

'I heard a noise just now, after the brakes on the road. It came from somewhere near, and sounded like an animal in pain. I'm going along the wall to find where it came from. It's the first sound I've heard that might have come from within the house.'

I walked on, keeping the wall at arms' length until I came to a bay window. The window was curtained. I tried to remember whether the unreal room with the magnificent furniture and the glittering candelabras was on this side of the house.

I thought not though. There was no sound from the heavily curtained room, nor did any light show through the material.

I put my hand out to the window frame and felt the roughness of paintwork scarred by sun and frost over many years.

I had some idea of pushing the windows up, but the sash windows were too firmly locked to move. The windows hadn't been opened in years.

The sound I had heard had sounded like a whimper. Something helpless and frightened, crying for help.

I came around the edge of the bay window, and there was a little light from the roads. That was when I stumbled.

The recording machine flew away into the rain and clattered on paving stones with what sounded to me like a series of gun-salutes. I cursed my clumsiness, then I felt the pain begin in my leg, just above the ankle. I had kicked some sort of metal protrusion. It felt as though I had a cut.

Again I heard that tiny whispering sound, and now it was very close, mewing and faint, still insistent.

I couldn't go back, not now.

I moved forward cautiously, feeling on the ground for the elusive machine. The metal protrusion turned out to be part of a grating left loose by the side of a coal-chute. I remembered about these old houses; in the autumn, they could have twenty tons of coal delivered for the winter months.

I peered around the edge of the wide, stone-faced hatchway, and there was a faint light that dimmed and dipped and flared softly in the unmistakable unsteadiness of candlelight.

I leaned forward, peering into the rectangle of light.

What I saw made me forget the recorder and everything else I had planned.

They were all there, Marguerite, her mother, the girls, at least a dozen in all; some I knew, some I didn't. Dozens of candles flickered in iron brackets all around the walls. There was so much light I could make out the lines of the flagstones of the cellar floor, the intent expressions of the girls' faces, and the calm, serene, evil countenance of the woman they all watched, the creature who had erased Miss Vardy.

All eyes were on the slim figure of the older woman.

Marguerite stood beside her.

They were together in a star-shaped

figure, with the girls all around them. Thick smoke belched from earthenware pots at the points of the star: I could smell the rank stench of the herbs — hellebore, rosemary, myrtle and the rest.

I heard the strange, mewling cry again. It came from the centre of the pentagon, where the writhing smoke hung in the air concealing the source of the sound. I could see, though, some kind of dais made of stone.

Horror held me terrified, for I was waiting for the beautiful, evil face to turn slowly in my direction, and for the haunting eyes to seek out my hypnotised stare; then I knew the creature's eyes would slowly start to spin, and I should be fully in her power again. For they must sense my presence. They must!

They *must* have heard the clashing of the recorder on stone. They must by now have seen my shocked face.

And yet none turned their eyes upwards to where I crouched.

It came to me slowly that they wouldn't see me, not when I was in darkness and they were looking out of a lighted area. I could see them well enough, but my spying would not be known.

I crouched more comfortably in the cold and considered what I saw.

I was watching a scene of Satanism, there could be no mistake. I had seen a Sunday colour supplement a year or two back with a set-up very much like the one in the candle-lit cellar. The painted star was a pentacle, one of the most powerful symbols of the witches' cult. The herbs burned in order to drug the senses and repress inhibitions, but apart from the pentacle and the aromatic herbs, where were the other appurtenances of Satanism? For, apart from the stone dais, there was nothing else to be seen. Just a dais, like an altar.

And that was the centre of attention.

I jerked suddenly as the smoke cleared and I saw that the dais was draped in black. I didn't want to look then, not closely, for there was a subtle change in the attitudes and faces of the onlookers. I saw Elsie Thacker's thin face become contorted, a snarl on her thin lips. Her thin, strangler's hands writhed in front of her.

Marguerite moved forward slowly with a trance-like step. There was a fearful sense of anticipation about to be fulfilled. Only the flickering of the light and the thin writhing of smoke gave the scene movement.

Then Marguerite began to speak.

She looked around the circle of entranced girls with her glittering, spinning eyes, and I found myself imagining terrible things: there was fire and blood and a golden promise of power and a rage of lust in those overpowering eyes, and even though I blinked against its force I felt my mind succumbing.

She spoke in a low, soothing voice, but the sounds were not any I could recognise as speech. It was a chanted incantation with a musical lilt, dreamy and suggestive of marvellous things and the girls responded with half-sighs and ecstatic exhalations as if some adored lover held them.

'Stop it!' I wanted to yell. 'Get out of there!'

I was watching, God help me, a ritual as ancient as sin. And it was all for a purpose, but what *was* the purpose?

My question was soon answered.

There was something else in the cellar.

It was just darkness at first, around the old woman and the dais. It gathered slowly, a thick solid dark that cancelled the yellow light from the thick candles all around the room: it was an impossible kind of darkness, for darkness is relative to light, and nowhere in the cellar was there an absence of light. But this thick blackness writhed into existence, seeming to absorb the candlelight and muffle it wherever it spread.

My utter concentration was matched by the complete absorption of the other participants in the bizarre scene — for I was, in some small way, a participant myself, as well as an onlooker: if they had previously been utterly entranced by the Friends, the girls were now absorbed by them. They were possessed by the hell-bitches. They lived only for what they saw in the thick, bitter darkness. Agonisingly, I forced myself free.

195

I wanted to prove to myself that I was not one with them, that the Friends didn't hold my soul in their power too. My fingers scrabbled for the recorder, then I remembered it was somewhere along the wall or in the long grass; instead, my fingers found the strap of the camera case.

I had to be sure I had some record of it all: I had to be sure that this time I had seen it happening, for even as I jerked the camera from the case the smoke writhed around the figures of the hell-bitches, and the darkness above the dais, as both changed subtly and slowly. There was the beginning of a shape in the blackness, and the two women were wrong for our age and time.

I wasn't looking at *here* and *now*.

The cellar was too large, too clean and dry; the women who called themselves Friends wore magnificent clothes, and their jewelry glittered with the authentic dazzle of polished stones.

The hell-bitch and her daughter were things that had returned from a previous life — there is a name for such beings, but at the time I couldn't find it. And these creatures had called something else from the Pit to share their bizarre ceremony.

My hands froze on the metal of the camera.

I forced myself to act. The shutter clicked with the appalling crash of a gun-blast, so it seemed to me, but the tiny sound was swallowed up in the steady splashing of rain, so I jerked at the mechanism, sighting unsteadily in a series of palsied movements.

Then Marguerite moved.

It was very quickly done, so that afterwards it took me some time to sift my memories to establish just what was the sequence of events.

One moment the old woman was standing quite still, with Marguerite very tense beside her; and in the next moment, Marguerite had jerked at the centre of the blackness, to come away with a black velvet cloth that she flung aside.

There was her smooth, rapid flicking away of the cloth, and then the older woman, with the same deft, practised speed, had raised high a long, wickedly curved knife and brought it down somewhere in the unearthly dark.

Something screamed. Once, that was all.

The Friends had the look of ferocious beasts, and a huge sigh came from the watchers; but Elsie Thacker alone had the same expression as the Friends. She flung her head back and bayed aloud with a sound that was like that of a hunting animal.

Something else happened too.

My memory tells me it was a shadowy blackness that flickered into brief existence around the dais where the night-creature stood. It hovered, a huge rearing shape, utterly black — so black it was difficult to look at; it seemed to me that I could see the kind of empty darkness that had once existed before the Universe knew light.

If the mystics were right, and there was a Pit for such things, then I was looking at a creature from Hell.

And the Friends bowed to it in humble homage.

I knew I should do something.

I had watched the total and absolute corruption of the teenage girls in the cellar, and I felt ashamed by my inability to move a muscle. Rain hammered at my back. The wind had shifted and I was soaked to the skin.

The girls swayed and moaned, echoing the incantation begun by the Friends, and the noise became louder and more insistent as the great, rearing shape assumed a more definite form.

'Christ help us,' I whispered. I couldn't move.

The dreadful shape in the cellar had frozen my blood and held my brain in an icy grip. I couldn't stop the ceremony. What a fool I had been! How could one over-confident and neurotic social worker believe for one moment that she could defy the Friends?

But the blackness began to fade, and I made myself move. I slipped the camera, very slowly, into my anorak pocket and began to feel around in the slippery wetness for the micro-recorder. 'Make a record,' I whispered to myself. 'Say what happened. Say it did happen.'

I scrabbled in the wet grass, and my hands closed on something but it was a pebble, hard and cold.

I looked back into the cellar, and saw only a vague outline of the terrible shape. I could see clear through the blackness to the dais.

A dark redness curled from the black stone. I didn't allow myself to think of it.

Almost without volition, my hands closed on the plastic case of the recorder. It had been very close all the time, against the wall. I kept my eyes on the scene in the cellar and began talking, low and fast, into the machine.

'I saw them call it down,' I said. 'There was a bundle on the platform. It was in a black cloth, but underneath it was alive. There's something in the cellar, hidden by the darkness. It has a shape, like a person, someone huge. A man's shape. But it isn't a man, it's made of darkness. And there's blood on the platform after the hell-bitch struck with the knife.'

I was stunned by what I had said.

'I saw the blood,' I went on. 'Under the black cloth.'

The spool wound on with the tiniest of sounds.

I looked back into the cellar, and saw the dark around the dais slowly clearing, and then the dreadful incantation slowed and stopped.

Elsie Thacker howled into the flickering candlelight, then Marguerite Friend's voice added to the hoarse, impassioned call. Together they sent out a plea that was full of humility, yet with a strange demanding, yearning quality that sent tiny convulsions chasing through my body, until I too wanted what they wanted, the return of the *thing* they had called down.

There was a stirring in the group below me, and I knew what would happen next, for I was sure that my presence had become known to them.

Slowly, the old woman gradually turned her face upwards to the lights.

She looked blind and venomous. And she sensed that I was near. The others followed her gaze as her head turned slowly to where I knelt. Her eyes were hooded, like a snake's.

'She's looking for me,' I whispered.

There was a noise near me now, quite distinct. I could make out clearly the tread of careful, heavy steps on the cold, wet path.

I half-turned and saw a blackness against the sky.

'Jesus be with me,' I said quietly.

Instinctively I moved away from the threatening shape, even though it meant that I was nearer to the opening where the lights flickered and the deadly woman searched for me. A scream started in my throat.

It stopped, for I was suddenly pitching forward for a tiny moment of time, and then I was jerked back, a hand over my mouth suffocating me and another hand heaving me backwards and sideways until I felt myself pinned savagely to the wet ground. *Hands*, I thought.

'For the love of God, don't start to fight!' someone hissed at me. 'Don't struggle, don't yell out! Do you hear me, Mrs. Knightson?'

Mrs. Knightson?

I gagged against the hand, and my

fingers clawed at the man's wrist. He cursed violently and slapped me once, twice, across the face — not hard, but sharp, stinging blows that stunned me.

'Be still!' hissed the man. 'Don't fight me — I'm here to help you! I'm Peters, Jarvis Peters. I've come to get you away — now, will you stop fighting me!'

I made a mewling sound. He let me take a breath.

My brain wouldn't absorb the information he was trying to get through to me. I was full of confusion and horror.

'They'll hear,' he said quietly. 'They know they are watched.'

It penetrated my shattered senses.

'Can you keep quiet if I take my hand away?'

I mumbled that I could.

As he took his hand away I took deep gulps of the night air into my lungs.

I was two or three paces away from the opening into the candlelit cellar where the hell-bitches were gathering their satanic powers to find the one who had spied on them and, I was sure of it, aborted their ceremony. My presence had disturbed the balance of the psychic forces they had called up: and they sought me. And I had almost pitched forward into their midst.

I shuddered, but I kept silent.

Jarvis Peters half-supported me. There were sounds now from the cellar. Sharp voices called, others answered. A stream of vile abuse followed, and I heard the hell-bitches shout in that distinct patois I had heard before.

'Come with me,' said Jarvis Peters urgently.

I took his hand and followed gladly.

14

'How did you get here?' he asked, as he harried me along the dirt track. 'Car?'

'Yes.' I looked at him, but all I could make out was a square face below a balding head, and a heavy, muscular frame.

'Where is it?'

'Not far. Ten minutes' walk.' I looked at him more closely. 'You are her son, aren't you?'

'Of course!'

'They were real, weren't they? I didn't imagine it all?'

'I didn't see much, but they were there. We'll talk about it at my hotel. Hurry!'

He increased his pace so that I had to run to keep up with him. I accepted that if he saw a need to get away quickly he was right.

'I don't think I can drive,' I said when we reached the car, but he was already taking the keys from my hands. He pushed me into the seat as if I were a child, and I was content for him to treat me so.

As he drove us to his hotel I shivered and tried not to talk. I knew what it was like to be a client, after so many years of helping people face their problems. It didn't seem ironical, not then nor afterwards when we were at the hotel and I was sitting in a deep armchair drinking brandy and hot water.

At the hotel he was confident and decisive. 'Send some hot coffee, two large brandies and some hot water,' he told the receptionist. He didn't mention me, and the woman at the desk didn't question my presence, half-drowned and white-faced as I was.

'Get into the shower,' he told me. 'And be quick.' I didn't argue. He threw a woollen robe after me.

When I came out, he was in dry clothes, and I could see how impressive he was.

He didn't look particularly tall, though he was only a little under six feet, but he was squarely built, with thick stooping shoulders and a deep chest. He wasn't handsome, just well-proportioned. He looked as square and as solid as a forest oak.

'I've seen you before,' I said.

'Drink some coffee, then brandy, then finish the coffee.'

He looked at me without embarrassment, and a stray thought about the women he had known crossed my mind. Dear God, I thought, this is one complication I do not want. But he seemed to know what I was thinking.

'We've a lot to talk about,' he said. 'I brought you here because there are no bad associations for you. I thought you'd feel safer where you're not known.'

It was delicately put.

'All right. Let me tell you where I saw you. It's a few weeks ago. You were standing in the shopping centre outside our offices. You were standing in a pub doorway, and you were looking up at our windows.'

'I was passing through town,' he said, trying to remember. 'I got a taxi out to The Meadows — '

'She was staring down at you!' I remembered the look of venomous hatred on Marguerite's face as she stared down, and the blind fury when she turned away from the window. 'She knew you were there!'

'The Friend creature?'

'Marguerite,' I said. 'Yes!'

'Sit down.' He stared at me for a while. 'I remember now. I must have felt her presence — I remember looking up.' He shuddered. 'I felt something fearful. We sense things. You. Me. My mother. She was afraid, like you. Like me.'

'So you do know about the Friends?'

'I know what it is to be psychic. I know there are creatures that walk in the world, as the Friends walk. And I know they have no souls.'

'Oh, Christ,' I whispered. 'Christ help us.'

Jarvis Peters looked at me with his piercing gaze. For a moment I could see Mrs. Peters' eyes staring at and through me, as if she were reaching back into a long-lost time and seeing things that were dust for hundreds of years. He was her son, no doubt of it.

'Christ help us?' he said. 'I wonder if anything can help us against the revenants.'

'*Revenants?*' The word had a dreadful, foreboding sound.

'Those who return from the dead,' he translated sombrely.

'But how can they?'

Jarvis Peters shook his head. 'I don't know. But I intend to find out.'

'Why?'

'They killed my mother.'

I'd known it, of course. She was a threat to them in some way, so they had murdered her. They had the power, and they had offered to place it at my disposal.

'She wrote to warn me,' he went on, anger replacing the anguish in his face.

Jarvis Peters would not forget, nor could he forgive. In his enmity, he would be implacable. Nor would he forgive himself for ignoring the warning.

'You said she'd written in your note to me,' I said.

'Yes. You were in the flat when I left the

note, weren't you?'

'Yes.' Why lie, now?

He nodded. 'It doesn't matter now. It's too late to help my mother, and it's too late to keep you out of it.'

'It was always too late for that . . . ' I paused as I was struck by a thought. 'You could ask for a post-mortem,' I suggested. 'On Mrs. Peters.'

He shook his head. 'It would warn them. And do no good.'

'I did no good tonight.'

He smashed a big fist into his other hand, and I could see the rage building up in him.

'We don't know enough about them. They're full of power, yet they must have weaknesses — they can build up an organization, yet they need human help. If I could find what they are, how they can live, if it can be called living; how they can reach out and leech onto the minds and souls of ordinary human beings — '

If it could be done, I thought. If there was a way of searching into the past of these creatures, then it might be possible to stop them. I felt a sudden surge of hope. I was no longer on my own.

I watched him, a bitterly bewildered and powerful man. He was so full of rage and anguish that he couldn't frame his thoughts, so I said,

'And when you know what they are, then what?'

'I shall know their weakness.'

'And then what will you do?'

His eyes narrowed, and his face was a cruel mask. In a low, vibrant voice, he said: 'Why, destroy them.'

I finished the brandy slowly.

'May I read your mother's letter?' I asked. 'We've a lot to talk about.'

15

I got back to my flat three or four minutes before Phil let himself in. I had a drink in my hand. A large gin and tonic.

'No drugs, if you can help it,' Jarvis had told me.

I was mulling over the long, intense talk at the hotel. We trusted one another, and could rely on one another. I had only known him for a few hours, but I felt as though I had known him all my life. When we talked, the words flowed easily, and the ideas merged sharply, without unnecessary explanation.

I had known only a few people I could relate to in that way. Pauline Hart was one. Then there had been one young man when I was at college, just before my parents were killed in a plane crash. He hadn't realised that a human being could feel such powerful emotions.

I frightened him by my very joy in his presence, so he had found himself a dull, beautiful girl and married her, and I had grieved for years. Then, after some diversions, there was Tony, a vain but delightful man who eventually bored me. And then Phil, who hadn't bored me at all, but who had betrayed me.

And now there was Jarvis Peters.

'But no future,' I told myself when I let myself in the flat. I'm not going to start all those 'If only I'd met him befores', there's no point to it. You haven't got him, but he's with you. Let that be enough.

And I sloshed in the gin and tried not to think of a shape moving around under the black velvet of the cloth, and another spectral shape forming in the eerie flickering candlelight.

Because it had all tested out, what I had seen, what I had recorded on the tape-recorder, and what Jarvis Peters had seen at the end, just before he caught hold of me. Those things had happened: we knew it: and the Friends had sensed our presence. And that was why I was back in the flat.

'Try to continue your normal routines,'

Jarvis Peters had told me. 'Hold out for a few days, maybe a week, and we'll be ready. But it's desperately important that they don't think of you as a danger.'

It was a slow, dragging business, forcing myself to drive back, to garage the car and make my way up the stairs to the empty flat, but I had done it. Minutes ahead of Phil.

I heard the key slide into the lock, and I froze. The aromatic drink spilled over my jeans. I waited in silence as the door opened, and I felt relief when I saw who entered.

'Phil!' There was more warmth in my voice than I felt.

I had told Jarvis about him, naturally, and he had been incredulous at first. 'He could use you in that ghastly way, and pretend regard for you at the same time?'

I looked at Phil's anxious face as he gazed around the flat and almost felt sorry for him. Of course he had used me, but wasn't he himself used in the same way? If anything, his was the worse situation, for he was intimately entangled with the revenant herself, whereas I had suffered only at human hands.

Jarvis had given me back my self-esteem, I suddenly realised. If I could feel pity for Phil, then I was myself a complete person again.

'Been far tonight?' he said.

'Why do you ask, Phil?' I parried.

'Oh, I just wondered. I rang earlier.'

'No, you didn't,' I said. His face had betrayed him, as it always would. She had told him what to say, but he hadn't the guile to carry it through.

I could almost hear her voice as she explained what he had to do, for there could be no question but that she had sent him.

The Friends had sensed a presence, maybe they had even smelled me out, for witches had that power; Jarvis Peters had doubted that they would have been able to exert those powers when we were at The Red House, though, for the effort of conjuring up the creature from the Pit had fully occupied them.

'They're not as secure as they wish,' he had told me. 'Don't ask me how I know, I just *know*. They're only at the beginning of their reincarnation, if that's what it is — they're weak and maybe vulnerable, otherwise why should they seek to bring another dark force into existence? No, they may suspect that you were there, but they won't be sure.'

And they had sent Phil to check on me.

Go to the pale-haired woman, Marguerite would have ordered Phil. Tell her this — and I could see the sharp intelligence directing poor glamourised Phil Walsh — and tell her this, and watch carefully for her reactions. And look for this, and look for that.

And then there would be the steely command: '*Return at once to report!*'

Phil had the uncomfortable look of an automaton in someone else's body. His gaze searched my face, as instructed, and then his eyes roved about the flat.

No Phil, I thought. You won't see anything of my wet clothes, for they're locked away in the wardrobe of the spare bedroom. You'll see me, apparently calm enough, having one more drink than is good for me, and hanging on your every word in the hope that you'll stay the night; but you won't offer to stay, I know. You'll have to go back to the hell-bitch to report.

He looked at me with distaste.

'I did ring,' he said.

'Not my number, Phil.'

'But you have been out. I mean, your hair's damp.'

I'd just towelled it again. 'Are you jealous, Phil?' I laughed. 'I do wash my hair some nights, you know. And what is this anyway — questions when you come round once a month, and not that lately? You don't own me, Phil.'

'Feeling neglected?'

'No. Deserted.'

'Blame the bugs, Di.'

'All right, let's blame the bugs. But don't start behaving like a husband.'

He flushed angrily. 'We always got on well together, Di.'

'So we did.' I didn't want to reveal the extent of my detestation of him — tempered as it was with compassion, so I tried to ease the situation. 'Like a coffee, or a drink of something else, Phil?'

He remembered his instructions. She

would have told him to look around the flat, check the bedrooms and the bathroom, find any small change in my routine: Jarvis had warned me to expect Phil to be inquisitive, and to make an excuse to search the flat. I had offered him the excuse; and he took it.

'I'd like a coffee. Di — oh, by the way. I think I left my brown shoes in the bedroom. I'll have a look for them.'

He went to the bathroom too. By the time I'd made him coffee, he'd had a chance to take a quick survey of every room. He couldn't open the locked wardrobe, and anyway it was always kept locked; there was no reason for him to ask for the key. I had thought of everything.

I was warming some milk when I saw him with the new camera.

'New, Di?'

I'd left it on my briefcase, behind the sitting room door.

'Yes,' I said.

'Nice one.' He examined the camera closely, taking it out of its case to inspect the stops. 'You could have borrowed mine. It's at least as good as this.'

'I suppose so. Here's your coffee.'

'Thanks. Is the camera for something special?'

I should have hidden it. 'Keep everything normal,' Jarvis had told me. 'Don't answer questions too readily. Expect awkward questions, and try to give yourself time to answer them. I expect you know how to do it anyway.' I did.

'Just help yourself to the warm milk.' I said.

'How about the camera?'

'How about it?'

He was uneasy, but any offer of information from me would have been an over-ready explanation.

'Have you taken any pictures yet?'

Prying questions. Her questions. And his too. But then Phil was a trained inquirer. The beginnings of the confidence I had felt when Jarvis Peters and I searched out one another's strength began to diminish. Fear came to me again.

Her voice seemed to be present.

'*Be aware of small changes, Phil,*' she

would have murmured. '*Watch her eyes when you enter a room. She'll immediately look at whatever she's trying to conceal. You're so much cleverer than her, but you must watch!*'

'Pictures?' I answered. 'Yes, why?'

'Some in here?' He was examining the case now.

He looked at me sharply, his mind on his task. 'I'll get them developed for you.'

I laughed. 'No thanks.'

'I'll take the film.' He must have sensed my fear, for he opened the back of the camera case.

It was empty.

'I've had them developed,' I said.

He nodded. Jarvis Peters had been right. He had insisted on taking the film himself. 'There's mud on the camera case,' Phil said.

'I know. I'm careless.'

He looked around the flat again. Nothing had changed though.

'Did you find your brown shoes?' I asked.

'Oh. No, Di. I was mistaken.'

I yawned in his face.

He was eager to take the hint, as I had known he would be. 'Well, if you're tired, Di?'

'I could sleep for a week.'

'I should get back to my bugs.'

'They'll miss you when you've finished.'

I missed the edge in his voice when he answered. He said: 'I'll kill the cultures. I'll have to.'

He was sweating slightly, but at the time I took his unease for guilt over his treatment of me. I *was* tired, and it had been a very large glass of gin. 'One for the road?' I said.

'Why not?' he said coldly. We drank together in a mutually deceptive celebration of our dislike and distrust of one another.

'I wish you could stay,' I said. I wanted him gone. He scared me now, for I had glimpsed again a look of loathing in his gaze. I thought of him with Marguerite Friend, and my skin crawled.

He shook his head. 'I can't stay, Di. And I'm going to be busy for quite a while. I'll call you when I can.'

'I'm sorry about your shoes.'

'That's all right.'

He couldn't look me in the eyes. She would be cold, like a snake, I thought. Cold.

He went, and I breathed out and gulped air in for two or three minutes. Then I threw my drink down the sink. I rang Jarvis after waiting for fifteen minutes of the half-hour we'd agreed on.

'He's just gone,' I said. 'You were right, he looked all over the flat.'

'Poor devil,' said Jarvis Peters. 'Can you cope?'

Fragments of our talk drifted through my mind as I asked myself if I had the resilience to go back to the office and live out the lie, all the time knowing that Marguerite Friend would be watching me.

I made my mind up. 'Yes, Jarvis. I'll do what we said.'

'Good. I'll be in Paris on Monday.'

'You'll ring when you get back?'

'I'll call as soon as I find anything important. If anything happens your end call the Paris number I gave you. I'll ring within six hours.'

'Then I'll get some sleep,' I said.

'Yes. Goodnight, Diana.'

'Goodnight.'

I pictured the heavy features and drew comfort from the memory of his tired, intent gaze, and his calm, deep voice. I wished he was with me.

I'd learned quite a lot about him. He was in his late forties, and he'd known I'd want to know if he was married or not. With quiet tact he'd told me he was long since divorced from a woman he'd known all his life, and that their marriage was childless. There was no regular woman companion, he'd told me that too: Jarvis had pointed out that a deep commitment to a partner would be a handicap, placed as we were. The information he had volunteered surprised me.

'I wasn't educated, as obviously you were,' he'd said. 'I started work when I was sixteen, and I've never regretted it. I still ski a good deal, though not as much as I'd like. Otherwise, I take my exercise at a club, squash and swimming. I read a lot. I keep my friends, but they aren't many. I drink but don't smoke. I never gambled. I like women. I can be thoroughly charming when I wish, but I won't try to charm you, Diana. I'm telling you all this so you'll be able to assess me.'

'I know.'

And then he had changed the tenor of our talk, for by then I was relaxed.

That was when he'd let me read Mrs. Peters' letter. I could remember most of it hours later.

She'd started by saying that a great evil hung over her, and that she knew her death was near: and that it was inevitably so. There was no one she could turn to, and she'd accepted the fact. 'But, I'm old, and Diana's a young woman, so help her,' she had told her son. 'She's strong enough to resist, I'm not.'

She hadn't blamed anyone, she said, and then her letter rambled into memory. There was one especially telling phrase, though, that sent me shuddering back to the half-full gin bottle.

'The Scorpion woman is deadly,' she had written. 'She is strong at night, but she fears the heat of day. There is another with her, and she has been through the fires of Hell. Beyond the two of them is a greater danger, and that is the one Diana must beware. It is the worst evil. It is from the Old Darkness.'

There was only a last greeting afterwards. The phrasing reminded me of an archaic form of benediction I'd heard as a child: 'Go with God,' she had written.

It was a half-mystical letter that didn't answer any of our questions, apart from one to which we already guessed the answer: I suspected, and now we both knew, that Mrs. Peters had become a danger to the Friends.

Marguerite must have suspected that Mrs. Peters was slipping from her control. There had been no one to help her. And yet she could somehow gather the strength to leave a warning for me. I looked down at the gin in fierce self-disgust.

I threw the drink away and tried to compose my thoughts for sleep, but eventually I took a Multival.

Whilst I was dozing, a picture formed again of Jarvis Peters' powerful frame. I could see how he would seize on a problem and worry and tear at it until he found the answer he was looking for.

'How did you find where the Friends lived?' I had asked.

'I know how to do those things,' he had told me. 'Money and patience. Some deceit too. But knowledge is the main thing, and how to use it. Most people are willing to part with information, and the Friends left traces.'

That was why he was going to Paris, for it all centred on Paris. Tendrils of phrases floated through my mind. There was a half-mocking, half-salacious, echo of Marguerite Friend saying, 'The really interesting things happened when the court was at Versailles.' Versailles, I thought. Yes, Paris again.

I heard an echo as the Multival drenched my brain with chemicals. 'Tell me.' It was Marguerite's cold voice, and she was staring at Mrs. Peters with her evil eyes. '*Tell me what happened in Paris!*'

And for that they had killed her.

Against Jarvis' advice I reached for the

dulling little bombs. Anything was better than the voices in my head.

Jarvis was right, though. I went to sleep at last trying to remember something he had told me. It was important that I should make sure of something — something very ordinary.

The Multival spun its web and I forgot.

16

Saturday was frantic.

I'd completely forgotten that I was on standby duty until the first call, at nine. Thereafter, I had no rest for twelve hours. Children absconded, aged women threw out their life-long companions, irate constables told me to hurry over to collect infested vagrants. I spent the day in pacifying parents, policemen, wardens of various homes, and calming down our clients.

For periods as long as fifteen minutes at a time, I could forget the private torment I had endured.

I took an hour off during the evening, then I put the receiver back on the cradle, and the whole mad circus began again. It was time for the drunks to start abusing their co-habitees, for the druggies to wind themselves up when they hadn't the money for their fix, and for the neighbours to realise that the screaming

228

next door was a child in pain. I was a very busy social work lady.

Phil didn't ring.

I'd had all the lights on in the flat all night long, but, amazingly, I hadn't woken till that first phone call at nine. I'd actually slept through the night, lights and all. And nothing had disturbed me, except for the dreams. Slow, vivid scenes unwound themselves through the night, and I was both participant and spectator. I heard the crying of the thing they had killed, again and again.

'A small animal,' Jarvis Peters had told me. 'Some young creature. It's part of the cult of Satanism. They use the blood.' I seemed to be one of the Satanists in my dreams. All night long the screams had echoed through my nightmares. I hadn't woken once, thanks to the Swiss laboratories that manufactured Multival.

Saturday night was a continuation of the day's madness. Saturday merged into Sunday, and at nine on Sunday morning I'd completed my standby duty for a month or two. I couldn't rest — I was past tiredness so I went out and visited my regular clients until I was exhausted. Some were glad to see me. Others were surly.

But they relieved the strain of waiting. I slept on until about five on Monday morning, when the phone began to ring. I blinked against the glare of the lights. There was hardly a dim corner in the room; I'd made quite sure that there would be no lurking blackness anywhere if I could help it.

'Yes?' I said.

'Mrs. Knightson? Police, Mrs. Knightson. This is the Duty Officer, West Road.'

The voice was polite and official-sounding. Police?

'Mrs. Knightson, there's been an accident.'

Jarvis?

'Oh Christ!'

'One of our cars is standing by to pick you up.'

He'd taken care to cover his tracks — he'd told me he hadn't got through directly to any of the agencies that could tell him where Miss Vardy originated, or what had become of her. He'd been utterly discreet. *Not him*. Please.

'I'm afraid your husband has had an accident, Mrs. Knightson.'

'Tony?'

'A Mr. Anthony Paul Knightson of Eighteen Poplar Avenue — '

'That's where he lived. He is dead, isn't he?'

'It's very serious, yes, Mrs. Knightson.' They can't come out with it straight.

'All right. How did it happen?'

As he told me, I realised that I hadn't once thought of Phil. I'd got him out of my system at last. And Tony. I listened to the policeman for a while, then it hit me that I was responsible for Tony's death.

'An accident?' I interrupted, as the man was talking about the Alfa-Romeo that was Tony's latest virility symbol. 'But how could it be an accident?'

Professional caution stopped the flow of information. 'Sorry, Mrs. Knightson, what was that?'

Ideas rang through my half-drugged brain. Memories clamoured to be heard. '*You needn't be troubled by men.*' The voice rang around my head. '*They die very easy, my dear!*' she had said. And now she had killed him.

Of course. It was my reward.

Phil had reported that I had been docile. I was no danger to the Friends, and they had remembered their promise. My cooperation had been rewarded. By Tony's death.

'Mrs. Knightson?' said the policeman. 'It is Inspector Tomlinson, by the way. We have met before, and I do know the circumstances of your relationship with Mr. Knightson. So it isn't quite the usual report to the next-of-kin'

'Then why call me?'

'We tried to contact Mr. Knightson's immediate relatives without success, Mrs. Knightson. It seems his parents are out of the country on holiday.'

'And?'

'Well, legally, you are his next-of-kin.'

They wanted me to identify him.

'How did it happen?'

'I'd rather leave that for my Sergeant to tell you. If that's all right with you, Mrs. Knightson?'

'All right.'

'And will you be available to make the identification?'

'You can send the car as soon as you like.'

Poor Tony, I thought. Wiped out on another spree. Whose bed had he lain in until the early hours? He had lain in so many. I wondered who would weep for him. Some would, I knew; but I wouldn't.

The Sergeant told me about it on the way to the hospital mortuary. He had been dead on arrival, taken from the wreck of the Alfa on a country road.

I felt a deep anger after I had seen his body. The face of my husband wasn't marked, but he looked so weak and thin, almost like a boy. I felt a deep anger for a few moments, and it showed.

The policeman took it for a show of hostility and began excusing himself. He was halfway to saying that Tony had been drunk, but my tears stopped him. 'Don't,' I told him. 'Please don't say any more.'

It was certain that they had killed him. For all his womanising, Tony Knightson was a careful and excellent driver who never took excess alcohol when he was at the wheel. I pictured him flicking the over-powered sports car around the winding roads, delighting in his skill and singing at the top of his voice. How had they done it?

It came to me almost immediately. Marguerite Friend would have had no trouble in glamourising Tony Knightson. He was susceptible to nubile young women — it would have been intensely exciting for him to have a beautiful seventeen-year-old making herself available. And then?

The spinning eyes. A rearing, terrible vision. I could see Tony fling his arms up in horror.

Poor Tony. I felt sorry for his parents and at the same time I knew I couldn't possibly meet them when they got back from holiday; I couldn't endure the acrimonious debates about our married life. It was over long ago.

Tony and I had been finished for years, and I refused to have the Knightsons inflict their guilt feelings on me. I had enough problems with the living: myself and Jarvis Peters, and the girls who had become the slaves of the hell-bitches. The phone rang as I started off for work. I let it ring.

No doubt it was the first of numbers of callers anxious to hear what I had to say about Tony's death.

'I won't weep for him,' I told myself, but it was only then that I truly realised that Tony Knightson — the man who had been my husband for five years — was dead. That extraordinarily vital, handsome, charming and irresolute man was a corpse. I did weep then.

Marguerite was there. I'd expected it, so I was prepared to hide my feelings when I heard her call to me as I went into the office.

'Di! Oh, Mrs. Knightson, I'm so sorry!'

She looked stunningly beautiful. There was the faintest of pink shades in her creamy skin as she came over to greet me. She wore the oyster-white she favoured, another new outfit that clung to the curve of her breasts and followed the line of her slim waist and slender hips. I was always amazed at her beauty.

'I heard about your husband, Di,' she

said. There was a hooded look about her eyes. A remnant of mistrust hung there, in the secret depths. I shuddered, for I was bitterly afraid of her. Nevertheless I forced myself to be natural.

'How did you hear, Marguerite?'

Pauline came up behind us. 'It was on the local radio this morning,' she said. 'I picked Marguerite up early and we heard it on the news broadcast. I'm more sorry than I can say, Di.'

I mumbled something, then a quirk of uncharacteristic aggression made me speak out. I regretted the words instantly, but they were gone from me in a moment. In spite of Jarvis Peers' warning, I blurted out:

'Did you go out to the house, Pauline? Marguerite's house?'

Pauline looked at me curiously. It was, after all, a surprising thing to bring up after their commiserations.

'Why, yes, Di. I went out to pick up Elsie Thacker. Mrs. Friend let her stay over the weekend.'

Marguerite turned the full force of her gaze on me. There was an arrogance in her smile now. I quailed before her strange eyes, retreating into a nervous laugh and a half-smile, all placatory and pleading that I meant nothing, nothing at all by my inquiry.

'I was very interested in what Marguerite's doing,' I gabbled. 'I know she's working hard with the Youth Community Services scheme — it's just that lately I haven't been in touch with it. I wasn't meaning to pry.'

'Pry?' said Pauline, puzzled.

'There's no secret about the scheme, Di!' Marguerite laughed. 'You can come out to see us at any time — of course, you've met my mother, haven't you? She's marvellous with the girls. She's taught them quite a lot in a very short time.'

'Taught them . . . ' I began. Taught them *what*?

Pauline smiled. 'Mrs. Friend is very much one of the middle classes, though it's unfashionable to say so, Di. But she has got breeding — tact and social ease, and general lady-like behaviour. Marguerite's mother has been channelling their energies — you know, teaching them how to handle themselves.'

Teaching them. Yes, that's what the Friends had been doing. Jarvis and I had talked it over, but that particular idea hadn't occurred to either of us. Marguerite was mocking me to my face.

'I expect Mrs. Friend can tell them about so many things,' I said slowly. 'She's very old, and she's seen so much.'

I felt the scarred, veined hands on my face again.

And I was back in time, hearing the vicious baying of a crowd and the gasp of breath as someone close to me felt the fire: I saw the flames again, and I almost fainted.

'Di!' I heard Pauline calling. 'Di, are you all right?'

I was sitting on a chair by then.

The moment of psychic insight wouldn't leave me. I gripped the sides of the chair and saw the flames die away and a new, darker scene, swim into my vision. At the same time, Jarvis Peters was talking to me. The scene was the cellar of The Red House, and the eerie dark figure had taken shape: I saw the ring of girls, white-faced and fiercely exultant mouthing the words the old woman chanted.

'*It fits with the record you made,*' Jarvis was saying. '*All of it. I got the same kind of vibrations when I was at a distance from the house too. And I saw what you saw — the girls were in a trance, and they did know about the blood, just as you and I knew about it. They saw the little animal die, and they knew it was an essential part of the ceremony. But all the time I felt there was something missing. At first, I thought it was our presence that had interrupted the ritual, but now I think it was something else.*'

'Are you ill, Mrs. Knightson?' whispered Marguerite. 'Tell me what's wrong.'

'No!' I shouted. 'There's nothing wrong.'

'It's shock,' said Pauline quietly, so I wouldn't hear. 'I'll make her some coffee.'

'Is it shock?' whispered Marguerite. 'Was it such a shock to you that Mr. Knightson's car crashed?'

I couldn't open my eyes.

And yet I had to do something to take

the pictures away.

'Well, Diana?' whispered the evil voice. It sounded like the older woman, but that was impossible.

'I'm sorry,' I whispered. 'I shouldn't act like this. So much has happened.'

'Di?' said Pauline. 'Here's some coffee.'

'Thanks.' I watched her honest, concerned face.

'What else has happened?' said Pauline. 'I heard you just now. You just said 'So much has happened' to Marguerite.'

I shook my head. 'There have been so many things. I'm so confused.'

'Is there anything I can do?' said Marguerite, in her sweet Cadet's voice, not a diabolical whisper.

'You've done so much,' I said. 'You have, Marguerite.'

I shouldn't have said it; I shouldn't have launched into my questions about The Red House and the bad girls. Jarvis warned me especially about raising issues that would make Marguerite suspicious again, but Jarvis didn't know about the death of my husband. He couldn't know the strain I was under. With very little effort I could be back where I was before Jarvis Peters had entered my life, on the icy slopes of the precipice called insanity.

'Oh,' said Pauline. 'You mean the girls.' She spoke too loudly and too reassuringly.

The speculation about my impending crack-up was back in Pauline's sharp eyes. She was wondering if I was going to start in on about what she believed to be my obsession with the missing Miss Vardy. But I wasn't! Oh, no!

'I've had a lot of deaths to face lately,' I said bravely. 'I don't want any more tragedies.' I looked squarely at Marguerite with what I hoped was a look of honest bewilderment.

'I was very fond of Mrs. Peters. I suppose both Marguerite and I let ourselves get too close to her. And now, on top of that, there's poor Tony's car crash.

'Oh, it was a crash, Di?' said Pauline. 'Yes.'

I admired myself for my sang-froid then, if at no other time. By no flicker of an eyelash, by no slight loss of pace, did I

241

for one moment let Marguerite know that she had told me she was Tony's murderer.

'He was fond of cars,' I added.

But I was thinking of what Jarvis had said about the ritual. There was something important missing in it.

'I'll find it in Paris,' he had assured me. 'That's where it all leads back to, so that's where it must have begun.'

Something missing, I thought as Pauline sipped her coffee.

'They didn't mention the cause of the accident in the news,' she said.

'No.'

But Marguerite had known.

She waited politely for Pauline and I to finish our coffee, and all the time ideas slowly surged around in my drugged head, for I had taken to the pills again; I'd had to. The chemicals kept the edge of tension away. They dulled me, but they made life bearable for a few days, until Jarvis got in touch with me.

As he would.

I panicked every time I thought of him now. Suppose he didn't ring? Suppose he simply decided to cut his losses and take a three-month vacation until the Friends had completed their self-appointed task? Suppose some quite ordinary accident left him with a broken leg, or a cracked skull, in a provincial hospital in France?

Suppose the Friends had already found him?

Another murder wouldn't trouble them.

They were interested only in maintaining their powers, and in reinforcing them by some hellish means. It was then that I understood.

'I see,' I said aloud. It wasn't much of an exclamation, but Marguerite was alert for the surprise in my voice.

'Is something wrong, Di?' she said, bending over me.

No, Marguerite, I thought. For once, something is right. Things fall into place at times, and that's what's happened now. I've just understood why the girls were reciting their words

They do the same thing in all rituals.

Rehearse.

What Jarvis Peters and I had seen was a dress-rehearsal for the big night.

I almost laughed in her face, for the

drugs had done what my normally fairly keen brain couldn't: they had disoriented me to the point where I could see beyond the immediate world and look through time and place to another, more sinister, reality.

I'd have something to tell Jarvis when he called me.

'You've both been very kind,' I told Marguerite and Pauline. 'You've helped me so much. Especially you, Marguerite. But you've the knack of helping others, haven't you?'

Pauline smiled. She believed all I said. I think she was proud of me too for coming round to her way of thinking about her protégée.

'We'll miss Marguerite when her time's up here. Yes, Di, I think she's been good for all of us.'

Don't, I ordered myself. Don't be sarcastic and don't antagonise the hell-bitch. Keep a check on your words, restrain the impulse to challenge her in her moment of weakness: for I could see that Marguerite was puzzled by what I was saying. My praise of her to Pauline, and my sudden moment of awareness had thrown her off-balance. I desperately wanted to believe Jarvis when he said that the Friends could be destroyed. And, until that moment, I had thought of them as possessing omniscience as well as supreme power. But they didn't know everything.

They didn't know that I had worked out their plan for the bad girls. So keep your glee under control, I told myself.

'I think Marguerite's been one of the successes of the cadetship scheme,' I said firmly. 'I've no doubt that if she wants to continue in this line of work she'll be welcome anywhere.'

Marguerite's eyes were on me as I left to clear up some loose ends from the hectic weekend's standby. I was fairly sure, though, that I had said all the right things.

I didn't notice that I'd left the micro-recorder on the desk. The drugs made me over-confident and, hence, forgetful. I could rely on Jarvis, I told myself. He was wary and strong, and they could not harm him.

Together we would confound the enemy.

17

No nightmares came to bedevil me over the next few days. The days dragged by with no call from Jarvis. I endured them, staying away from my flat in the evenings for as long as I could and only returning when I was exhausted. I looked at the phone for hours, but I didn't get as far as calling the Paris number.

Jarvis had enough to do in Paris.

It seemed that the Friends were satisfied with my conduct, for Phil didn't trouble to call or phone again. Tuesday and Wednesday passed, and it wasn't until Thursday morning that Jarvis rang.

I'd just finished my breakfast. The noise of the phone made me start.

'Who?' I said in a strangulated whisper.

'Jarvis Peters. Is that you, Di?'

'Yes.'

'No one with you?'

'No.'

'What happened on Friday night?'

'Nothing! Phil looked everywhere and he tried to bluff me into saying I'd been out but he didn't know, he was guessing.'

'And you — you're all right?'

'Yes, I think so.'

'And the Friend creature — when you saw her?'

'I'm not sure.' I hesitated. 'On Monday I thought she was satisfied. Oh Christ, you don't know about Tony. He was killed in a car crash. And they did it, Jarvis, *they did it*! It was my reward!'

'I'm sorry,' he said quietly.

I pulled myself together. 'Tony's dead, and I can't grieve. Go on.'

'I've found out a good deal, but there's more yet. Di, I believe I know what they are — what they were.'

Momentarily the glass and gold room formed around me, and I saw the beautiful, evil face of the old woman as she smiled and cajoled and threatened.

'Well?' I said harshly.

'You've heard of Madame de Montespan.'

'She was the Sun-King's mistress,' I said slowly, remembering lessons from school. 'A great lady who bore children to

Louis the Fourteenth. She was a Duchesse of France and the most beautiful woman at the court of Versailles.'

I could see the fire and hear the baying of the crowd.

I didn't need the direct link of touch to make my way back in time.

'*He saw a witch burn*,' I whispered. 'She told me.'

'Di, listen! Madame de Montespan employed sorceresses.'

'Yes, Jarvis, I know. The Friends!'

There was a long pause. 'You know? All right, Di. I think I understand. Now listen. The older sorceress was condemned to death. She was the worst of the two. She was to burn.'

'Yes,' I whispered. 'Go on.'

'They didn't trouble to change their name — La Voisin!'

'Christ!'

I remembered a childhood lesson. '*Neighbour*' or '*friend*' — that was the meaning of '*voisin*'.

'She didn't burn,' I whispered. 'She was marked, but she didn't burn.'

'Some accounts say she was strangled

and thrown on the flames, but there's another version, that says she escaped with her daughter.'

'With Marguerite. And?'

'I have to check more sources. It hasn't been easy, because I didn't want to alarm them — I had to use intermediaries to contact a group of Satanists who knew of them. But the Satanists wouldn't help. It seems that they too were afraid of what was to happen.'

I was confused, but I remembered what Marguerite had said, and then what Pauline Hart had innocently referred to.

A rehearsal.

And the older woman channelling the energies of the girls. It added up to a monstrous act of evil.

'What is to happen?' I asked Jarvis.

He sounded tired. 'I can't say yet. It's tied up with the court at Versailles and a priest who was the leader of the cult there in the late seventeenth century. The la Voisins worked with him, but he was a far more powerful sorcerer. So far I have just a name — there's so little information about him that I'll have to risk searching the old records myself.'

'His name, Jarvis! What was he called?'

I could see the dais in the cellar where the darkness began to coalesce into a rearing *thing* that nevertheless had the general shape of a man.

'He was called the Abbé Guibourg. He was the most dangerous magician and Satanist of his time.'

'And?'

'He was executed. There's no question of it. The King ordered his death, and he was strangled before hundreds of witnesses.'

I knew then what the terrible ceremony in the cellar meant, or, rather, what it would lead to.

'I know what you're thinking,' he said, and I was startled into almost a feeling of comfort. 'There *is* a link between them. The la Voisins and Guibourg were disciples and master. When he was killed they promised he would return in a new and frightful form. But *how*! I've talked this over with one of the Roman Catholic Church's eminent authorities on Satanism and devil-worship and he can offer no

250

more help or guidance than to tell me to keep my distance from these representatives of the Anti-Christ! I know, and you know, that they are working for the rebirth of this monster — '

'Jarvis!' I interrupted him impatiently. 'Jarvis, they're working through the bad girls. They are.'

'Bad girls?' Jarvis repeated. 'Of course.' He sounded tired. 'Yes, they would be used at a ceremony of invocation.'

'More than that! They summoned up the monster — it almost worked when they were just rehearsing!'

'I didn't want to tell you this,' Jarvis Peters sighed. 'I wanted to keep the proof from you, but you've worked out what they were doing. You must have strong psychic powers, Di, stronger than mine, stronger even than my mother's. But you're right. There's proof.'

My mind raced, and knew what Jarvis would now tell me.

The photographs.

'In the photographs?' I said hoarsely.

'In one of them only. Blurred and fogged — if I wasn't looking for the shape, I'd not see it.'

'Shape?'

'A cowled monk.'

'Christ help us,' I said slowly.

'We have to help ourselves now,' Jarvis said. 'I have to follow up one more line of inquiry, maybe the most important of all, for it could lead to a knowledge of how to overcome these *revenants*.' He gave the word a peculiarly French intonation that made me shudder. 'I think one more day will be enough. I'll be back tomorrow, Di.'

'Don't let it be more. Please, Jarvis?'

'I promise.'

'All right. Take care.'

'And you, Di — be very careful yourself.'

'I'll keep away from the Friend creature.'

Jarvis hesitated. He was troubled for me, I sensed it.

'Jarvis? What is it?'

'I had your — I had Philip Walsh investigated.'

'And?'

'The la Voisins were poisoners. De

252

Montespan and hundreds of others used their services to kill their enemies.'

'And Phil — ' I remembered the curious look on Phil's face when he was at my flat last Friday night. He had been tense, fearful, and arrogant and unsure. I'd asked him about his work, those bugs we had once joked about. 'I'll kill the cultures,' he had told me. *I'll have to.*

The cultures. A deadly and as yet unidentified killer.

'Philip Walsh is working in a laboratory. His research is in isolating one of a group of dangerous pathogens found in Madagascar,' said Jarvis. 'It could be — '

'Yes,' I said. 'It could be. It probably is.'

'Take great care.'

Or Phil might kill me. Lethal, he'd said.

'Now, go to work and act as normal,' Jarvis went on. 'I'm sure I'm on the track of something of the utmost importance!'

'You will come?'

'Trust me.'

I put the phone down, and at once it began to ring again.

I looked at it in astonishment, as if it

were a snake about to strike.

I let it ring and ring. I was completely bewildered.

Phil a poisoner?

Unliving *things* battening onto the bodies and minds of ordinary men and women, here in England?

Jarvis Peters searching for a means to destroy the night-things that he called *revenants*?

Of course it was all a nightmare. I picked up the phone.

'Who is it?' I said firmly.

'Pauline Hart,' said Pauline just as firmly. 'Have you breakfasted?'

She sounded so normal. 'Yes,' I said.

'Get in your car and come to the office. You're late.'

We believe what we want to hear, we see what we wish to see, we change the order of things so that we can keep our little delusions alive.

I wanted everything to be normal.

So, when Pauline sounded brisk and cheerful and ordinary, I pushed the whole ghastly series of incidents into a mental cupboard, locked it and hurled the key into the well of memory.

'I'm on my way,' I said, like a lamb. 'Right now, Pauline!'

Like a lamb.

Not once did I consider asking why Pauline Hart wanted me at the office only about twenty minutes after our normal starting time.

18

'Busy weekend, Di?' said Pauline.

We were in her office. She'd waved to me as I got through the door. Everyone else looked busy.

'I earned my pay. But what's so important?' I asked. 'Why did you call me?'

My scalp prickled. There had been talk of me, and only recently. In this room. I looked around involuntarily to see if anyone was behind the door. I sensed danger.

'I wanted you in to see about this report, Di.' Pauline said

She handed over a transcript. We use a standard form for our reports on clients. This was a photocopy of an original.

'The client isn't named, Di.' She tried to sound brisk and professional, but I could see the compassion behind the mask. 'I'm not sure what kind of inquiry it is, Di, though I expect it means something to you. We didn't quite know what to do with it. Where to file it, for instance.'

I shivered as I realised what I had done. Danger pressed all around me.

'I see it was the Friday before last,' Pauline said.

'Yes.'

'*September 3rd,*' I read, not aloud, but in the private echoing hell inside. '*Nine-twelve p.m. I thought it was earlier.*'

'Di?' said Pauline.

'Oh Christ,' I whispered to her.

'Sit down, Di,' she ordered.

'*I'm scared,*' I read. '*I think they can sense me.*'

'What's this about, Di?'

'I'm scared. I think they can sense me,' I whispered.

I flicked the pages whilst Pauline smiled at me nervously.

'*It's happening,*' I heard myself saying into the micro-recorder, and I could feel the chill of the rain and smell the sickening smoke from the open grating. '*I think the hell-bitches are getting to me.*'

'Maybe I shouldn't have brought it up just now,' Pauline said, and she was nervous. The politeness was gone, and I was a client, not a colleague and friend. 'Di, it's a very odd kind of report. It reads very much like a hallucinatory experience.'

I looked at her. My memory prompted me: I didn't quite know what I was saying. The words formed themselves, and it was only long afterwards that I knew I was quoting from the words I had recorded on that cold night.

'I don't know what my soul is except that I feel imperilled there. The hell-bitches don't make me just doubt myself, they make me feel I'll go on forever with this knowledge of evil. I think they could kill me and destroy whatever comes after that. I think they can do that, Pauline.'

Pauline snatched the sheets away.

'I'm a silly cow. I should have realised. Phil Walsh said you were unsteady, I should have known! I know Tony didn't mean much to you, but a sudden death has to be a frightful shock — I know you're working out your grief, and it's taken a strange form. It's made you doubt yourself and everyone around you!'

'Everyone? Like who?'

She didn't want to tell me.

'We'll put the report away. It hasn't got a name, and maybe you weren't thinking too clearly when you dictated the reports anyway. Look, I'll destroy it.'

She ripped it clean across.

I watched her, and even then I caught a phrase from that night: '*I am still in possession of myself,*' someone had typed, '*though I am sure that they know of my presence.*'

I had been so safe. Jarvis Peters and I could face the revenants.

But the mind-blowing terror was on me again, and I shivered in anticipation of the horror to come.

'Do they know, Pauline?' I said.

Pauline looked at me. There was a blankness in her gaze that I recognised.

I realised what I had done. I had set the winter wolves on me.

'Pauline? You didn't tell her, did you?'

'Tell who, Di?' Pauline shook herself. Doubt and compassion struggled for expression, and for a moment I thought she would break free of the hell-bitches' sway.

She couldn't.

'Who found the tape?' I asked.

'Why, Maggie Henderson, Di,' she said in relief. 'She had a blitz in the typing pool and gathered in every stray tape. She said she'd found a spool in the recorder you left on your desk the other day. She asked around to see if anyone knew what the report should be headed.'

I had forgotten to take the tiny cassette out of the machine after Jarvis and I had listened to it.

'I'm sorry, Jarvis,' I whispered. 'I tried.'

'Pardon, Di?' said Pauline.

'Nothing. Where is — Marguerite?' I choked on the name of the hell-bitch.

'Why I'm here, Diana,' she said silkily behind me. 'Pauline asked me to look in.'

I almost fainted. My legs gave way and my arms buckled, and my spine felt like paper. I think Marguerite must have lashed out with some jolt of psychic power, for I came to very soon afterwards to find those glaring pits into Hell fixed on me and I knew I was lost.

'Yes, Marguerite was helpful about the cassette,' said Pauline from a huge distance away.

I couldn't answer. She peered at me anxiously.

'So we'll do that, shall we, Di? Forget it all?'

'Yes,' said Marguerite.

'Yes,' I echoed. My voice sounded as sad as death.

'And we'll see you back in the office next week — if you feel up to it.'

'If I feel up to it, Pauline.'

'And Marguerite will see you get back home.'

I looked at her and saw the betrayal somewhere far back in her eyes. I tried to speak,

'Please don't — '

'I think Diana needs someone to be with for a while before she goes back to the flat,' said Marguerite, smiling

'No,' I whispered, but no one heard.

'I think Mother would be best,' said the thing that possessed the body of this young woman. 'Mother will be pleased to look after Diana.'

'I don't think she should drive her own car,' Pauline said. 'She's in quite a bad state of shock.'

'There's no need for her to drive, Pauline,' Marguerite assured her. 'It's all arranged.'

'I'm so glad you're here,' said Pauline.

Marguerite didn't trouble to answer.

I couldn't see any trace of humanity, or even a resemblance to humankind about her. She was as inhuman as a block of ice, without compassion, remorse or even awareness of my state of mind. She looked through Pauline and I into a darkness that was inhabited only by her own kind: she saw into the gulfs of space and through the emptiness of time, where only the shadows and shells of things like herself could exist.

I knew fully in that moment what Mrs. Peters meant when she wrote that the Friends lived in the worst evil.

The Old Darkness.

I wept silently, tears of self-pity.

'Come along,' the revenant said sharply. I stumbled into the outer office. No one seemed to notice me, and I might have passed through like a walking ghost if Maggie Henderson hadn't chosen that moment to drop a metal tray with an appalling clatter and for a second or two the terrible girl lost her hold on us all.

'Oh, Di!' shouted Maggie. 'I didn't know you were in — did you get the message?'

I shook my head.

Marguerite quickly looked from Pauline to Maggie and back to me, but her concentration was broken.

'It's in your message book, Di. Some-one called Gough. About a baby,' Maggie called.

I didn't know I had been given a chance to run. My mind rang with the memory of that vision of night and everlasting echoing emptiness that lay in store for me. Marguerite was, for a few seconds, unable to contain the situation; her psychic resources were overstretched, and, had I not been full of drugs, I might have been able to take the opportunity Maggie gave to me.

I didn't.

Self-pity overwhelmed me, and I

waited, like the dumb, brutalised creature I was, whilst Marguerite slowly recovered.

'Gough?' I said stupidly.

'She rang three times. Stupid sort of woman. She wouldn't talk to anyone but you, Di,' said Maggie.

'I don't know anyone called Gough,' I said weakly.

'Then it isn't important,' said Pauline decisively. 'I'll deal with it, if there's any need for action.'

'Move,' Marguerite grated at last.

I can't remember leaving the office.

The car was at the kerbside waiting for me. I looked at the driver, and I didn't feel anything at all.

'Sit in the back,' said Phil.

It all happened very quickly after that.

A brief, fast drive to The Red House, and then a muttered conversation.

'Drive up to the front door,' Marguerite ordered, after the consultation.

My mind ran on through the troubles of the clients I wouldn't be seeing again, and I felt guilty about some of them. What would become of them? I wondered, because it was my last contact with my job, who the Gough woman could be. An adoption? Or a request for a foster-child? Maybe, I decided, maybe something quite different. But none of it mattered.

I had stopped weeping when the car reached the house.

'Out,' said Marguerite.

Phil didn't look at me.

I heard the car start up. It went down the path a little way, reversed, and back towards us. I didn't turn to look at Phil even then. I saw the rotten framework of the huge French windows and looked inside the big room at the front of the house.

Oddly, the glass was completely opaque.

The door swung open and Mrs. Friend appeared at the front door.

She smiled invitingly at me, but I could see the utter detestation behind the mask, and for a fleeting moment of time, the fat, toad-like face, the lined and seamed skin, and the black stumps of teeth that were the original features of Catherine la Voisin.

I spoke to her first.

The words came out without reflection or prompting.

'You needn't have killed Tony,' I said. 'He wasn't a part of it.'

She answered me in English, and the words were apparently sympathetic and kindly.

'You've been badly hurt, Diana. We're going to change all that. Come inside, and we'll sit and talk for a while. I'm so sorry for you, my dear.'

The ordinary English words were lies. Behind them, I heard the grating, iron voice of the woman she had once been, in that barely understandable French of three centuries before.

'*Did she talk?*' the hell-bitch asked her daughter through the words she spoke to me. '*Did she speak of the* — ' and she said a word I had no knowledge of. It must have been a word no longer used.

Or some word of their own mystery.

Marguerite shook her head. 'Diana is quite safe,' she said, aloud and in English.

She didn't care that I might hear or understand.

'Go inside the house,' she said sharply

to me. 'Mother wishes it so.'

I walked forward hesitantly. I had no will of my own. 'What will you do with me?' I whispered.

The door closed behind me.

Candles blazed in the hall, many more of them. The faces of the hounds in the tapestry were cruel, and in the eyes of the quarry I saw a reflection of my helpless terror.

'Go in,' ordered the older woman.

I didn't need to be told where.

I gasped, though, when I saw the room once more. I again had the impression of years sliding away from me. Perhaps I was a traveller in time. The thought held no comfort for me.

'Well, Madame?' I said quietly.

She faced me, smiling confidently. She was a frail, old woman again. Charm and compassion radiated from her.

'There will be no more pain for you, Diana, not any more. Come and sit over here.' She looked up.

Marguerite was at the door, and, behind her, Elsie Thacker.

'Go,' she told them. 'Diana and I will

look at the cards together.'

'You needn't have killed Tony,' I said. 'Nor Mrs. Peters.'

'You've been imagining things, Diana,' the hell-bitch murmured, smiling at me, and all the time holding me with her terrible, spinning eyes. 'See,' she said, and she held my little office recording machine out to me. 'You're going to tell me about your imaginings. Listen!' she said, her voice like a whiplash. '*Listen!*'

'*There's something in the cellar, hidden by the darkness,*' I heard my scared whisper repeating.

The spool wound on for a second or two, and my voice went on,

'*It has a shape, like a person, someone huge.*'

'Enough, Diana?' the thing whispered to me. 'Is that enough of Diana, who went hunting by moonlight?'

'Yes, Madame,' I said.

'Sit there,' she said, indicating the gilt chair I had occupied on my last visit.

All was in place, as I remembered so well. The marble table glistened under the bright yellow candlelight. The cards gleamed. They hadn't been moved.

'We'll make a new recording, Diana,' the hell-bitch promised. 'But first we have to see what the cards hold for you.'

I was hypnotised by the glistening silk of the Tarot cards — for I knew now what they were; and what they would reveal too.

'Who is to be your Guide, Diana?'

'Why do I need a Guide?' I asked.

The malicious face turned to me. 'To show the Path, Diana.'

The Nine of Swords blazed on the table. '*That's Death*,' she had told me once. 'That's your card of Destiny,' she said.

Now, the withered hand indicated the card I had chosen but which was still face down on the table.

'You must have no more fear,' she said.

'No, Madame.'

'Turn the card.'

I wanted to finish it. I wanted no more pain.

I reached out and turned the silken card over. As I touched it, I saw the shimmering shapes of the men and women who moved in the silken forest. They seemed intoxicated with a furious, mocking delight. I put the card on the table.

And then I looked at it.

It showed a woman dancing. She was young and naked, and she danced towards oblivion with a branch of yew in each hand. *Graveyard flowers*, I thought. She had graveyard flowers in her hands and in her hair.

'Follow her,' commanded the creature who had once been Catherine la Voisin. 'Do you understand where she leads?'

'Oh yes, Madame. I know.'

I knew where the pale dancer led.

'And you know how to follow her?'

It was Marguerite who spoke now.

'I know,' I answered dully. There were clients who had spare bottles of drugs that killed pain; enough bottles to kill more than pain. They wouldn't know I had taken their drugs, not in the confusion in which they lived.

The hell-bitches discussed me. They didn't care that I understood.

'Now,' said the older creature. 'Now

you must leave a message on your recording machine.'

'Yes, Madame,' I said.

'And then take the Path.'

'Thank you, Madame,' I said gratefully.

Time passed.

I found myself alone by my car.

They had spared Phil the final act of betrayal, either because they had a use for him still, or, more probably, because they were sure of me.

19

I was still conscious when Jarvis broke the door down.

I heard it smashing free of its hinges with a huge explosion of noise, and my first reaction was one of anger. Who was breaking in on my very private self-killing?

He looked at me, picked up one of the bottles and pulled me off the bed.

'When?' he demanded.

I blinked, tried to concentrate and couldn't. I was full of a mixture of gin, brandy and vermouth as well as barbiturates. My words were an incoherent torrent.

'When did you take them?' Jarvis snarled at me. 'Answer!'

He hit me hard across the face with the back of his hand.

'Please don't,' I begged.

'Tell me then!' He raised his hand.

'What time is it?' I shouted back.

'Three-thirty!'

I remembered looking at the wall-clock in the kitchen when I'd gone for a glass.

'After three. Maybe three-fifteen. Don't hit me again!'

He picked me up and propped me against the kitchen wall by the sink. Quickly he located the salt, and in moments he was forcing me to drink warm salt water.

I gagged but he wouldn't let me stop. Vomit tried to rise, but still he pushed the salt water at me. And then I could have the relief I so much needed.

'They can't be in your bloodstream yet. You're sure it wasn't longer, are you? Di, answer me!'

I suppose the alcohol saved my life. I was able to bring up the mixture of chemicals and alcohol before I had absorbed much of either. I'd taken enough pills to kill me, I knew that Jarvis knew it too, and I could see his dilemma even as he bullied me.

'Answer.'

I could, at last. 'I'll live,' I said. 'I've done this before. Not me, I mean for clients.'

'You're sure?'

'Yes. I should be pumped out, but no one's going to do that and ask no questions.'

'No. Di, how did it happen?'

'They found the tape.' I coughed and spluttered and felt foul. 'I'll have to wash.'

'All right.' Jarvis frowned. He inspected the mess I had made and seemed satisfied. 'Get cleaned up, we're leaving.'

I went to the bathroom.

'Leave the door open!'

'All right, Jarvis,' I said. It was then that I realised I would be able to love again. No one would have done for me what Jarvis Peters had done. I ached from retching, and I was as cold as death, but I knew I wanted to live.

He took me to his hotel and made me walk the six floors up. I was weak and wobbly, and again I had to vomit, but I was nowhere near unconsciousness. If I had been poisoned I could not have kept awake; the barbiturates were mostly out of my system. Reaction hit me when we were in the hotel room and the door closed on the rest of the world.

'Jarvis, please hold me,' I said in a quiet voice.

He was very tender with me. Through the hour or more when I could do no more than sob out my fears and pour out a garbled history of the past days, he first held me then lay beside me and finally comforted me in the only way that could really help me. I was ill, I was near exhaustion, and I knew I was physically unattractive, but he told me I was a brave and good woman and that I was someone he could trust and admire and love.

I felt Jarvis' steady heartbeat.

We were lovers: in love. It couldn't be faked. Not between people so acutely sensitive. I lay back.

'I nearly died,' I said. 'And now I'm in love.'

He smiled at me. 'I loved you the moment I met you, Di. From the start I knew we'd come to mean a great deal to one another. There was always the bond of — of seeing beyond the immediate world.'

'Yes.' I felt the warm sheets become cold around me.

Jarvis sensed my change of mood.

'Di, we have these hours owing to us. We deserve just a little time together.'

I let myself respond to his warmth.

He wouldn't let me sleep. Jarvis reached across me and ordered soup and toast, then he sat up and looked at me for a while. Then:

'I found a record that escaped the destruction ordered by the King. This one account survived. I think it's an accurate record because it was made by someone who was present at the execution of the older La Voisin.'

I was instantly alert. With a certain amount of grim satisfaction I recognised that I wanted the Friends destroyed — they no longer held me in thrall. I was free to think for myself once more, and my thoughts were of hatred and vengeance.

Jarvis noticed.

'Catherine la Voisin was supposed to be burned, but she was given the rope as a measure of humanity.'

'And?'

'She wasn't dead when the executioner

threw her body into the flames. She clawed the burning rope away.'

I had closed my eyes for a moment, and the scene rose up before me. Flames shone on drawn swords; the rabble screamed as the witch clawed the rope; and, from a dark carriage, a masked woman in a blue dress watched. I saw a something writhing in the flames, and then a darkness came over the scene.

'That was all that was seen, for the smoke obscured the rest.' Jarvis broke off to touch me. 'Do you see it, Di?'

I nodded, shuddering.

'Mother saw things too. I sometimes hear sounds, but the images don't coalesce for me — it's too confused.'

'The darkness?' I prompted.

'Yes. My informants record says it wasn't smoke.'

'It wasn't,' I said. 'It was darker than any smoke.'

'Then they called it down,' said Jarvis slowly. 'And under its cover, another poor wretch was thrown into the flames, an old woman who resembled La Voisin.'

'To burn in her place,' I said slowly. For

a moment, the dreadful blackness parted and I saw a scrabbling movement like a creature in hideous pain moving away from the fire. 'Yes, she escaped. And Marguerite went too.'

'There's more,' said Jarvis. 'The document records a pact they made with the Abbé Guibourg. He was dead by this time, of course, and nowhere is there any report to the contrary.'

I could see the whole dreadful and cruel scene again.

'I'm cold,' I told Jarvis Peters.

He put the gown I had borrowed before around my shoulders.

'We have to exchange information,' he said. 'Listen to the rest. It's the centre of it all. The reason for the ceremony and everything else. The pact they made gave the la Voisins control over certain powers that the Abbé had mastered. But they brought a penalty. It was this: they had to live on, stealing a life where they could from a human being, ripping out the soul and continuing their own existence in the body, until they were able to gain enough strength to summon up the dead spirit of their master. They had to live on in a half-life.'

'As *revenants*,' I said, completing the sentence.

'It frightened my informant,' said Jarvis somberly. 'He was the Satanist I consulted earlier. He's certain that a monstrous thing would be born if the Friends accomplished their task. He has misgivings about bringing about the rebirth of the Abbé. The coven he belongs to will make no move to hinder them, but they will make no move either to assist the Friends. They fear their powers. Can you tell me what they did to you?'

'Jarvis, they made me say terrible things.' I could remember now some of it.

Jarvis got up and reached into the pocket of his coat. He dropped the micro-recorder onto the tumbled bed-clothes.

'You talked about it,' he said. 'You weren't making much sense when I reached you, but it was obvious that you had made a recording. You spoke about it here, in this room.'

A discreet tap on the door and the

arrival of the food gave me a few more minutes in which to re-arrange my fragmented thoughts. As I sipped at the hot broth, I kept telling myself that I deserved to live, and when I looked at Jarvis' strong face and the tender concern in his dark eyes I felt needed and loved.

'Di, let's get it all together,' Jarvis said when I had finished all the broth. 'I know why my mother was killed. She might have talked to me. We know why they killed your husband. It was a bribe. As for Miss Vardy, she was possessed — and somewhere the younger La Voisin obtained the body of the young girl you call Marguerite Friend. But you were a part of their plan too. Why do they want you dead?

'I think I know,' I told him.

He reached for the recording machine.

'No, wait,' I stopped him. 'Listen for a moment, Jarvis, whilst I have it clearly. They must have been trying for centuries to fulfil the terms of the pact — they've lived through life after life without succeeding in returning the Abbé to a living form. *Why not?*'

I thought of the ravening la Voisins, ripping and gouging at the souls of poor bedevilled creatures, robbing them of their pitiful lives and casting their souls into some nameless other-life. *'Why did they always fail, Jarvis!'* I cried out.

Jarvis was shocked, 'Di, what is it you see?'

I could see into that terrible Old Darkness, and in it there were lost husks of things that crawled about, lost and anguished, without hope of life.

The eerie half-seen images faded, 'I think you were right when you said the la Voisins were weak — they are. I believe they've almost forgotten the use of their powers, and that they needed someone with tremendous psychic energy to feed on. I think they drained others of these unguessable forces and made use of them.'

'Who? My mother?'

'Yes. And she knew it. I think they were able to grow strong on her spiritual powers.'

'And on yours, Di?'

I shuddered. I felt the things leeching

onto my soul, bleeding my spirit and growing arrogant with their new-found strength.

'I think so.'

'So you were no more use to them,' said Jarvis. 'My mother, and now you.'

'That's not all of it,' I said, quite sure of myself.

'Well?' Jarvis sounded vengeful and harsh.

'Listen to the recording, Jarvis. I don't think I can say any more.'

I had to lie back. The strange mood that had so suddenly overcome me had taken the last of my energy. I knew, vaguely, why the la Voisins wanted my death to be now: they had a use for me, even when they had gently guided me into suicide.

The words from my grave would protect them.

Jarvis looked at me for several moments, then switched it on.

I heard my voice as if it were a stranger's:

'*Forgive me if you can,*' came the calm, educated, troubled words. '*The first time it was a crazy impulse and anyway the child was ill. It would have died. I'm sure it would. I had to hide the baby. I couldn't help myself, I've never had a child.'*

'Christ!' groaned Jarvis.

'Leave it on,' I said. 'Listen to it!'

The terrible things they had made me say came back to me as my voice from the machine went shrill, and through the sobbed, tormented confession, I could see the faces of the two coarse-faced poisoners and sorceresses nodding to me and encouraging and threatening me at the same time, both of them half-snarling, half-smiling, revealing themselves for what they had once been: the hell-bitches of Versailles.

They had made me confess to horrible, perverse things, evil things of such a depth of depravity that I marvelled that the creatures who tormented me had ever been human.

I thought of a black-wrapped bundle and a ring of faces in the candlelight. Pain hammered through my skull, black waves of it: and visions of blood in the blackness.

'I was to be the scapegoat,' I said. 'They would go free again, and my death would hide what they had done.'

'But babies? Newborn children?'

'Isn't that what they always sacrificed?'

Jarvis glowered at me. 'Always. The la Voisins found the victims and the Abbé Guibourg made the sacrifice. They bought the newborn children of the Paris whores. Yes, I knew what they did, and I guessed what they might do. But to use you to cover their murders! God help me, Di, I'll wipe them from the face of the earth!'

'That night,' I said, 'could it be — was it a child?'

'Was it a child?' With a huge effort Jarvis strove to contain his fury. 'I've asked myself that a thousand times since I heard what they were and what they had done. But, if you have to know the truth, it's this. It was a child.'

'No!'

'They sacrificed a child.'

'Dear Christ,' I whispered, as the last, frightful truth came to me. 'Janet Gough.'

'Di!' Jarvis said intently. 'Di, for God's

sake, don't go off into nightmares again — tell me! Tell me!'

'Janet was one of the girls I had on case-load, eighteen months, maybe two years ago. She went North, to some godforsaken wilderness beyond Newcastle, where her grandparents hated her and used her as a slave. They sold her out to casual passers-by, and she aborted twice before she was fifteen. And, at the trial, she refused to give evidence about the way they'd prostituted her. She's a stupid and wily child, and the last time I saw her she was nearly nine months pregnant. Marguerite Friend was with her.'

'Poor child,' said Jarvis. 'Poor child.'

'She rang the office,' I said slowly. 'She saw me and she joined the others in mocking me, but she remembered that I had helped her, so she rang. And I didn't answer her. I deserted her when she needed me most of all. I left her baby to be murdered.'

I reached out to the micro-recorder again. 'Help me?' I pleaded.

'Leave it,' Jarvis ordered. 'You're Di

Knightson, nothing else! You became a tool of the revenants and now you and I will *destroy them*!'

I flinched away from him.

'Yes?' I said unsurely.

'For what they did, and for what they intend — *yes*!'

He dressed quickly. I watched in helpless amazement as he readied himself, and I did as he ordered without thought of what would happen next until I was dressed.

'Tell me what's happening, please Jarvis.'

He smiled grimly. 'You know already.'

'They won't trouble to check at the flat, will they?' I said.

'No, Di. So far as they're concerned, you're dead.'

It had occurred to me that the broken door and my absence would alert the hell-bitches, but all the time I had known that they didn't care what I might do: their time was short, and their arrogant lust was keen. They were swollen with power and fierce with desire for the return of the terrible master they served.

Jarvis reached across to his suit. He passed me a photo-wallet.

'You should see it,' he told me.

He opened the plastic case. I saw the great black shape. It was no more than a vague outline of shadow on shadow, but it was the thing I had seen gathering in the cellar. A cowled, black shape.

'It's tonight, isn't it?' I said.

'Yes.'

'We have to try?' I asked weakly.

I found I could control the shaking of my hands as Jarvis stared at me. Very slowly, I moved from the bed and dressed myself.

'I'm ready,' I told Jarvis.

Grateful for having found the gift of love; in great fear of what my dear Mrs. Peters had called '*the worst evil*'; and consumed with a fierce anger, I went with Jarvis into the early dusk.

20

We didn't talk on the way to the house.

Jarvis drove, so I had time to let my thoughts wander.

I went over and over every remark I had heard Marguerite la Voisin utter, from the moment when I had seen her in the office. Everything she had said or done was a part of the scheme. She had created a network of people and places with the speed and deadliness of a malignant spider.

I found myself amazed at the audacity of the plan to use the Social Services as a means of gathering together the facilities the la Voisins needed for their ghastly ends.

The remote house where they could hold their grotesque rituals in undisturbed secrecy.

Mrs. Peters' psychic powers, and, probably to their surprise, my own paranormal abilities: they had used me and Mrs. Peters as a power-source, and were ready to throw us away when we were used-up shells.

And then the impressionable girls.

The daredevil, exploited girls, like Jennie Webb, and the incautious, unheeding girls, like Janet Gough. And the evil girl, Elsie Thacker.

In a few weeks, the entire diabolical plan was brought to fruition.

The blurred thing whose terrible presence had registered on the film was waiting for the la Voisins' call.

They had been so cunning, so viciously direct. For they had hinged the whole corrupt scheme on me.

I laughed.

'Di?'

'I was laughing because I am sure.'

Jarvis reached out to hold my hand. He held it until we reached the turning for the cindered track.

He stopped the car. Traffic swished through the heavy rain. I noticed for the first time that we were in the centre of a late summer thunderstorm. The wind rocked the car, and I saw the dark clouds lit up by a brilliant fall of sheet lightning.

There could be no turning back.

Jarvis cut the headlights. My smooth little car purred forward across the deep water-filled ruts. Only the reflected light on the water from the sidelights placed us on the track.

Jarvis was tense.

His breathing was deep and steady, and his body rigid. I felt a deep tenderness for him.

It was in that moment that I knew I was stronger than him. In spite of my weaknesses, I felt a sudden release of tension, and a surge of jolting power running through my body and my mind and my spirit; so that I could feel every muscle of my body alive with an uncontainable force, and every part of my mind able to plan and direct and carry through the actions that the moment would need.

My psychic battery was fully charged. I felt as powerful as a juggernaut.

'Jarvis,' I whispered. 'Stop at the end of the drive.'

He turned to me. I could read his mind before he spoke. He was about to tell me to wait in the car.

'See,' I said.

The windows of the ground floor blazed with light. Through the slashing rain I could see the eerie yellow candle-light as the torrents of rain produced a shimmering, wavering, unearthly effect: there must have been a thousand candles ablaze in the great gold and glass room.

Jarvis shook himself free of the spell of the glittering sight.

'I must see it,' he said.

'Together,' I told him. 'You made me strong. Now I can make both of us strong.'

I was afraid for him, and he knew it.

'It's a very special kind of strength,' I whispered.

I honoured him for his courage, and tears swept coldly down my face. Without my special kind of new-found spiritual armour, he had tried to keep me from the la Voisins.

'Together?' I said again.

I sensed the presence of evil. All around

me, the sense of the outer darkness was present. It pulsed and heaved, without thought or form, yet it was here, and waiting for fulfilment in human shape.

And Jarvis was afraid to his soul.

I knew it, and I wanted to keep him from it.

'Now,' he said suddenly, and he stumbled out of the car with me following him through the biting rain.

A huge thunder-blast left me stunned.

He grabbed my hand, and we ran towards the fatal window where the candles blazed with a wicked violence at the buffeting storm. We slipped and splashed on the overgrown drive; thorns tore at us, nettles slashed, rotted trellises gave way and left bleeding scars on our legs: twice Jarvis kept me upright, and once, when a ghastly thing swept toward us I yelled words whose meaning I did not understand at it: and then we were clear and through the summer storm and at the frightful scene of evil.

It was as bright as a well-lit stage.

They had no need of the cellar now. The time for hiding was past — the la

Voisins were arrogant in their diabolical fulfilment.

The great room of glass and gold was full of movement. The candlelight cast no shadows as the two sorceresses moved in the pentacle, and the circle of girls swayed at their command.

I saw unfamiliar faces amongst the circle, and one face that would forever remain imprinted on my mind, that of the gloating child, Elsie Thacker; for she was in the middle of the circle too, and she held a bundle in her arms.

A black-wrapped bundle, that seemed to stir.

I had the sudden conviction that I was one of the circle too. My throat had dried, and my hands twitched to reach out to the star-shaped space of evil where the two gorgeously-gowned women mouthed their incantations.

I was one of the worshippers. The evil reached out to me.

I shuddered, as memories from a long-gone age splashed tormented scenes in front of my haunted vision.

'Blood,' I heard myself say. 'They

splash themselves with the blood. Just as they did before. Madame will make the celebration . . . the Great One will come . . . '

Jarvis dug me sharply in the ribs, and I gasped into quietness.

Thunder roared overhead, and the yellow lights paled in the immediate flashing of yellow-blue lightning. The old wooden windows shuddered in their frames, and, momentarily, the assembled worshippers paused.

In that pause, I heard a thin whimpering that trailed out and grew in strength until it was a half-uttered screaming sound, not loud, but full of pain, loss and grief. Then I saw the girl.

Jarvis and I were both rigid with shock.

The eerie room, the tremendous thunderclap, and then that sudden wailing, bubbling shriek, left us dazed.

I acted first. Janet Gough was crouched at the window — we had not seen her because she was almost hidden behind the framework of the bay — and her hands were raised upwards in supplication.

I reached out to grab her even as the elder sorceress turned towards us. The candles flared, and flames shot from the earthenware pots, heavy with smoke.

I sensed a darkness in the smoke as I held the rain-soaked girl and dragged her with me.

The blank-faced circle of girls turned to follow the pointing hand. Catherine la Voisin mouthed a name.

My name.

'Get her away!' I yelled, throwing the girl bodily away from me.

'Di!' yelled Jarvis, suddenly out of the shock that held him rigid. Janet Gough lurched into him, and the pair of them sprawled aside as I ran back down the drive.

I don't know what impelled me to act as I did. Much of what had happened in the weeks I had been enslaved by the hell-bitches remained a mystery to me: and much of my resolution at odd moments is at least an equal mystery. At times I was as helpless as a rabbit in a car's head-lights, whereas at others I could take my destiny in my hands and defy them.

As I did now. I did what I had to because, as I now believe, there is a fragment of spiritual resource in us all that persists no matter how it is overlaid with cynicism or disbelief: it is our heritage, this tiny spark of light.

Jarvis thought I was running away in blind panic.

'*Di!*' he yelled again.

But I was at the car by then. I raced the engine till it screamed. A weird back-glow of lightning illuminated every part of the scene: the overgrown flowerbeds, the sagging trellises, the rutted and holed drive, with its wide pools of water slashed at by the rain: and the two white faces in the car headlights.

I pointed the car at them.

Jarvis knew what I would do, and he moved fast. He threw Janet bodily aside and tried to reach me.

He crouched to one side of the drive as I pushed hard down on the accelerator. I kept to second gear. The car slithered under the fierce surge of power. I reached a high speed, and even then Jarvis tried to catch at the door-handle. I heard his body bounce on the metal as I tried to evade him.

I looked ahead in that last moment and saw the revenants glaring at me, their basilisk eyes huge and red: and behind them a towering Presence.

I raised both hands to ward it off. It was huge and grotesque and horrible.

Darkness covered me, and I could smell a dank, foetid stench all around me, and in the darkness there were scaled, clawing things that scrabbled to reach me.

And then the car smashed into the glittering room.

The metal buckled and screamed, but it drove on through the rotten wood and clear across the unreal room. I caught glimpses of girls throwing themselves out of its way, and I saw someone snatch at a bundle, black-wrapped, still moving; and I knew peace.

The car ricocheted off one wall, glanced at another and came to rest in the bright ruins, and I was still conscious, still able to see the vast shape that reared over the dais.

Not the la Voisins.

Just that shape.

Then the flames sprang up.

Someone screamed in a terrible agony.

I retched when I understood.

The fire was fierce, and the la Voisins were at its centre. It wasn't the unreal yellow light, or the ghastly flame from the smoking pots, but bright red flame, hot and purifying; and it burned them. I saw that the blackness was gone. And the shape.

The doors of the car had sprung open. Heat blistered the paintwork, and I remembered the distraught face of Janet Gough.

I saw — just for a moment, but it was a moment that I would relive daily for many months — the implacable hatred on the toad-like faces of the la Voisins as they burned. Then decay changed their features, as it had done once before in that hallucinatory room.

But the warning was there for me to see. They would pursue me through this life and destroy my soul.

There was no rest for me this side of the grave, nor beyond it. We were enemies forever.

'Get out!' someone was yelling at me. 'Out, Di!'

Jarvis pulled me with brutal force. Much of his thin hair was gone, charred to his scalp.

Behind him I saw someone else — a shocked, vicious face twisted in unbelief and hatred.

Elsie Thacker.

She had the bundle in her arms, holding it to the burning sorceresses. Her dress was on fire, but she didn't seem to notice. Flame licked the edge of the black cloth, and part of it fell away, to reveal the pink and wrinkled face of a new-born child.

I pushed from Jarvis and wrestled the child from the skinny hands. It wailed once and seemed to choke in the swirling smoke. Elsie tried to claw it back.

'Mine?' she said, pleading with me. 'For the Father — '

Jarvis pulled me away. I tried to grab at the burning girl but I couldn't reach her. She stepped towards the writhing squat figures at the centre of the conflagration with small, uncertain paces. I could see her skin burn.

I was half-carried away as timbers began to crash on the wreck of the Fiat and the remains of the la Voisins. The room seemed much smaller. Explosions high above showed how quickly the old timbers had given way. Girls sobbed all around me, maybe for themselves or perhaps for the gruesome things that had owned their souls; or even for the thin, evil girl who had walked into the fire with her arms outstretched.

Rain cooled my face.

A baby began to cry, and I saw that Janet Gough was nursing her child. I shuddered. Jarvis held me firmly.

'They used the skin of newborn children to back their books,' I said.

'Don't talk of such things.'

'They drank the blood. They will try again.'

'Di! No more!'

I was sinking into madness, and I welcomed it.

'I touched the hand of the revenant,' I whispered. 'The hand that once poured blood for a King's mistress. She serves Satan. And I touched her. She knows I fear her, and I know she will follow me. Jarvis, it will go on forever.'

I heard the baby cry, and I said the words I had once been told to say.

'*I couldn't help myself, I've never had a child.*'

Jarvis drew back his hand to slap me.

I looked up at him, and he let his hand fall. He was weeping.

The house exploded into a mass of flame that hissed under the driving rain. Far away, the thunder rumbled, but it was muted now. The storm-centre had moved.

'I'm sorry, Jarvis,' I said.

That was all I remembered for a long time.

21

Much of the next seven months remains to this day a complete blank in my life. I know that several people who were my friends called to see me, but how often they came and what transpired during their visits is lost to me; and probably will remain so, if what the competent young psychiatrist who was in charge of my addled brains says is true. I had decided to take in no more: and I had decided to wipe out the past.

I was successful in both for a long time.

Pauline called weekly. Sometimes she brought flowers, other times fruit. We talked about the food I was eating and the passing of time in the hospital; and about my progress in oil painting, crocheting and my reading of the novels of Anthony Trollope. Barchester, the Duke of Omnium, Lizzy Eustace: they were my companions, but they didn't help to bring me back to sanity.

Colleagues and friends remarked on my well-being. I knew they were liars.

I had aged by twenty years. My hair straggled, where once it had hung thickly in dark blonde bunches; my skin was blotched, and my nose looked sharp in my over-thin face. I couldn't bear to look at my eyes, they seemed so dark and frightened.

Nobody mentioned the past.

I was not in the least curious to enquire into the circumstances of my admission to what I was well aware was a psychiatric ward; nor did I wish to learn what had been my previous employment. Of course I knew that Pauline Hart was my boss. And I knew that when Maggie Henderson laughed at some joke of her own, she was recollecting other things that we had laughed at. Compassion flowed from the two of them; I was oblivious to its source.

I knew, naturally, that someone should call, someone who was dear to me; but I felt like some cardboard cutout princess in a storybook pop-up, that events would take care of themselves. No doubt my pasteboard prince would appear. I suppose the medication had made me smug.

Nothing penetrated into the ordered security of nineteenth-century Barsetshire. I painted vases of flowers, and I had no understanding of why the flowers were invariably flame-coloured. I worked from patterns and made neat placemats for whoever praised them: I chose scenes showing flowers in a grassy garden.

Six months drifted by.

I might be there yet if I hadn't heard the psychiatrist discussing me, in his only unguarded moments. His name was Frank Williams. We were Di and Frank from the start. I liked him. He was about my own age, very tall and thin, and unsmiling. I had the impression that I was his first genuine nut. I was right.

I'd wandered out of the ward in search of a book I'd left around, *Phineas Redux*. It was my favourite of the Palliser series. I thought Frank was talking about someone else at first, but I soon realised that I was the subject of his enthusiastic account. I waited in the curtained cubicle, out of sight of everyone.

I was 'Knightson'. And, it seemed, a schizophrenic. Not Diana, or Mrs. Knightson.

Knightson, I heard, was a textbook case of paranoia, with a high level of intelligence and a near genius level of rationalising ability. There was an amazing consistency in my fantasising. Early in his contact with me, Frank had read the accounts of my first ramblings. Apparently, I'd produced a wealth of evidence in support of my fantasy: and I'd confirmed these first statements under questioning.

I'd produced a delusion of phantasmagorical happenings, including a tale of occult intrigue and ritual. Clearly it was based on deep feelings of guilt, in connection with the deaths of a close colleague — a young girl, for whom I had felt a deep sense of identification — and another girl not much younger, this one a client.

I — Knightson — blamed myself for the deaths.

The listener was an older man. He asked friendly Frank if I was likely to recover.

Frank wasn't hopeful. I was a paranoid schizophrenic.

It was a last resort, but they'd try electric shock therapy. The listener didn't like it, but Frank asked what he'd do. It was unfortunate, the older man agreed. But necessary.

Frank pressed on with details. He was thinking of writing me up in a paper. How I'd worked in some of my clients and propped up my fantasy by combining the truth with the bizarre. Like the way I'd convinced myself that a Miss Vardy had become possessed by some reincarnation of a sorceress; Frank had personally checked on this one. Miss Vardy had existed! I'd been cunning, it seemed. I hadn't let it slip that Miss Vardy had died weeks before I'd met her. In Paris. A very ordinary heart attack, which the package deal firm had rightly kept very quiet about.

I heard the word *Paris*, and my months of absence from the human race came to an abrupt end.

Frank Williams' excited account went on.

I'd had an obsession about a baby. They'd had to sedate me very heavily for a long period of time. No, said my friendly psychiatrist, he didn't think it was anything to do with an earlier and unsuccessful pregnancy. Knightson had never been pregnant.

That could be half the trouble, the older man said.

I crept away and thought of these eager dabblers shooting my head full of shock-waves. I remembered who I was waiting for, but I wouldn't say his name, not even in my loneliest and remotest thoughts. Then I recalled the names of my enemies, and I tensed like a snared bird.

I was entirely alone.

I looked about the cheerful ward, and I smiled in response to the encouraging nod of the sister on duty.

Frank Williams and a distinguished-looking man in his sixties passed me. The older man regarded me with a keen, paternal air. Frank patted my shoulder. I flinched away from him. He was the man who would write up the case of one 'Mrs. K.', who saw ghosts from the Sun-King's court.

And how long would it be before the la

Voisins heard of the demented Mrs. K.?

I determined that I was safe until at least the beginning of May, for that was when the booby-hatch crowd have their get-togethers and compare nut-cases. So I began my recovery slowly, and convincingly too.

I didn't rush things.

I felt like screaming, and I felt like running, but I did neither. I confided in Frank that I had always wanted a child, and I asked if I'd talked much about children.

He was disappointed, if anything.

I think he'd liked the idea of cajoling me to the hot seat where the electrons were dispensed. But he listened, and he tried pills — which I sluiced away — and he at last let me work out my guilt feelings by showing me the newspapers for the days after the burning of The Red House.

It turned out that I was something of a heroine.

The girls had been trapped, and only my presence of mind had averted a major disaster. I'd smashed the windows through and released the girls. Elsie Thacker had died saving a child. The rest was glossed over, in the interests, no doubt, of the bad girls' futures.

I thought of Elsie Thacker offering the tiny figure to the half-formed shape of the Abbé Guibourg, and the way she had walked steadfastly toward the heart of the flames.

I rang a number I had memorized, but it was unobtainable.

I was numb with fright by the time Frank Williams decided I could face the world again. I wouldn't let him send for Pauline Hart. No, I told him, he'd given me the confidence to try again.

Would I work? Go back to the Department?

No.

I had no need, for Tony had been unbusinesslike at the end, and for all his attempts to take away my lawful share of what we had worked for together, he had left me his considerable fortune. He had not gotten around to changing his will before he died.

I tried again, thinking I had rung at the

wrong time, maybe rung the wrong number, maybe anything. But no, a French operator informed me impatiently, the Paris number was no longer in use.

I woke up early one May morning to find my bag packed.

Frank Williams came at eight and wished me luck.

There was no warning, and perhaps it's a humane system.

Psychiatric hospitals in this country discharge patients with no notice. Half an hour after waking, I was told I was able to leave.

I didn't go to the flat.

Fiercely I resisted the impulse to look for messages that would give me some hope; the danger was too great. I sensed that the la Voisins would have the flat watched.

I stayed for one night at the hotel where I had been almost a happy woman, and where I had learned to love again. It was as near as I could get to a relief from the pounding tensions of the hunt.

I let myself think for a few moments of

that strong back, and the gentle smile on the heavy face. Then I wiped out the memory. There was only vengeance left.

I made my arrangements quickly, and I learned what I had to know by making a few discreet phone calls.

Phil was abroad. He'd resigned, his work unfinished, for the laboratory had been destroyed and, with it, the cultures he was experimenting with. Fire again, I learned. Fire. Again. He could be with them still, God help him.

They had always been great poisoners.

He could be of use to them, no doubt, in their new lair.

I transferred funds to various banks, in England, and in France. I knew where the la Voisins had gone, naturally.

England was too dangerous for their macabre activities — it had almost been perfect, but they had been frustrated and enquiries would have been made. I knew that the newspapers would not reflect the whole of the story: much had been suppressed. The la Voisins were cunning enough to know it.

However, they needed another lair.

I checked my passport. It was good for another three years. I smiled bitterly. A few weeks would be enough.

I would find their old haunts, and they would be there.

I knew their ways. I could follow their tracks. My French wasn't quite perfect, but a few days would make me fluent again. I was trained for the work, a professional investigator, and I had more than enough money to bribe where I couldn't wheedle — I felt my strength returning, and I determined to make myself attractive to men again: I would not scruple to use people in my search.

'*Beware of Scorpios*,' the older la Voisin had told me.

I knew their bones had burned in the fire. Just as surely, I knew that their evil spirits would by now have found new bodily shapes. The revenants had the power of eternal renewal.

Diana would hunt, though. I would find their sanctuary.

I was full of a cold rage. *Let them beware!*

They were terrible in their bold

ferocity, but they lacked subtlety. They were impatient, and I trusted careless too. I would find them, and I would destroy them.

I left England on a cold and blustery May morning, with the chalk cliffs half-hidden in mist and the sea the colour of old iron. My hands were thin. I looked at them as they gripped the salt-stained rail. Then I looked up at the sea and mist, and the unseen French coast.

I sensed the brooding presence of the la Voisins, and my surge of confidence began to ebb. I felt doubt. I, who had endured the malice of the soul, was maimed in spirit. I tried to let my anger rage through me.

'Beware,' I whispered into the pressing mist. 'Beware the power in me.'

I looked down at the sea, and saw, even as I looked down, that there was another hand beside mine on the green-brass rail; and my heart thudded fast.

The wide, muscular hand closed over my hand.

My senses swam.

I saw calmness, glorious things, and

through a mist of sunlight I saw children dancing on a seashore: in the shallows, I saw three children regarding one another gravely: and dancing.

The children were mine.

'You know I couldn't contact you, Di?' said Jarvis Peters.

'Yes.' I *had* known. We cannot admit those things to ourselves, but we know.

'I heard you. Just now.'

'I meant it,' I said.

'Then let them beware!' said Jarvis Peters.

I knew too that he had seen beyond our coming time of trial. It is a power, a gift, a frightening thing.

It would sustain us. I knew it.

THE END